'Wonderfully dark and peppered with grim humour.

Alex Cross.'
SUN

'An ingenious and original plot. Compulsive reading.'
RACHEL ABBOTT

'As good as I expected from Paul Finch. Relentlessly
action-packed, breathless in its finale, Paul expertly weaves
a trail through the North's dark underbelly.'
NEIL WHITE

'A deliciously twisted and fiendish set of murders
and a great pairing of detectives.'
STAV SHEREZ

'Avon's big star . . . part edge-of-the-seat,
part hide-behind-the-sofa!'
THE BOOKSELLER

'An explosive thriller that will leave you
completely hooked.'
WE LOVE THIS BOOK

Paul Finch is a former cop and journalist, now turned full-time writer. He cut his literary teeth penning episodes of the British TV crime drama, *The Bill*, and has written extensively in the field of children's animation. However, he is probably best known for his work in thrillers and crime. His first three novels in the Detective Sergeant Heckenburg series all attained 'bestseller' status, while his last but one novel, *Strangers*, which introduced a new hero in Detective Constable Lucy Clayburn, became an official *Sunday Times* top 10 bestseller in its first month of publication.

Paul lives in Lancashire, UK, with his wife Cathy. His website can be found at www.paulfinchauthor.com, his blog at www.paulfinch-writer.blogspot.co.uk, and he can be followed on Twitter as @paulfinchauthor.

By the same author:

Shadows
PAUL FINCH

avon.

AVON

A division of HarperCollins*Publishers*
1 London Bridge Street,
London SE1 9GF

www.harpercollins.co.uk

A Paperback Original 2017
2

A catalogue record for this book is
available from the British Library

ISBN PB 978-0-00-755133-0
ISBN TPB 978-0-00-824812-3

Set in Sabon by Palimpsest Book Production Limited,
Falkirk, Stirlingshire

Printed and bound by CPI Group (UK) Ltd, Croydon CR0 4YY

For my children, Eleanor and Harry, who, even though they've now left home, are always available to bounce around a few ideas.

Chapter 1

The trouble with a really successful pub crawl – in other words, if you manage to hit *all* the hostelries on the proposed route – is that the team inevitably falls apart before you reach the end.

Oh, it'll start off in the usual high spirits, with much yahooing and backslapping as you excitedly barge your way in through the first few sets of doors. But as the evening wears on, and the decibels rise, and the golden nectar flows down gulping throats, heads become progressively muzzier and one by one, as the team weaves ever on to the next establishment, members will drop by the wayside. Usually they end up lingering behind because they haven't quite finished their pint, or because they've met a girl they know, or because they've lost track of where they're supposed to be going next. Or quite simply, in that mysterious way of pub crawls the world over, they've simply vanished from the face of the earth – at least for the remainder of that night, no doubt to show up the following morning in a garden or on a park bench or maybe slumped in a shop doorway, rain-sodden and with head banging.

Either way, by the end of the night, only the hardy quaffers tend to remain; that small band of iron-core loyalists who will always see things through.

Tonight, oddly, even though the rest of his mates were well-known on campus as big-time boozers, Keith Redmond had somehow found himself at the last port of call alone.

It was called The Brasshouse and it was located on Broad Street, where its reputation as a popular watering hole was very well deserved. On this occasion though, Keith arrived there in a fog of confusion, at least twelve pints of lager sloshing around inside him, and none of the four or five faces currently in there – when he could focus on them sufficiently – even vaguely reminiscent of his fellow rugby club members. In the way of these things, he wasn't quite able to work it all out. But as he ambled to the bar, filching his last tenner from his jeans pocket, he had some vague notion that the rest of the crew would catch him up in due course; either that, or they'd done what they'd said they were going to do some way back – namely not bother going the whole distance and, as it was only Wednesday, heading home early.

Keith wasn't sure which it had been.

As he stood there alone, the last few of the other midweek drinkers nodding their farewells to the landlord and his staff and drifting out, it irked him that he'd been marooned here. Though, as he downed his last pint of the evening in desultory fashion, he supposed he hadn't been marooned as such. If it had slipped his notice that they'd reached a communal decision to terminate the crawl early, then it was as much his fault as anyone else's. So, he couldn't really be angry with them. Not that this would stop him taking the mickey in the morning, or more likely in the afternoon, when he was finally fit to re-emerge, calling them plastics and phonies.

These things happened, he reflected, as he threaded his

2

unsteady way back across a central Birmingham awash with glistening October rain, and at this hour on a weekday almost bare of life. He wasn't sure what time it was. Probably around one. Which wasn't too bad. He had no lectures of note in the morning, so he could sleep until noon.

But he was only a hundred yards down the road, heading due southwest towards Edgbaston, when he remembered something important. It was quite fortuitous. A 'Poundstretcher' sign caught his eye, reminding him that he was supposed to draw some extra money out tonight. He was going home to Brighton this weekend, for his older brother, Jason's, stag do. Keith sniggered. There'd be no phonies tolerated on *that* seafront tour; any who thought they were going to try it would get dragged to the last few venues by their underpants' elastic.

Of course, Keith wouldn't be involved in any of that if he didn't have enough money. In his quest to find a cashpoint, he backtracked a little along Broad Street, and then crossed the canal, heading roughly in the direction of the city centre.

It was vaguely unsettling, even in his drunken state: there was literally no one else around.

That was partly because of the lateness of the hour, but primarily because rain was still falling in torrents: rivers gushed out of pipes and gurgled down drains; lagoons had formed at road junctions, the occasional passing vehicle kicking them up in spectacular waves. Keith was in his usual attire – jeans, trainers, and zip-up lightweight anorak over his T-shirt, though in truth that 'anorak' certainly wasn't protecting him tonight, his T-shirt already soaked through; at least that went with his jeans which were also sopping, not to mention his trainers.

On reflection, it might have been a better plan to have organised a taxi back this evening. This would usually be a last resort for Keith, who, as a student, preferred to spend what little cash he had on booze, but these conditions were pretty extreme by any standards. He could still try to flag one down, of course, but only after he'd drawn the money out for the weekend.

At least, one positive result of the downpour was the sluggish but steady return of sobriety. Keith's head was getting the full, unrestricted brunt of it, his short straw-blond hair dripping wet even as it lay plastered to his skull. It was amazing what a reviving effect that could actually have on beer-laden thought processes. By the time he'd crossed Centenary Square, those familiar post-party urges to chuckle pointlessly at nothing, or sing out loud or kick at the occasional can had long departed. He now found himself walking steadily and in a reasonably straight line.

And at the same time, as he came back to his senses, he wondered if perhaps this wasn't the best idea. His original intention had been to call at a cashpoint before they started hitting the pubs, or at least halfway through, when it wasn't too late and when there were other people around. Keith wasn't the sort of person who would normally expect to be robbed, but there was a particular story circulating at present that even he found unnerving.

He considered chucking it in and heading back to Edgbaston. But then another voice advised that there was a cashpoint not too far ahead, near the Town Hall, and if he turned around now when he was so close, he'd be an absolute idiot – not to mention a total wuss.

Keith puffed his chest and thrust out his jaw as he walked defiantly on. He didn't play wing-forward for the university seconds for nothing. He was six feet tall, and though, at the tender age of twenty, not exactly solid muscle, he was on the way to getting there. He'd make a formidable opponent even for some loser like . . . What was it they were calling this bloke?

Oh yeah . . . 'the Creep'.

Keith snorted with derision as he strutted determinedly past a row of silent shops, water pouring in cataracts from the canopies over their fronts. Even if the bastard showed up, it wasn't as if Keith was totally on his own here. There were lights on in some of the flat windows overhead. He even fancied he could hear music. And if he could hear them, they could surely hear him if he cried out for help.

Not that he *would* be crying out, for all the reasons he'd just underlined to himself.

Of course, it wasn't comforting that this guy – the Creep – supposedly came armed.

Keith shook the thought from his head as the object of his search at last slid into view. About thirty yards ahead, on the left, the bright green square of a cashpoint VDU revealed itself. He veered over there, turning his head and checking behind him as he did.

It was in the close vicinity of cashpoints, always late at night, where this nutball was supposed to hang around. Essentially, he was a mugger. He would stop folk in the street, produce his blade, and it was quite some blade, by all accounts, and demand the cash they'd just drawn from the telling machine – though apparently it was never quite as simple as that, or at least it hadn't been so far.

Keith's rain-greasy fingers fumbled at the buttons as he tried to bash in his pin number. For an absurd moment, he miskeyed and got a refusal notice. He hesitated before giving it another go, glancing around first. Pulses of heavy rain drove along the deserted street in a kind of choreographed procession. But he was still alone.

Unsure how many attempts he'd be allowed before it locked him out, Keith tried his number again, much more carefully this time. With relief, the transaction was completed and a wad of crisp twenty-pound notes scrolled from the slot. He crammed them into his pocket as he lurched back along the shopfronts.

It was about three and a half miles to his digs. That would be no problem normally, but though he wasn't exactly leaden-footed, his energy reserves felt as if they were dwindling – that was probably as much to do with the cold and wet as it was the booze. Again, he thought about trying to hail a taxi, except that, typically, there were none in sight at present.

It didn't matter too much. He was sure that he could make good time on foot if he got away from the town centre. That was all he needed to do, in truth. All the attacks had occurred in that inner zone, the areas around New Street and the Bullring; nothing had happened as far out as Edgbaston. As he walked down Paradise Street, and crossed Suffolk Street Queensway, his confidence grew that all would be well. The guy hadn't always struck as soon as the victims had drawn out their cash; apparently, he'd shadowed a couple for a few streets, until they'd hit more secluded spots. But there'd been absolutely nothing out in the residential districts.

Keith felt mildly critical of himself. It had been folly – drunken folly, needless to say – to have got himself into this predicament in the first place, but the reality was that he'd probably not been in any real danger. There'd only been three or four of these attacks, as far as he knew, and Birmingham city centre was covered by CCTV, so it couldn't be long before the lunatic was caught. Perhaps 'the Creep' had realised that himself and had already gone to ground. That was surely what any sensible criminal would do.

As he headed down Holliday Street, Keith casually glanced over his shoulder. And had to blink twice – as what looked like a dark figure about fifty yards behind stepped out of sight.

Keith halted and pivoted around to look properly, his heart suddenly jolting in his chest.

Seconds passed. There was no sign of anyone there now.

He walked quickly on, throwing more glances over his shoulder, but seeing nothing through the gauze of rain. Before he reached the canal, he cut left down a ginnel, unsure if this was the quickest route but determined now to keep heading southwest.

Could what he'd just seen have been a figment of his imagination?

He hurried down a covered walk, and emerged onto another main road, Commercial Street. From here, glancing left, he could see all the way to the point where it intersected with Severn Street. It was at least a hundred yards off, but a dark, upright shape seemingly waited at that junction. It was impossible to tell what it was from this distance – it could easily have been some kind of permanent fixture there, but on the other hand it might be someone loitering.

Keith hurried the other way along Commercial Street until he reached Granville Street. From here he had good vantage both to the left and right. Not too far away, a set of traffic lights sat on green; there were no cars to obey them, just more curtains of rain swishing over the empty crossing. He glanced back once to see if the figure at the intersection was still there, but it was impossible to be sure; again, the rain obscured all detail.

Low-key night lights were still on in various shops, he noted as he walked on. Funny how, when you were out alone at night that didn't really bring you any comfort, somehow enforcing the message that there was no one else here but you.

He turned onto Bath Row, lurching sharp right. The deluge still hammered down. Keith wondered if it was going to slacken off at all before he got back to the flat, not that it would make much difference now, saturated as he already was.

For what seemed like the umpteenth time, he turned and glanced behind.

And this time saw a figure about forty yards away and on the other side of the road, but heading roughly in the same direction that he was. As before, Keith felt as if he'd been struck. But then he had a couple of reassuring thoughts: firstly, although the figure was wearing heavy waterproof clothing, with the hood pulled up, concealing the face was hardly sinister on a night like this; secondly, he'd made no effort to duck out of sight again.

It must be someone else on their way home. Nothing to be worried about.

Even so, Keith increased his pace, jamming his hands into his anorak pockets, and more out of instinct than logic, on the spur of the moment, taking a detour down another alley, this one leading around the back of the Shell garage. Technically, he was heading northward again – not where he wanted to go, but he had to admit, he hadn't liked the way that other homeward-bound pedestrian had suddenly appeared from nowhere.

He peered backward as he trudged down the alley, its junction with Bath Row falling steadily behind. But no waterproof-clad figure strode past it as he'd expected. When the junction was a hundred yards distant, Keith still hadn't seen anyone.

And that felt wrong.

He pressed on urgently, and almost collided with the steel post of a street sign, which he must have made a blind beeline for without realising. He skipped aside, but in so doing, slipped on a greasy flagstone, and landed heavily on his back.

A great video for someone to post on YouTube, he thought as he scrambled back to his feet, insulated from the pain by his growing sense of unease. In actual fact, he hoped that somebody *was* filming. It might help them catch this Creep nutter.

When he stepped out onto a narrow, largely residential thoroughfare which he recognised as Roseland Way, it was a relief. He wasn't far from home now.

Within a few minutes, he'd worked his way down to the A4540, or the Middleway as it was known, a large inner-urban dual carriageway, which formed part of the Birmingham ring road.

On the other side of that lay Edgbaston.

He crossed the Middleway via an underpass, descending a flight of stone steps and heading quickly along the square cement passage, which led some thirty yards to the other side. The usual graffiti was there in abundance – 'Blues' and 'AVFC' – along with other vastly more profane slogans. Keith might consider himself a lad-about-town, but he didn't particularly like using these subways at night, especially not alone – they were damp, desolate and echoey. But tonight was an exception. He just wanted to get home, get showered and get to bed. Not long now.

He was perhaps ten yards from the end when a figure descended the steps in front of him.

By its height and shape it was male, but there was no real certainty of that because it was covered by a heavy black rain-slicker with the hood pulled down over the face.

It came straight along the passage, head bowed, hands buried in its pockets.

Keith continued forward too, didn't even falter in his stride. Partly this was due to surprise – it basically stupefied him; his brain, for all that he thought he'd sobered up, was still too sluggish to transfer immediate messages to his limbs. It was also, he supposed – somewhat fatalistically – because there was no turning back now.

He lowered his own head as he advanced, burrowing his hands deeper into his pockets, and at the same time moving slightly to the right. Drunk or not, he was still an athlete. He could still dodge and run. But the guy – who was quite clearly the same person Keith had seen before – now veered straight into his path.

They were about two yards apart when he looked up and met Keith face to face.

Keith couldn't speak. He was too mesmerised by the waxy-pale features and the deranged grin imprinted on them. In fact, he was only able to move when the figure drew something metallic and gleaming from inside its right-hand pocket – which clearly wasn't a pocket at all, because this thing came out inch after curved and glittering inch.

It wasn't as much a knife as an old-fashioned cavalry sabre.

Keith jerked himself backward – and slipped on some waste paper. For the second time that night, he landed hard on his spine. For the second time, he barely felt it as he attempted to crab-scuttle backward. The grinning figure followed with a slow, deliberate tread, raising the sword as though for a massive downward chop.

'*Alright!*' Keith shrieked, scrabbling frantically to his feet but at the same time yanking the wad of cash from his jeans pocket and waving it at the advancing shape.

Sword still hovering, the Creep – whose maniacal expression never changed – reached out a gloved hand, and snatched the cash away. Keith could only peer up at the gleaming steel. In part because he couldn't bear to lock gazes with those small and weirdly shimmery eyes – he'd read something in the paper about the Creep always wearing a demented expression and having a penetrating, glint-eyed stare – but also because he knew, he just *knew*, that awful blade would not be staying overhead. Even so, he never expected it to sweep down in a blur of speed, to deliver a murderous blow to the joint between his neck and shoulder, to bury itself deep in muscle and bone. Keith sagged to his knees, stunned by pain and horror.

But it was only when the blade was wrenched free that the blood fountained out of him, and he fell face-first to the concrete.

Chapter 2

Detective Constable Lucy Clayburn headed north along the M60, and at the Wardley interchange swerved west along the M61. It was just after ten o'clock at night, so even Greater Manchester's famously crowded motorway network was relatively quiet, enabling her blood-red liveried Ducati M900 'Monster' to hit a cruising speed of 80mph as she passed the turn-offs to Farnworth, Lostock and Westhoughton. She only slowed as she reached Junction 6, where she swung a right, entering the complexity of roundabouts and slip roads surrounding the Reebok stadium, the home of Bolton Wanderers Football Club.

From here it was straight north-west, first along Chorley New Road towards Horwich, and then north along Rivington Lane. Only now, on the northernmost edge of the Greater Manchester Police force area, with the great bulk of Winter Hill looming on her right – an amorphous escarpment on the star-speckled October sky – did the red-brick conurbation of the cityscape dissipate properly, to be replaced by the more pastoral villages, woodlands and stone-walled farms of rural Lancashire. In due course, she even veered away from this, riding east into the foothills of the West Pennine

Moors, dipping and looping along narrow, fantastically twisty lanes. A few minutes later, deep in Lever Country Park, in the close vicinity of the renovated Tudor structure that was Rivington Barn, she throttled slowly down. A famous meeting point for bikers from all across the north of England, this picturesque but isolated spot was for the most part deserted late at night, but now one particular car park – a small area about four hundred yards from the Barn, hemmed on three sides by thick belts of trees – was a riot of light and noise.

Lucy homed in on it, gliding in among the many bikes parked haphazardly across its gritty surface and the bodies milling there in blue denim and worn leather. As usual, they were all ages, from rangy, pimply-faced teens to characters in their fifties with capacious ale-guts, bald pates and grey fuzz beards. Women of various ages were present too – Hell's Angel type activity had never been exclusively confined to the guys.

Regardless of gender, the back of each jacket had been emblazoned in fiery orange letters: *LOW RIDERS.*

They fell silent as Lucy rode slowly among them, a natural alleyway parting for her. She hit the anchors properly at the far edge of the car park, where she turned the engine off and lowered her kickstand. She climbed from the bike, took off her crimson helmet and shook out her black hair, which tumbled glossily down her back and shoulders.

Immediately, there were wolf whistles, ribald comments.

Lucy didn't react. She was in her motorbike leathers, which while they weren't exactly skin-tight, were pretty clingy. Add to that her constant work-outs at the gym, which meant that she was in good shape. But when she turned and fronted them, and they recognised her as the copper she was, someone hawked and spat.

The Low Riders weren't just a motorcycle club. They were traditionalists, with an 'old-school' ethos: *Live fast, die hard.*

13

Leave us alone, and we'll leave you alone. We operate by our *rules, not yours.* All of which translated into a lifestyle of endemic lawlessness and a natural distrust of the police.

Yellow teeth had now appeared in nasty, defiant grins. Lucy saw bottles of brown ale, the scattered empties as well as those half-full and clamped in oily fists (even though most of these guys would be on the road in the next hour). She saw spliffs too; not many, but enough on brazen display to signify a challenge. Not that making a drugs bust was why she was here tonight – as they realised perfectly well, hence their brashness.

One of them came swaggering forward.

It was Kyle Armstrong, president of the Crowley chapter.

Lucy hadn't seen him for quite some time; he was in his mid-thirties now, but still the way she remembered him: tall and lean, with truculent 'bad boy' looks, a tar-black mane hanging to his collar, and thick black sideburns. In his tight jeans, steel-studded belt and leather jacket, which he almost invariably wore open on a bare, hairy chest, he had a raw animal appeal. He might be out of time, fashion-wise, but he'd always reminded her of one of those classy heavy rockers of the early days, an Ian Gillan or Robert Plant.

Of course, she'd never let him know that was what she thought about him. Armstrong's ego was already the size of a barrage balloon.

'New length on your locks,' he said approvingly. 'Just like the old days. Going plain clothes obviously suits you.'

Beforehand, when in uniform, a spell that had only ended about ten months previously, Lucy had always kept her hair cut square at the shoulder. She hadn't been overly fond of that style, and so Armstrong was quite correct; being a CID officer did have its perks.

Again though, she wouldn't admit this to him. Mainly because she wasn't in the mood for banter. Were it any other low-to-mid-level criminal who'd requested a meeting with her, she'd have told him that he was the one who'd have to travel, but she and the Low Riders' president had something of a shared past, which, being hard-headed about it, meant that a useful outcome here was marginally more possible than the norm.

Even so, she didn't have to pretend that she liked the arrangement.

'What do you want, Kyle?' she asked.

He stepped around her, unashamed in his admiration for her leather-clad form, which irked her, though it was insolence rather than an actual threat – and anyway it didn't irk Lucy as much as it did Kelly Allen, or 'Hells Kells', as Lucy had once scornfully (and secretly) known her, a busty beauty of a biker chick, famous in the group not just for her impressive physique, but for her waist-length crimson-dyed hair, which very much matched her temperament. Many years ago, Kells had zealously sought out Armstrong's personal affection, and when she'd finally secured it – and it didn't come easily – she'd defended that status like a tigress.

Kells currently watched from about ten yards away, not looking her sexy best in a raggedy old Afghan coat, but her kohl-rimmed eyes blazing under her blood-red fringe.

Armstrong, meanwhile, had moved his attention on to Lucy's bike.

'I heard you'd written Il Monstro off chasing some bad guys,' he said.

'Banged it up a bit,' she replied. 'Nothing that wouldn't fix.'

'How about the villains of the piece?'

'They're both doing life.'

'Ouch.' He grinned. 'Should've known better than to mess with you, eh?'

'So should you by now. What's this about?'

'Don't worry,' he chuckled. 'I'm not after rekindling that fire we once had together.'

'Good . . . because that's dead.' She could sense the rest of them watching her in expectant silence, which annoyed her all the more – it might be a police thing, but Lucy never liked being the only person on the plot who didn't know what was going on. 'In addition to which,' she said, 'it's late and I'm in Court tomorrow. So, whatever it is, make it quick.'

'All right . . . can we walk a little?'

'If you don't want the rest of the crowd to know what you get up to, you shouldn't bring them with you,' she said as they strolled along a narrow, moonlit path. 'Or is that like asking someone to go out without his pants on?'

'It's them I want to talk to you about,' Armstrong replied. 'Or one of them. But there's no point everyone being party to the nitty-gritty, is there?'

She supposed he was right about that. The rest of the clan would know that he'd asked her here to make some kind of deal, but the fewer of them who knew what it specifically entailed, the less chance there was that the info would leak out.

'The word is you're a big noise now,' he said. 'A *full-time* detective no less.'

'And?'

He turned to face her, his wolfish features saturnine in the woodland gloom. 'I need your expertise.'

Lucy had expected nothing less, but was still cheesed off about it. It was amazing how many of these outlaw gangs fell back on the law when it suited them.

'Don't look at me like that, babe,' he complained. 'We've never been enemies.'

'Really?'

'Look . . . we're on different sides of the fence, I agree. But we weren't always, were we?'

16

'I was young and stupid back then,' she said.

'Some might say you're stupid to do what you do now.' Briefly, he sounded stung by her dismissal of their former relationship. 'Lead a happy life, do you, Luce? Still see all your old muckers?'

'My personal happiness is irrelevant, Kyle . . . whether I'm stupid or not depends on my response to this favour you're about to ask.'

He didn't immediately reply, humbled again – firstly because she'd clearly guessed why she was here, which kind of gave her an advantage, and secondly because if he wanted to get anything out of this, he had no real option other than to be nice to her.

'One of our lot got turned over by Crowley Drugs Squad,' he said.

'Well . . . wonders never cease.'

'No, look . . . this is serious. Remember Ian Dyke?'

'Not sure. The memory plays tricks. All your idiots tend to blend into one.'

'He's been busted for possession with intent to supply.' Armstrong shrugged. 'It wouldn't normally be a big deal . . . he was only carrying some draw, a few ecstasy tablets . . . but he really doesn't want to go down.'

'What's that popular phrase?' she said. 'If you don't like the time, don't do the . . .?'

'I know all that. Listen Luce, Dykey's girlfriend's just had a baby and he's trying to get his life sorted. Got himself a proper job and everything. But this isn't going to help with that, is it?'

'If it's only a bit of molly . . . he won't go down for that.'

'But he *will* lose the job.'

'So, he'll have to get another.'

'Look . . .' Armstrong seemed inordinately frustrated. 'Of all my lads, Dykey's the last one to deserve this shit.'

'You telling me the Drugs Squad framed him?'

'Nah . . . that'll be his defence, but that's not what happened.'

'Well, then he *does* deserve it, doesn't he?'

'It was his *last* delivery,' the biker stressed. 'His very last one. After that, I was gonna cut him loose so he could start a normal family life.'

She eyed him with fascination. 'So . . . is this your guilty conscience speaking, Kyle? Is the untouchable general finally getting a complex about the good little soldiers he sends into battle for him?'

'Hey, I'm just trying to help a guy out who's been a good mate of mine for a long time.'

She pondered, mulling over whether she could turn this thing to her own advantage. 'Have we got a trial date yet?'

'Yeah . . . next spring.'

'Next *spring*?'

'He's at Manchester Crown.'

'He's at Crown Court?' That surprised her. 'And he was only delivering a few bits and bobs?'

Suddenly Armstrong couldn't look her in the face.

'Any other lies I should know about?' she asked. 'Like maybe he hasn't got a job? Maybe his girlfriend hasn't just had a baby? Maybe he hasn't even got a sodding girlfriend . . . that'd be more believable, knowing half of your lot.'

'Lucy, come on,' he pleaded. 'I can make this worth your while.'

'*Yeah* . . . how?'

He lowered his voice, and glanced back along the path to the lights of the car park. 'Maybe I can drop you a bit of intel now and then.'

'Oh . . . you want to be my informant?'

'For Christ's sake, keep it down!' he hissed. 'And no, I never said that.'

'But we'll give each other a back scratch every so often?'

'Come on . . . I know you do this stuff all the time.'

She contemplated his offer. 'Anything you can give me now?'

'No, but . . .' He shrugged. 'But when the time comes, you only need to ask. Come on, Lucy . . . you know me.'

Yeah, I know you, she thought. The Low Riders were reprobates through and through, and could hardly be relied on to give help to law enforcement. But they *were* connected, and if Armstrong – who at one time had been a lot more to Lucy than just an acquaintance, even if she had only been going through a 'teen rebel' phase – said he might be able to give her something now and then, there was always a chance it would be juicy.

She sighed. 'You say this lad's name is Ian Dyke?'

'Yeah. He lives on Thorneywood Lane.'

Lucy knew the place. It was yet another nice-sounding street on a Crowley council estate, which in actual fact was so run-down that it ought to be bulldozed.

'All I can do is speak to Drugs Squad,' she said. 'I've no clout . . . you understand that?'

'Sure.' He sounded happier.

'I may be a detective, but I'm still only a constable.'

'I know you . . .' He eyed her suggestively. You can be very persuasive when you want to be.'

'I *can't*.' she assured him. 'And I'm not going to be. Best I can do is have a word.'

They walked back to the car park, where Lucy pulled her helmet on, kicked her machine to life and spun it round in a tight circle. Before heading back to the exit, she pulled up alongside Armstrong and lifted her visor. The rest of the chapter looked on in silence, though Hells Kells had now come forward and firmly linked arms with her beau. She glared at Lucy with icy intensity.

'Let me know how we get on, yeah?' Armstrong said.

'There is no "we", Kyle. So, don't be pestering me. I'll call you if there's anything to report. And if we hit pay-dirt on this, I want something back.' She pointed a warning finger at him. 'I mean it.'

He shrugged. 'Promised, didn't I?'

'Yeah . . . you promised all right.' And she treated him to a dubious frown, before hitting the throttle and speeding out of the car park.

Chapter 3

Lucy Clayburn was known widely in the Greater Manchester Police as a biker girl, and as a deft handler of her Ducati M900. There was scarcely a colleague, whether male or female, who didn't in some way find this intriguing.

Most of the men, especially those members of the Motorcycle Wing, thought it majorly cool, even more so when they learned that Lucy was also a self taught mechanic. One or two of the more old-fashioned types were vaguely miffed, regarding it as a challenge to their machismo, but these were fewer and farther between each year in the British police service, so on the whole they kept quiet. There were equally diverse opinions among the women, a couple of the more serious-minded types dismissing it as a frivolous thing, accusing Lucy of trying too hard to win the men's vote by playing the tomboy. But most of the girls were impressed, liking the fact that she'd strayed unapologetically into male territory and quietly admiring the derring-do it surely required just to ride one of these high-powered machines through the chaotic traffic of the twenty-first century.

All of this was somewhat ironic, of course, because Lucy didn't take her bike out very often these days. Back in uniform, she'd regularly used it to travel to and from work, because when she was actually on duty back then she drove a marked police car. Now that she was in CID, she could either drive one of the pool cars – which often had interiors like litterbins, and stank of sweat and ketchup and chips – or she could drive her own car, which was easily the more preferable option. As such, she'd bought herself a small four-wheel-drive, an aquamarine Suzuki Jimny soft-top, which now provided her main set of wheels. The Ducati was still her pride and joy, but the bike shed where it lived and where all her tools were stored, was still at her mother's house in Saltbridge, at the Bolton end of Crowley Borough, while Lucy had moved into her newly refurbished dormer bungalow on the Brenner Estate, at the opposite end. As such, she rarely even saw the machine.

The previous night, when she'd headed up to the West Pennine Moors to meet Kyle Armstrong and the rest of the Low Riders, had been an exception; riding her bike to *that* meeting could only have helped to win their approval. But later on that night, when she returned to Crowley, she parked the bike back in its shed, and without bothering to pop indoors to see her mum, who by that hour was most likely in bed, she headed across town in her Jimny. First thing this morning, she was back behind its wheel, eating toast as she drove into central Crowley, not towards Robber's Row police station, but to the central Magistrates Court.

En route, she used her hands-free to place a call to the CID office, where she asked DS Kirsty Banks to sign her on for duty. And then placed a call to DCI Geoff Slater, at the Drugs Squad. Slater, whom Lucy had worked with in the past on 'Operation Clearway' – a non-drugs related case – was not available to take the call, so she left a message instead, asking him to contact her.

On arrival at the Court – an authoritative-looking

Victorian building, complete with tall, stained-glass windows and faux Grecian columns to either side of its front steps, and yet faded to a dingy grey through time and weathering – she parked in the staff car park at the rear, entered through the staff door and went down the steps to the police room and the holding cells.

'Where've you been?' DC Harry Jepson snapped.

'Why . . . I'm not late?' She threw her overcoat onto a hanger.

'I know, but I wanted to make sure we've got everything straight before we go up.'

'Listen, Harry . . .' Lucy checked her watch as she entered the kitchen area; they had a good twenty minutes before the trial commenced, '. . . if you tell the *truth* in Court' – she stressed the word 'truth' as if it might be a novel concept for him – 'then there's nothing to get straight, is there. We'll both be on the same page automatically.'

Jepson looked hurt. 'I *am* going to tell the truth.'

'Good.' She put the kettle on. 'So, what's the problem?'

After ten years working as a uniformed constable out of various police stations in Crowley, her home town, but also home to GMP's notorious November Division, or 'the N', as it was sometimes called, Lucy had made the long-awaited permanent move to CID the previous winter. To some extent, this had been a battlefield promotion, a result of the 'exemplary courage and resourcefulness', to use the words of the Deputy Chief Constable at her commendation, that she'd displayed during a long, complex and particularly dangerous undercover assignment, the now legendary Operation Clearway. Without any of this, it was highly unlikely that she'd ever have made detective. Long before Clearway, at a relatively early stage of her career, one spectacular foul-up had almost seen her kicked out of the job and had certainly looked as if it would follow her round forever. Even with

Clearway under her belt, it was mainly thanks to the persuasive powers of Detective Superintendent Priya Nehwal of the Serious Crimes Division, that the GMP top brass had finally decided to overlook her previous indiscretion. That was the good news.

The bad news was that, for her first posting, working out of the CID office at Robber's Row – Crowley's divisional HQ – Lucy had been partnered with Detective Constable Harry Jepson, who, though affable enough when it suited him, was a bit of a throwback.

Harry had already been a detective for fifteen years when Lucy came along, but in all that time he'd never once been promoted, which implied that his dual habits of cutting procedural corners and showing heavy-handedness with suspects did not always pay dividends. He was a reasonably good-looking bloke, fair-haired and with a big frame – like a rugby player – though he was now in his early forties and a tad beaten-up around the edges. He was also a divorcee, unhappily so, with several kids to support, which embittered him no end; he drank too much as well, was increasingly slovenly in appearance, and inclined to gruffness with those he didn't know.

Lucy occasionally wondered, though had never asked aloud, if her being partnered with Harry was deemed to be as much for his benefit as hers. Not that she was renowned for playing a totally straight bat, herself, she had to admit.

It was also a growing concern that she thought Harry might secretly be carrying a candle for her. She knew he was lonely and frustrated, and he was well aware that she too was a singleton. Though they enjoyed a productive working relationship, she'd several times caught him eyeing her approvingly when he thought she wasn't looking. Not that Lucy was in any way tempted. Harry wasn't unfanciable – he had a certain roughneck charm. But she had strict rules about mixing work and pleasure, much to her mum's helpless fury.

'Brew,' she said. It wasn't a question; she handed him a mug of tea, while still stirring her own.

'Ta,' he replied, distracted and flustered as he went through the details of the original arrest, noted in his pocketbook.

Lucy was quietly amused by that. Out on the street, he was as cool as they came – casually and confidently dealing with even the worst of the town's yobs and criminals; a good man to have in a tight corner. But confront him with a wall of bureaucracy, and he became childlike in his ineptitude; face him with officialdom, and he lost all sense of who he was – grew nervous and frazzled.

Giving evidence in Court was never less than an ordeal for him.

The defendant that morning was a certain Darren Pringle, a repeat violent offender whom they both knew of old. Lucy didn't think that Pringle had much chance on this occasion – he'd been charged with wounding, yet again. A habitually aggressive drunk, the previous August he'd come stumbling out of a Crowley pub, taken offence that a young chap was sitting at a nearby traffic light in a sports car, and with no provocation whatsoever, had walked around the vehicle, punched out its driver-side window and then punched out the driver, blacking his eye and splitting his eyebrow in the process. He'd then run for it, but Lucy and Harry, having taken various statements from onlookers and following a 'vapour-trail' of CCTV, had arrested him at his council flat the following morning, where they'd also seized his clothing, which had later proved to be covered with glass fragments and spatters of blood – both his own and the aggrieved party's. It didn't look good for him, but strange things happened in courtrooms.

They discussed the detail while they had their tea, and

then traipsed upstairs to the lobby, where they had a quick conflab with the civvy witnesses and the brief from the CPS.

After that, they sat down on a bench to wait.

'By the way,' Harry said. 'You know there've been a number of breaks on the Hatchwood?'

Lucy nodded. Hatchwood Green was one of the most deprived housing estates in the whole of Crowley Borough. Crime there was nothing new. But the recent spate of house burglaries had occurred at a remarkable rate, and a quick analysis of the various crime reports would reveal many similar characteristics between them.

'Well . . . from today onward,' Harry added, 'that's me and you.'

She glanced round with interest.

'Stan's had enough and wants it clearing up,' he said.

Stan Beardmore was the divisional detective inspector at Robber's Row, and Lucy and Harry's immediate senior manager.

Before she could question him further on this, the clerk appeared and called Harry into Court. He stood up, straightened his loosely knotted tie and brushed down the lapels of his crumpled jacket.

'Once I'm done, if I'm discharged I'll head back to the nick and gather the intel,' he said. 'So we can hit the ground running.'

Lucy nodded, and waited. As she did, her phone rang.

'DC Clayburn,' she answered.

'Lucy . . .?'

'Morning, sir.' She immediately recognised the gruff but friendly tone of Geoff Slater.

'How the hell are you doing?'

'Bumbling along, as they say.'

'Nah!' he laughed. '"Lucy Clayburn" and "bumble" can't fit in the same sentence together. Thought you'd have your stripes by now.'

Lucy fleetingly pondered that. The mere fact she'd made detective was miracle enough; the possibility of being promoted to sergeant, even though in her mind at least she'd earned it many times over, seemed light years away. Slater of course, had no such millstones round his neck. When they'd last worked together, he'd been a detective inspector on the Serious Crimes Division. Now he was a detective chief-inspector, though he'd needed to accept a transfer back to his original stamping-ground of the Drugs Squad before any such honour had finally been conferred.

'No way, boss . . . don't think my face fits as well as yours.'

'Bloody hell . . . if it was down to who's got the best face, you'd be the Chief Con and I'd be deputy bog-brush.'

'Flattery will get your everywhere, sir,' she said, 'as always. Especially when I'm after a favour.'

'Shoot. Anything.'

'You've got a case pending next spring at Manchester Crown . . . Regina v Ian Dyke.'

'Oh yeah . . . that little shit.' Slater chuckled darkly. 'Courier for the Low Riders. Well, he's gonna get what's coming to him, I'll tell you.'

'Facing hard time, is he?'

'With any luck. We've been trying to get into that lot for a while. We dropped lucky with Dyke. On his own he isn't worth too much . . . we offered him the usual deal, but he wouldn't bite. You know what bikers are like . . . they're a tight crew. Anyway, like I say, he wouldn't play, so he's copping for the lot.'

That explained everything, Lucy realised. She already suspected that what Kyle Armstrong was really concerned about was whether Ian Dyke would try to make a deal and drop the entire chapter in it. But a promise was a promise, especially if it might pay off at some point.

'I was just wondering,' she said, not entirely comfortable with this, but persevering. 'Well . . . if there was any way you might . . . well, go easy on him?'

There was a short but profound silence at the other end of the line.

'Lucy . . . the trial date's been set,' Slater said. 'April 3. And that was no small amount of gear we found on him.'

'It's just that it may be useful to one of my own enquiries.'

'I can't get the charges reduced at this stage, even if I was inclined to.'

'Sir . . . you remember that really crappy job you gave me during Operation Clearway? Going undercover in that brothel over in Cheetham Hill?'

'The job you lobbied me for, you mean?' he said sternly.

'Yeah, that one. And then remember how one of those bastards even threatened to blowtorch my nose off?'

'Don't try this on, Lucy . . .'

'I'm not trying anything on. I'm just saying . . . I did a job of work for you, that year. We took down a crime syndicate and arrested two serial killers.'

'For which you've been rightly recognised.'

'Sir, it's only a little thing I'm asking.'

'Lucy . . .' Slater sounded flabbergasted. 'Ian Dyke's a bad lad. He's been spreading the Low Riders' poison all over Crowley, and probably well beyond it, for years . . .'

'You've just told me he's a cog in a machine. Is it really going to advance the cause if you throw everything but the kitchen sink at him just because you can't collar the rest of them?'

There was another pregnant silence.

'Okay,' he eventually replied. 'I'll tell you what I can do. And this is purely on the basis of our friendship, which is on thin ice at present, my girl.'

'I understand that, sir . . . I'm very sorry.'

'Yeah, you sound it.' He paused, as if maybe about to reconsider. 'If Dyke changes his plea to guilty . . . and he might as well because he hasn't got a leg to stand on, I will personally write to the judge and point out that the accused has been helpful and cooperative throughout the case, has demonstrated genuine remorse and is seriously trying to get his life together. Now, you don't need me to tell you it won't necessarily save his neck, but it might mean that the judge will go a little easier on him . . . and, like I say, he's got to change his plea first, and that hasn't come from me, by the way . . . it needs to come from his legal team. So, the first thing Dyke needs to do is get onto his brief. Make sure he understands that, Lucy . . . the first move must come from him.'

'Okay, sir. I'll pass that on.' Lucy knew this was the best deal they were going to get. 'Thanks for your help.'

'I don't know what you're into with the Low Riders, love . . . but I advise you to be wary of them. They're not just some run-of-the-mill motorcycle club. They're a heavy crew and they're regularly involved in crime.'

'I know that, sir.'

'And that president of theirs, Kyle Armstrong – he's the worst of them.'

'I know that too, sir. Thanks.'

Slater harrumphed. 'See you round, Lucy. Take care.'

Chapter 4

Owing to Crowley's status as a one-time coal and textiles hotspot, its warehouse and factory district was almost in the town centre, primarily because that was where the main rail-yard was, but it was also only a stone's throw from the main shopping area.

As such, as recently as the 1970s, Crowley's 'inner ring' had been crammed with working mills and factories, their forest of tall chimneys pumping smoke into the air above the Greater Manchester township day and night. It had certainly given the place some character back in the day, and it did so now – to a degree – a succession of immense industrial structures towering over the red-brick terraced neighbourhoods which for so many decades had supplied their workforces.

Of course, in the twenty-first century such buildings were an anachronism. Some, rather ambitiously, had been renovated into blocks of 'desirable apartments' (many of which were still for sale), while others had become visitor centres. Of the rest, most had been boarded over and left. To some this was a blight on the environment, but others saw it as an opportunity. For example, it was in Rudyard Row, a weed-filled backstreet snaking its way between several of the most decrepit of these empty Edwardian monoliths, where Roy 'the Shank' Shankhill ran his 'business'.

Rudyard Row wasn't an alley you'd stumble into by accident, because you had to work your way through a warren of similarly-squalid passages just to reach it, and so most folk, even locals, didn't know it was there. In addition, there was next to no reason to go there. Some of the former workshops that lined it on either side were still used, but most of them were soulless facades of brick, with plank-covered windows.

It looked as dismal as ever on that dull, damp day in mid-October, when Malcolm Pugh showed up there. This was nowhere near his first visit, and highly likely it would not be his last, but he was no less nervous for that.

He'd come into town from Bullwood by bus. It was late-morning, rush hour long over, and so he'd travelled on the top deck alone, mulling endlessly over his plethora of problems. As he walked warily down Rudyard Row, he felt even more alone, but now he was frightened too.

In many ways, it was a good thing he was doing here today. He expected it to curry favour, but you could never be absolutely certain what the outcome might be when dealing with the Shank. He glanced left and right before knocking on the door to No. 38, the two numerals hanging rusty and limp amid strips of peeling paintwork.

What he neglected to do was look directly behind him, so he didn't see the door to the derelict building opposite swing silently open on recently oiled hinges.

Initially there was no sound from inside Shankhill's premises. Pugh was about to knock again when he heard what sounded like a rustle of newspaper on the other side of the door. He knew what that would be: Turk, that great slab of meat and bone that Shankhill called a minder, getting irritably up from his stool, rolling up whichever of the daily rags he'd been reading – probably something with lots of tits, bums and suspenders – shoving it into his jacket pocket, and . . .

'Yeah, who is it?' came Turk's voice through the wood.

It was a curious accent. Pugh couldn't place it. He'd always assumed from the guy's nickname, and because of his swarthy complexion and short tangle of oily black hair, that he'd originated in the Middle East somewhere. Not that it was important. All that really mattered where Turk was concerned was that he was six-foot four at least, and that he worked out daily, and/or did lots of steroids, which had built him a herculean physique. Reputedly, he liked nothing better than to imprint his many sovereign rings on the bodies and faces of those his employer took issue with.

'It's Malcom Pugh. I need to see Roy.'

A snicker of laughter sounded on the other side. 'You never get tired of it, do you?'

'I'm not here for a loan . . . I want to pay him back.'

'Yeah?' Turk sounded amused, as though this had to be a scam and he wasn't buying it.

'Seriously. Come on, Turk . . . Roy's expecting me.'

There were two resounding clanks as, first, a top bolt was drawn back, and then a lower bolt. The door started to open, and Pugh put his foot on the step only to be struck from behind as somebody barrelled into his back.

It threw him forward into the door, which bounced inward with tremendous force, impacting massively on the guy behind it. There was a *crump* of splintering wood and a garbled grunt from Turk, and Pugh – who was too stunned to know what was happening – was grabbed by the back collar of his anorak, a gloved hand slapped across his mouth, and forced inside.

The immediate interior was a narrow space at the foot of a steep, dank stairway. A single grimy fanlight only weakly illuminated its wet brick walls and the stool to one side. Turk lay sprawled backward on the foot of the stairs, the lower half of his face spattered crimson from a smashed nose. Pugh, meanwhile, had his legs kicked from under him, pitching him down onto his knees, as two burly bodies crammed into the tiny space behind him, moving with catlike stealth. The door closed with a thud, but its top bolt was shoved back into place as quickly and quietly as possible.

Blinking with shock and pain, Turk groped for the Colt Python he kept in the armpit holster under his tan leather jacket. But before he could reach it, the muzzle of what looked like a sub-machine gun was jammed against his chin. His hand froze.

Pugh cowered where he knelt, a crumpled adult foetus, only glancing up slowly and fearfully. The two intruders, who hadn't yet said a word, let alone shouted out a threat or warning, both carried automatic weapons with shoulder straps. Pugh had no clue what make or model they were, but they looked terrifying, especially as they had big magazines attached to their undersides.

The intruders wore zipped-up black leather jackets, black leather gloves and bright red woollen ski-masks with only narrow slots for the eyes. They were about average height and size, though one was slightly taller than the other. This taller one kept his gun under Turk's jaw. It was firm in his left hand, as he put the index finger of his right to the place where his lips should be, and said: 'Shhhh.'

Turk watched him balefully, but said nothing. Pugh, of course – a much smaller and older man than Turk, with a reputation even at home for being a weakling and failure – whimpered aloud, which earned him a vicious side-kick. The taller gunman leaned even closer to Turk, forced the muzzle into his Adam's apple, and pressing it in hard, dragged a glottal gurgle out of him. With his right hand, he rummaged around under Turk's jacket until he found the grip of the Colt Python and drew it out, slipping it into his own pocket.

He straightened up and backed off, but only for half a foot or so, the sub-machine gun trained squarely on his captive's battered face. 'Get up,' he said quietly.

Turk did as he was told. At full height, he stood several inches above even the taller of the two gunmen, but that scarcely mattered. He now fancied he recognised the weapon under his nose as a SIG-Sauer MPX. At this range, its 9mm slugs would cut him in half like a buzz saw.

'Arms out where I can see them,' the taller gunman said. 'Then turn around.'

Turk complied, spreading his empty hands and shuffling round in a semicircle.

'Upstairs,' the gunman instructed. 'Make a sound out of the ordinary . . . anything I think is meant to be warning, and you're on your way to Allah sooner than you ever imagined possible.'

Slowly, with heavy but careful footsteps, Turk ascended the stairs, the gunman close behind, the muzzle of the SIG jammed into his spine.

The second, shorter gunman nudged Pugh with his foot to indicate that he should go too.

'Please,' Pugh whined. 'I'm not even supposed to be here . . .'

A strong hand snatched Pugh by the collar and hauled him to his feet. Pugh headed up the stairs at a petrified stumble, the second gunman treading stealthily at his rear.

There was a corridor at the top, all loose boards and rotted, hanging wallpaper. Only one door led off it, down at its far end. The occupant of the room beyond, Roy 'the Shank' Shankhill, a hefty porcine individual with pinkish features, slit-eyes, a mat of lank, gingery hair, and as always, wearing a patterned house-robe over his stained shirt and scruffily-knotted tie, sat behind a broad, leather-topped desk, which, aside from the free-standing electric fire in one corner and the small, steel safe in another, was the only furnishing in an otherwise empty shell of a room.

Shankhill thought he'd heard a *bump* downstairs – he even put on his glasses, which normally hung on his chest from a chain, and squinted across the room at the half-open door. But no other sound had followed, and he'd soon written it off as Turk knocking over his stool or something. It might even be Malcolm Pugh arriving for his appointment – though frankly Shankhill would believe that when he saw it. It wouldn't be the first time the inveterate gambler had failed to show when he was due to make a repayment. Even if it *was* Pugh, it wouldn't be the whole whack. It was never the whole whack – and it wouldn't even suit Shankhill if it was. He could hardly have his debtors paying him back before they'd accrued some real interest. It wasn't like he needed full and immediate repayment anyway, as the heaps of used banknotes on his desk, which he was currently sorting into orderly piles, would attest – along with the chunky gold rings on all his fingers, the chains around his neck and the various bracelets adorning his wrists, not to mention his diamond-studded Rolex.

Then the door to his office slammed open, hitting the wall with such force that plasterwork flew, and Shankhill – a juggernaut of a bloke in physical terms – almost leapt from his seat.

Turk came wheeling in as though pushed, the lower half of his face a mask of glutinous blood. A balding, runty short-arse of a bloke – Malcolm Pugh, Shankhill realised – tottered in alongside him. The pair had been kicked through the door with such energy that both now fell onto all fours. Their two abductors came in behind them, also side by side, sub-machine guns levelled.

Shankill went rigid with disbelief, regarding the intruders through his lenses with a blank, fishlike stare, his podgy, sweaty hands hovering over the piles of money. Then he turned sharply – a Winchester pump was propped against the wall, perhaps only a yard away.

'Uh-uh!' the taller gunman said, cocking his weapon.

Shankhill scrutinised them intently, eyes almost popping behind his thick glasses.

Their guns hung from leather shoulder straps, making them immediately accessible. They'd spaced out so they were about two yards apart, making a more difficult target of themselves and yet at the same time easily able to cover the whole room. Their stance was solid, unflinching; they wielded their weapons with the look of expertise.

Professionals, then. Resistance would be extremely ill-advised.

The slightly shorter of the two stood on the left; he now circled around the kneeling figures of Turk and Pugh, before heading around Shankhill's desk, where he took possession of the shotgun. He backed away, cradling it under his right arm while balancing the SIG in the left, in effect, covering the three hostages with both weapons. The taller one, meanwhile, let his SIG hang from its strap, while he took a rolled-up black canvas bag from his coat pocket, shook it open, came forward and commenced sweeping the money off the table into it.

This took no more than twenty seconds. The kneeling captives could do nothing, fresh blood still trickling down the front of Turk's shirt, Pugh hunched forward, eyes screwed shut, a pool of yellowish fluid spreading out around his sodden knees.

When the taller gunman had cleared the desk, he dug into a large holdall alongside it, lifting out several more bricks of banknotes and cramming them into his sack.

'Do you know who I am?' Shankhill couldn't resist asking.

'I couldn't care less if you're Donald Trump's condom supplier,' came a voice from behind the taller intruder's scarlet ski-mask. 'Open the fucking safe.'

Shankhill pursed his lips and gave a tight shake of his head.

The gunman's eyes widened in the holes in his mask – not so much with anger, Shankhill felt, as with fascination. 'Seriously?' the guy asked.

'Seriously,' Shankhill replied in a stern but patient tone, like a teacher trying to impart a lesson. He'd decided that he was going to tough this thing out. 'You're on very fragile ice, boys, let me tell you. Time is not on your side, and if you actually *do* know who I am . . . you wouldn't even be here. Now, I strongly suggest you don't push your luck any more, and you get out while the getting out's good. As it is, you're going to be hunted for the rest of your life.'

The taller gunman regarded him with apparent deep interest. 'The safe?'

Shankhill shook his head again, slowly and deliberately.

The gunman seemed to consider this, and then whipped around, grabbed Turk by the collar of his jacket and yanked him up to his feet, before pushing him hard towards the far corner of the room. 'Turn around!' he barked.

Still with his arms out, Turk shuffled around until he was facing them, eyes expanded to an amazing size in a face not just bloodied but now pale and damp with fear. Without warning, the taller gunman raised the SIG and, single-handed, fired a deafening burst at his legs.

Both limbs were visibly shattered as the shells ripped through them, hammering into the wall behind, spraying it with blood and bone and meat. Turk fell full-length onto his side, gagging in almost unimaginable pain. Malcolm Pugh screamed in terror, clapping his hands to his ears, fresh streams of piss seeping through the front of his trousers. Shankhill, who'd banked that his temporary tough talk might do the trick, could only goggle in horror. He too had half put his hands to his ears, and now, as the echoes died away and the dust cleared, could do no more than blink in rapid-fire shock at the sight of his fallen comrade.

'He gets the next lot in the head,' the taller gunman said. 'After that, we start on the little fella.'

'No . . . please!' Pugh squawked.

'Be quite a fucking mess for you to clean up given that you run an unlicensed money-lending business from these premises,' the gunman added. 'And you won't even be able to call a friend when your own knees and elbows are shot through, will you? Because trust me, pal . . . we'll get round to you too before we leave here.'

Shankill's mouth sagged open as he gaped first at one, and then at the other.

This was serious. This was absolutely for real. Roy 'the Shank' Shankhill was being robbed inside his own office.

'The safe!' the taller one said again. 'You fat, greasy-headed fuck!'

The money-lender held his position for another moment – just long enough for the various bits and pieces to finally fall together inside his stunned mind. Beaded with sweat, he stumbled away from his desk to the safe and squatted down, where he adjusted a dial, turning it back and forth to listen to the requisite number of clicks. When the door *clunked* open, Shankhill rose to his feet and backtracked away.

At the far side of the room, the wounded Turk gave a low, animalistic whine. The gunmen ignored him, the shorter one stepping in front of Shankhill so that he could cover him with the SIG while keeping the shotgun trained on the fallen henchman. The taller, meanwhile, hunkered down at the safe, and began lifting out rolls and rolls and rolls of banknotes, all of which he shovelled into his sack. After that, he helped himself to jewellery – bracelets, brooches, necklaces – quality stuff too, not of the bling variety that Shankill generally adorned himself with, but platinum and white gold, embedded with diamonds and other gems. When he'd finished, he straightened up and turned to face the Shank.

He offered an empty hand. 'We'll take your neck chains and your rings, while you're at it. And the Rolex. Jesus . . . you wash your hair in chip-fat, or what?'

Shankhill scowled as he handed the valuables over. 'I'll find you,' he said quietly.

'Yeah?' The taller gunman stepped backward. 'Maybe my bootprint'll give you a head start.'

Then he opened fire at Shankhill's legs. A fusillade of lead shredded through muscle and bone, all but blowing the ungainly limbs away completely, hurling the overweight money-lender down onto the blood and urine-spattered floor-boards.

To prove he was a man of his word, the taller bandit concluded by stamping on Shankhill's pale, sweat-soggy face some two, three times. When he'd finished that, the two of them rounded on Malcolm Pugh, who wailed even more loudly than before.

'Shut it or you die!' The taller one stabbed a warning finger into Pugh's face.

But the little gambler was wild-eyed and wet-mouthed with fear. 'My inside pocket!' he gibbered. 'It's in my inside pocket . . . all of it. Take what you want . . .'

'We don't want *your* money,' the taller one said.

When Pugh filched a handful of twenties from under his jacket and waved it at them, the shorter one simply knocked it out of his grasp, sending it fluttering across the room, and then twisted his hands behind his back, causing him to shriek again, his time with agony, before binding them together with duct tape. He repeated the process with Pugh's ankles.

'It's dead simple . . . Malcolm,' the taller bandit advised him, when Pugh lay trussed in a corner. He'd read the first name on a credit card from Pugh's wallet, though he now reinserted the card into the wallet, and replaced it in the captive's pocket. 'You've survived this. You even get to keep your own cash . . . you'll be able to get yourself free in a few minutes. But it isn't over. We know who you are. So, you go to the cozzers about this . . . you even call an ambulance for these two goons, and we'll come back for *you*. And you won't need me to tell you . . . it won't just be your legs we shoot off.'

Pugh said nothing, closing his eyes against the stinging sweat dabbling his lashes.

When he finally risked opening them, the masked assailants had gone.

Chapter 5

Lucy was back in Robber's Row CID not long before one o'clock, the case against Darren Pringle proved and the regular offender finally in receipt of the custodial sentence he'd deserved for so very long. He'd been led down to the cells, looking totally stunned that four months' imprisonment now hung over his head, but Lucy knew that it was a minuscule punishment in reality. If he kept his nose clean, and he likely would given that he'd be in a short-stay facility where it was in everyone's interest to behave themselves, he'd be out in two. And then, not long after that – who knew, maybe at the end of his first-night-of-freedom party – he'd come reeling out of the pub plastered, and start throwing more drunken punches. If or when he did that, she wouldn't be too far away, and so they'd go through the whole dispiriting, time-consuming procedure again. But at least it wasn't her problem for the time being.

The detectives' office – or 'DO' as it was known locally – was its usual hive of midday activity, with many comings and goings, keyboards chattering, phones ringing.

'Result, Luce!' DS Banks shouted from across the room, briefly breaking off from a phone call. Lucy acknowledged with a thumbs-up, before stripping her mac off, draping it over the back of her chair and slumping down at her desk. Here, she found a note from Harry, explaining that he was now over on the Hatchwood, getting the ball rolling by re-interviewing the various burglary victims that DI Beardmore had linked together. She was welcome to join him whenever she was able to.

Before she drove over there, Lucy grabbed herself a cheese sandwich and a cola from the machine outside the DO's main doors, and opted to check through her emails.

Almost immediately, a piece of apparent junk offering cut-price Viagra caught her eye, the main reason being that it had slipped past the spam filter. She swilled cola and crammed down her butty as she made a note of the final few characters on its subject line.

TC – Borsd 1-15.

Meaningless to anyone not in the know, of course – more internet gobbledegook – but to Lucy it was as familiar as a street sign. She checked her watch. It was almost quarter past one now. The service would be departing the town centre imminently, which meant it would be calling outside the police station in the next ten minutes or so.

She got up and pulled her coat on. Technically, she wasn't supposed to attend meetings like this on her own. According to GMP rules, Harry ought to be present as well, but he wouldn't get back here from Hatchwood Green in time, even if he was able to set off straight away – which he likely wouldn't be if he was mid-interview. But it wouldn't be the end of the world. If anyone asked, she was feeling out a possible lead. If it looked promising, she and Harry could do this thing together, officially, later on today or maybe tomorrow.

She rounded the front of the building to Tarwood Lane and joined a couple of mothers with prams waiting at the bus stop there. She probably made a slightly incongruous figure, still dressed for court in a smart blouse and slacks, heeled shoes and her poshest beige raincoat, but if this was the way she had to do it, there was no real argument. Besides, she only had to wait a short time before the one-fifteen from Crowley town centre to Borsdane Wood turned up. The two young mothers clambered aboard first, Lucy assisting them with their prams. After she'd paid for her own ticket, she climbed the tight stairway to the top deck, where a single fellow passenger rode in the front seat – this was his usual position, mainly because the upstairs security cameras on this bus route were also located at the front, and thus unable to see the persons sitting directly below them.

There was no one else anywhere near, so Lucy slid into the seat immediately behind.

You wouldn't be able to tell it while he was seated, but Jerry McGlaglen was a tall man, about six-foot three and now aged somewhere in his early sixties. Almost invariably, he dressed in elegant fashion – flannel trousers and matching blazer and tie were his preferred combination, often with a carnation in the buttonhole – though this often jarred with his thin features, sunken cheeks and wispy grey beard and moustache, not to mention his mop of grey hair, which had something of the feather duster about it. When you spoke to him face-on, he had odd-coloured eyes, one blue and one green, and unhealthy, brownish teeth; his personal hygiene wasn't quite what it had used to be, either. As such, while he might strike an imposing figure from a distance, up close it was strange and rather scuzzy.

'Why are we persisting with this cloak-and-dagger stuff, Jerry?' Lucy asked quietly, after the bus recommenced its journey. 'Can't we just meet in the pub like everyone else?'

McGlaglen didn't look around. 'Because what I am giving you today, my dear, is the biggest tip-off you're ever likely to receive.'

Lucy nodded. She'd heard this kind of promise before, but to be fair to McGlaglen, he rarely offered anything that wasn't at least interesting. She clutched the horizontal bar at the top of his seat as they swung around a tight bend.

'A particularly unpleasant fellow,' McGlaglen added, 'a true reprobate and degenerate is in town.'

He'd been given to using flowery language for as long as Lucy had known him; he even delivered it in a dramatic, Shakespearean tone, all traces of his local accent suppressed. It was something to do with his past, she understood, though she'd never questioned him on it. Police informers came in every shape and size; all that mattered was the reliability of their intel.

'A true degenerate, eh?' she said. 'Go on. I'm all ears.'

'The Creep. You know of this beast, I take it? He's in the town now . . . as we speak.'

At first Lucy thought she'd misheard. 'Sorry . . . what?'

He neither looked round nor raised his voice. The one thing Jerry McGlaglen defended more zealously that his air of faded flamboyance was his right to anonymity; when imparting information to his police handlers, he was never less than exceptionally wary. He would do nothing whatso-ever to attract attention to himself from the ordinary public. To Lucy's mind that somewhat contradicted his manner of dressing and speaking, but when she'd raised this with him once in the past, he'd replied that his attire served its purpose as a double bluff.

They look twice, that is undeniably true. But when all they see is a well-known eccentric, they rarely look again.

'The Creep?' she said, puzzled. 'You mean the lunatic who hangs around cashpoints in Birmingham late at night, robbing people at sword-point. You say he's in town? You mean *here* . . . in Crowley?'

'This is the story I've been told, my dear.'

'Jerry . . . how is that possible?'

'Why . . . I'd imagine he bought himself a ticket at New Street, climbed onto a train and headed north.'

'Funny man. I'll rephrase the question. *Why* is he here . . . I mean in the Northwest?'

'How could I know? Perhaps he has relatives here. He was unlikely to linger in the Midlands after what happened during his last attack, don't you think?'

Lucy pondered the info with rapidly growing interest. Even though Birmingham was eighty miles south, she'd read all about the case on various bulletins. The offender was basically a mugger, but the West Midlands press had named him 'the Creep' because of his crazy fixed grin, which owed possibly to a mask or heavy make-up. A Joker lookalike, then; a comic-book madman. But there hadn't been much to laugh about for his victims, who'd not just lost wads of cash but, even when they'd complied, had been slashed with what appeared to be an old-fashioned but well-honed cavalry sabre. Invariably it had inflicted gruesome wounds, and in the case of the most recent victim, had proved fatal.

She leaned forward. 'How've you heard about this, Jerry?'

'Now, my dear . . . as you know, I never divulge such things. But as you also know, my sources are impeccable.'

'What's the Creep's name? I mean his real name.'

'This I cannot tell.'

'Cannot, or will not?'

'Cannot.'

'So where will I find him?'

'Alas, I have no answer for that either.'

'Jerry . . .' she leaned closer to his ear, 'you seriously think you're going to get paid for this? Passing on an unfounded rumour that this guy may be in Crowley . . . *may* be? And giving us nothing else whatsoever?'

'I suspected you'd be hostile. Ignorance, as always, breeds

contempt. I imagine I will only get paid if you apprehend this scoundrel . . . as per our usual arrangement. How you make that happen is beyond my control.'

'Do you have anything else on him at all?'

'It is my belief that he will have come here to work.'

'Work?'

'To continue his bloody reign.'

'Seriously?' Lucy wondered if he was winding her up. 'You think this bloke's on the run from a murder charge, and a few weeks later he's just going to blow all that by starting again only an hour up the railway line?'

McGlaglen shook his head. 'I know no more about this case than you, Miss Clayburn, but I have read sufficient disgusting detail to form an opinion that for this malefactor it is as much about the swordplay as it is the money. I appreciate that sudden fear has driven him to change towns. But really . . . how long can such a depraved individual resist temptation?'

Lucy had also read plenty of material regarding the Creep, and on reflection, it wasn't difficult to draw a similar conclusion. In each incident thus far, the offender had inflicted unnecessary violence; the slashing of the APs with his sword *after* they had handed over their wallets was completely uncalled-for, which implied that at least part of the abnormal gratification he drew from these attacks was from seeing first the terror of his victims, and then their blood. It might indeed be that this was *all* of it, the cash obtained little more than a bonus. And if that *was* the case, it seemed likely that he'd struggle to resist the impulse when it came. It could even be that, while here in Manchester lying low, maybe staying with friends or holed up in a B&B, he would feel more secure than he had in Birmingham, where the hunt for him was now really on, and so he might be even more encouraged to renew his violence.

46

'How long's this guy supposed to have been in Manchester?' Lucy asked.

'I only heard about him a couple of days ago, my dear,' McGlaglen replied. 'But it must be longer than that, surely.'

She considered this. The last Creep attack in Birmingham had made the papers about two weeks ago. Prior to that, he'd struck every few days or so. He could well be getting itchy fingers.

'Jerry . . . you're absolutely certain about this? People you know and trust are saying the Creep is in Crowley? I mean, this isn't some flight of fancy?'

He finally turned and frowned round at her, his odd-coloured eyes alight with intensity. On the basis of past information he'd provided, he probably had the right to look a little indignant.

'Okay,' she said. 'I'll go back to the nick and make this official.' She saw a stop coming up where it would be convenient for her to jump off. There was another one on the other side of the road; she could catch a bus back to the station from there. She stood up. 'If it happens, you'll get your usual fee. But if it doesn't . . . if we end up wasting a load of time and resources, they'll mark you down as a bad bet.'

McGlaglen sighed melodramatically. 'It is a sad state of affairs when a generally reliable man can only be allowed to fail once.'

'We're talking about someone who, for his hobby, hacks people up with a sword.' Lucy swayed her way to the top of the stairs. 'Forgive me, Jerry, if I'm keen to get it right.'

Chapter 6

He might have entered the criminal world relatively late in life, but Joe Lazenby had soon come to recognise this as a benefit rather than a drawback. It obviously helped that he didn't have a rap sheet, and it helped enormously that after years of normality, he didn't *look* like a criminal.

Whatever people said about the monsters in our society mingling easily and comfortably with the rest of us, that only really applied to the successful ones. As far as Joe Lazenby was concerned, some shaven-headed moron decked in cheap bling and wearing tattoos on his face and neck wasn't even going to enter a street-corner boozer without the punters edging away from him, so his chances of getting close to someone it was actually worth robbing or conning were beyond zero. Not that Lazenby went in for primitive tricks like robbing or conning, but in complete contrast to those tattooed, knuckle-dragging apes, he still regarded his 'ordinary joe' appearance as his best asset.

In fact, that was the street name he used: 'Ordinary Joe'.

He'd chosen it, himself, and almost unbelievably, it had caught on. Even so, as he sat here in the genteel environs of Hogarth's Cocktail Lounge, working through his daily accounts, no one would ever know what he was really up to. They'd just see a guy in his mid-thirties, slightly stout of build, average height, with curly brown hair and a neatly trimmed beard and moustache, a wedding ring on one hand, a none-too-expensive Nautica watch on the other, wearing black horn-rims and a three-piece suit, sipping Perrier water as he tapped away on a laptop; clearly an averagely successful businessman wrapping up the day's work with a few final, essential adjustments before winding his thankful way home – no doubt to a semi in the suburbs, where his pretty wife and two-and-a-half nerdy children awaited him.

It helped, of course, that most of the clientele at Hogarth's were cut from exactly that cloth, though mainly that was down to the time and place – late afternoon on a Tuesday, and Pearlman Road in the very centre of Crowley, where, for the most part, it was office and retail staff now disgorging from the workplaces close by.

Outside, the mid-October dusk was falling quickly, and with it the temperature. But Hogarth's prided itself on providing a warm, snug environment. The mullioned windows were shaded with velvet, the lamplight low-key, the various loungers and armchairs of the deepest, most comfortable variety. The music playing was easy jazz, while the real fire crackling in the grate threw cosy orange-gold patterns across the hardwood floors. There was no actual bar service in here; all drinks were supplied by waitresses, who would attend your seating bay or booth or coffee table, in response to the ornate Edwardian bell-pushes located nearby.

It wasn't too busy at present. No one would really expect it to be, but that suited Lazenby. He might be confident of his anonymity, but it was still easier to relax when people weren't constantly edging past your table, perhaps throwing covert glances at your laptop screen. There were perhaps six other patrons in Hogarth's at present, all dotted around, either alone or in couples, those together chatting quietly over drinks, the others reading evening papers, or, like him, fiddling around with electronic devices.

Either way, it left plenty of spare places all over the wine bar's comfy interior.

Which is why it was so annoying to Lazenby when another guy in a suit, someone he didn't know from Adam, suddenly inserted himself into the same booth and sat down on the other side of the coffee table, on top of which he nonchalantly plonked a large G&T.

Lazenby tried not to look at him, but couldn't help stealing a couple of irritable glances.

The guy was in his mid-fifties and sharp-suited, with an average build, lean features and silver-grey hair razored into a crew cut.

Lazenby didn't like his personal space being invaded for no reason, but for the sake of appearances – he was Ordinary Joe, after all – he didn't make an issue of it, merely nodded when the newcomer's dark eyes flitted towards him, and continued working at his accounts.

'You picked the wrong place to try and get some work done, I'd say,' the guy commented.

Lazenby didn't at first realise that he was being addressed. 'Sorry, what?'

'Noisy bar.'

It wasn't an especially noisy bar – not at this time of day.

'Didn't notice,' Lazenby replied, pointedly not looking up.

'Hard to concentrate.'

The air hissed between Lazenby's clenched teeth as he finally met the newcomer with his best blank-eyed stare. Ordinary Joe might value his average appearance and air of affability, but he was also a Scouser. He originated from Childwall, which wasn't a poor part of Liverpool, but nevertheless, in archetypical Merseysider fashion, he didn't take well to being hassled.

'Especially when people keep talking to me,' he said, 'and only politeness is preventing me telling them straight that I'm not interested.'

He went back to his laptop, pink-cheeked, but reasonably confident that the unexpected show of no-frills hostility would have done the trick. It couldn't be very often that tired, bored business guys encountered a straight-talking response like that in Hogarth's.

'You a polite guy, then?' the stranger said. 'Perhaps they should call you "Joey the Gent" rather than "Ordinary Joe"?'

Lazenby glanced up at him again, this time shocked.

The guy took a sip of his G&T, unfazed by the turn in the conversation. 'But hang on, I don't suppose that would work. "Joey the Gent" sounds like "Jimmy the Gent" . . . and wasn't he some kind of gangster? That would never do, would it?'

'Who are you?' Lazenby asked, instinctively closing his laptop to protect the information it contained.

'Me? Oh, I'm no one important enough to have a cool nickname.'

'You a cop?'

The man smiled to himself. 'I'm guessing they call you Ordinary Joe because you look and act like an everyday Charlie. Perhaps we should call you that, instead: "Everyday Charlie".'

'I could ring my solicitor right now,' Lazenby said, talking tough, though in truth his hair was prickling because he didn't know if he could; he had no clue how much the law might have on him. 'This is harassment.'

'Be my guest,' the guy said. 'Ring him.'

'I'll see you around, officer.' Lazenby did his best to look relaxed as he lifted his briefcase, slid his laptop into it, and clicked it closed. 'Come back when you've actually got something.'

He stood up.

'You know harassment's hard to prove,' the man said. 'I should know . . . me and my associates have made that call a few times. Never got anywhere with it.'

Lazenby was about to leave the table, when these words sank in.

He turned back, regarding the newcomer with careful deliberation, before sitting down again.

'You're the Crew, aren't you?' he ventured.

The man looked nonplussed as he sipped more gin. 'The Crew? Never heard of them.'

One second ago, Lazenby had been stiff and numb; his spine had gone cold – internally he'd been reeling with shock that the law had so unexpectedly caught up with him. He'd tried to brazen it out, praying that whoever this interloper was he was merely on a fishing trip. Now he felt only relief, though there was no guarantee he was on safe ground yet.

'Look . . .' he said warily, 'we don't need to have a problem here. I'm more than willing to do a deal.'

The man raised an eyebrow. 'Perhaps it should be "Co-operative Charlie"?'

'I know what this is about. I've got somewhere you can't. I'm selling all over suburban Manchester. Middle-class districts which you have no access to. I'm also in with the white-collar crowd in the commercial area. And believe it or not, they gobble the stuff like it's free.'

'Oh, I believe you.'

'But it isn't free.' Lazenby leaned forward confidentially. 'And I'm making good money without setting a single foot on the mean streets.'

This was an unashamed boast, and maybe that wasn't always advisable where the Crew were concerned. They weren't the Northwest's premier crime faction for nothing; internally, Lazenby's nerves were jangling. But it suddenly seemed important to him, if he was going to deal with these guys on an equal basis, to underline the fact that he was a real player who had something valuable to trade.

'Yeah. Everyday Charlie and his gentlefolk customer base.' The newcomer's tone wasn't quite derisory; he sounded vaguely interested. 'I've seen it actually, and I *am* impressed. Ice cream vans, pharmaceutical deliveries, driving instructors . . . touch of genius, all that. Great cover.'

'Look, I'll be blunt with you,' Lazenby said. 'For two reasons. Firstly, because I'm a straight player. I always believe in saying it how it is. That's how I've got where I am today, and I've no regrets about it. Secondly, because I figure you guys are smart enough to know what side your bread's buttered on.' He lowered his voice even more, increasingly confident of his position. '*You* can't get into the leafy parts of town. But I'm already there. So why don't we hook up? I don't have to move my own product solely. I can move yours too. I'll open a completely new market for you. But the terms have got to be favourable.'

The stranger mulled this over. 'Like you say, straight to the point. Least that'll make things easier.'

Lazenby made an expansive gesture. 'That's how I roll.'

'What's your annual turnover, just out of interest?'

'Well, in the last nine months alone, I'm . . .' Lazenby checked himself. It couldn't be wise revealing too much about his operation. But then again, if he wanted to win their trust and at the same time impress on them that he'd be a serious asset . . . 'In the last nine months, I'm two hundred-thousand net.'

'And you'll be looking at . . . what?' the stranger said. 'Ten per cent?'

'Erm, no.' Lazenby had to chuckle. 'I like to earn in a way

that's commensurate with the risk I'm taking. I'll take twenty-five, and that's being generous. That's out of respect for your status.'

'Twenty-five eh?' The stranger pondered this.

'And of course, it depends on the quality of the product you're pushing. I mean, I deal with discerning people. They smell chalk or talcum powder, it'll be no more dice from them and no more dice from me.'

'Everyday Charlie and his discerning customer-base, eh? I'll have to bear that in mind.'

Lazenby glanced over his shoulder before leaning even closer. 'What do you say? I was hoping to meet you guys anyway, at some point, so we could square this very deal.'

The man eyed him, for the first time closely; it was slightly disconcerting – there was steel in that gaze. 'You want *in*, basically?'

'Sure I do.'

'Into what, though?'

'The Crew. What else are we talking about?'

'There's no such thing as the Crew. Least, I've never heard of them.'

Lazenby sat back exasperated. 'Listen mate . . .' He knew he shouldn't do it, but he couldn't really control the snap in his voice. He needed to advise them that he was serious about his business. 'There's something you need to know. I'm not Mickey Mouse, all right . . .'

'No, you're Everyday Charlie.'

Frustrated that they were still playing this silly game, Lazenby grabbed his briefcase. 'When you find out who the Crew are, and more importantly, *where* they are, let's talk again.'

'I've got another deal for you,' the man said.

Lazenby stayed in his seat. 'I can do twenty per cent, but that's got to be it. That's as far down as I'll go.'

'Let's stop talking figures, and focus on responsibilities.'
Lazenby shrugged.

'Because, I think you've got me confused with someone else.' The man took another sip of G&T – in ludicrously genteel fashion; he even raised his little finger. 'You see . . . I don't have any product for you to sell. That's not my line at all.'

'So why are we having this conversation?'

'We're having this conversation because, like I say, I think you seem like a decent, straight-to-the-point kind of fella, and in addition, you've got this ingenuity thing going on. You're someone who deserves a bit of a heads-up.'

'To what?'

'Well, not to how much you're going to earn.' The guy treated Lazenby to that steely gaze again, now coupled with a wire-thin smile. 'But to how much it's going to cost you.'

'Ahhh . . .' It was several moments before Lazenby was able to work enough saliva into his mouth to reply properly. 'You're a tax collector, is that it?'

'No.' Though the man's smile broadened, it still didn't reach his eyes. 'I'm *the* tax collector.'

'You're Frank McCracken.'

'Never heard of him.'

'Don't they call you "the Shakedown"?'

To a degree, Lazenby was honoured, and not a little proud of himself, to have attracted the personal attention, not just of a senior lieutenant in the Crew, but the lieutenant whose main purpose it was to get the syndicate its cut from all those criminal enterprises in the Northwest of England that weren't actually their own. But he couldn't deny that he was unnerved too; his hands now shook, their palms moist. The approach had been gentlemanly enough, but Lazenby wasn't deceived. He'd heard some bone-chilling tales.

'So, let me see,' he said, biting down on his fear – this

was only going to end one way, so the best he could do now was try to affect some kind of damage limitation. 'I've got to source my own product, pay the advance on it, arrange importation, storage, security, distribution, delivery . . . with no input from you whatsoever, and you still get paid? Is that correct?'

The man who had to be Frank McCracken sat back. 'You make it sound like you don't win.'

'It depends how much.'

McCracken made a show of thinking this through – for about two seconds. 'I reckon sixty/forty's a fair split, to be honest.'

'Sixty/forty?' It could have been worse, Lazenby supposed.

'In *our* favour, of course.'

'In *your* favour . . .?'

'You sound doubtful, which I suppose is understandable.' McCracken thought it through, again. 'So, let's make it seventy/thirty. Until we get to know each other better. Oh, and we'll take our first payment from the two hundred-thou you've pulled in so far this year.'

'This . . . this . . .' Lazenby struggled to suppress his helpless rage. 'This always the way you do business?'

'Not at all. We'd normally be having this conversation out back. But out of respect for *your* status, I thought we'd do it differently today.'

'And I suppose if I say "no", those gloves will come off, will they?'

McCracken shrugged. 'No rush for that. But anything can happen.'

'I could've been a good friend to you.'

'You still will be, I'm sure.'

'You reckon?'

'You live off Mulberry Crescent, don't you? Nice part of Crowley, that.'

Lazenby didn't suppose he should be surprised that they knew where he lived. He said nothing, however, neither confirming nor denying it.

'Not as nice as Carrwood in Altrincham, mind you,' the gangster added. 'Or Bromley Cross in Bolton, or Worsley in Salford, or Ellesmere Park, or Hale, or Timperley . . .'

Neither, Lazenby supposed, should he be surprised that they knew his main sales areas.

'Nice places,' McCracken mused. 'Tree-lined streets, green lawns at the front of every house, couple of cars on each drive.' Suddenly, there was a mischievous twinkle in his eye. 'Be a real shame if things changed. You know, if the yobbos turned up . . . and the crackheads, and the gangbangers, and the boy-racers. Looking to party every night up and down those quiet streets. The residents would call the fuzz of course. Probably again and again. I mean, they're not used to that kind of disorderly conduct. But is that really what you want, Joe?'

'And let me guess . . . if I pay my taxes, none of that happens?'

McCracken finished his drink and stood up. 'There are no guarantees in this line of work. But if I was you, I'd hedge my bets. I mean, you may be a refined kind of guy, you may live in a detached house and mix with culturally correct people, but I reckon you're a gambler too. I'm sure you know a safe option when you see one.'

He edged around the table, to leave.

'I'll think about it,' Lazenby said.

'No, you won't.' McCracken backed towards the cocktail lounge door, still smiling. 'You're not that stupid.'

Chapter 7

Detective Inspector Stan Beardmore was a short, squat chap in his mid-fifties. He had snow-white hair, which he always kept close-cut, and was habitually clean-shaven and well-groomed, though this tended to clash with his shabby tweed jackets; he had a brown one and a green one, and he alternated them on a weekly basis – even though both had seen better days, with frayed cuffs and leather-patched elbows. He was a good boss, though. Lucy had quickly come to realise that his affable nature masked a sharp mind and years of experience. On top of that, rather than being a stickler for paperwork or procedure, he was trusting of his detectives and encouraged independence of thought.

On this occasion, however, he seemed a tad dubious.

He sat behind his desk in his own office, an annex to the DO, and leafed through the pile of print-outs that Lucy had handed him. For the most part, these were selected extracts from the policy file of the Major Investigation Team down at West Midlands CID, mainly crime-scene reports and glossies, witness statements (for what they were worth, which wasn't much), several e-fits, and a detailed psychological profile, as prepared by a forensic psychologist.

'So, West Mids were happy to share?' Beardmore flipped pages but only really skimmed what they contained.

'Think they're keen to wrap this thing up,' Lucy replied. 'Any help GMP can give them and all that.'

'And what exactly do we know about this Creep fella?'

'According to the notes, he's a biggish bloke. About six-one, six-two, heavy build. The psyche profile makes him a young-to-middle aged male, most likely white, probably out of work or in low-paid employment.'

'No kidding.' Beardmore turned one of the e-fits around; it depicted a pale moonlike face under a heavy hood, with tiny, narrow eyes, a near non-existent nose and a jack-o'-lantern grin which split the visage from ear to ear. 'Thought they'd be queuing up to recruit this fella.'

'I spoke to a DS Broadhurst, who's Document Reader in the West Mids MIR,' Lucy replied. 'He says they reckon this Creep business is a bit contrived. The manic grin, the sword . . . it's his theory that they could be looking for someone a bit more stable than that suggests.'

'Someone who's capable of putting an act on?'

'Yeah.'

'And if that's the case, why do we assume he's going to reoffend while he's on his holidays up here?'

Lucy paused before responding. She'd been through all the November Division crime reports taken that last week, and though there was the usual quota of assaults and street robberies, none were like-for-like with the attacks in the West Midlands. As such, with no actual crime for Crowley CID to investigate, she was now proposing that they put some spotters on the street at night in anticipation; maybe even use decoys. If the Creep's past form was anything to go by, he'd commit his offences in proximity to town centre cash-points. Lucy had even produced a map of central Crowley and had earmarked certain hotspots they could prioritise.

'In answer to your question, boss,' she said, 'we don't know whether he'll reoffend while he's here, or not. But just because the psyche evaluation suggests he's an organised offender, that doesn't mean he doesn't have mental problems. It also, see . . .' she indicated a particular paragraph, which she'd underlined with red biro, '. . . it proposes the possibility that, whoever he is, he's suffering from Antisocial Personality Disorder.'

'So, he's a sociopath. There's a surprise.'

'At the very least he's a sociopath, I'd say. Look at *this* section.' She read aloud: '"The offender demonstrates a considerable degree of delusion. For example, taking precautions to avoid identification but at the same time not realising that such a distinctive and exaggerated MO will in itself narrow his chances of remaining at liberty. The same conclusion may be drawn from his chosen attack-zones, the vicinities around cash machines, which any ordinary thief would surely expect to be progressively more heavily policed. Highly likely, the offender knows right from wrong, and is thus able to function normally when it pleases him, which will be most of the time. However, there are clear indications that when his desire to inflict violence becomes overwhelming, there is little to hold him back."'

Beardmore looked to be lost in thought.

'In other words,' Lucy said, 'it's quite possible that when he slips back into this deluded state, whether he's down in Brum or up here in Crowley, he'll go straight back to work, as Jerry McGlaglen calls it.'

'That McGlaglen's an oddball. Are we sure he's given us everything on this he's got?'

'Well . . . we're never sure of that, are we.'

'He's grassed for us a few times, hasn't he?'

'Been good as gold up till now.'

Beardmore eyed her carefully. 'What does Harry Jepson think?'

She shrugged. As Jerry McGlaglen's joint handler, Lucy had spoken about it to Harry on the phone, but in truth he hadn't been especially interested, pointing out in his usual frustrated way that they had more than enough work to be getting on with already.

'He thinks it sounds promising,' she lied, feeling certain she could pull Harry along.

'Well . . .' Beardmore planted both hands on the spillage of paper in front of him. 'I can see you've done quite a bit of spadework on this, Lucy. An impressive amount, given the short time you've had available.' He arched a busy white eyebrow. 'But I can't help wondering what it's got to do with the burglaries I assigned you and Harry to look into on Hatchwood Green?'

Her cheeks coloured, but she'd been expecting this. 'Harry's still over there.'

'I wanted *both* of you over there.'

'I'll be going there soon . . . I just thought you'd want this bringing to your attention.'

'Hmm.' He pondered. And then sighed. 'Crowley CID certainly hasn't got the time or resources to mount a surveillance on every cashpoint in town on the off-chance this nutcase breaks his cover. But . . . DI Blake may be a different story.'

'DI Blake?' Lucy was a little surprised. 'You mean the Robbery Squad?'

'Why not?' Beardmore scrabbled the various documents and photographs together. 'They're in trouble, aren't they? Could be just what they need, this, a big case to get their teeth into. A result wouldn't do them any harm, either.'

No, Lucy thought to herself, somewhat ruefully. *Nor me.*

Chapter 8

Crowley Robbery were a branch of Greater Manchester Police's Serious Crimes Division, and were formerly the Manchester Robbery Squad, whose original purpose was to investigate commercial armed robberies across the whole of the Greater Manchester area. However, the current age of cascading budget cuts had seen them reduced significantly in size and divided into smaller units which were now allocated to GMP's various divisions. Highly likely even that wasn't the end of it; as Beardmore had alluded to, with police expenditure still being slashed across the board, talk was rife that Crowley Robbery – like Salford Robbery, Rochdale Robbery, South Manchester Robbery and so forth – were luxuries that local law enforcement could not really afford, at least not currently.

Despite this, Crowley Robbery – or 'Robbery Squad' as they were still referred to in rank-and-file parlance – were highly valued by most CID officers, who saw them as an elite outfit. Headed up by the highly decorated Detective Inspector Kathy Blake and, in the short time they'd been operating from out of Robber's Row, already responsible for taking down a number of high-profile blaggers, Lucy in particular had been fascinated that the fabled bunch of thief-takers were suddenly working only a couple of floors overhead.

Not that she wasn't nervous in their presence, even with Beardmore by her side.

Though she'd passed various Squad members in the station corridors and the canteen, this was the first time she'd been up close to them, particularly to their mythical leader, whose desk she and Beardmore now stood in front of, though she also felt vaguely surprised. Lucy had half been expecting a policewoman with DI Blake's reputation to be a real hard-bitten toughie. But in fact, she was attractive and looked rather refined. She was also surprisingly young. Lucy was thirty-one, but she doubted DI Blake was more than a year older than her, if that. In addition, she was short – perhaps no more than five-six, whereas Lucy was five-eight. She had long, honey-blonde hair, which she wore in a ponytail, and was 'peaches and cream' pretty, with a dusting of freckles and intense green eyes. In fact, DI Blake's unblinking, laser-like gaze was something Lucy had heard about before; even the most rugged customers were said to have struggled to meet it during interrogation.

However, that intense gaze was now directed downward as she rifled through the heap of documentation that Stan Beardmore had brought up from CID.

Lucy glanced around the Robbery Squad office, while she waited. It was a big room, which had been put to lots of different uses in the past, but currently was cluttered with desks, tables, filing cabinets, VDUs and whiteboards covered in scribble, its walls adorned with paperwork and pictures. One thing she noticed in particular was an entire section of room that appeared to have been cordoned off with work-benches. Two detectives were currently in conflab there, discussing a series of blown-up CCTV screen-grabs pasted onto a Perspex screen and apparently depicting an armed robbery in progress: two figures in khaki fatigues and stocking masks were unloading money bags from a G4S security van on a shopping centre forecourt. The security staff lay face down, and were covered by two other masked figures, one wielding a pickaxe handle, the other a sawn-off shotgun.

DI Blake's desk was at the opposite end of the room from this, set against the wall, to an extent lost among the desks belonging to the bulk of the lower ranks, and certainly no larger or grander. However, one thing that was different was the wall behind it, on which a series of large square photographs had been pasted in seven orderly rows. Each one depicted a face, the bulk of them ugly and brutish – clearly the headshots of known criminals, one or two of whom Lucy thought she recognised straight away – but approximately half of them defaced by a big red X, which had been drawn in vivid marker-pen, and with some vigour.

It fleetingly distracted Lucy from DI Blake herself. But not for long. While most of her team wore casual gear – jeans, sweat-tops, trainers and the like – the DI was almost formally attired in a neat grey skirt-suit, pearl blouse and heels. She tapped her pen on the desk as she checked through the last few pages that Beardmore had supplied her with.

'Do you trust your informant, DC Clayburn?' she suddenly asked.

'I suppose so, ma'am,' Lucy replied.

'He's no track record for giving you duff intel?' Blake wondered.

'Not so far. This one's thin on detail though, I must admit.'

'Well . . .' Blake had another long think, 'technically, these are robberies and that puts them in our ballpark.' She glanced at Beardmore. 'I think we can run with this for a couple of weeks, Stan. But we haven't got the resources to cover every cashpoint in the borough.'

'I anticipated that, ma'am,' Lucy said, unfolding another sheet of paper, this one a street-map of central Crowley. 'That's why I suggest we focus on these particular cashpoints here.' She spread it on the desk, indicating ten separate locations which she had marked with biro crosses.

DI Blake stood up to assess it properly.

'Ten of them,' she said. 'Only ten?'

'I guessed we'd have to concentrate our resources to a degree,' Lucy explained. 'So, these, to me, will be his most likely targets. I've chosen them on the basis that he'll do his research. He'll have to – he's a stranger in town, or at least he's not a resident, so he's not going to be overly familiar with the layout.'

She glanced at Beardmore, who remained studiedly indifferent. She could imagine that he wasn't best pleased at the amount of attention she'd clearly been paying to this particular case, when she was supposed to be concentrating on something else. On the other hand, he ought to be a little proud that she was now demonstrating to the head of a specialist unit just how thorough and professional his own divisional officers could be.

'Go on,' Blake said. 'I'm listening.'

'Well . . . all of these work in his favour, ma'am,' Lucy said. 'They're all in areas extensively covered by CCTV, but he's got a hood. And the fact it's a mucky October means he can walk the streets with his hood drawn up and not attract any attention. So, he's got that base covered. In addition, they're all out in the open.' She moved her index finger from one point to the next. 'A high street, a junction with traffic lights, the edge of the market square . . .'

'And that's an advantage to him?' one of Blake's underlings asked.

Detective Sergeant Danny Tucker had been summoned over to join them by Blake as soon as she'd learned about the case.

Lucy had spotted him walking around the station before, but hadn't really known who he was. This was the first time they'd been up close together, let alone had spoken. It was perhaps a minor distraction that Danny Tucker was just about the best-looking guy Lucy had seen in the job for quite some time. Of West Indian extraction, but by the sounds of it born right here in Manchester, he was tall, about six-three, with hair cut short and an athlete's build, which was visible even through his figure-hugging polar-neck sweater. He had a square jaw, high, strong cheekbones, and bright, intelligent eyes.

'Well, yeah,' Lucy said. 'He attacks late at night, and not many people are likely to go out to a cashpoint late at night unless they feel relatively safe. These particular cashpoints, because they're out in the open, will probably be deemed safer than most.'

'So, if he hangs around these, there's basically more chance he'll get lucky,' Blake said.

'That's my reading of it, ma'am, yes.' Lucy's finger roved further across the street map. 'These points also benefit from having getaway routes everywhere. A side passage through to a pedestrianised shopping mall, from where there are half a dozen other points of egress. A subway . . . An overpass that leads to a housing estate. Plus, and this could be very important, they're all in close proximity to free on-street parking.'

'You think he's mobile?' Blake said.

Lucy shook her head. 'I don't know, ma'am. You dress up like a lunatic, pick someone at random, cut them down with a sword and just run off into the night, in most cases leaving them alive to shout for help . . . you'd normally be asking for trouble. I mean that wouldn't just draw attention to the scene of the crime, but to you and to whichever route you've used to get away. That would normally be the trademark of a disorganised attacker who's doomed to get nicked pretty quickly. Unless, as we've already said, it's a part of an act, the purpose of which is to conceal the fact he's actually a very organised offender indeed. I mean, while the cops are running around looking for a grinning maniac, he's removed his disguise and miraculously become an ordinary citizen again, happily driving home to his house in the suburbs . . . or something like that.'

Blake contemplated this.

'Of course, he's not going to leave his motor on an actual car park,' Lucy added. 'I mean, they're covered much more intensively by security cameras than on-street, and that would reveal his VRM.'

'You've really done your homework on this, haven't you?'

Lucy shrugged modestly.

Blake sat back on her swivel-chair to chink. 'DC Clayburn? Aren't you the lass who arrested Timothy Lennox? Cleared up a whole bunch of historical murders?'

'That's right, ma'am. Last winter.'

'Good collar, that. You also led the undercover op that brought down the Twisted Sisters over in Longsight, didn't you?'

'I didn't *lead* the op, ma'am.'

'She was a leading light in it,' Beardmore grunted. 'They couldn't have done it without her.'

Blake chewed on her pen. 'Have you ever thought about coming to work for me in Robbery Squad?'

Beardmore pointedly harrumphed – a message Lucy received loud and clear.

'It's certainly something I'd be interested in, ma'am,' she said. 'But well, I've got quite a bit of work on in CID at the mo.'

Blake shrugged. 'We haven't got any vacancies at present, anyway. But if something comes up, I'll get Danny here to give you a shout, so you can get your application in early.'

'I will, ma'am. Thank you.'

'Okay.' Blake shuffled the paperwork. 'Leave this lot with me. I'll keep you informed.'

Lucy nodded and smiled, and as she left the office, walking side by side with Beardmore, felt completely re-energised. It was always a thrill to think you'd made an impact on someone who counted.

But they were only halfway down the stairs, when Beardmore said: 'Don't get any ideas about that. Robbery Squad are an effective unit, but you know what things are like. One day the money's there, the next it isn't. Friday night, they lock up a load of blaggers. Saturday night, they celebrate it. Monday morning, they've all been shunted back to Division.'

Lucy wasn't sure how to respond, but she knew that he was right.

'Hey, Lucy!' someone called down from the top of the stairs. They turned and saw Danny Tucker descending.

'Sarge?' she replied.

'Quick word?' he asked.

Taking the hint, Beardmore turned and continued down. 'Just remember, the jobs are piling up,' he said over his shoulder.

Lucy turned back to Tucker, who grinned, displaying a neat row of pearly whites.

'This is good stuff you've brought us,' he said. 'Thanks very much.'

Unsure how to reply, she nodded.

'We're actually working a big case at present,' he said.

'Yeah, I saw the pics. That's the Saturday Street Gang, isn't it?'

'Oh, you heard about that?'

'How could I not? Seven cash-in-transit robberies in two months. But I didn't know Saturday Street had done any jobs on the N.'

'Well . . . they haven't,' Tucker admitted. 'But when we were still the Manchester Robbery Squad, our unit was getting very close to them. It only seemed reasonable we should continue the enquiry after they broke us up. It'd be a feather in our cap if we could pull those bastards in. But it's the same with this case you've brought us. I mean, we're busy . . . but we can never be too busy at present, if you know what I mean. Got to justify our existence somehow. Anyway . . .' Fleetingly, he seemed awkward, as if he wasn't quite sure what to say next. 'You've done a lot of groundwork for us here. This is great, so thanks very much for that. I'll keep you clued in, let you know how we get on.'

'Thanks, sarge.' Lucy couldn't help wondering why he'd come downstairs to repeat DI Blake's promise.

'Hey, listen . . .' He smiled again, which he seemed to do a lot – and why not, it was far from unattractive. 'This is Robbery Squad. We don't do titles. Call me "Danny".'

'I will . . . thanks.'

He headed back upstairs. Lucy watched him go for a teensy bit longer than she perhaps normally would, before turning and walking on down to CID.

Chapter 9

Ordinary Joe Lazenby didn't particularly want to go home that evening.

Immediately after the incident in Hogarth's Cocktail Lounge, he drove aimlessly around the town for perhaps an hour. All along of course, he'd known that there were higher powers in this world he'd infiltrated. Yet, things had gone so smoothly for so long that he'd begun to feel, perhaps not invincible, but certainly a master of his own destiny. During the working day, he headed up a relatively lowly admin department at Crowley Technical College. He earned a reasonable wage from it, and he was treated with civility and taken fairly seriously by the academics on campus, even if in truth he suspected that they thought him a jumped-up little jobsworth who was no more than a glorified paper-pusher. But he made an okay living. He owned a large detached house on Coxcombe Avenue, which was on the Cotely Barn estate on the edge of Crowley golf course, an affluent part of town; he drove a decent enough motor – a metallic beige Ford Galaxy; and he and his family went on a nice holiday once a year – cruising was the in-thing currently, and they'd so far done the Western Med, the Eastern

Med, the Caribbean and next August they were looking forward to doing the Norwegian fjords. On the surface, everything was hunky-dory.

But in actual fact, this commonplaceness was the problem.

For quite some time, Joe Lazenby had been deeply frustrated by his none too awe-inspiring status. Throughout his adulthood, he'd felt that, unless he was to diversify into something much more lucrative, and dare he say it, dangerous, he was never going to fulfil his lifetime's ambition, which was to be a man of substance, of ingenuity, of latent but undeniable power.

And so he *had* diversified, and it had been a rocky road – he'd taken chances, both financial and actual, first getting into the drugs-importation market through former school-friends who'd long ago taken to crime and shipped their produce in through the Liverpool docks. But having earned the trust of his Colombian suppliers by providing all the cash required upfront and on time, and wowing them with tales of his previously untapped middle-class market, he had completely divested himself of those awkward, insolent middlemen. Lazenby got a huge kick from this alone, convinced that his forward-planning was second-to-none, and that his nose for a deal and an innate working knowledge of the real world made those elitist, muddle-headed book-dwellers at the college shrink to child-like insignificance. He'd been running his low-key op for three years now, the money had poured in, and the respect he'd so long yearned for had finally arrived; perhaps not up there in the surface world, but certainly among those who mattered.

And then today had come along.

When Lazenby got home that night, he couldn't settle. His wife, Geraldine, had already made dinner. He was late and so it had gone cold, but she didn't comment about this because she knew he was putting in such enormously long hours at the college these days – at least, that was what he told her – which meant they were far better off financially than they'd ever been before.

After dinner, Lazenby kissed his two children, Maggie and Joseph junior, and Geraldine put them to bed. The normal process now would be for Lazenby and his wife to shower, change into their pyjamas, slippers and dressing gowns, and snuggle up on the sofa in front of the real-flame gas fire and mid-evening TV, sipping mugs of cocoa and commenting casually on the events of their respective days; Geraldine cosy in her knowledge that they were living the middle-class dream, Lazenby cosy with thoughts of his secret but ever-expanding empire.

But tonight when Geraldine came back downstairs changed, her husband was still in his work clothes and sitting stiffly in one of the armchairs. He looked pale-faced and distracted, and even though watching the day's second instalment of *Coronation Street*, he clearly wasn't following the events on screen; his eyes were almost glazed. When Geraldine tried to speak to him, he was curt to the point of being dismissive. A few minutes later he apologised, explaining that he'd had a tough day and that there were some difficult decisions to make in the department. She perched on the chair's armrest and tried to cuddle him, cooing that it would be all right, that he was a good departmental boss and that he knew what was best for everyone. She even tried to massage his shoulders through the back of his suit jacket, but he remained rigid as a board, his eyes locked on the TV screen despite not seeing anything that was happening there.

'It's just, I wish . . .'

He'd been about to say: *'I wish things were as normal as*

that. That all I had to do was either sack someone or put them on a warning, or something.'

But even if he had said that, it would have been a lie. Because deep down he didn't wish for normality at all. He wanted his dukedom back; he didn't want to suddenly be a servant again.

Which started him on a new train of thought: How much of a servant would he actually be?

The Crew must see some value in him, otherwise they'd have – what was it McCracken had said? – had the meeting 'out back'. That encounter could have been a lot more frightening, and perhaps considerably more painful. Maybe this meant that an equal partnership still awaited him somewhere up the line? Assuming he proved his worth.

But how far up the line? How much would he have to demean himself to make this happen?

How much more humiliation could he go through when he'd thought he was past all that?

But then, did he even have a choice? It wasn't as if Frank McCracken had been negotiating. If anything, he'd been laying down ground rules. And how had McCracken even known that Lazenby would be in Hogarth's, or who he was for that matter? Had they been following him?

Lazenby's anxiety grew exponentially, his shoulders stiffening even more under his wife's fingers.

'My God, Joe . . . you really need to try and relax,' she said.

Lazenby couldn't answer; his mouth was dry, his teeth locked.

They clearly knew everything about him. How else would they have closed in on his business affairs so quickly? But there was still no need to panic. This was the Crew, after all, not some bunch of drugged-up nutcases. But even so, why make it easy for them?

Abruptly, he stood up.

'What's the matter?' Geraldine asked. 'I didn't hurt you, did I?'

'No, it's fine.' He walked across the room, opened the door and went out into the hall. When he reappeared, he'd donned an anorak over his suit. 'I'm going for a drive.'

'Joe, what's the matter?' she pleaded. 'Tell me what's bothering you.'

'It's nothing . . . it's really nothing. There are some things I need to work out, and to do that I need to get some peace and quiet. Okay?'

She regarded him worriedly. 'Do you want me to get Mrs Gallagher to sit in, so I can come with you? We can talk about it.'

'For Christ's sake, no . . . it's fine!'

As he climbed into his Galaxy on the drive, he realised that that parting shot had been far sharper than he'd intended it to be. He loved Geraldine and the kids. He loved everything about his family. They were the ones he was doing this for. He wanted them to share in the dream, even if they didn't know about it. And by the look on Geraldine's face after he'd snapped at her, he'd upset her, which he regretted – but that couldn't be helped at present.

As he drove out of Coxcombe Avenue and onto Mulberry Crescent, and then onto Leatherton Lane, the main thoroughfare connecting Cotely Barn with central Crowley, he wondered if he was now about to do something he'd come to regret even more.

Only slowly, after driving a mile or so, did he finally conclude that he probably wasn't.

The Crew hadn't become who they were through cowboy antics. Okay, working on the basis they already knew everything there was to know about his operation, it was safe to assume they would soon twig what he was up to now – if not tonight, probably as soon as tomorrow. And they wouldn't like it; it would certainly inconvenience them, but perhaps, being arch-professionals, they'd expect nothing less. Surely, they'd anticipate that he'd try to protect his own corner at least a little bit? It might even impress them, and from his own point of view, though it would be no more than a gesture – as effective an act of defiance as flipping them a V-sign – he might even feel that he'd regained a little bit of what he'd lost.

In truth, he might regain even more than that.

He and McCracken had been talking in round numbers earlier on. The Crew might know an awful lot, but it wasn't as if they had access to his secret accounts, for God's sake.

Unless they'd hacked him.

That was an ugly thought. It would also explain a lot. But all Lazenby could do was shake it from his head. What would be would be, and anyway, unless they were still following him, there was no way they could know what he was up to at this moment. He checked his rear-view mirror, but it was half past nine at night: the streets, which were dark and wet from the rain that had fallen earlier, were deserted.

'It could be you're flattering yourself,' he said under his breath. These guys ran what amounted to an underworld corporation. 'Don't kid yourself into thinking you're so important that they'll watch you every minute of the day.'

He told himself this with growing conviction. It was a realistic assessment of the way things were. But his hands still sweated on the steering wheel. Until this evening, everything had been fine. Now his road felt much, much darker.

When he arrived at the Bellhop Industrial estate, it was nearly ten.

At this time of night, there was nobody around, the corrugated metal warehouses and workshops all standing in darkness, their windows and entrances covered by roll-down security shutters. There would be CCTV in operation, of course, but Lazenby was not an unfamiliar figure on the site – he'd been a regular visitor in the three years since he'd taken out a lease here for one of the privately rented lock-ups – so if anyone was watching from a security office somewhere, or a mobile patrol made an unexpected drive-by, his presence, even at this hour, would draw no comment.

In truth, if you wanted absolute certainty that your goods were in strong safekeeping, the Bellhop wasn't the ideal spot – there were certainly safer facilities in Crowley, but having lots and lots of officialdom around would hardly have suited Lazenby's purpose. In any case, from the outside, the lock-ups here looked like old garages and so were unlikely to be tampered with by opportunist thieves, while those who knew there were personals stored here would also know that, because of the low rates, it was mostly rubbish: old furniture, moth-eaten clothes, a few corroded car parts. Slim pickings indeed. Nothing worth bothering with.

From Lazenby's perspective, such anonymity was ideal. Because in his private little depot, along with various knick-knacks he'd installed to provide window-dressing, he also stored the bulk of his product, and just in case there was ever a real emergency, a supply of liquid cash.

On this occasion, he approached with more trepidation than usual, turning his Galaxy slowly into the narrow lane between the last two rows of lock-ups, half expecting to find the roll-down door to No. 17 jemmied open and all his goods, or what remained of them, scattered on the tarmac – though an inner voice kept telling him that this was unlikely. No one knew that he kept his stash here. Even among his electronic records, all of which were meticulously coded, there wasn't a single reference to it, and he'd taken out the lock-up lease under a fake identity. The only way the Crew could have come to know was if they'd been following him around, and while he suspected they'd done a bit of that, surely they hadn't been doing it for weeks on end; he hadn't been here for at least a month and a half.

He rounded the corner and halted, his headlights flooding the straight ribbon of tarmac running ahead of him, the brick backs to the penultimate row of lock-ups on the left, the row of garage-like doors on the right. It was bare of life. The shutter on No. 17, which was three doors down, was locked in place, as it should be.

Relieved, Lazenby edged his Galaxy forward. The motion-sensitive lights overhead activated. So far so normal. He drove past his own unit, and parked across the entrance to No. 16. Climbing out, he looked around and listened. The only sound was a distant thrum of night traffic. There were no voices, no metallic clatters as other shutters were opened or closed.

He peered once more to the far end of this particular lane, seeing only the distant boundary wall. Satisfied, Lazenby opened the back door to his car, took out the overlarge sports bag that normally travelled there, and emptied his unused squash gear into the footwell; he hadn't played squash in ages, and only kept his kit in the car as cover for keeping the bag, which he always wanted handy in case of occurrences like this. He took his keys from the ignition, closed the car and locked it, and, squatting down, opened the padlock at the base of the shutter.

The shutter wasn't heavy and he was able to lift it easily, its own momentum pulling it up the last few feet, at which point a steel catch clicked into place.

The interior of the lock-up was rectangular, about twenty-five feet by twelve, enclosed by breeze-block walls. When he hit the light switch, an electric bulb shuddered to life, exposing what he thought of as his 'knick-knacks' but which, in reality, was a clutter of junk expanding wall to wall and comprising all the odds and ends he'd assembled over the last few years: from disused garden furniture and dated, dust-coated office-ware, to boxes of second-hand books that he'd bought cheaply at auction for this sole purpose. Even the hooks on the walls had come in handy, and now dangled with rusted, cobwebby tools, both of the garden and DIY variety.

The good stuff was right at the back, but even if some intruder managed to navigate his way through to that distant point, all he would see, jammed between a rusty fridge and a stack of propped-up bamboo matting, were two ratty old armchairs. The one on the left had a cardboard box crammed with video tapes on top of it, but underneath this, and underneath the cushion, the chair's base had a false bottom, and a hidden compartment in which there was a steel strongbox containing twenty rubber-band-wrapped blocks of clean twenty-pound notes, each one totalling around £8,000, an overall sum of one hundred and sixty grand. The chair on the right was weighed down by a long-broken television, but the strongbox concealed inside it contained the real gold in Lazenby's stockpile: eight one-kilo bricks of cocaine wrapped in cellophane, the street value of which came to just under half a million pounds.

He unzipped his sports bag and went first to the chair on the right, loading the bag with the eight bricks of coke. When he'd finished, he moved to the chair on the left. One-sixty K wasn't humongous money in gangland terms, but it would serve to give him some kind of safeguard, a final fall-back if everything else went pear-shaped. He got it all into the bag, which was now heavy and cumbersome, but he was still able to zip it closed and lug it back through the junk and out into the fresh air, where he humped it round to the Galaxy's boot.

He wasn't overly keen on taking this stuff home with him, but it would only be for one night – tomorrow he'd find somewhere else, somewhere better.

'That would be ours, wouldn't it?' a muffled voice said.

Lazenby spun around, startled.

Two men faced him from about ten feet away.

He hadn't heard them approach, which was probably no surprise given that he'd been banging around inside the lock-up, lost in his thoughts. But even if he had, it didn't look as if there'd have been much he could do – their intentions were pretty clear.

The one on the left was of average height and broadly built, while the one on the right was equally broad but a little taller. Both wore dark clothing, including black leather jackets, but also scarlet woollen ski-masks with holes cut only for their eyes. Each was armed with what looked distinctly like a sub-machine gun, the two weapons levelled on him.

Strangely, almost as quickly as the shock had hit Lazenby, it subsided.

All along, he'd perhaps expected something like this. It hadn't seemed terribly probable, not in that safe, average, everyday world that Lazenby's success had lulled him into believing he still occupied. But there'd still been that constant, nagging doubt, which is why the stuff had been ready to move at a moment's notice.

'What . . . what do you mean, this is yours?' he stammered, breathing hard from his exertion. He hadn't yet given up on the idea that a deal could be made. Maybe they were simply testing him here?

'Just what we say, arsehole,' the taller one said. 'The bag.'

As if to emphasise that this wasn't a joke, the shorter one raised his weapon to chest height and squinted along its barrel. Helpless to do otherwise, Lazenby rocked forward on the balls of his feet, and hurled the heavy sports bag over the two or three yards between them.

The taller one let his firearm swing from a shoulder strap while he hunkered down and tugged the holdall's zip open. Almost immediately, he glanced up. Lazenby could only see his eyes – which were colourless in the dimness – but he had no doubt there was a smile behind that woollen visage.

'Good lad,' came the voice.

The taller one drew something out of his jacket pocket, which, when he unrolled it, turned out to be a black canvas sack. Almost casually, he began cramming the blocks of cash inside it.

'Seriously?' Lazenby said as he watched. 'This is the whole plan? A chicken-feed robbery? I thought you guys were supposed to be businessmen. Have you any idea how much money we could make if we reached some kind of agreement?'

They didn't bother to reply.

Lazenby's sweat rapidly cooled in the October night. His thoughts swam like directionless fish. There was still no need for despair. They weren't for playing ball at present, but that didn't mean they wouldn't do in due course. These two were just crude muscle, no doubt; a pair of paid thugs. Making deals didn't figure in their remit. And that really could *not* be the end of it. The Crew hadn't got to the top of the criminal tree by knocking off a bit of bent gear here and there.

But throughout these ruminations, Lazenby increasingly found himself distracted by how small their canvas bag was. It didn't look big enough, not for the coke as well. And indeed, once the money was loaded, the bag was zipped closed and kicked backward into the shadows. Lazenby watched, increasingly bemused, as the taller bandit now zipped up the original sports bag, with the coke still inside it, and tossed it back into the lock-up.

Were they simply here to teach him a lesson then? Taking every spare penny he had as a down-payment on future deals? He supposed that might be one underworld method.

But then something even more bewildering happened.

The taller bandit walked around to the other side of the Galaxy, bent down and picked something up. There was a metallic *snick* – the sound a cigarette lighter makes when being struck – followed by a burst of wavering light. When he came back, he was carrying a two-pint glass bottle full of greyish liquid, with a burning rag stuffed into the neck.

'What the fu . . .' Lazenby shouted, diving out of the way as the guy flung it into the lock-up.

It exploded furiously, the blazing payload engulfing the old clothes, the decrepit furniture, and the bag containing the cocaine.

'*Are you fucking nuts!*' Lazenby screamed, scrambling back to his feet and trying to approach the open doorway, but inevitably being driven back by the heat of the flame-filled interior. '*There's over four-hundred grand's worth of dope in there!*'

He never noticed the reply coming – in the shape of a sub-machine gun's walnut stock, which slammed into the side of his jawbone with such force that he literally saw stars as the world cavorted around him, and the damp tarmac rushed up to his face.

As Ordinary Joe Lazenby lay there, groggy, only half aware of the hot blood filling his mouth, a wool-clad face appeared next to his ear, and whispered: 'Not anymore.'

Chapter 10

Lucy clocked on at eight the next morning, and found a memo on her desk from DI Beardmore.

Report to Robbery Squad at 1st opp.
Liaise with DS Tucker
(they've got you for one week – after that, we reappraise)

Lucy stood up from her desk just as Beardmore entered the DO.

'You sure you can spare me for a week, boss?' she asked.

'No, I'm not,' he said, pulling a face and stripping off his coat as he headed into his office. 'But you started this thing, Lucy. Only seems fair you get a sniff of wherever it's leading.'

She halted in his office door. 'What about the break-ins on Hatchwood Green?'

Beardmore rustled distractedly through the usual pile of bumph that always seemed to accumulate on his desk during the hours of darkness. 'I'm sure Harry can carry that for a few days.'

'He'll whinge.'

'He always whinges. One thing he never does, though, is

whinge to someone who cares.' The DI didn't look at her as he slumped down into his chair. 'Go on . . . shoot up there before I change my mind.'

Lucy mounted the stairs with that usual mixture of elation and trepidation that always accompanied inclusion in major enquiries. It was a curious feeling, to be truthful. Most divisional CID officers had to juggle three or four minor investigations at any one time – sometimes more. It certainly kept them on their toes, but quite often it was routine stuff.

But the major investigations, or the 'monster hunts', were something else. On these occasions, you were after real predators, soulless psychopaths with an overwhelming urge and a huge potential to cause damage, deranged felons whose swift capture was deemed to be so important that you had to focus entirely on them, leaving everything else on the backburner. The thrill of these special investigations was often a reward in itself. This was certainly what Lucy had joined the police for.

The Robbery Squad office wasn't too busy at this stage of the day. However, DI Blake and DS Tucker were already present, poring over a series of street maps spread on a desk in a corner of the room directly opposite from the one dedicated to the Saturday Street enquiry. Lucy also noticed that some maps had been tacked onto the walls, alongside photographs of the cashpoints she herself had earmarked as possible attack zones, plus the alley entrances and subway mouths in their vicinities. The majority of these were professional surveillance shots, taken from multiple high angles so as to fully recreate on film the anatomy of each environment. It might be early, but the Squad had clearly been busy.

DI Blake glanced up. 'DC Clayburn . . . welcome.' She herself had dressed down today, wearing only a jumper and jeans. 'Glad you could join us.'

'Delighted, ma'am,' Lucy said, approaching the desk.

'For the duration of the time you're with us, it's Kathy,' Blake said, with half a smile. 'Unless I need to pull rank on you. Which I'm sure I won't.'

Unseen behind his boss's shoulder, Tucker winked at Lucy.

'I hear you're a bit of an expert when it comes to under-cover decoy work,' the DI said.

'I've done my fair share,' Lucy replied.

Tucker grinned. 'That's putting it mildly, isn't it?'

Lucy smiled coyly. 'The last time it worked out quite well, I must admit.'

'I'm guessing you know what I'm going to ask you?' Blake said.

'You want me to visit some cashpoints late at night?'

'Correct.' Blake indicated the spread of documentation, in particular the maps and the photos. 'You've laid your plan to catch the Creep out pretty well for us . . .'

'Thanks.' Lucy nodded in sobre appreciation.

'No, it should be us thanking you.' Blake gathered up some sheets of what looked like work schedules and shuffled them together. 'I was impressed at the time, and I'm even more impressed since we haven't really been able to improve on it. It only seemed right that you should be in for the takedown. Assuming there is one.'

'I just hope I haven't caused a lot of fuss for nothing.'

'Not a bit of it. I think your reasoning was pretty sound.' Blake pursed her lips. 'As long as you trust your informant and the psyche profile from West Midlands isn't way off the mark, I think it's a reasonable bet that this lunatic will strike again. And in case he's only *half*-tempted, well . . . we're going to put it on a plate for him. Now, speaking of madmen, we're also closing in on the Saturday Street boys. I anticipate that we'll be making arrests in the next couple of days.'

'Oh, wow . . . that's great news.'

Blake nodded. 'Yes, but it's going to keep me and quite a few of the rest of the Squad pretty busy. So, I'm giving you all the resources I can, but that isn't many. Danny's going to take point, and I can spare you four other detectives. After that we're using spare bodies from Uniform.'

'No one else from divisional CID available?' Lucy asked.

'I think you're pretty pulled-out down in the DO. But me and Stan go back a bit; at least I was able to get you.' She gave another half-smile.

DI Blake was a distinctly warm presence, even if she wasn't especially demonstrative.

'Don't worry about it,' Tucker chipped in. 'Uniform jumped at it. We're only taking a couple from each relief, so we're not thinning them out too much. The younger lads and lasses can do the decoy stuff, the older heads can ride in the support cars with us.'

'You'll be working awkward hours, of course,' Blake said.

Lucy shrugged again. 'Only to be expected.'

'We're looking at nine in the evening till five in the morning,' Tucker added.

'We've also had it cleared that we'll be working clean through the next fortnight,' Blake said. 'No days off, but overtime will be paid as per the norm.'

Lucy nodded. That made sense too, but it was impressive that the DI had managed to pull this off. She might be supervising a unit whose existence was under threat, but she clearly still had influence.

'You can get off home for now if you want,' Tucker said. 'Take a few hours R&R. Briefing in here at nine p.m., operation goes live at ten-thirty. Alternatively . . .' He tapped a stack of bulging buff folders on top of the filing cabinet next to him. 'Since we've copied West Mids in on what we're doing, they've sent quite a bit more paperwork through. So, if you're bored, or you fancy a quick shuftie, it might be of some interest.'

As it wasn't inconceivable that her life could be in danger during this operation, Lucy agreed that the new material would probably, at the very least, be worth a skim-read.

She found a spare desk, and laid the folders in front of her.

'Oh, ma'am . . . Kathy!' she said, as Blake and Tucker wandered away.

The DI glanced back.

'You say we're on this for two weeks. But DI Beardmore says he can only spare me for one.'

Blake gave another of those bland but warm half-smiles. 'Like I say, Lucy . . . me and Stan go back. Let's see how it plays out.'

As Lucy expected, the new stuff from West Mids mainly comprised copies of crime-scene observations, forensic and medical reports, witness statements and plenty of additional photographic material. There was also an updated e-fit.

Lucy found herself staring at this long and hard. The face looking back at her almost seemed inhuman; its eyes little more than slits and yet possessed of an eerie glint, its mouth curved upward in OTT fashion, creating the most extravagant image of pantomime villainy she'd ever seen. As far as she knew, this picture, or others like it, had been screened regularly on the news bulletins, and had been appearing in all the papers and online ever since the most recent attack. Surely, if there was anyone walking the streets whose face even vaguely resembled this bizarre image, he'd be in custody by now?

Definitely a mask. It had to be.

'No wonder they call him the Creep, eh?' a voice said.

Lucy glanced up and, fleetingly, her enthusiasm for working with the Robbery Squad flagged.

Detective Constable Lee Gaskin had just come in, and now stood alongside the desk. He hadn't changed much since she'd last worked with him, standing about five-ten with a stocky frame, a thick neck, broad, sloping shoulders and big arms with heavy-knuckled hands. What remained of his hair was thin and mouse-brown, while his face was notched and pitted all over as though he'd had chickenpox as a child and had vigorously scratched – Lucy had never thought any face could exist that was so well suited for the scowl Lee Gaskin habitually wore. On this occasion, ironically, he wasn't scowling, but smiling. It was cold, though, and it offered more than a glimpse of the nicotine-yellow teeth clamped together underneath it.

'DC Gaskin,' she said. 'What a delight.'

She had already known that Gaskin was a part of the Robbery Squad. She'd glimpsed him several times in other parts of the building during the intervening weeks since the Squad had set up its base here, but so far had managed to avoid him.

'I heard you'd finally got your long sought-for CID post,' he said quietly but intensely. 'Un-fucking-believable. Anyway, the good news . . .' He stuck his thumb in the direction of the door. 'The local DO's downstairs. There can't be anything up here for you, so don't trip on your way down. Or rather, *do* trip . . . but make sure you fall all the way to the bottom, so *they* have to deal with your body rather than us.'

'You sure you're not confusing me with one of your prisoners?' Lucy wondered, standing up, determined not to be cowed by him. 'Isn't that what normally happens to them?'

'Whoa!' he snorted. 'A smarty-pants too since she's put her civvies on. I'll have to be on top form from now on.'

'Well . . . first time for everything.'

'And a last.' He leaned forward, bringing his scabrous face

right into her personal space. She was resolute that she wouldn't flinch, difficult though this was. 'Whatever you're up here for, love,' he said quietly, 'I really, really hope it's nothing to do with this big obbo we've got starting tonight . . .'

Lucy glanced across the office to see if anyone else had noticed the altercation, but they were all too busy, and Gaskin was still keeping it low key.

'But if it is,' he added, 'and you have another cock-up . . . well, I'll just have to make sure the boss knows damn well that you've got a long track-record for that sort of thing.'

'You finished?' she said. 'Because if you have, get your rotten fag-breath out of my nostrils . . . right fucking now.'

Grinning almost ghoulishly, he stepped away from her and turned.

Slowly and precisely, Lucy replaced the West Mids paper-work in its relevant folders. Re-stacking them on the filing cabinet, and checking again that no one else had observed the minor incident, she walked from the room.

'Why does it have to be him?' she said under her breath.

She could ride this complication out; she knew she could. But it undeniably put a dampener on things. Why the hell did it have to be *him*?

'Now, stranger,' Lucy's mother said from over the counter at the Saltbridge MiniMart.

Cora Clayburn was fifty-four now, and since her long fair hair had finally started running to silver, she had begun cutting it to shoulder-length. She was still a handsome woman, though – Lucy remembered her as a stunner in her younger days; she could even make the unflattering blue smock and heavy plastic 'Assistant Manager' tag look good.

'Thought I could take you for lunch,' Lucy said.

'Ooh, had a pay rise or something?'

'No, it's just . . .' Lucy shrugged. 'You know.'

Cora eyed her suspiciously, sensing something untoward. It was always the same; Lucy had once successfully lied her way into the inner sanctum of the two most dangerous female gangsters in Manchester, but she could never fool her own mum.

'You trying to bribe me?' Cora wondered.

'It's not really a bribe.'

'But there's something you need to tell me and you want to sweeten the pill?'

'Mum . . .' Lucy tried her most plaintive voice. 'I don't live with you anymore, so you wouldn't have known about this otherwise, but I don't like hiding things from you.'

'Hmm.' Cora busied herself along the counter. 'Let me guess . . . you're off on another suicide mission.'

'It's not a suicide mission. It's just undercover work.'

Cora pointedly said nothing. Neither of them needed reminding how badly Lucy had been injured and frightened the previous time she'd gone undercover.

'But it's going to be nothing like last time,' Lucy added hastily. That was completely true, but she didn't bother to explain that, whereas last time she'd been standing with those suspected of committing violent crime, this time it would be the other way around – she'd be out there with the prospective victims of it. 'It's with the Robbery Squad. Which means I'll have big, hard blokes with me at all times. Plus, it's here in Crowley . . . it's only round the corner.'

Cora didn't look mollified, but she didn't raise any further objections.

It had never been the case that Lucy and her mother 'didn't get on'. Cora, a single parent living in Saltbridge, one of the older terraced districts in the town, which had suffered deprivation even into the twenty-first century, had raised her daughter alone, and with the odd exception of a few 'wild child' phases during Lucy's youth, had turned her at length into a model citizen. However, Lucy's joining law enforcement at the age of twenty had been a bone of contention between them, which had persisted for the last ten years. It was not that Cora disliked the police per se, but she considered that she'd seen some terrible things in her time – she knew 'what went on', as she was fond of saying. And every time her daughter climbed into her uniform, or now, as it was, plain clothes, she feared that something awful was going to happen. But, these days at least, these were concerns that Cora only paid lip service to, which Lucy took as a sign that she was at last getting used to the fact that her daughter was a copper for life.

Lucy left her Jimny in the MiniMart car park, and they walked together across the road to the Wagon & Horses pub, which, though popular with both factory and office workers at lunchtime, usually had a couple of tables spare. Today was no exception.

Cora ordered tagliatelle, Lucy a small portion of salad with poached salmon.

'You eat like a rabbit,' Cora said disapprovingly. 'I don't know where you get the energy from to do your job.'

'Don't like filling myself up at lunch,' Lucy replied. 'Makes me sleepy in the afternoon.'

'Does that matter . . . if you're working funny hours again?'

On reflection, Lucy supposed it didn't, given that she was mainly going to be on nights. It would probably help if she could get some kind of shut-eye today, even if it was only short-lived. But she still wasn't hungry, and that was probably down to the excitement of her forthcoming assignment.

'I just didn't inherit your miraculous metabolism, Mum, that's all,' Lucy replied.

Cora gave a sweet smile. Before spotting someone she knew across the pub, and waving.

'All right, Cora . . . looking gorgeous today, as always!' a burly builder shouted as he and his mate trundled across to the exit in their dingy overalls and heavy, dust-caked boots.

'That Jimmy Ogden?' Lucy said after he'd gone. 'Now . . . he *has* put weight on.'

'And he probably puts in a tougher day's shift than the two of us together,' Cora replied. 'Just goes to show . . . we're all different, lovie.' She leaned across the table and playfully patted Lucy's cheek. 'So don't feel inadequate.'

'Get out of it,' Lucy chuckled.

They continued in this fashion for the remainder of the meal, enjoying each other's company, easily and idly avoiding any risqué subjects. Until inevitably, almost unavoidably, Lucy sat back, dabbed her lips with a napkin and, after the barmaid had taken their empty dishes away, asked: 'I don't suppose you've heard anything from *him*, have you? He's not tried to contact you?'

Cora looked unperturbed by the question. She wore her readers as she perused the sweets menu. 'Not at all. He said he wouldn't, didn't he?'

'And *he's* the kind of guy who keeps his promises?'

'He kept them for thirty-odd years, love.'

And that, from her tone, was the end of this particular matter.

The 'he' in question was Lucy's estranged father, who in so many ways signified a distant but dark past that still haunted and embarrassed her. Long before Lucy was born, Cora went through a wild child phase of her own, leaving her family home under such a cloud that she'd never speak to her parents again, and finally earning a living by performing nightly at a strip-club called SugaBabes on the other side of Manchester. She'd only been in her late teens at the time, and had been easily smitten by a handsome bouncer at the club, with whom she'd commenced a romantic relationship. However, when she unexpectedly fell pregnant with Lucy, she re-evaluated everything, and drew the conclusion that these underworld figures with whom she was increasingly involved could never be part of her daughter's life. She thus packed the stripper job in, broke it off with her boyfriend, who was surprisingly amicable about it – most likely because he could (and did) take his pick of the rest of the girls there – and crossed the city to commence a new, more respectable life. In time, the ex-boyfriend, as he rose through the ranks of the mob, doing worse and worse things and yet reaping ever greater benefits, contacted Cora again, offering financial assistance in the raising of their daughter. But Cora, always an independent soul, continually resisted. In due course, she lost touch with him altogether . . . until last year, when unusual circumstances brought him back into both her and her daughter's lives with shattering force.

It was a particularly horrific experience for Lucy, learning that her father was a villain. She'd grown up with the lie that her real dad had been a cheeky-chappie bus driver who'd abandoned them both because he couldn't face the responsibility of parenthood. Of course, it didn't make it any better that she was now a police officer; in fact, it made things a whole lot worse. If word of this revelation had got out, both father and daughter would find their respective careers imperilled. As such, they'd agreed to keep it quiet, and even now only a very tight circle of select acquaintances knew the truth.

Not that this prevented Lucy losing sleep from time to time.

Against her better judgement, she occasionally had to raise the subject with her mother. Even when, as now, it was patently obvious that Cora didn't want to discuss it, Lucy just had to check that there had been no further contact from her long-absent father, aka 'The Shakedown', Frank McCracken.

Chapter 11

As always with decoy duty, the menacing prospect of suddenly encountering the offender you were trying to lure was juxtaposed against the many hours of tedium that in actual fact *would* fill your shift.

The previous year, as part of the now legendary 'Operation Clearway', Lucy had gone undercover as a prostitute, walking the highways and byways on the outskirts of town. Though to a degree that had been worse than this – because, even though she'd been intelligence-gathering rather than presenting herself as a potential target, she'd been dressed in demeaning clothes and had been subject to the disdain of the general public, not to mention the potential violence of those nocturnal wanderers who existed only to hate and hurt – she'd mostly been in the company of other girls and had been able to spend the dark, wet nights in chatty conversation. Here, in the centre of Crowley, despite it being superficially less dangerous because she was now just an ordinary woman in jeans and an anorak – albeit wearing a concealed Kevlar stab-vest and carrying both a radio and a CS spray, with a support car never too far away – the main problem was that all-pervading boredom.

Lucy had been allocated four cashpoints in the obbo's so-called 'central zone', which was mainly the district in closest proximity to Robber's Row police station. They were all cashpoints that she herself had specified, each one located about a mile and a half away from the next. This worked well because it wouldn't have done for them all to be close together. It was highly possible that the Creep, if he was here at all, would allow for the fact he was on foreign soil by scoping things out before launching an attack, and if he spotted the same lone female making constant rounds of the cashpoints, he'd soon get suspicious. As such, she'd commence her first walk at 10.30p.m., making a casual but lengthy circuit of the four cashpoints, starting at the RBS on Brunton Way, in the town centre, then moving on to the Co-op on Goodwood Drive, the NatWest outside the Lidl and finally the branch of Lloyds at Broadgate Green, drawing a minor amount of money from each one of them.

At the end of this, at around midnight – it was a timed circuit, and it was important that she kept to the schedule – she would wander idly into the car park at the rear of the Plough & Harrow, the only pub in Broadgate Green, where she'd get into the support car for some sandwiches and a flask of coffee.

At 12.30, the whole process would repeat itself, as it would at 2.30. They'd wrap things up with a debrief at the office at 4 a.m.

For the first five nights, nothing happened at all. In fact, it reminded Lucy of her very earliest days in the job, when, as a probationary constable, and regardless of the weather, she'd invariably be allocated the long-haul of foot-patrol in the town centre. It had been an even longer haul during this particular op, because out of uniform and to all intents and purposes a civvy, there were no calls coming over the radio to send her to an emergency, no one to summon her across the road to report a noisy party next door or prowlers at the back of their house, or just to invite her in for a cuppa. Not that Lucy could complain. This had been *her* idea after all – and anyway, it wasn't as if she was completely alone: there were several other officers, two males and three females, all going through exactly the same process in different parts of the borough, thus far to no gain.

A couple of times that Monday night, mainly during her first circuit of the cashpoints, Lucy saw other pedestrians heading home from wherever they'd been. A couple were walking dogs. A middle-aged man hummed to himself as he tottered along, beer fumes wafting in his wake. But during the second circuit, which commenced at 12.30a.m., the streets were empty.

The strange thing was that, though well aware that this particular hour was the optimum one for an attack, Lucy, also knew that, even though they were planning for it to happen, it was still unlikely. As she drew money out of the RBS, then the Co-op, then the NatWest, and then headed down for what was perhaps the most far-flung of her four locations, the Lloyds on Broadgate Green, she tried to mentally calculate the odds of this thing actually coming off – especially after five nights on the trot and the Creep still a no-show. They weren't looking good.

Okay, they had Jerry McGlaglen's assurance that the Creep was in Crowley – that was worth something, no doubt about it. In addition, they had the psychological profile, which suggested that, if he had come up here to Manchester to escape the heavy police presence on his home patch, he would still struggle to resist the urge. But it seemed a long shot that it would occur in the skinny timeframe they'd allowed themselves, if at all. As with all serial offenders who'd suddenly gone to ground, there was always that possibility that he'd been sent to prison for something else, or had become ill, or had even died. There was also a chance that, because he felt the heat was getting too much, he'd decided to let it go for a while. Whatever the experts said, it was entirely possible that he maintained *that* degree of self-control.

All kinds of things were possible, in truth. There were no fixed rules in psychosis.

As Lucy walked along the dark hedge bordering the grounds of Crowley Grammar School, and pondered all this, it occurred to her that the Robbery Squad had actually invested a lot of faith in the tip-off she'd brought to them. Not that they would blame her particularly if nothing happened. So much policework relied on hunches and tips and 'information received'. If this specific job failed to produce, and DI Blake had to account for her wastage of time and manpower, there'd be no hard feelings; it would be accepted as an occupational hazard. But then there was the Lee Gaskin factor.

Of all the detectives involved in the operation in Borsdane Wood five years ago, an occasion when Lucy had taken her eye off the ball for half a second and one DI Mandy Doyle nearly died as a result, Gaskin had taken it the worst.

That had been Lucy's first CID assignment. She'd been in plain clothes a week when it occurred, and had been kicked back to Uniform straight afterwards, but it had been implied to her at the time that she was lucky she was still in a job. Most of those involved had been content with that punishment, apart from Doyle, who had never been happy from the outset with Lucy's attachment to her otherwise all-male team, and Gaskin, who, for some reason best known to himself, had hung onto Doyle's every word. Lucy hadn't known either of them especially well back then, but in that one week she had seen enough to know that if Doyle had said to Gaskin, 'Jump, you soppy little twat!' he'd have replied, 'Of course, ma'am . . . how high?'

Clearly, even five years later, this irrational devotion hadn't diminished, and the bastard was now well-placed to do some dirt on her if he wanted to. Lucy had no doubt that Kathy Blake would already know about her past indiscretion, but if this op *really* went pear-shaped, and Gaskin made enough of a stink about Lucy and her intel not being all they'd hoped for, it wasn't impossible that it would make a negative impression.

As Lucy pondered these thoughts, she cut across a now sleeping housing estate, walked down a passage between two clusters of maisonettes, and set off across Broadgate Green. This was a triangle of grass in what was an otherwise heavily built-up area of council housing. On the Green's north side stood a row of six shops, in the very middle of which was the Lloyds branch. There was a raised terrace in front of the row, paved and fenced off from the road with a crash barrier, while to the west of it, Halpin Road, one of Crowley's larger thoroughfares, though at this late hour it was quiet.

Lucy crossed the Green and glanced once over her shoulder as she ascended the steps to the shop-front terrace. Tonight, the support car, Danny Tucker's Vauxhall Passat, contained both him and a Robbery Squad DC called Ruth Smiley. Lucy had already known who Ruth Smiley was before any of this started, because, aside from Kathy Blake, she was the only other female in the Squad. She was in her late-thirties and ex-military, a veteran of both Iraq and Afghanistan. What was more, she carried this aura around with her, looking and sounding both tough and efficient. She wasn't tall but was in visibly good shape, and yet, though her short, dark-red hair was shaved at the sides, almost like a crew cut, and her usual attire of polo shirts, slacks and flat shoes rather than dresses, skirts and heels, gave her the air of a toughie, up close she was alluringly pretty, with bright blue eyes, pink lips, and a button nose. She was notoriously curt and forthright in her conversation, but that hadn't stopped a lot of the guys at the station hitting on her (and getting knocked back). At present, however, it was Smiley's renowned competence at the job that was of greatest value, and both she and Tucker were displaying it amply: the Passat had shadowed Lucy's every step this evening, yet never once had she spotted it.

She trudged on along the terrace to the cashpoint, glancing over her shoulder again and peering directly across the Green to the mouth of the alley that had brought her here. It was a small relief to see that a vehicle, most likely the Passat, had pulled up at the far end. It showed no lights, but it hadn't been there a moment earlier. It was perhaps a little further away than Lucy would have liked, but that said, Tucker, who was physically fit, could probably cover the distance on foot pretty swiftly if he needed to.

Lucy went through the usual motions, inserting her card, tapping in a key number and then waiting patiently. From somewhere behind, there came the echoing double-thud of what sounded like a door opening and closing. She withdrew her card and a couple of tenners, before it occurred to her that what she'd just heard could well have been the support car.

She spun around.

The figure was only about fifteen yards away.

It had approached silently along the terrace from its eastern end. It wasn't especially impressive in height or breadth, but it wore a black, heavy cape, too big for it really, which covered it from shoulders to ankles like a voluminous, waterproof shroud. The hood was pulled down over the face, which could not be seen in any case because the head was bowed.

Even under normal circumstances, the sudden sight of this spectre in such close proximity might have made Lucy jump. It did more than that now: a yelp caught in her throat and she stumbled backward, bracing herself against the cashpoint ledge with her hand.

And yet the figure came straight on towards her, the cape so long that it was almost gliding.

Though momentarily transfixed, Lucy caught movement in the corner of her vision. She assumed it would either be Tucker or Smiley emerging from the alley on the far side of the Green, having seen what was happening before she had. But she couldn't take her eyes off the advancing form, which now was only five yards away. With escalating alarm, she noticed that both its hands were concealed. She tried to say something, but her mouth was too dry. Belatedly, she stuck her hand into her anorak pocket, scrabbling for her CS spray. She could now sense someone running full-pelt across the Green, but still at least a hundred yards off.

The figure now stopped directly in front of her, slowly lifting its head, and at the same time drawing one of its hands from under its capacious folds.

But the hand, when it came into view, and which was little more than a curved, bony claw, was empty, and in fact cupped. The face, which was wrinkled and wizened, was familiar to her.

'*Armed police!*' Danny bellowed, as he reached the northern edge of the Green, his Glock drawn and levelled two-handed. 'Stay where you are! *Don't bloody move!*'

'Danny, wait!' Lucy shouted, raising a warning hand.

She again glanced at the figure in front of her, at the docile, non-comprehending eyes of Sally Skegg, one of several of Crowley's resident homeless; a mentally challenged but otherwise completely harmless street-woman. Lucy peered past her and at the distant east end of the terrace saw what looked like a rusty shopping trolley full of discarded cans.

'It's okay, Danny! False alarm.'

Warily, he lowered his weapon.

Lucy turned back to the bag lady, who didn't even seem aware that Tucker was present.

'God's sake, Sal!' Lucy said. 'You can't be wandering the streets this late. Not in October. Here . . .' She dug into her pocket for some change, and dropped it into the cupped hand.

On the Green, Tucker shoved his pistol back under his jacket. He lifted his chequer-banded baseball cap and scratched under his hairline. There was a screech of gears from somewhere nearby. Ruth Smiley was trying to find a quick way around to them, and by the sounds of it, she wasn't succeeding. As Sally Skegg glided back towards her trolley, counting her handful of newly acquired coppers, Lucy moved to the barrier to speak with Tucker. Before she did, she glimpsed more movement in her peripheral vision, and looked to the west end of the terrace.

Another figure was standing there; this one too was heavily coated and hooded.

Lucy didn't immediately react. Initially, she assumed that it was one of Sally's friends. Perhaps the strange old woman had been traipsing the streets in company. But then something about this second presence struck Lucy as odd. For one thing, it was man-height – at least six foot. For another, by the breadth of it, this one *was* a man, and by his ramrod-straight posture, a man in relatively good nick. And the more Lucy assessed that posture, the more something else about it struck her; it wasn't just straight, it was rigid – as if this guy, whoever he was, had just received a shock.

She glanced to where Tucker was busy on his radio, still wearing his hi-vis baseball cap and, over his jumper and jeans, the firearms jacket with POLICE stencilled across it.

When she glanced back, the second figure had gone.

'Shit,' she breathed. 'Shit . . . *Danny, he took the bait!*'

She started running.

'Hey . . . what? *Lucy!*'

She called back over her shoulder as she raced west along the terrace. 'It's the Creep . . . I've just seen him! He must've gone around the back of the shops!'

'You sure?'

'I'm bloody positive!'

There was a howl of brakes as the Passat finally roared around a corner and skidded through half a dozen puddles before stopping. Lucy looked briefly back as Tucker dived into the front passenger seat, and with another loud and protracted squeal of rubber, the vehicle took off, pulling a rapid three-point turn – there was only one way a car could get to the rear of the row of shops, and that was via the access road at the east end of the terrace.

Lucy, looking to stay on the suspect's heels, took the footway around the west end at such speed that she almost lost her footing on the mossy paving. But she barely broke stride as she regained her balance and pounded down another narrow passage, at the end of which she entered the lot, where, aside from a huge metal dumpster and a few scraps of waste paper drifting on the breeze, there was nothing to catch her eye.

She halted, breathing hard, sweat pinpricking her brow.

The far boundary of the lot was edged with undergrowth and a slatted wooden fence. Beyond that, there were more houses. But Lucy had worked in Crowley long enough to know that this was deceptive. There was actually a public footpath on the other side of that fence, a narrow one, separating the shops from the next estate – and she knew where it led to.

She hurried on across, the point where her quarry had penetrated the fence sliding into view. It was in the far west corner and was partly concealed by a clump of evergreens. The reason she hadn't heard him breaking wood was because the gap was already there: a few of the slats had simply rotted and fallen away. As Lucy hared towards it, an engine revved and strong lights flooded the tarmac behind her.

She half-turned, seeing Tucker leap out of the Passat.

'He's got through the fence!' she shouted. 'There's a footpath . . . he'll either go left or right, but right will only take him back to Broadgate Green. So, I'm guessing left. That's Halpin Road and there's a bridge over. Get the car to the other side quickly, and you can intercept!'

Tucker nodded, clambering back into the Passat and gabbling into his radio.

Lucy ducked through the hole in the fence, at the same time digging out her own radio.

The narrow path beyond wasn't pitch-black, but the high fencing on either side, for all that it was slatted, permitted minimal street lighting. She stumbled left anyway, following the beaten-earth trail, which gradually curved right, until she saw the lights of Halpin Road.

The footbridge also came into view, arching across the dual carriageway, the path leading straight onto it. And this *was* the way the suspect had come – the bridge was caged to stop idiots dropping things off it onto the traffic below, but she could still see as far across it as its apex, which gave her a momentary glimpse of a dark shape vanishing down towards the other side.

But this wasn't the only thing she could see. As Lucy pelted out onto the bridge, great rectangular outlines, ghostly grey monoliths, emerged from the dimness on the far side of the carriageway. She'd forgotten that on the other side of Halpin Road lay Reddington Hall, a sprawling complex of high-rise and low-rise flats, all now condemned and standing as derelict shells. There were any number of hidey-holes and rubble-filled crawlspaces over there, where an escaping fugitive might conceal himself. More to the point, there was no easy access to Reddington Hall for vehicles. When Lucy got there, she'd be alone.

Chapter 12

The Reddington Hall flats had been empty for nearly five years while debates raged at local authority level about refurbishment or demolition. It had eventually been decided that they'd face the wrecking ball, though that time hadn't come yet, and they'd been closed ever since, towering tomb-like edifices of grimy concrete, their windows covered with corrugated metal, the unlit passages winding between them strewn with rubbish and cinders.

As a uniformed copper, Lucy had been fairly well acquainted with Reddington Hall. Even when occupied, it had housed plenty of known offenders, and since it was emptied had been regularly used by squatters. A year last March, she'd been part of a raiding team put together to flush out considerable numbers of heroin addicts who'd been using it as a shooting gallery.

The upshot of this was that the Creep, a native of the West Midlands, oughtn't to know his way around the place as well as she did. That gave her a kind of advantage, she supposed, but it would still be dark and labyrinthine in there, and crammed with refuse and grot and God knew what else. She alighted from the bridge on a concrete ramp, which swept down to what had once been the forecourt of Reddington Hall 'A', the first block. Here, a mesh fence blocked any further progress. It was about ten feet tall, with coils of barbed wire along the top. This was a relatively new addition to the site. As the demolition date approached, Crowley Borough Council were taking ever stricter measures to ensure that no one could get in. But, by the looks of it, they weren't strict enough. Directly in front of Lucy, the fencing had been sheared open from head-height to floor, the wire-mesh sliced through as though made from string.

'DC Clayburn to Foxtrot Alpha,' she panted into her radio.

'*Go ahead, Lucy . . . where are you, over?*' came Tucker's response.

'You're not going to believe this, Danny. I've chased him across the footbridge into Reddington Hall, and the new perimeter fence the Council put up has been chopped through. What's this guy using, a sword or a chainsaw?'

'*That sword must be bloody sharp, Lucy . . . take care, you hear?*'

'Roger that.'

'*You got a visual on him?*'

'Negative.' Her gaze roved the vast, desolate structures. 'Probably working his way through to the other side, as we speak. Anyway, I'm going in . . .'

'*Negative, Lucy!*' It was an uncharacteristically sharp response from Tucker. '*Stand by until we get over there. ETA five.*'

Frustrated, Lucy stepped through the slashed meshwork, but waited inside the fence, still scanning the buildings for any sign of movement.

'*Received, Lucy?*'

'Roger, received.'

Health and Safety was a big deal in modern-day law enforcement. Though everyone acknowledged that police work was different from anything else in civilian life, and that allowances must be made when life-or-death decisions needed making, you still weren't supposed to enter situations you couldn't control, or take undue risks – even if that meant letting a felon escape, which had always seemed contradictory and un-police-like to Lucy. Wasn't this what you joined the job for? To protect life and limb, to take down villains? There was rarely a circumstance where it was going to be risk-free. Indeed, there was another school of thought which long predated H&S but which had still been kicking around in the job when she'd first joined, eleven years ago; namely, that you were a copper, not a security guard, and if you had a chance to grab some lowlife committing criminal offences, you grabbed him whatever the circs – and from that point on, the only excuse for letting him go was if he knocked seven colours out of you.

But time moved on, and so did attitudes – whether rightly or wrongly was not for Lucy to say. And so she waited, the seconds ticking by as she watched the first block of flats.

In the sodium-yellow glow of the street lights behind her, its pebble-dashed façade was eroded by weather, many parts of it crumbled, exposing the brickwork underneath. All its window apertures were blocked off with metal, but on ground-level, just beyond a clutter of battered, burned-out hulks that had once been cars, she spotted the front doorway – and that, unusually but maybe because the Creep had kicked it in – stood wide open.

Right on cue, Lucy heard a metallic clatter from somewhere inside. She advanced a couple of feet before stopping again, her sense of duty nagging at her.

He was still on the plot, then. Still within reach.

She'd half-assumed that he'd have taken full advantage of her waiting for support, and would by now have got clean away. But clearly, he hadn't.

'DC Clayburn to Foxtrot Alpha,' she said quietly, sidling between the scorched, broken cars. 'Danny . . . I'm going in.'

'*Lucy, stay put!*' came Tucker's terse response. '*We'll be two minutes, tops.*'

That didn't win her to his cause. He and the other support units he'd summoned might only be two minutes away – but whereabouts on the Reddington Hall boundary would they arrive? All told, it was about a mile and a half in circumference, and it was anyone's guess which side they'd approach it from.

Suddenly, there was no question in Lucy's mind that unless she acted now, the Creep was going to elude them. She advanced, only hesitating at the gaping doorway.

'*Lucy?*' Danny persisted.

'Received,' Lucy replied. 'Stand by.'

As she'd suspected, the door had been kicked from its hinges, which were nothing more now than stubs of corroded metal. The chain that had been fastened across it still hung at waist-height, a padlock, attached to two rusted ring-handles, suspended in the middle. The blackness beyond was so complete it was almost solid.

Lucy ducked under the chain, reaching to her back pocket for her phone. Its light might come in useful, but she didn't activate it straight away, as it might alert him to her presence. The stink of the place embraced her as she stepped inside: dampness, decay, that indefinable but repulsive reek you always found in ruined buildings, like rotted vegetables, or faeces.

Her eyes gradually adjusted. A shaft of pale moonlight filtering through some partly obscured aperture high on the right revealed a footway of litter-strewn asphalt leading forward between two rows of plastic wheelie bins and dumpsters. Ancient black bin-liners, bulging with foul trash, had been loaded into them or jammed in between, turning it into a virtual valley of garbage. As more came into view, Lucy hesitated again. She recognised this as the entry point they'd taken during the raid nineteen months ago. Back then, they hadn't met much opposition on ground-level, but it had been infested with rats – she could still hear faint scuttlings – so even the most degraded of the town's dropouts hadn't fancied sleeping down here. Of course, tonight's opponent was of a different ilk. On top of that, Lucy was alone. Last time, they'd come here team-handed, and in a blaze of torchlight, clad with body armour and visored helmets, and carrying shields and expandable batons. By comparison, now, she felt naked.

She wondered if that scratching she could hear was really the sound of vermin, or the stealthy movement of someone hiding. As she scrutinised the mountains of rubbish on either side, her eyes fell on a fragment of metal, an old beer can lying trampled in the middle of the footway.

I heard something clatter in here, she reminded herself.

She saw the rest of the beer cans. They'd spilled from a torn bin-liner a couple of feet away. This bag also sat on the footway, having been dragged out of a gap between two skips on the left. Had this happened some time ago, perhaps during the drugs raid all those months back? Or more recently? The space between the two skips was probably still jammed with refuse, but not necessarily jammed solid. A space had been made in there, but space enough for a man to hide?

Everything else in the cave-like darkness melted to irrelevance, as Lucy gazed at the narrow slice of black. She didn't notice that a large, hooded figure had slid out of concealment behind her. Had he not set his foot on a rat, which scampered off, squeaking, she'd never have noticed.

She twirled around just as the curved steel exploded towards her, a glimmering blur in the moonlight. She dropped to the floor. It swept past, *thunking* into the plastic side of a wheelie bin, laying it open like a human corpse, foul detritus disgorging like entrails. Lucy made a frantic forward roll away from her attacker, but as she leapt back to her feet, he came at her again, this time with a backhand slash. She jumped backward, just evading it. As before, the blade sliced into the nearest bin, more filth spurting from the wound.

Lucy caught a flying glimpse of the face under the hood; it looked unnaturally pale, and yes, she could see that fixed Halloween grin that so many who'd survived the Creep had reported. As he wrenched the sword free, she spotted that it had a guarded hilt at one end, just, as the reports had said, like an old-fashioned cavalry sabre.

Lucy backed away from him, retreating deeper into the innards of the sepulchral building.

'I'm a police officer,' she warned him, breathless. 'You cut me with that thing, you're gonna be in bigger trouble than you've ever known.'

With face in shadow, he advanced at a half-crouch, sabre held loosely in his gloved right hand, blade turning slightly, back and forth, back and forth, a clear indication of how flexible a tool he found it.

Lucy retreated more quickly, trying to recollect what she could about this place. If her memories were correct, there was a single flight of stone steps somewhere behind, leading up to the first level, at which point three corridors ran off between apartments, one on the left, one on the right, one straight ahead.

'I'm warning you,' she said again.

He lunged at her, this time a thrust rather than a swipe, trying to skewer rather than slice, forcing her to jump aside but at the same time throw herself forward, grappling with him chest-to-chest. He was so startled by this that he temporarily froze – and wasn't remotely prepared for the blast of CS agent she directed into his face.

Lucy had used this weapon many times, and always there was gasping, choking, gagging, the assailant tottering backward, hands clawing at streaming eyes. But this time it made no difference. He didn't so much as flinch – which surprised her, and instead grabbed her throat with his free hand, flinging her sideways, her spine jolting against the brick jamb of an interior doorway. The next blow he aimed at her was two-handed, and would have severed her head from her torso, had she not struck down at him with the only heavy device she had to hand – her radio; she swung it from on high, crunching it into his collar bone.

He gave a grunt of pain and tottered, his own blow going askew, the blade's edge skittering along the bricks. Lucy rolled away along the wall, and almost by accident passed through the doorway into the next section of the building, where she saw the lowermost steps of the flight she'd remembered. She scampered up it, jabbering into her radio.

'DC Clayburn to Foxtrot Alpha! Immediate assistance required . . . I'm in "A" Block, Reddington Hall, under attack. I'm uninjured, but haven't yet found a secure position. Armed suspect very close behind me . . . urgent assistance, over!'

Grunting and panting, she heard her assailant commence the ascent.

She gasped as she reached the top of the stairs, and found the three corridors leading off in opposing directions, each one dark, dank and, though zebra-striped with moonlight from the broken-open doors along them, looking almost impossibly sinister.

One of these routes led to an exit. She remembered that much, as she lurched down the corridor on the left. This was the one she wanted, she was sure.

She blundered through patches of moonlight, stumbling over broken furniture and gutted mattresses, skidding in pools of slimy water.

And with heavy, lumbering footfalls, he came after her.

'That's it . . . don't quit on me,' she breathed.

She even slowed down, so that he was no more than fifteen yards behind, puffing and panting as he hobbled along but able to see her. Ahead, meanwhile, the corridor looked as if it came to a dead end, a blank wall of shadow – but this was deceptive. What was really here, concealed in blackness, was a wooden fire-exit door. Also concealed, just to the right of this, was the entrance to the last flat. Of all the squats they'd broken into nineteen months ago, this one had been the best defended, because when they'd entered, they'd found that it wasn't just a shooting gallery for smackheads, but a drugs den, where the dealers stored their merchandise and weapons. The door itself had been lined with steel and fixed with brand-new bolts. The police raiding party had assailed it with sledgchammers and eventually a hydraulic ram, which had not just brought the door down, but the lintel too and all the surrounding bricks and masonry.

What remained now was exactly what Lucy remembered: a jagged, cavern-like entrance, only blackness and rubble lying beyond. All around the edges, loose bricks hung from rotted mortar. Lucy didn't waste time choosing one. She grabbed the first she could, waggled it free and swung around with it, bringing it up and over her shoulder like a cricket ball, and as the Creep came at her, smashing it into his face, jarring her shoulder, but dragging a surprised and horrible squawk from out of him.

He didn't drop his sabre, but for a second was completely off balance. His head hinged backward as he toppled. He managed to throw a punch with his free hand. It missed Lucy, but only because she ducked it, striking the jagged

112

brickwork with her shoulder but using it to stabilise herself as she edged around him. He'd clearly been hurt, now taking time to brace himself against the opposite wall. When he glanced up, the moonlight caught his face, and it fleetingly looked as if she'd inflicted a terrible injury. The whole of his right cheek, right eye socket and right temple had been crushed and now sagged inward. But as he clawed at it, she saw it coming away in pieces.

A mask after all, then. By the looks of it made from wax, and with a strip of sticky cellophane across the inside of the sockets to create those eerie, reflective eyes. Great for inflicting terror, no doubt, and maybe for keeping off the worst effects of CS spray (that cellophane strip again). But not much use against stone-throwers.

With half the waxen visage gone, Lucy could distinguish a dark pattern of blood and bruising on the right side of the Creep's real face, though the eye on that side was not damaged; in fact, it widened as it fixed on her, perhaps blazing with indignation that she had dared to fight back. He barrelled towards her again, drawing the sword back as though to run her though rather than cut her down. But the advance was clumsy, his feet stumbling on rubble – at the very least, he was dazed.

She dodged the sabre, and it drove past her, plunging into the mildewed wood of the fire door, sinking to half its length and wedging.

With strangled grunts, the maniac wrenched at it, working it back and forth with both hands to try and get it free. Lucy retreated along the corridor. Her chance had come. All she needed to do now was run.

At the Creep's back.

Over twenty yards, she hit full speed.

He never saw her coming – not even when she lofted into the air with a flying kick and struck him between the shoulder blades. The force of it slammed him into the door, which was so decayed that it erupted outward.

The next thing he knew, he was falling.

Because what he hadn't known and Lucy had, was that there was no fire escape here. The drugs gang who'd utilised this corner of the building had removed it as a security measure.

He dropped fifteen feet, turning head over heels. When he landed, he did so in another skip filled with yet more rubbish bags. His impact on these was heavy, and some of the bags doubtless contained solid items, so they didn't cushion his fall well.

Lucy, who had clutched at either side of the doorframe to prevent herself hurtling after him, peered down. She could just about distinguish her assailant's shape. At first, he lay unmoving, but then, slowly, began to twitch.

He was alive, at least. She supposed she ought to be glad about that – it was an odd thing that she'd barely considered his chances of survival when first luring him here. That was the fight or flight mechanism in full flood, she realised. But without any doubt, this was the best outcome.

Wiping away sweat, she lurched back down the corridor, spinning left at the first junction and hammering down the next passage, half-tripping on debris, but at last reaching another fire door. She rammed it with her shoulder and this too burst open. On this side of the building, there *was* a fire escape. She hurried down it, and ran along a narrow passage, finally, turning right into the alley where the skip was located.

From here, she advanced warily as a shaken, groaning wreck of a man now, rather than the walking embodiment of terror, eased himself over the edge of the skip, and slid down onto his feet, where he leant against the huge, cast-iron receptacle at an awkward, painful angle.

The alley was only dimly lit, the yellowish glow of the

lights on Halpin Road filtering through the rabbit warren of encircling passageways. But it was sufficient to show fragments of the broken door scattered on the alley floor. Lucy even spotted a glint of metal where the bastard's sabre had landed, though that too was now in pieces.

It also revealed more of the Creep.

Bits of the wax still clung to his face, though most of it had gone. His hood had fallen back and, as she approached, she could distinguish the features of what might be an everyday householder: a receding hairline, pudgy cheeks, a small mouth, a thin moustache. She put him somewhere in his early forties, and not even in good shape given the swell of flesh under his jaw.

Her own breathing drew his attention to her. He jerked upright when he saw her. Even though this brought a crease of pain to his face, he backed away towards the end of the alley.

'You're done, pal,' she said, padding after him, but already she could see that his strength was resurging, the adrenaline kicking back in. As the grogginess subsided, he took longer, steadier steps. Any second now he'd turn and run. The foot chase would be on again. But before he had a chance, a third party appeared, a tall, strongly built silhouette stepping into the light at the alley's far end.

Caught between the two of them, in the very act of turning to flee, the suspect froze.

His gloved hands flexed at his sides like jittery spiders.

'You all right, Lucy?' a voice called. It was Danny Tucker.

'I'm fine,' she called back.

'This him?'

'This is him.'

Tucker advanced quickly – to the point where both she and the suspect could see the pistol he was training on the suspect.

'Don't you fucking move!' Tucker warned. 'Not one fucking muscle.'

The suspect glanced back at Lucy, his wounded face beaded with sweat, eyes bright with fear.

'Yeah, try it,' Tucker said, drawing closer. 'Make a break for it . . . but I warn you, I've never been good with leg shots.'

The suspect was clearly half-considering it. Perhaps if he ran straight at the young policewoman, he'd make it difficult for the armed officer to chance a shot, and maybe could trust to his bulk to bounce her out of the way. But if that was his line of thought, he gave it up when a second police-woman appeared at her side.

It was Ruth Smiley, and she too was wielding a firearm.

Slowly and resignedly, the suspect raised his hands in surrender.

The officers closed in over the last few yards, grabbing him all together, slamming him backward against the brick wall facing the skip. Tucker took a step back but pinned him there by jamming the muzzle of his Glock into his collarbone, while Lucy and Smiley patted him down. The Creep slumped where they held him, eyes downcast, mouth trembling.

In the background, Lucy could now hear the shouts of other support units working their way across the estate. 'How do you fellas want to proceed with this?' she asked, breathing hard.

'Hey . . . *your* call, love,' Smiley said.

'Totally,' Tucker agreed, a pearly-toothed grin splitting his handsome, ebony face. 'Your case, Lucy . . . your collar.'

Chapter 13

'It was very difficult,' the prisoner said in a matter-of-fact voice, 'to keep resisting the urge. I'd come up here to Manchester to lie low. At first, it was to help my brother do up his new flat . . . he's lived in Crowley for a while, but it wasn't long before I realised that was an excuse. I knew that if I kept at it in Birmingham, I'd get nabbed eventually.'

'When you say "kept at it,"' Danny Tucker asked him, 'you mean if you kept robbing people at sword-point and then attacking them with the sword afterwards?'

The prisoner nodded. 'That's correct.'

Lucy watched him through the two-way glass of the interview room mirror. His name was Ray Spellman and the most extraordinary thing about him was how unextraordinary he was. Without his heavy coat and hood, not to mention his devilish mask, he was as suburban as they came: a mid-to-late forties everyman, bland of feature, with a small, neatly trimmed moustache, overweight to the point of being dumpy – the sort of guy you literally wouldn't look twice at in the street. Even now, dressed in a white jumpsuit, hands still cuffed, as he faced Tucker and Smiley across the interview room table, the duty solicitor next to him scribbling notes, it looked like a mistake; you were tempted to say: 'Come on, this can't be the guy.'

But he'd come clean about his murderous alter-ego, 'the Creep', almost from the moment of his arrest. Not exactly relieved, not as if he was unloading something hideous from his soul. But because he was clearly of a logical bent and had recognised that his time was up. He'd had his fun and now it would be better for all if he simply co-operated.

Kathy Blake had not joined Lucy in the darkened viewing room, because it was after 3 a.m. and she was on an obbo at six. But two other officers who were currently off-duty were present: Stan Beardmore, and their overarching supervisor, Chief Superintendent Charles Mullany, a tall, lean man with a shock of white hair and thick, snow-white eyebrows. Normally famous for his immaculate uniform, he maintained a regal bearing even in his late-night attire of sweater, slacks and loafers.

'And when you say "resisting the urge," Ray,' Smiley asked the prisoner. 'Do you mean the urge to rob? Were you short of money?'

'No, it wasn't really about the money,' Spellman replied. 'I never needed the money . . . though there were times when I tried to tell myself that anything I earned from these robberies was my fee for the risk I'd taken.'

'Your *fee*?'

Spellman shrugged. 'You sound pissed off, but don't be. I was kidding myself. Trying to justify walking away with these people's cash. It was never about that, you see. When I say the urge, I mean the urge to attack someone.'

'So, what was it?' Tucker asked. 'A kind of sexual thing?'

Spellman gave that serious thought. 'Maybe. I never had an orgasm or anything. But it gave me this incredible feeling of power. Especially when I was out hunting. The chase was better than the catch, I suppose you could say.'

'And you were the arresting officer, were you, DC Clayburn?' Chief Superintendent Mullany's dry, nasal monotone cut across the viewing room. It wasn't just surprising because they'd actually heard him speak, the guy being such a distant, remote presence on the N Division, but also because he'd actually addressed Lucy by name without needing some kind of gazetteer to identify her.

'Yes, sir,' Lucy replied, 'I was.'

'You're in a rich vein of form . . . Keep it up.'

Beardmore raised his eyebrows at her; this was praise indeed from their omnipotent divisional commander, whom everyone else, with no little justification, assumed had no interest whatsoever in any event occurring beyond the confines of his own palatial office suite.

'Who'd have thought it?' Ruth Smiley said, when Lucy joined her and Danny Tucker in the charge office after the interview had terminated. She read from her notes: 'Ray Spellman, forty-six years old, of Whitefield Lane, Shakespeare's Corner, Warwickshire. In case anyone was wondering . . . Shakespeare's Corner is every bit as nice as it sounds. Thatched roofs, mullioned windows. Ray is a happily married man, he has four kids, two of whom are at university and two of whom are still at school. By trade, he's a small businessman. Runs a DIY shop in his village, and one in Stratford-upon-Avon . . . both of which are being searched as we speak. Ray is also a regular churchgoer, a choir master and a boy-scout leader.'

'Nothing surprises me anymore,' Lucy replied. 'I've learned the hard way that real monsters rarely look the part.'

'Monster and sicko, I'd say,' Tucker said. 'The lad he killed in Birmingham was only carrying a hundred quid. I mean seriously . . . you kill a guy for a hundred quid!'

'Well, like he said,' Smiley replied, 'it was more about the violence than the theft.'

'Good thing he likes violence,' Lucy said. 'It'll all be coming the other way now. They're gonna love him in the high-security wing.'

'Either way, it's a terrific collar,' Tucker said, signing off a form at the charge desk and handing it to the custody sergeant.

'It is,' Lucy agreed. 'But you didn't have to give it to me. I know you guys need the arrests.'

'It's not like you didn't earn it,' Smiley said.

Tucker nodded. 'It'll still get written up as a Robbery Squad op. But it's only fair you get a share in it. You made the running, Lucy. Quite literally . . . which, in other circumstances, could have got you in trouble with me.' He arched a mildly disapproving eyebrow.

'Yeah, sorry about that,' Lucy said. 'I couldn't let him get away.'

'Don't worry, I hear you. Anyway, it's West Mids who are *really* going to steal your glory. They'll be the ones who charge him with murder.'

'They on their way up now?' Lucy asked.

'Sure are,' Smiley said. 'They weren't too pleased.'

Lucy wasn't completely sure that she blamed them. GMP had locked up on their behalf within a week of joining the enquiry, whereas West Mids had been hunting this offender for several months. It didn't make them look great.

'Anyway . . . as SIO, I'd better hang around,' Tucker said. 'If the rest of you have got your statements in, you can knob off early. Nothing else to do round here.'

Smiley nodded, looking pleased at the suggestion. She gave them both a mock-salute, and headed for the door.

'Do you think he's fit to stand?' Lucy wondered, as the room emptied.

Tucker shrugged. 'I think they'll want to assess him. Seems

like a bit of a split-personality to me. But you never can tell. Anyway . . . I thought you were going home?'

She pondered that. Technically, there was still another hour and a half of her shift to run. Tucker's offer to send her home early was irregular but generous – especially as it would mean he'd be left here alone, waiting for the West Midlands Major Investigation Team to arrive. No doubt he'd have plenty more paper to fill in, but that wouldn't be much consolation.

'What time are you expecting them to pick him up?' she asked.

'This time of day, should only be a couple of hours on the motorway. But if they're anything like us, probably take an hour and a half just to get their shit together.'

'You'll go out of your head.'

'Nah.' He grinned again. 'I've got a certain pal up in the office who's used to keeping me company. Ever met Detective Jim Beam?'

She chuckled.

'You're free to join us, if you fancy it,' he said.

Lucy gave it some thought.

Everything about DS Danny Tucker was attractive. Not just his appearance or his easy, likeable manner, but his air of efficiency. Laid-back affability was more the sort of thing she'd associate with cops like Harry Jepson, who habitually and unconcernedly got things wrong. But there was no sign of such incompetence with Tucker. He was a rare beast indeed. Even so, though it would disappoint her mother no end, and tempted as she herself may be, Lucy remained adamant that she would never mix work and pleasure.

'Thanks, Danny,' she said. 'But while you're letting me go home early, I'm taking it. Stan Beardmore will want me back on Division some time tomorrow.'

'No probs.' If Tucker felt disappointment, he didn't show

it. 'See you around.' He moved away along the charge desk, to liaise with the custody sergeant.

Lucy left the Custody Suite still wondering if she'd done the right thing. Would a little nightcap have done any harm? Seriously?

Not that it mattered.

'Probably got a girlfriend already,' she told herself. She hadn't spied a wedding ring on his finger, but it seemed unlikely that he wouldn't have a partner of some sort.

Her thoughts were interrupted in the corridor outside, when she encountered Lee Gaskin.

He'd just come in through the personnel door, having also been involved in the stake-out for the Creep, though in his case up at Cotehill Crescent. As usual with officers unused to working anything other than daytime shifts, which was Robbery Squad's normal form, he looked sallow-cheeked and drained. But he carried his firearms jacket over his shoulder, revealing the brown leather strap across his chest, and the Glock still holstered under his right armpit.

'Well, well,' he said, in his usual sneering tone. 'If it isn't Jane Bond herself. More crazy hi-jinks? I guess we're just lucky your pretty little face didn't get messed up this time.'

'You could have been there to make sure of it,' she replied. 'But as usual, you weren't.'

His eyes, already bleary with fatigue, narrowed. 'But I suppose where we're *really* lucky is that no one got badly hurt . . . none of our lot, I mean. Because that's your usual style, isn't it?'

Suddenly, the weight of the hour began to tell. Not to mention the physical and emotional strain Lucy had put herself under for the arrest. In any case, one thing she couldn't stand was gobshites blundering into situations they had totally and utterly misread.

'Take a fucking hike, Lee.' She tried to step around him. 'You're the last idiot I need at this time of night.'

To her surprise, he slid sideways, blocking her path and leaning into her face.

'You what?' His voice was genuinely aggressive, his breath rancid with cigarette smoke. 'You think because you got lucky tonight, you're entitled to use my first name? You think we're equals?'

'Oh . . . stop *acting*,' she said, tiredly.

'Acting?'

'What *was* Mandy Doyle, *Lee* . . . your mother, your missus? Like I say, stop acting.'

'Don't get cocky with me, you little bitch.'

'*Oy!*' a voice bellowed. Danny Tucker had just emerged from the Custody Suite and overheard. 'What's going on?'

Gaskin's belligerent expression sagged. 'Nothing to do with you, this, sarge . . . it's personal.'

'The hell it's nothing to do with me!' Tucker stalked towards them.

'It's okay, Danny,' Lucy said. 'DC Gaskin's just letting his mummy issues get the better of him.'

'*Fucking bitch!*' Gaskin pushed her.

Now Tucker leapt between them, shoving Gaskin backward.

'For Christ's sake, Dan!' Gaskin pleaded, seeming surprised by the intervention. 'Don't tell me she's fooled you an' all?'

'What the hell's going on?' Tucker demanded.

'Are you seriously telling me you don't know how much of a fucking liability this one can be?'

Tucker looked baffled. 'She did a job and a half for us tonight!'

Gaskin rounded on Lucy. 'You live a charmed fucking life, Clayburn, that's all I can say.'

'That's enough,' Tucker growled. 'Now you watch your mouth . . . all right?'

'It's okay,' Lucy said. 'He's just ticked off because he had a gander in a mirror.'

'I'm warning you . . .' Gaskin snarled.

Tucker grabbed his collar and slammed him back against the corridor wall. 'I said *that's enough*! You know the rules, Lee . . . we don't have shit in Robbery Squad. Anyone stirs it, they'll find themselves out on their earhole, you understand?'

'And that'll be down to *you*, will it, Sarge?'

'It'll be down to DI Blake, who I'm sure won't take very kindly to hearing one of her fellow female officers referred to as "a bitch". Especially when the officer in question has just pulled out a real plum for us.'

'Just . . . *get the fuck off me!*' Gaskin wriggled free and backed away. 'Tell me something, Danny . . . you're not thinking of bringing her into the Squad *permanently*? Do me that favour at least.'

'I'm not doing you any favours. Now you do as I say, you dozy little pillock . . . get home and get your head in gear. I don't want to see you around here until DC Clayburn's had a written apology from you.'

'Yeah . . . that'll be the day Hell fucking freezes.' Gaskin turned and stumped away.

'And check your pistol first!' Tucker shouted, to which Gaskin replied with a V-sign over his shoulder.

Tucker turned and eyed Lucy, who was still doing her best to remain unflustered.

'You want to tell me what all that was about?' he asked.

'It's not a short story.'

'Better if you get *your* side in first, trust me.'

She nodded, acknowledging the wisdom of that.

'Still sure you don't want that late-night tipple?' he asked.

Lucy pursed her lips. Under the circumstances, she was no longer sure of any such thing.

Chapter 14

'Before he joined the Robbery Squad, Lee Gaskin was the adoring student of a certain DI Mandy Doyle,' Lucy said.

Tucker frowned as he tried to recollect the name. 'Think that rings a bell.'

'It ought to. It was quite a scandal.'

He'd slumped in the swivel chair on the other side of his desk, fingertips playing round the rim of his whisky glass, which contained several inches of reddish/amber liquor. Apart from Lucy, who'd also pulled up a chair and had a tumbler of the good stuff in front of her, the Robbery Squad office was empty.

'About five years ago, I was part of Mandy Doyle's team too,' Lucy explained. 'It was my first CID assignment. I had a dangerous suspect in custody. We'd locked him up for forcing entry to his elderly neighbour's house, raping her and half beating her to death. It transpired that he'd already raped and murdered two other women. We didn't know that at the time, but obviously he was still a high priority for us. In a nutshell . . .' She sighed, always embarrassed at this admission. 'In a nutshell, I allowed him to overpower me and get hold of a gun he'd stashed beforehand. As such . . . DI Doyle got shot.'

'Whoa . . .' Tucker sat slowly upright.

'She survived but was crippled and had to retire on a medical.'

He leaned forward. 'I defo remember it now.'

Lucy shrugged. 'I copped most of the blame for it. Got kicked back into uniform. Thought that was it for me, but in due course I was advised that it hadn't entirely been my fault. Doyle mismanaged things. She'd given me a hard time from the start – never understood her really. Strange kind of policewoman. She liked fellas. I mean in the team with her. Didn't really want any other girls on the plot.'

'What . . . she was some kind of queen bee?'

Lucy shrugged. 'Not really. But . . . she liked to be in charge of blokes. She'd worked her way up through the ranks, and that was back in the days when women were second-class citizens in the job. It was a response to that, I suspect. Other policewomen – especially youngsters, like I was at the time, were just a distraction to her, an irritant. But a lot of the guys didn't see it that way at all. They just thought she was great.'

'And Gaskin was one of them?'

'Yeah. He'd been with her a few years. Saw himself as her protégé, I suppose. He was only a young detective, like me. But whereas she put nothing but obstacles in my path, she was grooming him for great things. At least that was what *he* thought.'

'And then suddenly his number one mentor is gone? And he blames you?'

'Correct.' Lucy gave a crooked smile. 'And he wasn't the only one. There are detectives scattered across GMP who still resent me because of what happened . . . who think I really bolloxed it and should be chucked out of the job.'

Tucker sat back. 'You've obviously made up ground since.'

'I like to think so. But only in recent years. And Lee Gaskin clearly doesn't agree.'

'Well . . . to be honest, Lee's a bit of a prat.' Tucker paused as if unhappy bad-mouthing his fellow Squad member, but perhaps thinking it was sometimes necessary. 'He likes to get stuck in, so on one hand he's a useful team member. But he has views that are . . . shall we say, not entirely conversant with police-think in the twenty-first century. Kathy's had to rein him in on occasion.'

'I'm surprised she tolerates him,' Lucy said.

'His background isn't the best, you know.'

Lucy shrugged.

'No one told you?'

'No . . . but then, I suppose I never asked. When a guy vehemently hates you, how much more about him do you want to discover?'

'That's probably true.' Tucker sipped some bourbon. 'The thing with Lee is . . . he came into the job for very personal reasons. And they're all kind of tied in with the origins of the Robbery Squad.'

Lucy sat up. 'Wait a sec, you're not saying . . .' It was vaguely disconcerting that suddenly she thought she might know something about this, after all. '*That* was a PC Gaskin, wasn't it?'

Tucker nodded sombrely.

Lucy sat back again. She breathed out. 'Oh . . . wow.'

Sometime in the early 2000s, an armed robbery had occurred at a branch of the Halifax Building Society in central Manchester. The gang got clean away, but only because, when a patrolling constable confronted them as they left the premises, one of them shot him at point-blank range, killing him instantly.

'It was Lee's older brother, Tony,' Tucker confirmed.

'Jesus,' she said slowly.

If her memory served, the formation of the Manchester Robbery Squad had followed about a year later, certain of the murdered officer's colleagues refusing to accept that, because funds were tight, the investigation should be relegated to the 'cold case' division, and lobbying the GMP top brass for some kind of dedicated anti-armed robbery unit in the style of the Flying Squad in London. When journalists and local MPs got on the case as well, it finally happened.

'Tony Gaskin had been my tutor-con when I first joined up,' Tucker said. 'Absolute top bloke. When he died in 2002, I was divisional CID at the Crescent, Salford. Just around the corner from where it happened. I couldn't believe it . . . best lad in the job, gone in a blink. I felt we had to do something. Couldn't let it go unanswered.'

'You were part of the original lobby group?' Lucy asked, fascinated.

Tucker shrugged. 'That's right. A few of us made a big pitch. Ended up going nationwide. Manchester was supposed to be a happening place, and rotten press like this didn't look good. In the end, they couldn't refuse us.'

'So, you were in the Squad right from the beginning?'

'Yeah, but that's not the point.' He frowned, in some way disappointed with himself. 'We still didn't catch the bastards, did we? No matter how many others we put away. Going back to Lee, he was doing an apprenticeship when Tony died. A plumber, I think he set out to be. Only a young lad, but . . . a devastating blow, obviously. Put him on a new course in life. Brought him into the job, where he's been pretty . . . well, *zealous* would be one word.'

'Yeah,' Lucy said under her breath.

Suddenly, things were a lot more explainable to her.

One dead cop who was very, very close to Lee Gaskin and then a nearly dead cop who was close enough to him.

128

Clearly, they were indivisible in his mind. And those responsible, the unknown killer of Tony Gaskin and the cop whose negligence almost caused the death of Mandy Doyle, were near enough one and the same. It was a delusion on Gaskin's part, Lucy realised. A big one. But at least his attitude was now understandable, even if not excusable.

'Best solution's just to stay out of his way,' Tucker said. 'Kathy likes there to be a good atmosphere in the team. No personal issues, if you know what I mean.'

Lucy was intrigued to hear him talk as if she was already a permanent attachment to the Squad: was that something he *hoped* would happen, or was he actually party to conversations that had been held?

'Well . . . you're done with me now, anyway, aren't you?' she said.

Tucker smiled. 'We're *done* with you?'

'I mean we got our man. You've no further use for me.'

'Well . . . you're right, we got him.' He raised his glass in an impromptu toast. 'Everything else about today is unimportant compared to that.'

They sipped together.

Rather dolefully, he added: 'Whether we've got any more use for you depends on whether the brass have any further use for us.'

Lucy thought again about the shadow hanging over them. 'Surely, if the Squad does get discontinued, you'll all get good gigs elsewhere?'

He shrugged. 'You'd like to think so. But I reckon we've got a good set-up here. I mean, when we were the Manchester Robbery Squad, it was better. We had more manpower, more resources. We took some big teams down. But we're doing all right here too.' He nodded across the room to where the current major op was in progress. 'Kathy's been tracking this Saturday Street mob. They're real heavyweights. If we pull *them* in, especially after serving the Creep up to West Mids . . . well, it'll show what we're capable of.'

Lucy glanced further across the room, this time to where DI Blake's own desk sat anonymously amid the work stations of her rank and file. The only thing to mark it out was that gallery of faces on the wall behind it, blown-up mugshots of some of the region's most notorious armed robbers. Among them, she recognised Jason Demetrius, whose MO had been to inveigle his way into city-centre hotels and rob the guests in their bedrooms, Donny Costello, who had launched a solo crime wave in the Stockport area, robbing three banks and, in one case, shooting and crippling a young clerk, and Julius and Anton Vrozak, who'd lain in wait for a bookie at his Altrincham home, tied the guy up alongside his wife and then ripped the wife's toenails off with pliers in an effort to get him to open the safe. All four of those hoodlums were among those who'd been crossed out in red, which clearly represented their apprehension, conviction and imprisonment.

It impressed Lucy no end. And yet, it confused her too.

'DI Blake seems like a conundrum to me,' she said.

'How so?' Tucker wondered.

'Well . . .'

'You mean because she looks like she's just left a ladies' finishing school?'

'She's a girlish figure, I suppose. Seems very refined too. Sounds more like a doctor than a DI. I mean, I know there are lots of college girls in the job these days, looking for a lucrative career. But DI Blake seems different.'

He chuckled. 'She's going places, that's for sure. Destined for the top floor. But I've been in the job for nineteen years, and she's the best boss I've ever worked under. How often can you say that you actually look forward to coming in to work? Because *we* do. She's got a great management style . . .

very efficient, very clipped, but affable, accessible, easy to get on with. But that's only part of it. She's also a real detective, if you know what I mean. She wants to rise through results, not because she's always got one eye on the next promotion board. These characters up here.' He indicated the photo gallery. 'We call that "Kathy's Hall of Fame". She doesn't put those pics up. *We* do. Every one of them a total bastard . . . never done an honest day's work in his life, yet most of them minted through robbing and brutalising the innocent. But, as you can see, Kathy's working through them like a whirlwind. And that's something every mucker in this room is happy to go along with.' He smiled. 'Now you see where we get our *real* job satisfaction.'

And Lucy did. She was tired now, and yet she was enthralled by what she was hearing.

Danny Tucker wasn't an especially demonstrative guy, but his energy and enthusiasm imbued his every word. In addition, he was selling something Lucy really wanted. She again took in Kathy's Hall of Fame. A strong desire to bang the region's most hateful scum behind bars had certainly been her own key motivation when joining the Greater Manchester Police, and so tackling its *crème de la crème* had to be the ultimate goal.

'What you see is what you get, with Kathy,' Tucker said. 'She doesn't slap backs when it's not needed, or tell everyone how wonderful they are just to be popular. But she appreciates good work, and she looks after you . . . if you've earned her trust, you've got it for life. And if you *do* fancy coming up here to Robbery, well . . . you've already gained a lot of ground with her.'

'I *do* want to come up here,' Lucy said.

'Won't be much opportunity for promotion, mind.'

She shrugged. 'That's CID all over.'

'No, I mean . . . seriously there's zilch opportunity inside the squad. Kathy's the only brass we need, hence she's the only one we've got. And she isn't going anywhere at present.'

Lucy smiled. '*You* could get promoted out of the squad. That'd leave a DS vacancy.'

He feigned hurt. 'You mean you'd want to stay in if I left?'

She smiled and finished her drink. 'I think we're getting a bit ahead of ourselves now.'

'Seriously, Lucy . . . you've impressed me. Not just tonight, but living on your own beat. I commute thirty miles a day to and from Chadderton, and I'm quite happy with that. I wouldn't want to know what's *really* going on in the next street to where I live.'

Lucy finished her whisky. 'I think it's helped my effectiveness over the years.'

'You know Crowley well?'

'Inside out, I think it's safe to say.'

He studied her. 'The more I look at you, DC Clayburn, the more I want you . . . I mean in the Squad, obviously.'

'Erm . . . thanks.' She stood up; she knew he'd only been joking, but there'd been a mischievous, flirtatious edge to it, which she wasn't well-equipped to handle this early in the morning. 'Time for me to go, I think.'

He didn't stand up with her, but waved in lazy fashion. When she was halfway across the room, he said: 'Don't be a stranger, Lucy.'

'Sorry?'

'Whenever you've got a spare five minutes, come up and see us, have a chat. Keep registering your interest. Put the message over that this is where you want to be.'

She nodded, her feelings about Tucker decidedly mixed, but otherwise delighted with the way the day had gone. However, halfway down the stairs, she met someone whose mere presence brought her back to earth with a bump. It was the last person she'd expected to see at five o'clock in the morning, though unsurprisingly, he was pale-faced and red-eyed with lack of sleep, his jacket and tie scruffy, his hair a dishevelled mat.

'Harry!' she said. 'What the hell are you doing here?'

He yawned. 'That's a welcome and a half.'

'Tough. The question stands.'

'Well . . . as I've been working these burglaries on my tod the last few days, I've been putting in some extra time so I can get the paper straight.'

'I mean what are you doing up *here.*'

'Well . . .' He looked sheepish. 'I was sort of looking for you. I saw your Jimny outside, realised you were still on. Soon as I got in, I heard you'd nabbed your suspect. Thought some congrats might be order.'

'Well, cheers . . . ta.'

Lucy didn't totally believe that explanation. It wasn't impossible that he was simply being nice, but inevitably that old suspicion reared its head again; that he fancied her. That would be inconvenient enough, but if he started getting possessive about her too, then they'd have a real problem. So much so that she didn't even want to consider it at this moment.

She walked on down the stairs. 'I'm done here and I'm off to bed. Tell Stan I'll be back in the DO this afternoon.'

'Yo, Lucy!' someone called from the top of the stairs.

They looked up and saw Danny Tucker descending. He was grinning broadly.

'You won't be going anywhere without these,' he said, tossing her a set of car keys.

'Bloody hell.' Lucy shoved them into her anorak pocket. 'Told you I was ready for the sack. Listen . . . see you all later.' She continued down.

'Hiya . . . Danny Tucker,' she heard Tucker say to Harry. 'Robbery.'

133

'Harry Jepson,' Harry replied, maybe with a grudging handshake. 'I work with Lucy.'

'Lucky you.'

Lucy didn't glance back, just rounded the corner at the foot of the stairs and headed out.

Chapter 15

Lucy wasn't required back in the divisional DO until eight on the Wednesday morning. She received a call from CID Admin to advise her of this just after nine o'clock on the Tuesday morning, and so after grabbing a couple of hours in the armchair, she managed to fight her way through the rest of the day, bug-eyed with fatigue but just about staying this side of the human/zombie divide, and finally got to bed at a normal hour.

As such, come Wednesday morning, she was able to go back to work, as Stan Beardmore was fond of saying, 'full of piss and vinegar'.

On her way in, she took a phone call on the hands-free. It was from Kyle Armstrong, who didn't sound best pleased.

'Thanks for nothing,' he grunted.

'Excuse me . . .?'

'That so-called favour you did us.'

'*So-called!*' Lucy had delivered the message from Geoff Slater to the Low Riders by leaving it on Armstrong's voice-mail. She hadn't expected him to ring her to offer thanks for it, but even given the biker president's usual truculent attitude where law enforcement was concerned, she hadn't expected *this* either.

'Dykey's still talking to his solicitor about changing his plea,' Armstrong said. 'But seriously . . . the best we get is a letter to the judge?'

'Perhaps you thought you were going to get one of those anyway?' she snapped, as she drove into the personnel car park. 'Perhaps you thought that, out of the sheer goodness of their hearts, the Drug Squad were going to recommend your lad for a smack on the wrist rather than the good slap round the head he so richly deserves. It may come as a surprise to you, Kyle . . . but there are certain people based in offices not very far from the office where I work who've really got you lot marked as a pile of dog-shit, and can't wait to see you shovelled up and chucked into the nearest bin.'

'Fuck 'em. We feel the same about them . . .'

'The difference is they can do something about it,' she said. 'And they aim to, the first chance they get. Now, in light of all that, I think your lad, Ian, got a good deal here, don't you?'

There was a long, surly silence – she could just picture his handsome, feral face as it twisted with indignation that 'a mere lass' had him on the backfoot.

'So . . .' she said, 'can I assume that in reality you're actually eternally grateful for this, and are now looking for any way you can to scratch *my* back in return?'

He muttered something foul-mouthed but inaudible.

'Eloquent as ever, Kyle. Don't worry . . . I'll be in touch soon.'

By eight-thirty she and Harry were ready to hit the road. They left the nick by the personnel door, and were traipsing across the car park when a commotion caught their attention at the main gate. They stopped to watch as the barrier lifted, and a Trojan unit – a heavily armed troop-carrier – came trundling in, with firearms-response officers in full armour and helmets, their MP5s held crosswise at the chest, trudging in front of it.

DI Kathy Blake came next. She was in scruffs, but also wore a Kevlar vest and shoulder pads, and a high-visibility baseball cap. A Glock was holstered on her right hip, and she was talking on the phone. A divisional prisoner-transport van followed, a firearms officer walking on the nearside of it, a Robbery Squad officer walking on the offside. Three more firearms guys walked into the car park behind the van, and then came a couple of the Robbery Squad's unmarked cars, both loaded with detectives, all of whom, from their faces, seemed to be in a very good mood.

DI Blake was too busy on the phone to notice Lucy and Harry, as she veered away towards the Custody Suite's outer door, which swung open in advance of her reaching it. The prisoner-transport peeled from the cavalcade and followed her, pulling up right alongside the door. The troop-carrier and the detectives' cars halted a couple of dozen yards away, their personnel spilling out and hurrying across the yard to form a cordon.

'Now this is what you call a result,' Lucy said, half to herself but loud enough for Harry to hear.

The prisoner-transport's rear doors swung open, as did the cage doors inside them, and pairs of men began scrambling out, four of them in total, in each case a Robbery Squad officer handcuffed to a suspect. Lucy didn't need to look at the suspects, who, to a man, were brawny individuals with close-cropped hair and prison tats to match, to know that this was the fabled Saturday Street Gang.

One by one, they were taken inside. Danny Tucker now appeared, stepping out from the Custody Suite and having a quick word with the inspector in charge of the firearms-response team, who nodded and indicated that his men could climb back into their vehicle. Tucker spotted Lucy, and gave her a thumbs-up before going back inside, slamming the door behind him.

'You want to avoid that fella,' Harry grunted. 'Don't like him. Too flash. Don't trust any of these flash bastard specialist departments.'

Lucy glanced round at him. 'You can't argue with their results.'

'Yeah, but why do you think they're under the microscope at present?' Harry chuntered on as they walked across the yard towards his silver-grey BMW. 'All they do all day is focus on these teams of blaggers – who might do a job once every six months. Meanwhile, the rest of us wear down shoe-leather chasing the odds and sods of Crowley, who're at it twenty-four-seven. Small scores on paper, but in the long run we're the ones who are cleaning up the frontier.'

'You know,' Lucy said, as they climbed into the car, 'uniform probably think the same way about CID in general.'

He didn't bother to answer as the BMW grumbled to life.

'We're all on the same side, Harry,' she added. 'Chill out.'

There was nowhere quite like Hatchwood Green for reminding you that most policework took place a long way from the pseudo-glamorous world of stake-outs, fast cars and high-end villainy that the Robbery Squad occupied.

It was the archetypical sink estate, which under the steady drizzle of a dull, grey October day looked even more depressing than usual.

Lucy hated the place, partly because she had to visit it so regularly, but also because it was architecturally hideous, not just comprising run-down, past-its-sell-by-date housing stock, but also faceless tower blocks and rows of dingy deck-access flats. If all that wasn't bad enough, the council's original policy of gathering together on the Hatchwood what looked like every antisocial element they could find – problem families, drunks, addicts and other known criminals – in effect turning this already declining neighbourhood into a human dustbin, had been sheer folly, as it had created a ghetto atmosphere where resentment festered.

Harry parked his BMW on Edward Terrace, in the very middle of the estate, and then sat and fiddled with his phone, playing *Candy Crush Saga* while Lucy leafed through the crime reports he'd put together for her as rain dotted the windows.

'Most of these APs are quite elderly,' she observed.

Harry grunted. 'That's hardly unusual, is it?'

'Wouldn't be unusual if we were talking robberies with the householders assaulted or told to get out of the way . . . but these are burglaries, break-ins when they're not at home. That's obviously these perps' thing. But OAPs, because they're not employed, tend not to keep regular hours.' She pondered. 'Whoever these lads are, they obviously know the estate pretty well, keep an eye on the comings and goings.'

Harry shrugged as though once again this was hardly a revelation. 'I'm perfectly prepared to believe it's *local* industry. Look at the stuff being taken. It's hardly high-end.'

Lucy had to admit that whoever the burglars were, they weren't getting away with life-changing hauls. In most cases, it was cash and jewellery, but it rarely amounted to much. The most recent break caught her eye. It had occurred on October 22 at 19, Durkin Crescent, the bungalow of a nonagenarian war veteran widower called Reg Murgatroyd, whom she knew personally. In that case, the loss comprised two rings, his late wife's wedding and engagement rings. Lucy doubted it would earn the thief much on the black market, but it could be a crippling blow to the old man.

'Cynical opportunism,' she said. 'These breaks aren't planned in advance. That means they . . . or *he* know the area well – because he knows where the OAPs live, and he patrols it regularly looking for his chance. But how can a gang of lads, or even one lad alone, do that without someone getting suspicious and reporting them?'

Harry grunted again.

Lucy felt vaguely aggravated. Ever since she'd returned to the DO that morning, Harry had seemed distracted and irritable. She knew that he was embroiled in constant legal tangles with his ex-wife, and he moaned endlessly about how much of his income drained away in maintenance payments for three children he never even got to see. That was bound to have preoccupied him to an extent. But she also suspected that he was manifesting some resentment about her recent dalliance with the Robbery Squad. At one time, Lucy's own future in the police had looked bleak, with zero chance of a permanent detective role. But all that had now changed. In the last year, the good results had rolled in and suddenly she was the girl everyone was interested in. Harry meanwhile, through his own numerous gaffes, was still rooted firmly on the first rung of the ladder. It was easy to see how that would peeve him. But while it might serve as an excuse in Harry's mind, it was hardly helpful when they had a shedload of work to get through.

'Harry . . . how much have you actually done on this?' she asked.

He turned a stony expression towards her. 'I've had *other* stuff to get on with too, you know. While you were galli-vanting round town all night with idiots like Danny Tucker and Lee Gaskin.'

'Trust me, I wasn't gallivanting with Lee Gaskin.' She took a breath. 'But the point is taken, I wasn't here . . . so, let me rephrase . . . how much progress on this have you managed to make?'

'Well . . .' he slipped his phone into his raincoat pocket, 'I think you're right. I'm pretty sure there's only one of them.

We've got no dabs anywhere, but there are three separate instances where footprints were detectable: one in a flower bed, one on a lawn where there's not much grass, one on a kitchen floor. Before you ask, in no case was a tread identifiable. Probably wearing worn-down boots or trainers.'

'But they were all the same size?'

'Yeah. Nine-and-a-halfs.'

That fitted, she supposed. Eight times out of ten in the UK, burglary was committed by male teenagers or male twenty-somethings.

'But that's not the main thing,' Harry said. He spread the crime reports on his lap. 'Here's my thinking . . . these are the ten breaks on the Hatchwood we were assigned to look into.' He separated the paperwork into two piles, one smaller than the other, patting the larger one first. 'These are the eight we *should* be interested in.'

'Those eight are defo connected?' Lucy said.

'I think so.' He handed her the other two reports. 'The victimology in these two is not the same.'

Lucy rustled through them. It was true. Whereas the victims in the other eight cases had all been OAPs, the latter two were a single mother and her child, who'd been away on holiday in Blackpool when the burglary occurred, and an Irish barman who'd been home in Dublin for the weekend.'

'Okay . . . but there has to be more to it than that.'

'There is,' Harry said. 'Both the single mum and the Irish barman's properties got trashed during the break – typical pillhead job. Total jerks looking for anything they could to score. You'll note that both medical cabinets were raided.'

Lucy skim-read the reports again. 'Yeah . . .'

'Well . . . in the other eight, they weren't. In fact, there was no unnecessary or gratuitous damage at all.'

Despite her earlier annoyance with him, Lucy had to give him marks for this; it was a good spot.

'So, whoever did these eight OAPs is a more organised offender?' she said. 'But that doesn't tie in with the opportunist element.'

Harry shrugged. 'Maybe not. But just because he's organised, that doesn't make him Raffles. Look . . . if nothing else, he knew what he was looking for. In each case the intruder went straight to the place where the goodies were stored.'

Lucy re-checked the eight connected burglaries. On second assessment, there were distinct similarities. In the case of Reg Murgatroyd, for instance, the intruder had gone straight to a bedside cabinet where the two rings were kept, and removed them. According to the sit-rep by the PC who'd first attended, there was no other evidence of damage in the bungalow, apart from the forcing of a rear window. Whoever it was, they had not needed to search for valuables. It was the same story with the others. None of the premises had been ransacked before theft.

'At first, I thought this had to be someone who'd been inside the houses beforehand,' Harry said. 'You know . . . who'd had a good mooch around legitimately.'

'You mean like a tradesman?' Lucy said. 'A builder, a decorator?'

'Yeah. But none of these eight have had any work done recently. And anyway, it wouldn't have taken us long to follow that line of enquiry. He'd surely know we'd nab him.' Harry pursed his lips. Now that they were back on the job together, he seemed relaxed again, more focussed. 'So, the question remains . . . how does he know where the good stuff, such as it is, is stashed?'

It was a conundrum, for sure, and one they'd both need to apply their thinking caps too.

'I take it you've already done a door-to-door?' Lucy said.

'Canvassed half the bloody estate. No one curious hanging around anywhere.'

No one curious, Lucy thought to herself. It was always a problem when you asked questions like that. The reality was, as proved not two nights ago by the Creep, aka a podgy everyman called Ray Spellman, that the guys who really made this kind of living work were those who shielded themselves behind a façade of inoffensiveness. Again, Harry ought to know that, but as she'd reminded herself before, he had lots of other things on his mind. Anyway, she was here now, which meant they could split up and cover more ground.

Lucy's first port of call was 19, Durkin Crescent.

She had already met Reg Murgatroyd twice before. In her uniform days, she'd interviewed him after he'd witnessed a brawl at Hatchford Green Railway Club, which had seen someone glassed and badly disfigured. Thanks to his evidence, she'd made an arrest and a well-known thug called Keiron Penrose had subsequently gone to prison. It had been brave of the old soldier even to make a statement, given the reputation of Penrose and his family, but the loss of their violent son seemed to take the wind out of their sails, and there'd been no repercussions.

During a follow-up visit to Murgatroyd's home, he'd treated Lucy to a cuppa and to some of his old war stories, most of which concerned his days as a Desert Rat. He'd also told her that he still lived in the bungalow he and his late-wife, Daisy, had first moved into not long after he was demobbed, but complained that during the decades since, he'd been forced to watch his formerly beloved Hatchwood Green degenerate, using his own words, 'into a cesspool'.

Even now, as Lucy plodded up Reg's front drive, of all the houses on this particular road, his bungalow was the best-kept, the woodwork recently painted, the brickwork re-pointed, the tiles on the roof realigned.

The interior was as immaculate as the exterior. Typical of

a former military man, she supposed. There wasn't a great deal of furniture inside the house – Reg was ninety-five after all, and hardly rolling in wealth – but there wasn't a hint of dust or damp.

The old man hadn't initially clicked that Lucy was a police officer until he saw her warrant card, but then it was three years since they'd last spoken.

Reg himself hadn't changed a great deal. Never the tallest man, no more than five-six, he'd doubtless once possessed a solid, soldierly build, but great age had reduced this. These days, he was shrivelled, his white shirt hanging on his short, skeletal frame in loose, empty folds. Even though they were patently too large for him, his trousers possessed no front button, his braces alone serving to keep them up.

'I don't suppose you recognise me, do you, Reg?' Lucy said, as he walked with a stoop into the spick-and-span living room ahead of her.

'Oh yes, love, of course,' he replied, though she suspected he was just being polite.

He studied her as he settled into a low-slung armchair. He had a full head of white hair, though it was thin and lank, while his cheeks were pale and had sunk in on themselves. When he peered at her through the pebble-thick lenses of his glasses, there was no clear recollection in his rheumy eyes.

'DC Clayburn.' She showed him her warrant card a second time. 'It's about the break-in you had on October 22.'

Reg stiffened a little, his armchair's springs groaning. This he clearly *did* remember.

'I've not got anything to report yet,' she added hastily. 'I just wanted you to know that we're still investigating it.'

'Do you think you'll catch them?' His voice was shrill, almost squawky.

'I think there's a reasonable chance, Reg. My colleague, DC Jepson, came here to see you, I understand?'

Reg nodded, but didn't say anything.

She wondered why he seemed tense. His spine was stiffly upright, not resting on the cushion of his armchair. She noticed that the fingers on both his hands had dug into the fabric of the armrests.

'Is this burglary really bothering you, Reg?' she enquired. 'Because I saw from the crime report that you didn't want a visit from Victim Support, but we can easily change that . . . you might find it helpful. In addition, I can near enough guarantee that, whoever it was, they won't come back. I mean, they got what they came for straight away, didn't they? Apparently, they didn't make a mess looking round for anything else.'

'No . . . they didn't make a mess.' He rummaged in his trouser pocket, producing a lump of crumpled tissue. Lifting his glasses, he dabbed at his eyes. 'They got what they came for, all right.'

'I'm sorry,' she said. 'I know this is a big loss for you.'

'Well . . .' With a visible struggle, he tried to get himself together. 'Bits of metal at the end of the day. Not like they took Daisy herself, is it?'

He dabbed his eyes again.

Lucy could do nothing but sit and wait while he recomposed himself.

'Not be long before I join her,' he said. 'Then it won't matter, will it?'

'Oh, I think you're good for a few years yet. Can I make you a cup of tea, or something?'

'No . . . it's all right, love. I'm going out soon. Still get up to the Railway Club of an afternoon. Regular as clockwork. Even weekends. Legs haven't gone yet.'

He made a show of sitting back, as if trying to get comfortable, and readjusted his glasses, all the time watching her.

He's waiting for me to leave, Lucy realised.

That was unusual. Old folks, particularly those who'd suffered at the hands of criminals, were normally glad of police company; they'd tea and biscuit you to death just to keep you on their property. But this situation was clearly different, and most likely that was down to the loss of those precious mementoes.

'Okay, my love.' She stood up. 'I just wanted you to know that we're still on the case. We'll keep working it till we get some kind of result.'

Outside, Lucy wandered down the drive and halted by the gatepost.

As a rule, the average householder in the UK was more frightened of burglars than any other kind of criminal. On one hand, there were viable reasons for this; but on the other, there were equally viable reasons why they should actually be much less afraid.

There was no doubt that the prospect of some stranger trespassing in your home, usually after they'd forced entry while you were out, and rooting through your personal stuff, was quite horrifying. It was also a commonplace crime; it happened a lot and at all levels of society. All of this made burglars as feared as they were hated. Any man so callous as to force his way into your house had to be one of society's worst, a fearless law-breaker who'd think nothing of brutally attacking any householder that got in his way. This was a person to be terrified of, right?

Wrong.

Most burglars in Lucy's experience were skinny little wimps. Drug-addled teenagers, or inadequate adults who stole from other people because they were too weak and ineffectual to hold down a job, and who broke into dwellings because they were easy targets. And more likely than not, they'd run for their lives if they ever met someone there.

Of course, none of that made vulnerable, elderly people like Reg Murgatroyd feel any the less besieged on dreary housing estates like Hatchwood Green.

Even eleven years into the job, it made Lucy's blood boil that a chap like Murgatroyd, who, in his own youth, braved the bombs and bullets of Rommel's Afrika Korps now had to eke out his final years in this state of oppression. If that wasn't enough to move you to tears, the guy's stoicism certainly would. Reg might have been a tad unfriendlier than she'd seen him previously, for some reason ill-at-ease to have her in his presence, but he still represented that stiff-upper-lip generation, who, having shrugged off the horrors of a war that killed sixty million, were clearly not going to let a few minor disasters in civilian life inconvenience them.

'Bits of metal at the end of the day,' he'd said.

Bits of metal, Lucy thought.

At first, she didn't understand why this seemed relevant to her.

And then the penny dropped.

She stepped away from the gatepost, tingling. At first it seemed unlikely, if not plain ridiculous. But the more she thought about it, the more that unlikelihood diminished. She grabbed her phone and banged in Harry's number.

'Yep,' he replied. By the background hubbub, he was at the chippie, buying their lunch.

'Harry, I know how he's doing it.'

'Ta, my love . . . keep the change. Sorry, Luce . . . what did you say?'

'He's using a metal detector.'

'He's . . . *what*?'

'He knows exactly where to find the valuable stuff because he's using a metal detector.'

'Hang on . . .' To say Harry sounded dubious would be an understatement. 'Lucy, what're you . . .?'

'Look, they're not difficult to get hold of. You can buy them over the counter.'

'That would work?'

'Why not? If they can detect rusty old swords ten feet underground, surely they can tell you which drawer the money's in or which shoebox under the bed contains jewellery.'

There was a long pause before Harry spoke again.

'Clever little bastard, eh?'

Chapter 16

Andy Northwood's house was well placed to be the party capital of Crowley.

In truth, it was only just inside the Crowley border, in the southwest corner of the borough, where it adjoined Cheshire, and was located on Millwright Lane, a B-road with a semi-rural atmosphere because on its south side, it ran along the northeast edge of Chat Moss, an extensive area of natural heathland. Northwood's house, none-too-subtly named *Golden Roost*, was a lavish, seven-bedroom mansion – all red brick and white stucco – and boasting an indoor swimming pool and sauna area, its own tennis courts, and substantial mature gardens to the front, back and sides. It was situated on high ground, at the top of a winding, seventy-five-yard drive, which, in addition to the thick wall of conifers in front, ensured that it couldn't be seen from Millwright Lane itself.

Wednesday night parties at *Golden Roost* were so regular an occurrence these days that they'd become known in certain circles, with Northwood's encouragement of course, as the 'Wednesday Night Specials'. This wasn't just because Northwood himself led a wild lifestyle – even though as one of Greater Manchester's leading pimps and drugs dealers, he certainly did – but because he had ambitions to be much more, and in this day and age, with high-end crime in the Northwest of England as strictly controlled as it was, that didn't mean kicking and pushing your way to the top, but wheedling your way: making friends, not enemies; being nice to people, entertaining them. And if there was one thing Andy Northwood did very well, it was entertain.

In some ways, Northwood, himself, was a walking advert for this.

In reflection of his firm conviction that he was a player, 'Flash Andy', as they tended to call him, always adopted the playboy look: lots of gold and jewellery, big Hawaiian shirts, loafers, light-coloured linen pants. He even wore this kind of gear in winter; the impression he sought to make was that he was the kind of guy who, at a moment's notice, might hop onto a private yacht and sail off into the sunset. Purely in physical terms, he was a big bloke – six-three, and well-built with it, despite his forty-five years. His red-gold hair implants matched his fake tan, and he worked out regularly to ensure that he stayed trim around the waist. His tattoos – and he bore many on both arms – were strictly of the ultra-expensive variety. But for all this self-evident ego, he was genuinely a good-looking guy, and he was undeniably generous to his guests.

Every Wednesday night, divorcee Andy, whose ex-wife, Raimunda, had already taken him for the apartment in Malaga, would invite five or six different but always important local faces to attend his house, where, to start with, there'd be poker (for big money of course), but also an amazing spread; each week he bought in the most expensive champagne and hired a different chef from one of Manchester's swishest restaurants to provide an exquisite buffet. In addition, there'd be cocaine, lots and lots of it, and the usual bevy of the most beautiful girls his high-class stable could provide, who would taunt and flirt with the guests all evening, stroking their cheeks, cooing into their ears, and finally, after performing full stripteases and dancing naked while a drunken 'girl-auction' was held, going upstairs one by one with the highest bidders.

On this Wednesday evening in particular, the five guests were the usual assortment of powerbrokers, though perhaps not from the topmost league.

Paddy Drinkwater was a music promoter and nightclub owner, who'd once courted controversy by being the first club boss outside London to introduce 'lap-dancing' to certain of his establishments. Eric Klinsman was a successful sports agent who several times in recent years was alleged to have been involved with match-fixing in football, though thanks to the expertise of his legal reps, this had never been proven. Mervyn Grimshaw, a general-purpose entrepreneur, was a particularly close associate of Flash Andy's, who'd mainly made his money importing marijuana from Morocco. Lenny Carmichael was a real estate hustler and the region's unofficial go-to man for dodgy deals in that business. And lastly there was Mo Newman, superficially a successful road-haulier but also a fraudster, fence and the trusted 'handler' of several highly placed and very corrupt police officers.

Individually, none of these men were hugely valuable to Northwood, but 'spreading the love' was his buzz phrase. Each Wednesday Night Special saw him wining and dining a different set of such pals and would-be pals at *Golden Roost*, so that he gradually built up an extensive network of nefarious but reasonably empowered characters, who could, at any time in the future, be in a position to look on him favourably.

And it wasn't as if the Wednesday Night Specials were too expensive a deal. Okay, the food and drink didn't come cheap, but his girls usually earned so well from the tips they received that they didn't need anything extra from him, while the drugs always came from his own stash. And on top of that, he very often made a lot back from the table; Flash Andy was a dab hand at poker himself, and if he won every so often, who would complain, he being the host? That night of October 25, he'd already acquired seventy grand by nine o'clock, and so thought it politic to withdraw from the game and supervise the rest of the evening instead.

It was dark outside and drizzly, but given the time of year, though it was chilly, it was not bitterly cold. On some occasions, regardless of the weather, there'd be a host of bodyguards, brought by guests and dotted around the exterior of the premises, often packing more hardware than he was comfortable with. But that wasn't the case tonight. None of these guests were highly enough placed to have brought anyone with them, relying instead on Northwood's own security arrangements, a single employee called Rob Hoon, who would operate the front gate from a dedicated security booth, a small prefabricated structure on the west side of the house, and who, thanks to the horseshoe of video screens around him, would keep an eye on other sections of the property as well. Hoon was an ex-cop who'd been sacked from the job and briefly jailed for child pornography offences. Northwood didn't really hold with that kind of thing, but if nothing else, it meant that Hoon would know his way around computers, was completely without scruple, and as he was virtually unemployable anywhere else, was never likely to let him down, even though he was paid a pittance. The guy had also at one time been a trained firearms officer. What more could a gangster ask?

It was therefore a surprise at around ten past nine that evening, to hear a loud knocking on the front door when there'd been no call-through from the security booth to let Northwood know that another guest had arrived. In fact,

Northwood only heard the knock because he happened to be coming downstairs, having just visited his gold and marble bathroom to relieve himself of some champagne. If he'd been inside his eighty-foot by thirty-foot lounge, where the Wednesday Night Specials took place, he wouldn't have heard anything, because the raunchy music from the boom box in there and the wild, booze-soaked shouts of encouragement from the guests as the girls bumped and ground on the temporary stage in front of the screened front windows was loud enough to drown out anything.

Even so, Lori, one of two maids on duty that evening, got there before him. She was in the process of bringing a tray of empties from the Games Room on the other side of the hall.

Lori wasn't a real maid. She and Kerry were two pretty barmaids of his acquaintance, who regularly worked this occasion for him specially attired in sexy French uniforms with stocking tops showing under indecently short, pleated skirts. His one full-time domestic servant, Ms Fothergill, the housekeeper, was always given Wednesday evening off, as she would doubtless disapprove of such shenanigans.

'Lori, wait up!' Northwood said, descending the last flight of stairs quickly.

He'd just checked his phone, and he was correct – there had been *no* alert from the security booth, and that bothered him. But Lori had already unlatched the huge front door and had opened it by a couple of inches. She heard her employer, but screamed before she could react as the beaten, bloody-faced form of Rob Hoon was pushed semi-unconscious on top of her. She collapsed beneath his weight, still screaming, but the two figures that piled in through the door behind him were even more terrifying.

Northwood went rigid at the sight of men in black leather jackets and gloves, dark jeans and full-head woollen ski masks, blood-red in colour.

Both wielded what looked like sub-machine guns with silencers fitted to the muzzles.

Northwood launched himself back up the stairs with great lanky strides, covering three treads at a time, only for a volley of suppressed gunfire to burst up the staircase in pursuit, blasting out every spindle in the bannister. Still only halfway up, Northwood hurled himself down into a ball, arms wrapped around his head. With thudding footfalls, one of the intruders, the slightly shorter of the two, hurried up after him, grabbed him by the collar, yanked him to his knees and pushed, sending him rolling back down the stairs.

At the bottom, the second of the two men had got Lori back to her feet and now held her tight against him, his gloved left hand clamped across her mouth. Her eyes bulged under sweat-damp strands of hair, as she regarded her boss with a mixture of horror and bewilderment.

'Look . . . just take it easy,' Northwood stammered as he rose to his feet; it wasn't clear whether he was talking to Lori or the intruders. He tried to keep his voice level, but his eyes almost popped as they fixed on the weapon trained one-handed on his face. 'For fuck's sake . . . just chill, yeah?'

The taller intruder didn't reply, but watched the closed door to the lounge for several tense seconds, in case someone in there had heard the commotion and was about to come out to see what it was. But thanks to the raucous music, that clearly hadn't happened. The tall blagger finally glanced up the stairs to his compatriot, and nodded. The other intruder responded by scampering to the top and commencing what Northwood could only presume was a rapid search of the upper floor, checking the rooms for any other staff and/or guests. Northwood glanced sideways at Hoon, who lay twitching on the carpet. The guy was alive, but his eyes were closed and at this proximity his face looked like raw meat.

'Okay, look . . . what do you fellas want?' he asked, though in truth it seemed obvious. It had never been much of a secret that there was plenty of green stuff on these premises come Wednesday night.

The taller intruder didn't bother answering; instead, his liquid brown gaze bored into the host. There wasn't a hint of stress or tension in him, his woollen mask completely inscrutable. Feet now rumbled down the stairs as the shorter of the two returned and nodded.

The taller one nodded back in acknowledgement.

Again, Northwood tried the blokish approach. One of the many things he prized himself for was his gift of the gab, his ability to smooth things over. He might be a big, burly guy, but apart from his schooldays when he'd commenced his criminal career by extorting money from smaller kids in the playground, Northwood considered that he'd always been more of a cooler than a bouncer.

'Listen, fellas . . .' He attempted a friendly voice, as if he was partly with them on this. 'I can see you're on the job. I've no doubt you're het up, coiled like springs, ready to go . . . yeah?'

The eyes in the scarlet woollen mask continued to spear into him.

'I admire your guts and daring.' He shrugged. 'This kind of thing, good old blag . . . bit of a lost art these days, eh? And you've clearly done your homework. You must've done, to get past security. Thing is . . . I hate to tell you this, but it's better you know beforehand rather than stumble into something you can't handle . . . there's no way there won't be repercussions if you see this thing through. You understand what I'm saying? We've got some top men here tonight. They won't take this lying down.'

This was a lie. As Wednesday Night Special guests went, this particular crowd were more toothless than usual. Okay,

155

they were all connected, but none had form for calling in the heavies. Not that the blaggers needed to know this.

'I admire your professionalism,' Northwood continued. 'I really do. But on this occasion, you've got to think "self-preservation" first.'

Lori whimpered behind the hand plastered over her mouth, as if she couldn't believe that this was the best he was doing to protect her.

'It's all right, love.' Northwood palmed the air placatingly. 'They're not here for *you*. You'll get out of this unhurt, whatever happens. So . . . what's it to be, fellas?' He looked the taller one full in the eye and nodded at the closed door to the lounge. 'We go in there, and you're looking over your shoulders for the rest of your lives? Or you walk away right now . . . and I never need mention this to anyone else?' He smiled, raised his eyebrows – as though he was helping them, as though he was the teacher and they were his errant but likeable pupils. 'I won't even charge you for the banister rail.'

When neither of the intruders replied, he tried again.

'Look . . . I respect you. I'm serious. I'm almost envious. This was the way we *all* did it, one time . . . before we got old and creaky.'

He let that last phrase hang, arms outspread, not just smiling now but grinning.

'You finished?' the taller one asked.

'I . . . what?'

With a clatter of steel on bone, a sub-machine gun barrel cracked against the back of Northwood's skull, knocking him to his knees. A second such blow sent him to the carpet; the hallway a dizzying whirl of figures and shapes and wallpaper patterns. He lay groaning, for a brief time only vaguely aware that the shorter intruder had hurried off again, disappearing and reappearing as he checked all the other ground-floor rooms apart from the lounge.

156

'Two things,' a harsh voice whispered into his ear. 'One . . . we *know* you've got people here who matter. That's *why* we're here. Trust me, it wouldn't be worth the effort if there was only a pipsqueak ponce like you. Two . . . you open your yap one more time without being spoken to first, and it's the fucking graveyard.'

Northwood was dragged groggily but unceremoniously to his feet and hurled at the door to the lounge. It burst open, and he staggered through, still in a daze.

Lori, was thrown in after him, her whimpers rising to a panic-stricken shriek.

The two bandits followed, unscrewing the silencers from the ends of their barrels, and drilling thunderous gunfire into the lounge ceiling and then across the room into the boom box mounted on the wall, which exploded in a shower of wiring and circuitry.

There was brief stunned silence, which immediately blew apart in a percussion of screams and shouts. The three girls on the podium to the bandits' left, all of whom had been gyrating naked apart from their jewellery and high heels, froze like mannequins.

'*Get on the fucking floor!*' the taller bandit bellowed at them, entering the room properly, kicking the stumbling Northwood in front of him. '*Face down, now!*'

A secondary blast of gunfire raked the top of the walnut sideboard, destroying the crystal goblets and bottles of champagne arrayed there, not to mention the dishes and plates piled with delicacies. At the end of it, a generous mound of pure white powder sat on a silver platter, along-side several pre-rolled fifty-pound notes. It turned to fog as the slugs hit it.

The guests – Drinkwater, Klinsman, Grimshaw, Carmichael, Newman – the other maid, Kerry, who had a tray of canapes in her hands, and three girls who, not yet having taken turns

157

to strip, were still in their party dresses, had clustered in front of the podium, egging on the performers, but now fell on top of each other in their haste to hit the deck.

'Stay down and no one gets hurt!' the tall bandit barked, at the same time kicking Northwood viciously in the backs of both his legs.

The householder, still in a stupor, blood streaming down his face, tumbled to the carpet alongside the others.

The shorter one let his weapon swing by the shoulder strap as he hurried the length of the hangar-like room. At the far end, the poker table was set up, a huge trove of cash and jewellery still heaped in the middle of it. He drew and unravelled a black canvas sack, and shovelled it full of goodies. As he did, there were moans and doglike whimpers from the cowed victims. Acrid smoke from the gunfire and the bitter dust of the coke mingled in a hanging curtain which stretched clear across the room.

'Shut your fucking mouths!' the taller one instructed, and for emphasis, landed a savage boot in Northwood's stomach.

The gangster gasped and gagged, blood-laced vomit splurging from his mouth.

'Okay . . . the rest of you!' the taller one added, as his mate came back down the room, his sack now clinking with valuables. 'Everything you've got. Wallets, watches, jewellery . . . *do it now!*'

The shorter one scuttled around them like a crab, holding open the mouth of his sack, as, white-faced and teary-eyed, they knelt up and threw what they could into it.

'Don't be clever,' he hissed at Paddy Drinkwater, grabbing him by his mass of shaggy, dyed-yellow hair and yanking his head from side to side. 'Wedding ring!'

'That's personal stuff,' the club owner protested.

'So personal, it nearly stops you shagging the arse off every grateful little dolly bird that gets through your exclusive front doors, eh?' the taller bandit sneered, stepping in and dragging Drinkwater to his feet by his tie. 'Most of 'em underage, I've no doubt . . .'

'That's a lie . . .' Drinkwater tried to protest, but the taller bandit dealt a right-hook rocket to his temple, the resounding *smack* echoing from the bullet-ravaged walls as the club owner dropped to the carpet. The bandit then pinned his hand down with a foot, covering the rest of the hostages with his sub-machine gun, while his shorter confederate worked the ring off Drinkwater's finger with brutal efficiency, unconcerned that he tore flesh and snapped bone in the process.

The other captives wept and gibbered, hardly daring to watch.

'Anyone else fancy holding out on us?' the taller bandit wondered.

Now, even the strippers coughed up, depositing platinum anklets, pearl necklaces and golden earrings in the bag. But when Lori and Kerry, the two maids, tried to hand over the few quid they had in their purses, the shorter bandit prevented it with a raised palm.

'You two . . . sit over there,' the taller one said, indicating an armchair across the room.

Sniffling fearfully, they did as he told them.

With the canvas sack now heavy at his shoulder, the shorter bandit retreated to his companion's side, re-training his firearm on the captives.

'All you ladies,' the taller one said. 'You beautiful babes who just live to show it off to scum-sucking pigs like these . . . get up.'

The strippers, both naked and dressed, did as they were told, watching their captors through terrorised, tear-sodden eyes.

'Right side of the room . . . on the sofa!' he said.

They hurried to comply.

'We can't all fit,' said a buxom redhead with a nasally Salford accent.

He chuckled. 'If you can squeeze into that cute little dress, darling, you can squeeze into anything . . . now *do as I say!*' He drilled another blast into the ceiling, plasterwork erupting downward.

With frantic yelps, the girls scrambled all over the sofa, and each other, skilfully and sinuously managing to accommodate themselves.

'Now, the rest of you,' he said to the men. 'Get up! Left side of the room.'

Northwood, who, after vomiting his entire day's intake of food and booze, had come around sufficiently to glare balefully at the intruders through the one eye that wasn't glued shut with congealing red slime, was the last to rise to his feet. Even then he hesitated to follow orders.

'You've gone too far,' he said. 'I warned you, crackhead fuckers . . . you're seriously gonna regret this.'

'What did I say about that yap of yours,' the taller bandit retorted, lifting his sub-machine gun and gazing through its sights. 'You fucking plankton who thinks he's a whale . . .'

'All right!' Northwood shouted, raising his hands, shifting over to the bullet-riddled sideboard, where his other guests stood bunched together.

'What've you separated us for?' Drinkwater asked, tears coursing down his sunbed-bronzed cheeks. Even his right eye, which had swollen like a purple plum, blinked frantically. 'You've got what you wanted . . . why don't you just leave?'

'You don't need to do this!' Klinsman stammered, in growing terror of what he suspected was about to happen.

'They don't need to, but they're going to do it anyway,' Northwood said in a low, tight voice. He hoped the blaggers hadn't noticed that both his hands were behind him. 'Because

160

now I'm suddenly thinking this is what *they're really here for!*'

He shouted those last few words hoarsely, as he yanked a Walther P99 out from the shattered drawer behind his back, and dashed diagonally across the room for another door on the far side of the sofa. He opened fire as he did, pegging wild, uncoordinated shots at his captors.

Two rounds punched the curtains behind the podium, but several feet above the heads of the two blaggers. They barely even needed to duck, and when they returned fire, of course, it was far more accurate, cutting Northwood down before he'd even made it halfway.

Gobbets of flesh and blood flew in a vortex as he spun to the floor.

The shorter bandit cursed aloud, though it was lost in the dirge of screams.

'Not what we planned,' the taller one said, as they advanced into the centre of the room. 'But shit happens.'

They turned to face the rest of the huddled, cowering men and, resuming the plan they'd first come here with . . . shot the legs off the lot of them.

Chapter 17

Harry glanced at his watch, and groaned to see that it was nearly ten o'clock at night.

'Jesus, I've wasted some hours in this job. But this has to be the worst ever.'

'It's still the best lead we've got,' Lucy replied.

'What's his bird's name again . . . Janet O'Dowd?' Harry was behind the steering wheel of his BMW, but as they were parked on a stretch of muddy waste-ground, he'd been able to push his seat back in order to accommodate the various print-outs on his knee. He leafed through them. 'Are we actually sure this lass is Burke's girlfriend?'

'All we're sure is that she's *one* of them,' Lucy said. 'At least, one of the most recent.'

'How do they do it, these little scrotes . . . get their own harems together? I mean look at this twat . . . he's five-foot-nothing, he's a weed, probably a druggie, probably a pisshead, never done an honest job in his life.'

Lucy looked out across the darkened road to the nearest line of council houses. It was named Duke's Row, and it was located at the west end of the Hatchwood. Each of its dwellings now showed lights, including No. 8, which sat in the very middle, but otherwise, there was no sign of life

The 'twat' that Harry referred to was a certain Jordan Burke, a well-known tea leaf, who Lucy had latched onto whilst carrying out a door-to-door on Epsom Close, the street behind Durkin Crescent. Initially, the metal-detector lead had felt like a long shot; but then she'd spoken to a middle-aged woman called Eileen Winterbottom, who said that sometime around mid-afternoon the previous Sunday, she'd got curious about a workman she'd spotted coming down one of her neighbour's drives. He'd been youngish – in his early twenties, with greasy red hair and walking with a limp. His age was what had first alerted her, because even though he was wearing overalls and carrying tools on a utility belt, she'd thought he'd seemed young. On top of that, it was a Sunday, and how often were workmen busy at weekends? However, she'd enquired later on with the neighbours in question, and though they hadn't been having any repairs done, there'd been no break-in and nothing had been stolen. Happy with that, Mrs Winterbottom had taken it no further.

Of course, the helpful resident had not realised that the house in question also happened to back onto a bungalow in the next street, said bungalow belonging to one Reg Murgatroyd; or, that on the day in question, Sunday October 22, mid-afternoon, when the old man made one of his 'regular as clockwork' trips to the Railway Club, his bungalow was burgled. When Lucy produced her iPad, and called up a few images of basic tools, Mrs Winterbottom was able to identify several as having been attached to the young workman's utility belt. These included a brace and bit, which no good burglar should ever be without. But more importantly still, he was wearing headphones around his neck, while over one shoulder he also carried an item the lady did not recognise until Lucy showed her a specific picture of it; with its long

163

metal stem, touchpad controls, comfy armrest, and flat search-coil at one end, it was clearly a metal detector.

After that, a quick search on the database for an active burglar, aged around twenty, with red hair and a pronounced limp, had brought Jordan Burke to their attention.

He was the perfect fit: twenty-one, but already an experienced house-breaker, and well-known for employing innovative methods. But he was an opportunist thief too, content to trawl for likely victims among the depressed housing estates of his hometown, Crowley. If that wasn't enough boxes ticked, he knew Hatchwood Green and its residents well, having a girlfriend, Janet O'Dowd (with whom he'd had a child), who lived there.

A visit to Burke's own address that evening, a poky little flat on the Bullwood estate, which he shared with his alcoholic grandmother, Karla Jones, paid no dividends. Jones, a wrinkled, gap-toothed wreck of a woman, who looked much older than her sixty years, was having a bottle of gin for her tea, but had not been obstructive. Well-used to police attention, she'd given them permission to look around, even inside Burke's bedroom, which had been unoccupied for quite some time. Karla Jones claimed that she hadn't seen her grandson for several weeks and that, not only was she unconcerned by this, she was actually glad; apparently, he was 'a thieving little shit', who always helped himself to her booze when he thought she wasn't looking.

Their next port of call, perhaps inevitably, was Janet O'Dowd's address. Given that the girl actually lived in Hatchwood Green, it seemed possible that, if Burke wasn't currently crashing at her place, he was using it as a centre of operations. However, this time they weren't simply knocking on the front door. Instead, it was a waiting game, the two cops parked just across the road from the house, hopefully innocuous among the various other vehicles there.

Though, so far, there'd been nothing. On first arrival, at around seven that evening, there'd been no one home at all, the house lights switched off. But some fifteen minutes later, O'Dowd, an overweight bottle-blonde in a lilac shell suit, had showed up, pushing a pram. She'd gone indoors, hitting light switches, but after drawing all the curtains, she'd been the last sign of life they'd seen. Now, five hours after their shift had supposedly ended, Harry was increasingly frustrated.

'I mean . . . how can Burke even afford it?' he complained, still referring to the mystifying fact that Jordan Burke didn't just have this particular girlfriend to shack up with, but had had lots of others previously, and probably had others on the go even now. 'Don't you have to buy girls presents and stuff? A bunch of flowers now and then?'

Lucy didn't respond, but the comment made her think about Kyle Armstrong, the only real boyfriend she herself had ever had. Okay, she'd only been a teenager, and Kyle certainly hadn't been one for flowers and chocolates, but they'd had a wild time together, brief as it was.

'*Aren't you going to miss all this?*' he'd asked her, that hot summer night in the car park of the Jack of Diamonds pub, where they'd all been lolling on their bikes, slugging beer.

The moment she'd broken the news to him that she was off, he'd been visibly dismayed, remaining utterly (and satisfyingly) oblivious to that beautiful, bloody-haired harpy, Hells Kells, who was already hovering in the background.

'*It's just not for me,*' Lucy had replied.

'*Since when? Raising hell, ripping the world a new one . . . what else were you born for?*'

'*I can't answer that, Kyle . . . because you wouldn't understand.*'

'*We're perfect for each other.*'

165

'*I'm not a kid any more, Kyle. I have to do adult stuff now.*'

'*I don't believe you're actually gonna be a copper. There must be someone else.*'

That had been typical of his suspicious nature. And yet, amazingly, there hadn't been a hint of violence or rancour in his voice; he'd simply sounded bewildered by the whole business. And not a little bit saddened.

'No,' she'd assured him. '*There's no one else.*'

'*You realise this'll mean we're enemies? Not just exes, but actual enemies. There'll be no choice in the matter for either of us.*'

'*I know that.*'

And that had really hurt at the time, she reflected. It genuinely had.

Sensing the conversation was over, she'd put her helmet on and kicked the Ducati to life.

'*You weren't made to be alone, Lucy!*' he'd said, face finally hardening. '*None of us are. You may think you can hack it . . . but you're not so tough.*'

That parting shot had barely made an impression on her at the time. But there'd still been a kernel of truth in it: humans are not solitary by nature; everyone needed some romance in their lives. Not that this negated Lucy's personal standards. As she'd replied so often to her mother's repetitive enquiries, there was no point entering a relationship with someone unless you had actual feelings for them. It wasn't just about a guy being tall, well-built and good-looking. Plenty of that sort had hit on her over the years. It was about whether you connected with them. And somehow or other, Lucy never did – or never allowed herself to.

'*Guess I'm just unlucky,*' she'd told her mum more than once. '*I haven't met him yet.*'

'*That's because you're not looking hard enough,*' had come

the disapproving reply. *'You're married to that job. Any self-respecting bloke'll be intimidated by what you do for a living . . . unless he's a copper himself, of course, and you've told me a dozen times you won't date other coppers.'*

It was a painfully old-fashioned attitude, Lucy supposed, but again, there were some truths buried there. She had, on occasion, been wooed by civvy guys who she'd thought she might be interested in, only to see their ardour cool when they learned that she was in the job. And there was no question in her mind: she was never going out with a fellow cop. That would be the biggest distraction possible. At least – this had been Lucy's view until recently.

While Harry chuntered on in the background, she slipped her phone from her coat pocket and glanced again at the text she'd received forty-five minutes ago:

> *Saturday Street boys charged. Squad party tonight.*
> *Fancy it? Danny.*

She sighed aloud at the uncertainties of life.

Harry, mistakenly detecting a kindred weary spirit, glanced sidelong at her.

'How long are we giving this?' he wondered. 'We said ten, didn't we?'

'We did.' Lucy checked the dashboard clock. 'And it's still only ten to. And on the subject of how Burke can afford the women in his life . . . we already know the answer to that, don't we? Let's not forget why we're here.'

'I'm not forgetting anything.' He squinted across the rain-wet street. 'I'm just wondering where the hell he is.'

'If we don't get him today . . . we'll come back tomorrow. We'll nab him at some point.'

'I'm also wondering where you and me stand?'

Harry phrased this like it was any other question, like he

167

was wondering whether she could lend him an umbrella. Lucy cocked her head towards him. He scanned the far side of the road, pointedly not looking at her.

'What was that?' she asked quietly.

'Wondering where you and me stand?' He glanced round at her, but it was too dim to tell if he seemed in any way embarrassed. 'Wondering if there's any chance, like?'

Had Lucy's heart not sunk at the sudden arrival of this long-dreaded moment, she might have been faintly impressed by the business-like bluntness of his approach.

'Harry?' she said. 'What're you talking about?'

'Come on, Lucy . . . we're both adults. Don't make me spell it out.'

'It's because we're adults that you *should* be spelling it out. Every single word.'

He shrugged. 'I want to take you out. On a date . . . for a drink and all? Is that so bad?'

'Are you actually serious?' Despite having expected this, she still managed to feign a tone of incredulous outrage.

He looked genuinely puzzled. 'I'm not such a bad catch. Only a bit older than you, not married any more, no nasty skeletons in the closet . . . I don't think.'

'And are you seriously asking me out *now* . . . while we're at work?'

'What time would be better? We've nothing else to do except sit here.'

She turned back to the front. 'You should know better, Harry . . . you really should.'

A couple of seconds later, he said: 'So I'm guessing the answer's "no"?'

'Of course it's no. I mean let's get this thing cleared up right away . . . it's *no*.'

Another few seconds passed, before he ventured a further enquiry. 'Can I ask why?'

168

'I've told you a dozen times . . . I don't mix work and pleasure.'

'And is that the only reason?'

She glanced at his hopeful expression, exasperated.

'Look, Harry . . . it's supposed to be a two-way thing. I get it that you fancy me . . .'

'Who doesn't fancy you?'

'Erm . . . thanks.' She was unsure whether feeling flattered by that was the correct response. 'But the point is . . . I don't really fancy you.'

He adjusted his collar, straightened his tie, jutted out his jaw. 'Only because you've never seen me spruced up.'

She half-smiled, but then decided that this too was an incorrect response. She and Harry got on; not always, but most of the time. For that reason, she felt a tad regretful being harsh with him like this, but it wouldn't be doing him a favour to lead him on.

'Please accept the answer I've given you,' she said. 'It's no, okay? Sometimes it just doesn't click between people. And that's what's happened here. So, let's not talk about it again, eh?'

He clamped his mouth shut and exhaled through his nostrils, before turning away.

Though rejection by females could hardly be a new experience since he'd split from his wife, the 'grump' was now on him. Like so many blokes Lucy knew, Harry Jepson could sulk for England if he felt it would serve a purpose.

She closed her eyes and pinched the bridge of her nose. Sometimes you just couldn't win; it didn't matter what good you tried to do, it always backfired. More to the point – she checked the dashboard clock, and saw that she still had three minutes of this torture to endure. There really were occasions when you simply had to give yourself something to look forward to, just to lift yourself out of the intolerable fugue of the present.

As covertly as possible, though it wasn't difficult with Harry determinedly looking elsewhere, she slipped out her phone, and keyed in a quick reply to Danny Tucker's invitation:

What time and where?

Chapter 18

The Aspinall Arms, a tall, narrow red-brick building, part of a cobbled, terraced backstreet at the rear of Robber's Row police station, had been a police pub for as long as Lucy had known it. Even in the days before late-night pub licensing, it had maintained a covert twenty-four-seven service, officers coming off duty able to slip in through the back door when the front doors were closed and the blinds drawn. Invariably, it was crowded and noisy, though partly this was down to its small, cramped rooms, and to its town centre location, which meant that at lunchtimes it also got busy with office and factory workers.

The one group that didn't populate it, perhaps inevitably, were the town's hoodlums. The underworld could sense the presence of coppers without needing to spot the regulation shaved-to-the-bonce haircuts, or glimpse the partial uniforms still worn under civvy jackets. Even so, when there was a special event to be celebrated, and sometimes even the police could be choosy about which colleagues they drank with, there was a function room upstairs, which could be booked for private parties.

Lucy only needed to stick her head into the taproom at

ten-thirty that evening, for Vic Haverstock, the licensee (an ex-bobby himself, as if his six-foot-six inches and salt-and-pepper mutton-chop whiskers didn't give that away) to catch her eye and point at the ceiling.

She went upstairs in a state of trepidation, but also frustrated with herself.

Like some religious mantra, she repeated the inner assertion that she didn't have a crush on Danny Tucker. Okay, he was ridiculously handsome, his easy, laid-back manner was appealing in itself, and he seemed interested in her – but this was her work environment, and all these people were her colleagues. The last thing she needed now, when things were looking up professionally, was to start muddying the waters by attracting gossip.

But if Lucy genuinely feared this potential outcome, she wondered why she'd touched up her make-up in the locker room before coming over here and had changed into clean jeans, a new sweater and a nice pair of heeled boots?

On the pub's top floor, a blackboard stood on an easel outside the function room. On it, someone had chalked the message:

TONIGHT ONLY
ROBBERY SQUAD
AND MATES
(you know who you are)

Inside, it was difficult to say how long the party had been in progress; at least since early/mid evening, she surmised, judging by the scene of good-natured chaos. Lots of figures, mostly male but with one or two females, were grouped around the scattered tables or propping up the bar. The lighting was low-key, the background music hard rock. In the far corner, under a single bright lamp, there was a pool table. Here DI Blake, still in the same scruffs she'd been clad in that morning, minus her weapon and body armour of course, though still wearing her chequer-banded firearms cap – probably at the insistence of her troops – only now at a jaunty angle, was pocketing balls in every direction, to the accompaniment of riotous cheers from the men gathered there.

Yet again, Lucy was impressed by the DI's mere demeanour.

Kathy Blake was such a girlish figure, and yet she wasn't 'girlie', if such a distinction could be me made. She moved and spoke with a confidence that only stemmed from being completely in her comfort zone even in this most macho of police cultures. Her natural authority evidently owed to her personal knowledge and expertise, but there was more to it than that – there was sexual control too. Units like the Robbery Squad, who by their nature tackled the worst the underworld could throw at them, tended to appeal to some of the roughest customers on the force. But while DI Blake might be doing the ladette thing now, that clearly wasn't her normal style. Lucy had seen her dress smartly and attractively for formal occasions; she'd seen her neat blonde ponytail, her tasteful make-up. Kathy Blake could clearly do it either way. She was a pretty woman in a man's world, which often made the men concerned feel good about themselves, but by the same token she knew what she was doing, which meant that she could make decisions and pull rank whenever she needed to. They might not admit it, but the guys would like that about her too – good, firm leadership was always popular. Plus, if she decided it was time to get raucous and rough it with the troops, she could do that as well – and they would like that about her most of all.

'You look nervous,' someone said alongside her.

Lucy turned and saw Ruth Smiley in a black polo shirt and tight jeans, with what looked like a different exotic cocktail in each hand.

'Not nervous exactly,' Lucy said.

'Good.' Smiley took a long sip from the straw on her left. 'Because trust me, some of this lot can sniff out a prey animal from five-hundred paces.'

'Just wondering whether I should even be here.'

Smiley guffawed. 'Get out of it . . . this is a do for the Squad *and* friends.' She nodded across to the far side of the room. 'So, *you* certainly fit it.'

Lucy glanced over there and saw Danny Tucker working his way through the tables towards her.

Smiley chuckled to herself as she melted away into the crowd.

'Glad you could make it,' Tucker said, looking surprised but elated that Lucy was here.

'Least I could do, once you'd invited me,' she replied, as they sidled to the bar together. 'What'll you have?'

'Put your money away,' he said. 'It's all on the DI.'

'Really?' Lucy glanced at him, amazed.

'She's a happy bunny . . . and so she should be after the last few days.'

'I really *do* feel honoured,' Lucy said, as they moved away, bottles of lager in hand. She scanned the room, looking for anyone else from the ordinary world of Division who might have received an invitation; there were none as far as she could see.

'If you're looking for Lee Gaskin, don't fret,' Tucker said. 'He's on an obbo tonight. I made sure of it.'

'I'm not worried about *him*.' That was mostly truthful; if Lucy was to progress her interest in the Robbery Squad, she knew she'd have to get used to being around a hostile entity like Gaskin, but some small part of her was glad that he wasn't here this evening.

'Anyway, you're the woman of the hour,' Tucker said. 'How could we *not* invite you?'

An explosion of shouting drew their attention back to the pool table, where DI Blake, having despatched her opponent, had thrown out a general challenge to the rest of the blokes encircling her. 'Minimum price is twenty,' Lucy heard her shout. 'Gotta pay my bar bill somehow.'

They responded with roars of approval, half a dozen hands waving the requisite banknotes.

'DI Blake certainly keeps you guys on your toes,' Lucy said.

'She's something else, isn't she?'

'She's young. Was she fast-tracked?'

'No way.' Tucker seemed amused she would ask such a question. He kicked a couple of stools out from under an empty table, so they could sit together. 'Hasn't got a degree, or anything. Rocketed her way up through the ranks under her own steam. And no airs and graces, you know. A copper's copper, as they say.'

Lucy thought about the gallery of notorious faces on the section of office wall behind Blake's desk, and how many of them had been etched out with a big, blood-red X.

'She certainly gets results. You all do.'

'Listen . . . I've been around a bit in this job.' He leaned forward, to be heard over the hubbub. 'I mean, I know I was part of forming this outfit, but I've transferred round a bit . . . yet I've always come back. This was always a good team, but since Kathy took over, it's been the best team I've ever known.' He shook his head, unable to hide his disappointment. 'Telling you, Lucy . . . it almost makes me cry when I think how they're planning to shut us down.'

'Is that definitely going to happen?'

He shrugged his big shoulders. 'Who can say? But the very fact it's on the table's an outrage, in my view. We've rolled more blaggers in GMP than the Crime Commissioner's had slap-up dinners. Last year alone, we sent over fifty seriously bad people to jail.'

'With results like that, you'd have thought it a no-brainer.'

'Once the accountants take against you, it doesn't matter how many results you get.'

'What's their justification?'

'They say we're not cost-effective. I mean, I don't know how some bunch of suits stuffed with straw can seriously evaluate what *we* do? How can you put any kind of price tag on the removal of vicious toe-rags from law-abiding society?'

Lucy had heard similar opposition to much of the top-down reorganisation in the modern police and, ultimately, it would be the same with the Robbery Squad. They were an expensive unit, and though fifty convictions a year was impressive, it wasn't massively impressive when seen purely from a statistical point of view, especially when stacked against the costs – but then that would not take into account the high-level criminals they targeted, nor the very serious crimes that would not be committed once these career-felons were in prison. For quite some time now, there'd been a popular phrase among the rank and file: 'The job's fucked'. Lucy didn't quite see it in those stark terms, but she was often disheartened.

Though not as much as Danny Tucker seemed to be.

Fleetingly, the guy who every time she'd met him thus far had been upbeat and chipper, grinning broadly, effusing enthusiasm, seemed down and morose. But then, as if remembering who he was, his mood changed.

'Shit, listen to me!' he laughed. 'Going off like an old woman. Hell, nothing's been decided yet. It may never happen and tonight's a party. Let's just enjoy ourselves, yeah?'

They clinked bottles, drank some more lager, and chatted in that cosy, convivial way more normally found when the participants have known and liked each other for years. Lucy discussed her childhood in Saltbridge, one of Crowley's poorer quarters, but spoke in glowing terms about her mother, Cora, how she'd been a single parent, but how she'd always worked, and had leaned on Lucy relentlessly during her education, inspiring her to become a useful member of society. Lucy told Tucker that she'd only had one real boyfriend back during those days, a ne'er-do-well – she did not name him as Kyle Armstrong, or mention the Low Riders – whom Cora had never approved of, though ultimately the relationship had expired from natural causes.

'Nothing to do with you joining the job?' Tucker said with a disarming wink.

'Sort of, I suppose.'

He nodded, as if he fully understood.

'Do I detect something similar in your background?' she wondered.

He smiled. 'Similar kinds of pressures. I grew up in Hulme . . . we lived in the Crescents.'

'Good Lord . . .'

And when Lucy said that, she meant it.

Hulme Crescents had been notorious by almost any standards. Already one of the most deprived inner-city districts in Greater Manchester, Hulme had been made fifty times worse in 1974 by the imposition on it of the Crescents, one of the least successful public housing schemes in the history of England. It commenced life as four gigantic U-shaped blocks of concrete flats, supposedly providing new homes for over thirteen thousand people, but so badly was it designed and constructed that within two years of opening, it had degenerated into a dark, dank, crime-infested slum. In the words of a famous journalist at the time, 'if you want to take a look at science-fiction's beloved dystopian future, visit Hulme Crescents'.

'My mum died when I was four,' Tucker said. 'My dad was a bin-man, so there was some money coming in, but not much. My grandma looked after us most of the time. She was from Anguilla originally.'

'So, she swapped an island paradise for Hulme Crescents,' Lucy said.

'Well . . . it wasn't that much of a paradise, from what I've heard. She was great, though. Good Christian lady, kept a tidy flat, had a firm hand. Gave us a good smack if we needed one. That was me and my two brothers. Bunch of reprobates back in those days, I suppose. But it did the job. We all went on to reasonably good things. Our David runs his own joinery firm, our Adam's a nurse at Manchester Royal.'

Lucy nodded, impressed.

'I came into the job after GMP visited our school,' Tucker said. 'It was a travelling police roadshow type thing, looking to encourage ethnic minorities to apply. I didn't think there was much chance. I mean, this was around '94. Not as bad as it had once been, but still a bit of a "them and us" thing going on with the cops. But . . . something happened that day, you know.' He paused, peering into his own past. 'They gave us all the usual propaganda . . . posters showing blonde cutie WPCs having cups of tea with little old ladies, or big square-jawed uniforms standing at zebra crossings, holding hands with schoolkids. But I'd grown up watching telly. I'd seen shows like *Hill Street Blues*. That had a particular resonance where we lived . . . it was like the same bloody ghetto. And I'm watching these hard-arsed detectives kicking butt, bringing the scrotes in. And I thought: I can do that. So, I said to one of these fellas, one of these bobbies on the roadshow, I said: "I don't want to show kids across the road, I want to be a detective." Anyway, he took a few of us like-minded lads into a room and says: "Okay, this is what it's really like. You want to go to war with these people who are ruining your estates? Tired of seeing your neighbours

178

getting burgled? Tired of hearing that nice old Mrs Jones who lives three doors down has been mugged coming home from bingo? Tired of seeing gang-tags everywhere, drugs being sold. They're not doing it in posh areas, you know."'

Tucker's eyes flashed at the mere memory.

'*That* made an impact on me,' he said. 'I've never forgotten that bit. He says: "They're not robbing the rich to give to the poor, they're robbing the poor to give to themselves. You sick of all that? You want to settle that score? Then, lads, *we* are the job for you." The day I left school and posted my application, I found that half the kids on our block suddenly hated me. But what did I care. It worried me a bit when they said: "You'll be the token black face. They'll pretend to like you, but really you'll only be there to make 'em look good." But even if that last bit was true, when I got into the job, I *wasn't* the token black face. There were lots of black faces, and we were as good at it as any of the whites, maybe better because we *had* to be better. And anyway . . .' He smiled self-consciously, suddenly awkward with his show of emotion. 'Here we are now . . . making that very same difference they talked about all those years ago.'

Before Lucy could reply, she saw the door open and Kirsty Banks from the DO come in, paperwork in hand. Midweek, divisional CID would often run with a skeletal staff on nights. As such, when Lucy had checked in after the unsuccessful obbo on Hatchwood Green, Banks had been in the office alone, engrossed in her laptop. She was a plump, doughy girl, with limp fair hair and pale, pudgy features. But she was a good sort, a smart detective, popular with her colleagues and always ready with a roaring laugh.

She stood in the open doorway, rolling back the sleeves of her cardigan as she looked around. When she zoned in on DI Blake, she made her way over there.

'Don't look now, but something's occurring,' Lucy said.

Tucker straightened up where he sat, to get a better angle. 'Always the same, isn't it?' he said. 'You clear out one set of a villains and another bunch pop up.'

Banks was now deep in conversation with Blake, and showing her the document she carried. Whatever info she imported, and it clearly was of some importance, Blake turned and passed it on to those detectives standing around her. The music was switched off and the DI climbed onto a stool.

'Can I have everyone's attention?' she shouted.

The rest of the room fell quiet.

'Anyone in here who's not too bladdered to do some work?'

There were mumbles of uncertainty.

'Okay . . . anyone in here who fancies pulling some overtime tonight?'

The mumbles in response to this were more assertive.

'We've copped for a job,' she said. 'But I want honesty . . . anyone cross-eyed and stinking of ale, go home and get some kip. Sign on in the morning as usual. Anyone who thinks they *can* work, get some coffee down you . . . briefing in the office in ten.'

Lucy stood up as the Robbery Squad began to bustle, some drinking up, others adjusting collars, mopping back sweaty hair. Tucker left Lucy's side, sauntering over to speak with DI Blake, while Kirsty Banks came the other way.

Lucy accosted her near the door. 'What's going on?'

'You're not going to believe this,' Banks said. 'Andy Northwood's been shot and killed.'

'Flash Andy?'

'The same. And in his own pad, would you believe.'

Lucy was fascinated but puzzled. 'How does that involve Robbery Squad?'

180

'By the looks of it, it's a robbery. A home invasion. DCS Billington's at the scene as we speak. Stan's on his way too, and so is DSU Nehwal.'

Detective Chief Superintendent Roy Billington was head of CID on November Division, while Detective Superintendent Priya Nehwal was second-in-command of GMP Serious Crime, which meant that this was a gold-standard response to a robbery/homicide. But considering the AP was Andy Northwood, a career criminal rumoured to be affiliated to the Crew, it was perhaps understandable.

'Apologies but we're ending the party early,' Tucker said, reappearing.

'I've heard,' Lucy replied. 'Andy Northwood, eh?'

'Just goes to show . . . there's always a bigger fish. Poor Flash Andy, eh? How upsetting.' Tucker wasn't obviously being sarcastic, but neither did he look even vaguely aggrieved by the news. 'But we shouldn't gloat too much. Apparently, it's a real mess. Multiple shots fired, lots of serious injuries.'

'And you're on it?'

'Assuming the Squad gets assigned. Kathy's up for it . . . she'll take any job at the mo if it keeps us in business.' He glanced enquiringly at Lucy. 'You okay to drive home?'

'I've only had one lager.'

'I'll walk you down to your car.'

She shrugged, and went out with him. Her normal response to an offer like this would have been to bridle with indignation, but she knew he hadn't meant it the way it sounded. Danny Tucker was well aware that if there was one thing Lucy didn't need, it was a chaperone. They walked down through the pub and around into the station's personnel car park. At this late hour, there were only one or two vehicles dotted around. Lucy's Jimny sat alone.

'Heard a rumour you were a biker chick,' Tucker said as they strolled over there.

'I've still got the bike, but it lives in my mum's shed these days,' she replied.

'Oh.' He sounded disappointed.

'It's not neglected. I take it out for a spin now and then.'

'That's good to know.'

He was attempting to register interest, but she knew that his enthusiasm was not for her Ducati.

At the car, she turned to face him. He stood with hands jammed into his jeans pockets. He was several inches taller than she was, but they met each other with a mutually penetrating gaze.

'The way I see it,' he said quietly, 'we've got about twenty-five seconds before everyone starts piling out here.'

He leaned down towards her, only for Lucy to step backward.

'Danny . . . I . . .' She was surprised how much of a struggle it was to get these words out. 'I kind of have rules about this.'

'Yeah?' He sounded bemused.

'You and me . . . we'd see each other every day. Especially if I can wangle my way onto Robbery Squad, which you know I'm keen to.'

Now, he looked bemused too. 'And that'd be a problem?'

'I don't know . . . I really don't.' It irritated Lucy how hapless she sounded. 'I need some time to think about it.'

'Well . . .' He checked his watch. 'We've now got ten seconds.' He smiled again, but the normal good humour was a little lacking. There was no hiding the disappointment he clearly felt.

'I'm not saying "never",' she said. 'I'm not even saying "no". But this has all happened really quickly for me. I don't know if I'm ready. I've gotta give it some thought.'

Across the yard, the station's personnel door opened and

figures emerged, pulling on coats, talking loudly. More came in through the car park entrance.

'It's okay,' he said. 'Seriously.' He palmed the air for calm. 'Whenever you're ready, yeah?'

He winked, and then turned away to join his colleagues.

Lucy climbed into her Jimny and sat behind the steering wheel, watching as ten or eleven Robbery Squad detectives milled around, arguing about who was fittest to drive, before saddling up in three cars and pulling out one by one. DI Blake came last, now having removed her firearms cap and wearing a heavy anorak. She was deep in conversation with Tucker, who'd gone back inside to grab his own coat. They spoke animatedly, as they climbed together into his Vauxhall Passat.

After they'd gone, Lucy kneaded the back of her stiffening neck. It had been a long day, but she was wired rather than tired; her body felt weary but when she got home she wouldn't be able to sleep easily. There were too many crazy ideas rushing around inside her head.

She knew she wanted to join the Robbery Squad. She was quite firm on that. They didn't just lead a more interesting life than Division. These guys, having already banged up one murderer this week, along with a bunch of prolific armed robbers, would shortly be on the trail of another big league team, a real set of desperadoes if they'd taken out a player like Northwood.

But then there was the Danny Tucker factor.

Back in her uniform days, Lucy had been asked out several times by a CPS prosecutor who she'd occasionally liaised with at Crowley Magistrates. His name was Larry Dawson, and he'd been a nice enough guy, roughly her own age and presumably on a good wage. But he hadn't done anything for her; there was no spark there, no feeling. The fourth time he'd asked her out, she gave up trying to fob him off with polite excuses, and said that it was nothing personal but she

183

didn't want anyone else in her life at that stage, she didn't *need* anyone.

That was the way she had felt ever since, if she was honest. Until Danny Tucker had come along.

However, Dawson had got cross, and responded by calling her 'a statue', 'a chunk of bloody marble', saying that she was 'beautiful, flawless, but cold' and 'destined to spend a lifetime alone'.

Of all the occasions when Lucy had dismissed the unwanted attentions even of eligible men, that had been the most upsetting thing that any had ever retaliated with. Mainly because it echoed her mother's viewpoint, namely that everyone needs someone eventually, and that insisting on going it alone purely from some misguided ideal about independent womanhood would, in the long run, leave her high, dry and very unhappy.

It all came back to that phrase again: 'Married to the job'. 'That isn't me,' she said to herself, peering across the personnel yard.

The irony was, of course, that she'd finally, after all this time, found someone she liked. And yet it would be far from straightforward, working in the same nick as him. The gossip alone would drive her nuts.

She tapped her fingers on the wheel, struggling to see a way forward.

It wasn't impossible that the Robbery Squad would be shut down and the problem, if not exactly taken away, at least lessened. It would certainly make a relationship easier if Danny was working in a different part of GMP. But did she honestly want the Robbery Squad to fold when she felt close to getting on board?

Some situation she'd found herself in: a leap forward professionally, or a leap forward in her love life? It could be one or the other. But apparently not both.

She switched the engine on, put the Jimny in gear, and caught her reflection in the rear-view mirror.

Mum was beautiful too when she was young, Lucy thought. *Or so I've been told. So beautiful that she didn't think she'd need a proper education, a proper job – and it almost was the ruin of her. But when she had a really difficult decision to make, she got it right.*

But Lucy could hardly go and ask her mother's advice now. Already, she could hear Cora's words of wisdom ringing in her ears: *'Are you kidding, love? Ditch the job, go with Danny, have his babies. If nothing else, you'll make me happy in my old age.'*

'It's different now, Mum,' Lucy said as she drove out of the car park.

But was it?

Was it really?

Lucy Clayburn, the girl who'd always prided herself on knowing her own mind, drove home that night aching with indecision.

Chapter 19

In his capacity as Chairman of the Board, in other words head of the Crew, and therefore boss of bosses in the Northwest, Bill Pentecost rarely had to shout and bawl. His rep went before him. He'd started out strictly small-time, as a backstreet money-lender, but he'd always ensured that he got paid in full and on time, mainly through his propensity for crucifying malefactors to their own front doors or to bits of their furniture.

It has long been said that you can't keep a good man down. But a more unspoken truth is that you can't do it to a ruthless man.

Pentecost's willingness to use the most sadistic violence to achieve his ends had earned him the nickname 'Wild Bill' back in the day, and had cleared a pathway for him to the mid-ranks of the Manchester underworld before he was thirty. After that, his organisational and diplomatic skills came into play, when he recognised that small-to-average-sized outfits like his would never rise to prominence if they didn't stop fighting each other. He was into all the usual rackets by then – drugs, protection, gambling, illicit alcohol, illicit sex – but constantly waging bloody war against his rivals on the next Moston housing estate ensured that this empire would never expand. As such, he commenced the formation of the Crew, which in due course – though it took a long time and only came together with much more of the same crazy violence that Pentecost had sought to eliminate – emerged as the region's overarching crime syndicate.

What was more, even now, at sixty years of age, Bill Pentecost was still top-dog, the guy who ultimately was in charge of everything. Though he'd never looked an especially brutish individual, facially he was stone, with pinched, pale features, curious wire-brush hair, and narrow grey eyes, with which he'd spear people through a permanent pair of square-lensed, steel-rimmed spectacles. He was tall, six-two, and thin – but it wasn't an unhealthy kind of thinness. You only needed to look at Pentecost, to suspect that, despite his advancing years, he still had energy and virility. This aura of strength was only enhanced by his Tom Ford suits and Grenson Albert shoes, by his easy, confident gait, by his near-infectious lack of humour.

It was often said of Bill Pentecost that he could turn a room ice-cold simply by entering it. But on the morning of October 31, this was tested on two fronts; firstly, because it was already a very cold day, and secondly because it was a scene of intense, exaggerated emotion.

They'd just buried Andy Northwood.

It was the usual extravagant inner-Manchester affair, a team of six handsome horses drawing a glass-sided hearse crammed so full with floral tributes that they almost concealed the huge, black-lacquered coffin, as it made its stately way from the Anglican church in Whalley Range that Flash Andy had attended as a schoolboy (no one could think of a church he'd attended any time since), with family, friends and general well-wishers walking behind it in a slow, reflective procession the whole mile and a half to the municipal cemetery. News crews and TV cameras were present of course, tolerated because showy occasions like this always needed to be broadcast to the outside world, so long as they kept a respectful distance – which they did, though it didn't prevent them seeking out celebrity faces half-hidden in the crowd; as usual, there were plenty of those, and not just of the criminal variety.

After the burial, Flash Andy's mother, Carole Northwood, a well-known personality in the old neighbourhood, and still, despite her sixty-five years, beautiful in a black silk Versace dress, led the party back around the cemetery to the official reception, which was to be held inside a vast pavilion set out in the beer garden at the rear of Paddy O'Byrne's Bar.

This part of the long goodbye was to be joyful, in honour of Northwood's favourite film, *Live and Let Die*, the perambulating horde entertained all the way by a jazz band playing from the back of a slow-moving lorry, Carole Northwood encouraging everyone to sing and dance en route. For once, the late-October weather facilitated this. The air was fresh and cool, but the day settled quickly into a golden haze of mellow sunlight, which brought out the full greenness of the verge-side grass, and the deep red of the crinkly leaves strewing the gutters. More lively entertainment was planned for O'Byrne's, though almost inevitably by this time, that first flush of brave-faced defiance was waning as reality kicked back in. Carole and her late son's two sisters, Sheena and Charmaine, as equally gorgeous in sultry black as their mother, greeted everyone on entry, sniffling into black-lace handkerchiefs as each heartfelt embrace brought a new and effusive rush of tears.

However, when Bill Pentecost strolled into the tent, hands clasped behind his back, with the usual clutch of minders at his rear, Carole Northwood made an especially brave effort to get herself together, hurriedly lifting her veil.

He graciously lowered his head, so that she could peck him on the cheek.

'Thanks so much for coming, Bill. Andy would've appreciated it.'

'I'm only sorry it's in these circumstances,' Pentecost replied in his slow, emotion-free voice.

'What can I say?' She dabbed at her eyes, fighting off more tears. 'He would never listen to me. I can't say I always approved of the things he did, but he was my boy . . . my only son. I ask you, Bill . . . who would have the gall? Who would dare?'

'We'll have to find that out, won't we, my love?'

'I mean I've spoken to the coppers a couple of times. They've put that bloody Robbery Squad on the job. But I don't know how seriously they'll take it. Set of bastards. I got the feeling they were laughing behind their hands at me.'

'The coppers may come up with something,' Pentecost replied, managing to say this as if he actually believed it. 'You never know.'

'I'm gonna keep on at them, Bill. I'm gonna keep haranguing them. I'll not let this go.'

'Nor should you. Like you say, Carole . . . he was your only son.'

The boss of bosses allowed her to hug him one more time, before disentangling himself and padding away through the crowd, finally taking up a place close to the buffet table, where Frank McCracken and his own personal sidekick, the six-foot-nine mountain of brawn and brutality called Mick Shallicker, unobtrusively nibbled on cheese sandwiches.

'I take it the little bastard didn't die owing us anything?' Pentecost asked quietly.

McCracken shook his head. 'His bills were all straight . . . for once.'

They stood in silence, nodding at the occasional greeting thrown their way from the ever-expanding crowd.

'So, what do we know?' Pentecost asked from the side of his mouth.

'What are we supposed to know?' McCracken replied.

'Flash Andy might not have died owing us,' Pentecost said. 'But we earned from him all the same. At least, we used to. And now we don't . . . and that's not very satisfactory, is it? Especially as I'm now hearing whispers that there's been more than one incident like this.'

'We're hearing those whispers too, Bill.'

'We need to focus on Flash Andy first. But it may also pay to start asking questions a bit further afield, assuming these *incidents* are connected.'

'I've put some feelers out,' McCracken said. 'But no one has a clue at this stage.'

Pentecost shook his head as a slim, black-clad waitress offered him a glass of sparkling wine from a tray. When another member of staff chanced by with goblets of still orange, he took one of those.

'I'm not sure that's good enough, Frank.' Pentecost still spoke in that drawling, menacing monotone, which routinely flummoxed anyone who was trying to work out his mood. 'I don't know whether this was personal or just business. And when I don't know things, it gets on my wick. I'm aware this doesn't fall strictly within your remit – Benny B's on the job too. But *you've* got a whole network of people out there who keep their ears to the ground for this sort of thing. As such, I find it hard to believe that any kind of blag – particularly a blag like this, with automatic shooters – could've escaped their attention, or the attention of anyone they might know.'

'If you want my honest view, Bill,' McCracken said, 'I'm not sure Benny B's solution is helping us much.'

'Benny B', or Benny Bartholomew to use his real name, another lieutenant in the Crew, was their official Head of Security. Even as they discussed him, he stood only five yards away, his paper plate heaped with sandwiches, slabs of cold meat, chicken drumsticks, spare ribs and wedges of quiche, all of which he was now in the process of shovelling into his mouth, at the same time as guzzling from a plastic pint-pot that was at least as full of froth as it was lager. He was a huge, square-shaped man with ham-shank arms and a tree-trunk neck, the width of him alone putting massive pressure on his straining suit, though he wasn't as imposing a figure as Shallicker because much of his youthful muscle had now run to fat. His face was plump and flabby, while his eyes, already oddly tiny, looked tinier still behind the lenses of small, circular-framed glasses.

The 'solution' that McCracken referred to was a general reward that Benny B had announced some five days ago – fifty grand, no less – for information leading to the robbers who'd killed Flash Andy. Almost inevitably, with so much money on the table, this had led to a rash of accusations and counter-accusations, and plenty of vigilante activity, not just aimed at the cash-stealing community, but at anyone the accusers happened to have a grudge against; when the Crew were looking for answers, it was always a good opportunity to settle some scores.

'In less than a week, it's turned into a bloodbath,' McCracken said. 'Lots of fingers getting broken, lot of heads kicked in.'

'You have a problem with *that*?' Pentecost sounded amused, though as always, it was an icy kind of mirth. 'You of all people, Frank?'

'What I have a problem with, Bill, is the lack of info it's generating. Half these idiots are chancers. Fifty K's a lot of dough. They'll do anything to get their mitts on it. Chuck baseless rumours around, name names that have got nothing to do with it . . . they'd try to beat a confession out of Mickey Mouse if they thought they'd get paid. The one thing they're not doing is getting to the truth. If anything, they're muddying the waters till we can't see a fucking thing.'

If Pentecost took McCracken's criticism of Benny B's scheme as indirect criticism of himself – after all, he had okayed it – he didn't show any irritation. Instead, he replied: 'Perhaps you now realise why I think *your* team should be more involved.'

McCracken nodded. 'I'll ask around a bit more.'

'Do so, Frank. Put the pressure on. And the sooner the better. I'd hate to have to call a board meeting over this.'

'Doubt there'll be any need for that, Bill.'

'Do you?' As always, it was impossible to read emotion into Pentecost's frosted features. 'We'll see. If this is some new outfit seeing a soft target and going for it, then it's purely about what we're owed – and I've no doubt you're the man to get it, so I'm not worried. And if this is something Flash Andy's got paid back for – and Christ knows, he got on our nerves enough, so I'm damn sure he's done it with a few others! – then we tax the bastards for not going through the correct channels. I'm not worried then, either. But if this is something bigger, Frank . . . I mean, if this is something we actually *need* to worry about . . . well, anything can happen then.'

Chapter 20

Lucy and Harry had now been on and around the Hatchwood for seven days, primarily keeping watch for the elusive Jordan Burke.

Though Janet O'Dowd's address on Duke's Row was the priority, they'd also needed to maintain surveillance on Karla Jones's flat over in Bullwood. They'd sometimes divided these chores between them, though they'd also, on occasion, been able to requisition some uniforms and change them into plain clothes – all without a result. It was as though Burke had dropped off the face of the planet, though more likely he'd simply received a tip-off that they were onto him. Both Lucy and Harry were trained to carry out covert surveillance, doing everything in their power to blend into whatever sordid background the circumstances dictated, but with such a high proportion of criminals living in these particular neighbourhoods, you could never be sure that you hadn't been clocked.

The obbo wasn't made any easier by an unexpected upsurge in reported violence in recent days. This was unusual because, though Crowley was a high-crime borough, the figures normally took a slight downward turn as the winter months came on. 'PC Rain' was infamously great for keeping the Friday and Saturday night hooligan element indoors, but colder, wetter nights had a similar effect on the real criminals too, particularly the sneak-thieves, the muggers, the joy-riders, those general-purpose opportunists who liked nothing better than to trawl the streets or loiter with intent.

But at present, with a spate of seemingly unconnected but nevertheless very violent attacks in progress, including GBH, arson, attempted murder and aggravated burglary, local police bosses had no option but to organise a much more proactive response than usual. DI Beardmore, having compared notes with neighbouring divisions, and learning that they were also recording higher numbers than expected of violent offences, had convened a couple of special meetings with the brass and was demanding more personnel and longer man-hours; as a direct result, divisional detectives like Lucy and Harry had not just been increasingly denuded of support officers for their obbo, but had regularly been diverted from it themselves.

It was all in the job, of course; juggling several investigations at the same time was part and parcel of routine inner-city policing. But it meant that it felt as if Jordan Burke was slipping out of their grasp, which made this a frustrating duty as well as a monotonous one.

'Get many trick-or-treaters round your neck of the woods last night?' Harry asked.

They were parked up again on the waste-ground off Duke's Row, just opposite Janet O'Dowd's house. The last few times they'd planted themselves here, they'd alternated cars so as not to make it too obvious, but today they were back in Harry's BMW. It was an unusually bright morning for the first day of November. A cloudless blue sky arced overhead, though it was cold; the dashboard barometer read only five degrees.

'Mum gets them . . . not so many round my neighbourhood,' she replied.

'Used to take our three trick-or-treating,' he said. 'Well, Abi and Toby. Sal was too tiny.'

He spoke with a melancholy air and yet a dreamy expression, as he gazed into a past that must have seemed light years ago. In the week since Lucy had rebuffed his advance, he'd never mentioned it again. Oh, he'd been sullen for the first two or three days, but gradually, as usual, this had lessened until now he was back to normal. Not that it was ever easy to be sure what 'back to normal' meant with Harry Jepson. It could be the softer him, the one Lucy was seeing now: relaxed, affable in his conversation. But then, in an instant, everything could change, and the harder, more embittered personality could emerge.

'Unusually decent weather,' Lucy said, trying to steer the conversation away from her partner's unhappy personal life. 'Even makes the Hatchwood tolerable.'

'You want to know what would make it more tolerable? An eighty-megaton blast . . .'

'*Whoa!*' She snatched his wrist.

They watched as a lone male figure, wearing jeans and a ragged sweater, sauntered casually up the street, an old-fashioned gym bag dangling over one shoulder. He stood five-eight and was lean to the point of being lanky, with a mop of red hair. More important than any of this, he walked with a pronounced limp.

'That's *him*, isn't it?' Lucy whispered. 'Burke?'

Harry rustled through his paperwork. 'Thought we were looking for a workman?'

'His overalls are probably in that bag . . . along with his burglary kit.'

The redhead reached the entrance to No. 8, glanced once over his shoulder, and walked up the path to the door, which he opened with a key.

'Perfect,' Harry said quietly.

195

There were no warnings for Jordan Burke on the PNC. He wasn't considered to be a weapons-user, or known for his violence or his determination to always escape. But he clearly had boltholes he could disappear into – so they didn't take any chances.

Calling divisional Comms to send uniform back-up, they approached the house immediately, Harry working his way round to the alley at the rear, and Lucy walking up to the front door.

'Police officers, can you open up please!' she called, the second time she knocked.

There was a loud kerfuffle inside. Lucy struck the door with her shoulder. It broke open on the third impact, and she barged in.

The living room smelled of bleach and was almost bare of furniture: a shabby sofa was positioned in front of a TV balanced on an overturned crate. And that was it, aside from a few toys strewn across the carpet.

There was no sign of Burke, but Lucy immediately came face to face with Janet O'Dowd, who stood in the middle of the living room with the baby in her arms, but responded to the forced entry with barely a hint of surprise, let alone outrage.

'Just be quiet, if you can . . .' she said. 'And try not to make a mess.'

'Where is he?' Lucy demanded.

The question was answered by a noise from the kitchen, the sound of the back door being wrenched open. Lucy dashed through, just in time to glimpse Burke, now kitted out in grey overalls, as he scarpered into the rear garden. She dashed outside too – onto a patch of scruffily overgrown lawn, in the middle of which someone had dumped a moth-eaten sofa. Burke, who clearly wasn't too badly hampered by his limp, vaulted over it and opened a gate in the middle of a rotted fence.

On the other side of that, Harry was waiting, grinning broadly.

Burk retreated until the backs of his thighs met the sofa. When he spun around, he met Lucy.

'Shit,' he said.

Harry grabbed him by the collar.

'I'm guessing you're Jordan Burke?' Lucy said, as they steered him back up the garden. 'Don't bother denying it, we know you are.'

Again, Burke seemed to reflect the general rule that housebreakers tended to be inadequate little squirts rather than hulking, scar-faced brutes He was a complete drip; the overalls he'd been wearing to do the jobs hung loose on his bony frame; his ferrety features were those of a truculent schoolboy just asking to be slapped.

'You're being arrested on suspicion of burglary,' Lucy said, as they re-entered the house. 'For a whole bunch of burglaries, in fact, which have occurred on this estate over the last few weeks. You don't have to say anything, but it could harm your defence if you fail to mention something you may rely on in court. Anything you do say, will be given in evidence.'

'I understand,' he replied, his tone implying that he wasn't looking to give them any trouble.

'Anything you want to tell us about these jobs straight away, Jordan?'

'Can we speak off the record?' he asked.

'Nope.'

Burke was banged to rights. There was nothing surer. Not only did he go quietly when the prisoner transport arrived at his girlfriend's address, but he gave an indication that he was willing to make a full admission once he was down at the station. He again tried to wangle some kind of deal for himself, but Lucy told him to save it. On top of that, on his direction, they searched an upper room in Janet O'Dowd's house, where inside a single wardrobe which had rather ingeniously been wallpapered into a recess, they found many of the goods he'd stolen from various of the houses he'd broken into. Later on, in the meter cupboard downstairs, they found the gym bag containing his burglary kit, and a Garrett Ace 250 lightweight metal detector.

They promptly summoned another police van, and some extra evidence bags.

'Not a bad job, this,' Harry said, as they loaded it all on board. 'Pity it took us so long.'

'Couldn't help being sent off the plot every time it kicked off somewhere else, could we?' Lucy replied.

As the van pulled away, Lucy turned and caught sight of Janet O'Dowd standing in the front window. She still had the baby in her arms, and was feeding it formula from a bottle.

'We should pull her in too,' Harry said. 'There're any number of things we could charge her with.'

'I suggest we leave it for now,' Lucy replied, as they climbed into the BMW.

'Not getting soft in your old age, are you? Never looks good bringing a baby into the Custody Suite, but it wouldn't be the first time.'

'No, but if we leave her be for the mo, it might give us some leverage.'

Harry grinned. 'You mean, if Burke decides he doesn't want to play ball after all, the long arm of the law might feel his girlfriend's collar too?'

'He wants a deal, doesn't he?' She shrugged. 'That's the best one he's going to get.'

'You crafty little minx.'

But Lucy's thoughts were already elsewhere.

'You ever known a time when there were as many violent offences as we've seen in the last few days?' she commented as they drove off the estate.

Harry shrugged. 'Comes in waves, doesn't it?'

'It's serious stuff. Kickings, beatings, knifings . . . people getting done in their own houses. And they're all scrotes. The APs, I mean. There's not one we've seen all week who doesn't have form himself.'

'Yep. Upside to everything.'

'Harry, I'm being serious.'

'So am I,' he said. 'Who cares about those shitheads? We've just investigated a whole raft of burglaries where the vics were mostly OAPs living alone. After that, you expect me to worry about a bunch of gangster wannabe tosspots twatting each other? It's probably a fallout over drugs, or whatever. It usually is.'

'Stan thinks it may be more than that,' she replied. 'He's trying to put a team together to look into it, but we're all a bit busy.'

'Should ask for some help from Robbery Squad. They were quick enough to call on you when *they* needed some help.'

'To be fair, I took that job to them.'

'Yeah, but it wasn't just you. They got other bods off Division as well.'

'I think they're a bit buried under this Andy Northwood murder.'

Now that it was mentioned, the robbery/homicide at Andy Northwood's house started Lucy thinking. Nearly all the other recent incidents, most of which they'd heard about over the radio while they'd been engaged on the Hatchwood, had involved assaults, sometimes *vicious* assaults, on known members of the Crowley criminal community.

Could the Andy Northwood murder be connected to that?

Harry, meanwhile, snorted with disdain. 'Too busy admiring themselves in the bathroom mirror, you mean. Too busy counting the brownie points they collect each time they pull a major crim in, simply because they haven't got any other distractions . . . apart from making daisy-chains out of paper-clips, of course.'

Lucy couldn't help feeling stung by that; on Danny Tucker's behalf of course, and maybe on her own if future plans came together, though she wasn't comforted that it was a week since she and Tucker had chatted properly. 'I think they're pretty good at what they do.'

Before he could reply, there was a crackle from the radio.

'*Attention all units on November East and West! PC requires immediate support at O'Halloran's Snooker Hall on Peak Street! Fighting in progress . . . officer already believed injured. Anyone to attend, over?*'

Lucy glanced at Harry, but he'd already hit the accelerator.

Peak Street, Dunnington, was less than half a mile from their current position.

'DCs Clayburn and Jepson en route from Dunnington Road, over,' she shouted, digging their detachable beacon from out of the glove compartment.

'*Roger, Lucy, thanks for that. And take care . . . this sounds serious, over.*'

Chapter 21

O'Halloran's Snooker Hall, which they reached within four minutes, was one of those single-storey 1970s-built structures which could have been put to almost any use, from carpet-sales to bingo, so long as it didn't matter that it possessed the drabbest exterior imaginable. It was windowless, constructed from basic brick, but covered with stucco-type whitewashed plaster, much of which was now rotten, damp and dirty. The roof was flat and probably pooled with rain-water, its outside walls littered with the rags and tags of illegible fly-posters.

As they swung into the car park, they'd expected to find full-scale fighting in progress, or at least a few bodies strewing the tarmac. But none of that was in evidence. Only one or two cars were there – which was probably about normal for early afternoon on a Wednesday – but one of these was a divisional patrol car, which was parked skew-whiff across two bays, its driver's door hanging open. Harry cruised warily forward, only for three men to come sauntering out of the building's front door.

Lucy's immediate impression was that this was no group she'd like to cross.

The first two were white guys, but stood a minimum six-foot-three and were almost as big across the chest and shoulders as they were tall. The first was bearded, the second clean-shaved, but their faces – what she could see of them, because they wore hoodies and baseball caps, with the hoods pulled up over the top – were hard, angular and fixed in concrete frowns.

Her second impression was that she recognised the third member of the trio. This guy, about ten yards behind the others, was black and shaven-headed. He was taller than the other two, about six-five, and quite a bit leaner but very muscular, as revealed by his green string-vest. If this wasn't threatening enough, he was carrying what looked like a broken-in-half snooker cue.

Despite the cautious advance of Harry's BMW, complete with flashing beacon on its roof, the threesome walked casually around the abandoned police car towards a blue Hyundai Civic parked in the far corner. The bearded white guy produced a fob and unlocked it, and he and the second white guy climbed in. The black guy walked after them, but as he did, he very casually, as though it made no difference to him in the world, launched the snooker cue in Lucy and Harry's general direction.

It clattered across Harry's windscreen, inflicting a massive spider-web crack.

Harry almost choked with rage. 'What . . . *what the fuck!*'

He rammed his foot down, gunning his BMW across the tarmac, tyres blistering as it homed in on the missile thrower.

'Harry, that's Leon Royton!' Lucy shouted, as it came to her. 'He's a Crew enforcer.'

'*Was* a fucking Crew enforcer!' Harry retorted.

Despite his size, Royton danced dexterously aside, just managing to evade the speeding car, before falling and rolling. Harry yanked at his handbrake, the BMW pulling a screeching one-eighty turn, so that when it came to a rest they were facing the snooker hall. A fourth figure had now appeared from the building, leaning sideways against the door frame. It was Don Cooper, the PC who'd answered the emergency call; the entire front of his T-shirt and stab-vest had been torn open, and his face was a mask of glutinous blood.

Lucy leapt out of the car, but didn't run over to him; she had an inkling what was coming next. 'Don?' she shouted.

It took vital seconds for Cooper to recognise the blue light on top of the BMW, and to focus on Lucy.

'Get . . . those three bastards!' he stammered. 'GBH'd two lads in here . . . really bad . . . gave me a tonking too . . .'

His words dissipated under a massive rending of gears from the other side of the car park.

Lucy turned around as the Hyundai, now carrying all three suspects, spun through its own rubber-melting semi-circle and bulleted out of the lot, hitting the road with such speed that vehicles forty yards away braked to screeching halts.

'Lucy, get in!' Harry barked.

'Go!' Cooper shouted. 'I'll be okay!'

Lucy jumped back in, while Harry lugged the BMW's wheel around.

'DC Clayburn to November Four, urgent message!' she shouted into her radio.

'Go ahead, Lucy.'

She relayed as much info as she could, summoning ambulances but at the same time describing the offence, the target vehicle and the suspects, naming Leon Royton, who was well known to police forces across the north-west, and because of his usual connections, requesting firearms support.

Meanwhile, Harry wove smoothly but dangerously through the traffic on Peak Street, blues and twos fully activated. The Hyundai was visible about a hundred yards ahead, waiting at a set of lights; they closed on it rapidly. As a police officer, Harry Jepson had many flaws, but his driving wasn't one of them. A British Cadet Kart champion in his youth and a junior recruit to the McLaren Young Driver Support Programme before he chucked it all in to join the cops, he now had a reputation for being exceptionally good behind the wheel.

But as with so many other things he did in life, he was inclined to take risks.

Lucy secured her belt and braced for impact, as, with reams of cars bottled up ahead of them, Harry cut left onto the pavement, which thankfully was empty of pedestrians – though she didn't see how he'd had the time to check that – and sped forward, separated only from the main traffic by a single crash-barrier, flying past one shopfront after another.

'Harry, for Christ's sake!' she shouted.

'I'll teach the bastards,' he snarled. 'Smashing my fucking windscreen.'

Forty yards ahead, the Hyundai, its driver spotting the fast-approaching police car, jerked through the red light, causing vehicles to shriek and swerve, and spun a sharp left.

'Suspect vehicle left onto Danson Road,' Lucy shouted, interrupting the dirge on the radio. 'No index yet, over.'

'Bastards!' Harry said.

The crash barrier ended, and he bullocked back into the traffic, pulling a handbrake-turn as the lights switched to green, smearing rubber about thirty yards behind him as he raced up Danson Road. In her wing mirror, Lucy saw another flashing blue light encroaching from behind. It looked like another divisional patrol. Up ahead, the Hyundai made an unexpected move, slicing sharp left, through an open gateway onto the slip road leading into the Tesco Superstore car park.

They both instantly knew what this meant.

It was midday, so the place would be busy; there'd be lines and lines of cars and lots of shoppers with trollies, which had catastrophic potential. But the reason the fugitives had taken this desperate action became clear a second later, when a divisional police van appeared from the opposite direction, reaching the Superstore entrance before Lucy and Harry did and swinging onto the slip road.

This was a slower, clumsier vehicle than Harry's BMW.

'Out the fucking way!' Harry bellowed as they trundled behind it.

When they entered the car park proper, the van went left, Lucy and Harry going right, accelerating past the entrances to the aisles lying between the rows of parked cars.

'Tesco Superstore, off Danson Road,' Lucy yelled into her radio. 'As much support as you can give us, please. We might get the bastards boxed in. And don't forget that Trojan!'

If the three suspects were armed, they hadn't pegged any shots at the pursuing cops yet, but Lucy didn't expect that they would unless they found it essential. She'd already identified Royton as a Crew soldier; highly likely the other two were similarly employed, which meant that they were professionals and had been sent to O'Halloran's to do a specific job, not to indulge in freewheeling criminality. Shooting at the police would be the last thing their paymasters would want. The assault on Harry's windscreen had probably been as much about trying to slow their pursuers down as wanton vandalism.

Harry banged his foot to the floor as they blasted up the

next aisle. The Hyundai was at the far end, in front of the supermarket's paved forecourt, where shoppers were still milling about, unaware of the encroaching police activity. Its driver spotted Harry in his rear-view mirror and pulled another left, before squealing to a halt and hitting reverse. A second divisional police car, an Astra this time, had also entered the car park, racing up the exit road the hoodlums had thought they were going to use to escape, cutting them off.

'Got 'em!' Harry hollered.

But of course, it was never going to be that easy.

On the Tesco forecourt, shoppers staggered out of the way, shouting and screaming, as the Hyundai backed into their midst at high speed, trying to make a three-point turn and smashing into a flower-seller's stand, sending petals and greenery and splinters of woodwork in every direction. The flower-seller himself only just darted out of the way. With a deftness of touch even Harry would have been proud of, the Hyundai pulled a right and screeched back down another aisle leading to the opposite end of the car park – only to find the divisional van ploughing up towards it, blocking the thoroughfare.

Harry swung in behind the suspect vehicle.

'Index Mike-Victor-one-six,' Lucy relayed into her radio. 'Lima-Hotel-Bravo. Received over?'

'Roger that, Lucy. What's the status of the pursuit, over?'

'The status is he's fucked!' Harry shouted triumphantly.

The driver of the Hyundai had reached the same conclusion. With the van about twenty yards in front and Harry's BMW even closer behind, he dropped his anchors, the car sliding sideways, clipping the front of a parked Golf, shattering its nearside light cluster, ripping off its own bumper bar. Before it was even stationary, the hoodlum trio were out of it and scattering across the car park in different directions,

threading between parked vehicles, knocking yet more innocent shoppers out of their way.

Lucy and Harry jumped out as well. Perhaps because he
was the one she knew, Lucy found herself focussed on Royton,
who clumped off towards the car park's eastern edge. He'd
donned a heavy khaki jacket, which could easily be concealing
weapons, but she gave chase anyway, encouraged to hear
the shouts of officers behind as they attempted to apprehend
the other suspects, and to see Harry as he also chased after
Royton.

Lucy was lighter, and a whole lot fitter, but she'd no sooner
rounded the next vehicle than she collided with a shopping
trolley, which almost upended her. She sent it skittering away
with multiple profane curses, but it meant that Harry got
ahead of her.

Royton, meanwhile, had slowed to a weary trudge. There
were so many police personnel on the car park now that there
was minimal chance he could weave his way back to the
entrance on foot, while directly ahead of him stood the superstore carwash, two flags billowing alongside a high, prefabricated
canopy. A Range Rover was parked underneath, three Asian
lads in heavy waterproofs giving it a going-over with high-
pressure jet washes. Beyond this point, a brick wall marked
the boundary of the car park. It was ten feet tall at least, but
even if Royton could have got over it, there was a thirty-foot
drop down the other side into the Bridgewater Canal.

Seeming to realise this, Royton stopped and turned when
he reached the canopy, his muscular neck and exposed chest
gleaming with sweat. Almost as soon as he did, Harry was
in front of him, shouting at him to give it up and that he
was under arrest.

Royton responded with the sort of swift precision one
would expect from a professional enforcer. Harry was a big
guy but he went in unguarded, and caught a bone-crunching

knee in the groin. He doubled over, and Royton, clamping his hands together in a single giant-sized fist, bludgeoned him in the middle of the back. As Harry tottered, agonised, the big guy caught him with such a powerful uppercut that it lifted him upright, blood spattering skyward, and then a short, hard left, followed by a roundhouse right, the meaty *smack* of which echoed across the car park.

Lucy got there just as Harry hit the deck, Royton spinning to face her.

His face was terrifying simply because it was blank. There was no rage there, no fear, no desperation; he'd just beaten someone unconscious, and it made no impact on him at all. Because this was his job, this was what he did for a living. And now he was about to do it again.

He lurched towards her, all six-foot-five of him.

Lucy backed off involuntarily, before sensing one of the two Asian lads standing nearby, gawking in disbelief at the unfolding situation.

Instinctively, she snatched the jet wash from his hand, and turned it on Royton, angling it into his face. Taken by surprise, he gagged and gasped, batting at the intense stream with both hands. Lucy advanced as she trained it on him, blasting it into his eyes, pushing him backward. Royton ducked and wove like a boxer, to no avail.

As Lucy came alongside the second of the three car-washers, she grabbed his jet wash as well – now she was hammering the bruiser with *two* high-pressure sprays. He crashed into the Range Rover and sank to a crouch, arms over his head, trying to work his way along its flank, only to slip and fall to his knees.

Lucy kept blasting him, getting as close as she dared. He tried to crawl away on all-fours, but then, though she at first thought he was squawking and spluttering, she realised that he was actually laughing.

By now, uniform support had arrived. They clambered all over Royton, one officer hooking an armlock around his neck, another cuffing his wrists behind his back.

Lucy dropped the hoses and ran to Harry, who lay face down in a puddle of blood-filled water.

'You think this is funny, Royton?' she shouted over her shoulder. 'You fucking *won't!*'

Chapter 22

Cora Clayburn always took a half-day on Wednesdays. She was back home at her terraced house in Saltbridge by two in the afternoon. When she got there, the central heating had already come on, thankfully. It was the first day of November, so no one would expect it to be mild, but even though the sun was out, there was a raw, icy edge to the breeze.

She showered, dressed in a house-robe and slippers, wrapped her long silver-blonde hair in a towel and went down to the kitchen, where she sorted out a ham salad for lunch, at the same time switching on Radio Two – for which reason she didn't at first hear it when someone knocked at the front door. The second knock was louder. Assuming it would be the postman or maybe a parcel delivery, Cora turned the radio down, went along the hall to the front door, and opened it.

It was a full-on shock to see Frank McCracken standing there. Smartly groomed as ever. Silver-grey hair short and neat. Lean, aquiline features wolfishly handsome despite their age-old scars. Wearing a thick gabardine coat over his sharp suit and tie.

Cora sucked in a tight breath, checking up and down the street to ensure that he hadn't parked his black Bentley Continental saloon anywhere close by. In this neighbourhood, a motor like that would have curtains twitching in every house. There was no sign of it.

'We agreed that you were going to stay away!' she hissed.

'Yeah, well I had to break that agreement,' he replied. 'And before you ask me why, do you really want this conversation on your doorstep?'

Stiff-backed with indignation, still glancing up and down the street to ensure there was no one hanging around who might wonder why this well-appointed stranger was calling on her mid-afternoon, Cora stepped aside to admit him, slamming the door closed when he was inside.

In the living room, he unbuttoned his coat and peeled it off as if he'd popped in for a daily cuppa. 'Nice and warm,' he commented.

'Enough niceties, Frank,' she snapped. 'You don't do them very well.'

'Okay . . .' he draped his coat over the back of an armchair, 'let's cut to the chase. The situation's simple, Cora. I *have* stayed away . . . for as long as I was able to. But now something's gone wrong, and it's in all our interests that it gets fixed.'

'*All* our interests, Frank . . . really?' She didn't find it difficult sounding sceptical.

'Lucy's joined CID, I understand?'

'Don't you dare start prodding me for information, Frank McCracken.' She jabbed a finger at him. 'It was bad enough what happened last time. My life won't be worth living if I gossip with you about her job again.'

The previous year, terrified that Lucy was getting in too deep during an undercover assignment, which just conceivably could have threatened one of McCracken's own operations, Cora had contacted the gangster, explaining their daughter's role in it and begging for her safety. Lucy's life had been spared, but her cover was blown and weeks of careful police-work wasted. At the time, Lucy had been quite sincere when swearing at Cora that she would never speak to her again. Events had eventually conspired to bring them back together – if somewhat stiltedly, though it was not a scenario Cora wished to revisit under any circumstances.

McCracken looked unconcerned by the outburst. 'Has she mentioned anything in passing about a bunch of cowboys doing shoot-'em-up blags around Manchester?'

'Are you not listening to me?' Cora retorted. 'I said I can't talk to you.'

'Cora . . . this is serious.'

'Oh, it's always bloody serious . . . at least as far as *you're* concerned. And what is it you do, Frank? Oh yeah, Lucy told me. You extort money from other criminals.' She made no effort to conceal her disgust. 'And if they don't cough up, you have them killed. Is that what this is about? This new bunch of maniacs . . . the Crew not getting their cut? So they've sent you along?'

'For once, love, this is not about money. These men are wreaking absolute bloody havoc. They're highly dangerous . . . they carry sub-machine guns, for Christ's sake! And they're not frightened to use them. Now, if Lucy hasn't mentioned these guys already, she needs clueing in at the first opportunity.'

'You what?' Cora scoffed. 'You're here to give her a heads-up? Is that what you're saying? I mean, how stupid do you think I am?

'Look, I've done some digging around this, and at present these bastards can outgun anyone . . . *anyone*. Are you hearing that, Cora?' He gave her a long, flat stare. 'At some point soon there'll be an absolute massacre. And it could easily be that the dead bodies are coppers.'

Cora glared at him, lips clamped but visibly trembling. At length, she turned away and sat on the armchair. McCracken walked around to face her. He knew from previous conversations that the one chink in Cora's armour was her daughter's safety. In truth, he didn't think there was much chance that the police would get into a firefight with these new kids on the block, but Cora was tortured night and day by worries that something bad might happen to Lucy when she was on duty.

Even so, *this* reaction was more than he'd expected; she'd literally gone pale with fear.

'Hit a nerve, have I?' he said curiously.

'You're not lying about this?' she said in a terse voice.

'Do you really think I would?'

'I've seen nothing in the newspapers about these robberies.'

'Doesn't the name "Andy Northwood" ring a bell?'

A nervous near-flinch indicated that she *had* heard about this crime. At least one tabloid had led with the somewhat indelicate splash:

> BLOW-N AWAY! *Gangster gunned down*
> *at wild cocaine party.*

'What exactly has alarmed you?' McCracken asked.

Cora tangled her hands into a tense knot, before sighing long and hard, and replying: 'Lucy doesn't tell me much, as you know. But she *did* say something about doing some work with the Robbery Squad. Here in Crowley, I think she said.'

'What work with the Robbery Squad?'

'I don't know . . .' She shook her head, before abruptly standing 'Anyway, I wouldn't tell you even if I did. This is

213

exactly the opposite of what we agreed last year, Frank. You're not supposed to come here.'

'I'm here to warn her . . .'

'You're *not* here to warn her!' Cora grabbed his coat and threw it at him. 'Because if you wanted that, you'd go and tell her, yourself. You know if I let it slip that you've been here again, it'll be the end of mine and Lucy's relationship forever. I've already said too much.'

Reluctantly, he pulled the coat on. 'If you hear anything else, call me.'

'I'm not your grass, Frank McCracken.'

He moved out into the hall. 'You know, Cora . . . last time *you* came to *me* for help, and I gave it.'

'You gave it in the end . . . when you had no other choice.'

'Because of the action I took, Lucy caught two murderers and got that CID job she'd been angling for.'

'I won't help you kill people.'

'Very Christian-minded of you, Cora.' He checked his reflection in the hall mirror, straightening his tie. 'I'd heard you were a churchgoer, these days. Trouble is . . . you refuse to help me, and people will probably die anyway. What will God think about that?'

She pointed at the front door. 'You should go.'

He nodded, pecked her on the cheek – to which she made no response except to glare at him – and left. The banging of the front door echoed behind him as he walked down the street.

McCracken's Bentley waited on the car park at the back of a nearby pub, The Anvil. Mick Shallicker was slouched behind the wheel, playing on his iPhone.

He sat up when McCracken climbed in. 'How'd it go?'

'How'd you think?' McCracken grunted. 'She bloody flew off on one.'

'Birds, eh?'

McCracken was silent for a moment, as he pondered.

Despite the innate loyalty of all his men, he only had one personal confidant when it came to really sensitive matters, and that was Shallicker, who'd never been merely a minder/enforcer, but a bosom buddy as the two of them had risen through the ranks together. The big guy had many times proved his unswerving support since, but McCracken most likely wouldn't even have trusted Mick with the knowledge that his estranged daughter was a police detective had the guy not been around when he himself had first learned about it. That made the deputy only one of four people privileged enough to know about this, the others being McCracken himself, Lucy and Cora – it was the ultimate inner sanctum – but if it ever occurred to McCracken that Mick Shallicker might one day seek to feather his own nest by blowing the gaff on them, he simply put it from his mind. He couldn't afford to do anything else.

'There *is* something,' McCracken said. 'Sounds like our Lucy's been working with the Robbery Squad.'

'Yeah?' Shallicker looked impressed. 'Talk about going up in the world.'

'Don't know what she's doing with them . . . whether it's a full-time appointment, or she's just been seconded, or whatever it is they call it. The point is, there may be something in it for us.' He thought about it again. 'Put a tail on her, Mick. Not all the time . . . just when it's convenient, and not so obvious that whoever it is gets caught. Remember, she's no stone fucking jug. Let's see where she goes, who she talks to. Build up a dossier. Just between us, of course.'

Shallicker switched the engine on and put the car in gear. 'Even if she is on the Robbery Squad, she won't necessarily be working these blags.'

'We won't know until we pay some attention, will we?'

Shallicker drove out of the pub car park. 'She gets around, that lass of yours . . . I'll say that for her.'

'She's no lass of mine. Better remember that, pal. Or we'll all wind up in the Ship Canal.'

Chapter 23

Though she'd made two pretty good arrests, Lucy's day went downhill from late-afternoon.

It wasn't all bad news about Harry. Aside from whiplash, facial bruising, three loose teeth and eight stitches in his bottom lip, he hadn't suffered any serious contusions, and the scan revealed no fractures or brain injuries. Even so, the staff at St Winifred's wanted to keep him in overnight because of concussion. Lucy couldn't afford to spend too much time with him, just sufficient to hear his groggy griping as he was wheeled up from casualty to one of the short-stay wards, all the way pleading with her to take him home and look after him, herself – at which point he called her Sandra, his ex-wife's name, which sealed the deal that he needed at least a couple of days on the sick. But the upshot of this was that, when Lucy got back to Robber's Row, she had two prisoners to deal with, and the custody clock was already ticking on both of them.

DI Beardmore said that he wanted to interview Royton personally, but promised that the big hoodlum would be written up as one of Lucy's prisoners. She was happy with this arrangement, as it meant she'd still get credit for the arrest but would now have more time to work on Jordan Burke, who she interviewed in company with DC Ken Birch, a hard-bitten, grey-haired veteran of the DO who was standing in for Harry.

At first, despite his earlier co-operation, the thief was evasive, clearly hoping for a deal. Lucy responded to this by steering the interview towards any accomplices he might have used during the burglaries, asking if he thought anyone would believe that stolen property could be stored in Janet O'Dowd's council house without her knowing about it. Sensing where this was leading, Burke requested a break and a private consultation with his solicitor, after which he admitted everything, assuring her that he had been the only person involved and that Janet was too busy looking after Baby Caleb and 'too fucking dozy anyway' to have any clue what he was keeping in the unused upstairs room. He even went so far as to offer to work through a list of the stolen items, indicating which houses he'd taken them from.

So far so good. It all looked like a clean job – until a glitch appeared.

Lucy was able to marry up every single piece of stolen property with one of the complainants on Hatchwood Green, except for a diamond-studded Rolex watch.

'You say you stole this from 19, Durkin Crescent?' Lucy said, remembering that this was the home of old Reg Murgatroyd.

'Sure,' Burke replied. 'Surprised me too, little house an' all. But it was well-kept. Had a quick shuftie round the downstairs with the metal detector, and it was in the drawer under the telephone.'

Lucy glanced at Ken Birch, who looked equally bemused.

'Jordan,' she said, '19, Durkin Crescent belongs to an OAP who, even though he keeps a tidy house, probably never has more than a few bob to spend, and most of that goes on mild and bitter. How's he likely to have come into possession of a Rolex watch?'

Burke shrugged. 'Dunno, but it was there. Not gonna forget a piece of kit like that.'

The main reason this anomaly concerned Lucy was because it suggested the suspect was still holding out on them, and that he may have done another job on a higher calibre property, one that had proved more rewarding to him. It would be the irony of ironies if they missed something like that because he'd lulled them by coughing to a bunch of lesser crimes.

'You know, Jordan,' she said, 'we've already agreed that we may TIC some of these offences . . . the smaller ones, where you didn't take much. But we won't be able to extend that to a major break if one suddenly emerges late in the day.'

'Major break?' Burke seemed genuinely bemused. 'Don't know what you're talking about.'

'You didn't get this Rolex watch from a council property on the Hatchwood, did you?'

Lucy was certain of this, because as well as the sheaf of paperwork they'd been working through with the suspect, she also had a copy of the original crime report in front of her, and the stolen goods listed at 19, Durkin Crescent did not include a Rolex.

Burke regarded her warily, as if she was trying to play a game with him.

'I swear I did,' he said.

She stared back at him. He was a lifelong thief; for all that he was apparently assisting, his promises and assurances meant very little. There was no reason on earth to believe him. But if this was an untruth, it was a pretty ridiculous one.

She briefly wondered if the Rolex might indeed have

belonged to Reg Murgatroyd. Was it conceivable that he'd been awarded it by some kind of old soldiers' association, or something?

Pausing the interview, she went down to the Evidence Store, a vault-like cellar accessible from a stair in the Charge Office, where she rustled through the various exhibit bags, finally pulling out the Rolex, turning it over and over in her hand, examining it through the clear plastic. There was no question about its value; it was Rolex Day-Date, done in what looked like rose gold, with diamond studs around its dial. This was a pricy item. Not the kind of thing you'd expect charitable groups like the British Legion to donate. And even if they had, surely that would have increased its value to the owner, making it impossible to imagine that, when it was stolen, he would either not notice or fail to report it.

She went back upstairs and along the corridor to CID Admin, where she spent half an hour rooting through files, both paper and electronic, but was unable to locate any outstanding theft of a Rolex as reported locally in the last two years. Deeply puzzled, she traipsed back to Custody, where DI Beardmore was now pacing the Charge Office wearing a disgruntled frown.

'Don't tell me he's not having it?' Lucy asked. 'Royton, I mean.'

'No, he isn't,' Beardmore said.

'Seriously? I *saw* him clobber Harry . . . happened right in front of me. And surely we've got statements from the witnesses at O'Halloran's and Tesco?'

Royton and his unknown associates (the latter two of which, equally fit and powerful individuals to him, had used the distraction of the carwash fight to get clean away, fleeing through the supermarket itself) had apparently battered two young blokes senseless at the snooker hall in what other people who'd been there had described as an unprovoked attack.

'He's not having anything,' Beardmore said. 'He says he'll only talk to the arresting officer.'

Immediately, Lucy had an inkling why. Was Royton banking that a young female cop would be more malleable, less likely to get something out of him they could run with?

That was a challenge she would normally have risen to. But not at present.

'Stan, I've got to close this burglary case.' She glanced at the clock above the Charge Office desk. 'I've got nineteen hours left, admittedly, but a complication's arisen and it needs looking into.'

Beardmore frowned. 'I thought it was a straight-up job.'

'So did I,' she said, walking out.

Reg Murgatroyd, blinked several times at the Rolex watch in its transparent exhibit bag, but it was the blinking of a rabbit in headlights rather than an elderly man trying to adjust his rheumy vision. In truth, he'd been twitchy since Lucy had returned here. More so than previously. As before, even though seated in the armchair in his own living room, he sat bolt upright, his arthritic hands hooked into the armrests on either side. The last time this had happened, Lucy had assumed it was the simple shock of having been burgled. Now, she was wondering if Reg Murgatroyd himself had something to hide.

'That's not mine, love,' he said. 'No, I couldn't afford a watch like that?'

'You know what kind of watch it is, then?' she asked, not yet having put it into his hands so that he could examine it closely.

'Well, erm . . .' Again, he faltered. 'It's a Rolex, isn't it?'

Lucy studied him. She very much doubted that he could

see from the other side of the room that this was a Rolex, which meant that he was already familiar with it.

'Reg,' she said, 'I've got absolutely no doubt that you've done nothing wrong here.'

'I hope you haven't.' He gave a fluting, clearly fake laugh.

'But somehow or other, a Rolex watch – worth nearly £30,000 – was stolen from this house during a burglary.'

'Who says? The burglar? You surely don't believe him over me?'

That was a valid point, but old Reg's tone had turned waspish. It might be that he was outraged to now find himself, the victim of a crime, under questioning. On the other hand, it might be a defence mechanism because he actually felt guilty about something.

'I must admit, Reg,' she said, 'the suspect I have in custody is probably a better and more experienced liar than you are. But that only makes me all the more curious. Where did you get this watch from, and why are you pretending it's not yours?'

He worked his moist lips together. A sheen of sweat glimmered on his brow.

'Reg . . . I'm sure you're not going to get into trouble over this.'

He still made no answer.

'But the best chance of us ensuring that . . . is if you tell me what's actually happened.'

'Can I . . .?' he ventured 'Can I ask you a question first?'

'Go on.'

'Is there such a thing as theft by finding?'

'You're saying you found it?' It wasn't completely implausible, Lucy supposed.

He didn't say anything, just awaited a response to his own question.

'It depends on the circumstances,' she said.

'It's just that, a lad who was in the forces with me . . .' He dabbed at his brow with a handkerchief. 'He joined the police when we came home. And I remember him telling me once how he'd lifted this fella because he'd found a wallet with fifty nicker in it – that was a lot of money in those days, you know – and he took it straight to the pub, buying all his pals a drink.'

'Was there a chequebook in the wallet, credit cards?'

'I believe there was, yeah.'

'In that case, the man *did* commit an offence,' Lucy confirmed. 'Because the real owner of the property was easily traceable. But I'm not sure that would be the same situation with this watch, Reg. There's no name on it. There is a serial number if you look at it with a magnifying glass, but you couldn't have been expected to know that. But you still need to have taken reasonable steps to find out who the owner was. And there's one other problem . . .'

She pinioned him with her best interview room gaze.

'I've checked with Rolex themselves, and the serial number on this particular watch has never been reported missing. And that means anywhere on earth. So, no one lost it, did they?'

'But if I'd stolen it, wouldn't it have been reported missing then, too?' he said.

Lucy conceded that. At present, none of this made sense. But only Reg Murgatroyd could give any kind of answer.

'Doesn't that *prove* I didn't steal it?' he said. 'If I had, wouldn't I have tried to dispose of it? I could've sold it or anything, but I didn't.'

'I'm more interested in how you came by it?'

He hung his head for a second. 'It was given to me.'

'Given to you?' Lucy arched an eyebrow. 'And who was the exceedingly generous donor?'

'This is the bit you won't believe . . . I don't know.'

Lucy sat back. 'Reg . . . someone you don't know gave you a thirty-grand watch?'

A ripple of fear crossed his face. 'I knew you wouldn't believe me. Look, if it was someone I did know, don't you think I'd have questioned it? Who do I know who'd give me a present like that? Someone up the Railway Club? My daughter, who works as a part-time carer? My carpet-fitter son-in-law?'

Lucy regarded him carefully. 'What were the circumstances?'

'Like I say, whoever it was, they were anonymous. It was a couple of days before I got robbed. They shoved it through my letter box in a plastic bag. Hand-delivered it, like. No name and address on it, or anything.' His face creased, with bitterness as well as worry. 'Thirty grand, eh? The only thing I've had in my life that's valuable, and now you want to take it off me.'

'They hand-delivered you a Rolex in a plastic bag?' It was still a struggle not to sound sceptical.

'Take the piss if you want,' he grunted. 'But that's what happened. I got up in the morning, and there it was on the doormat. No sign of anyone around.'

'No note with it?'

'Nothing.'

'Have you still got the plastic bag?'

'Give over, love. It went in the bin with all the other rubbish. Look . . .' He raised the handkerchief again, but now to dab tears away; the emotional stress of this whole thing was becoming too much for him. 'I can see you don't believe me. I'd struggle to believe it too, if someone told me. But I'm not the only one this has happened to.'

'You're not?'

Before he could reply, her mobile vibrated in her pocket. She checked it and saw that the call was from Beardmore.

'Sorry, Reg . . . I have to take this.' She walked out into the hall. 'Stan?'

'Custody want to know what you're doing with this prisoner, Jordan Burke,' Beardmore said. 'Are you going to charge him or what?'

'I'll be back in in fifteen,' she said. 'There's still an irregularity, but that won't stop us charging him.'

'Okay . . . good. I also want you to interview Royton.'

'Royton, boss?' Lucy couldn't conceal her frustration; she'd hoped this one would have been dealt with by now.

'He still won't talk to anyone else.'

'You realise he's just playing games?'

'Course, I do. But sit down with him for ten minutes. See what you can get.'

'Will do,' she sighed, cutting the call and going back into the living room. 'Reg . . . we may need to talk about this some more, but for the moment I'm going to make further enquiries. What I need from you now is an explanation, and a quick one if you don't mind . . . what do you mean when you say you're not the only person this has happened to?'

Murgatroyd shifted uncomfortably in his chair. 'These are only rumours, you understand?'

'I understand nothing so far. It's a big puzzle.'

'Aye.' He nodded glumly. 'This is why I was nervous . . . I mean about you thinking I might've done something wrong. Because good things like this don't happen, do they? Not to the likes of us. Because what we're supposed to get in life is all the rubbish. And if we don't . . . if something good comes along, there must be something bad behind it, wouldn't you say? Must be something very, very bad.'

Chapter 24

'You sure you don't want a solicitor present, Leon?' Lucy asked.

At the other side of the table, the underworld enforcer, still a menacing figure even now in his custody whites and with his hands cuffed behind his back, shrugged.

'Don't need one,' he said. 'Gonna come clean with you.'

'I imagine that'll be some kind of first,' she replied. 'Especially after the way you held out on DI Beardmore earlier.'

Royton shrugged again.

As Lucy had already told herself, she knew what the suspect was up to here. Beardmore, an experienced DI, had given him the third degree, looking for anything he could find on the wider crime wave that had recently struck Crowley. Lucy was in no doubt that Royton possessed information about that, but guessed he'd have resisted talking about it to protect all those others involved, finally requesting a younger, newer detective – an 'eager young lass', like herself – who he could give half a story to, maybe confessing to the assault, in effect chucking her a crumb, which she'd consider a result and which the likes of

Beardmore would grudgingly accept in lieu of having anything else.

Lucy glanced sidelong at Kirsty Banks, who nodded that she was ready.

'You realise you're still under caution, Leon?' Lucy said.

'Sure,' he replied. 'Look . . . I'm sorry about them two coppers. I didn't mean to hurt 'em. But they came at me first, you know.'

Lucy pursed her lips to consider this. Given that Royton beat people up for a living, such remorse was most likely as big a pretence as his seeming willingness to co-operate. He knew he was going down, and was now trying to mitigate the severity of it. But if nothing else, it would make the interview less stressful.

'You're referring to Police Constable Don Cooper and Detective Constable Harry Jepson,' she said, 'both of whom you assaulted today, yes?'

'If you say so.'

'Well, I wasn't witness to the incident involving PC Cooper, Leon, but I certainly was present when you clobbered DC Jepson into semi-unconsciousness. So, I *do* say so, yes.'

'Old habits.' Royton shrugged a third time; it seemed to be his preferred gesture. 'Like I say, they both got into my face. I had to put them down.'

'So, just to be clear,' Lucy said, 'you admit you assaulted both officers?'

'Yeah, like I say. It's all on me, this.'

So far, this was just as Lucy had predicted.

'What about the two men you assaulted at O'Halloran's?' she asked him.

'Yeah, that was a bit naughty too.'

'Why don't you tell me about it?'

'We were having a game,' Royton said simply, 'and these two tearaways started giving us a bad time.'

'We have witnesses who will strongly refute that, Leon,' Lucy said. 'In fact, we have at least two statements which will assert – as in the witnesses are absolutely sure! – that you and your two associates came into the snooker hall, made no effort whatsoever to start a game – even though there were plenty of tables free – and immediately started what's been described as a "shouting argument" with George and Charlie Benton.' She paused for effect. 'But it didn't remain an argument for long, did it, Leon?'

'They were pushing their arses around.'

'What do you mean by that?' Banks asked him.

'They were giving us grief. You're right, there were other tables free, but we wanted that table, and they wouldn't budge even though they'd just finished playing. Started getting in our faces, pissed up, shouting. How else was I supposed to react?'

Lucy observed him wryly. 'Not a good day for you, today, was it, Leon? All six-foot-five of you. Everywhere you've been, someone's got into your face.'

'Yeah, but I shouldn't have overreacted. I've already said that.'

'You call it overreacting, Leon . . . but do you know how badly injured George and Charlie Benton actually are?'

He gave one of his customary shrugs.

'You must have some notion. After clubbing them to the floor with snooker cues, you and your two mates punched and kicked them for so long that the snooker room attendant called 999 shortly after you'd started, and when PC Cooper got there, you were still doing it. So, we're talking very severe injuries indeed: multiple broken bones, vital organs ruptured, massive internal bleeding. What've you got to say about that?'

Royton averted his eyes. 'I agree. That happened. Went a bit OTT.'

'Who were the other two men with you?' Banks asked.

'Can't help you with that, I'm afraid.'

'You went to play snooker with two guys you didn't know?' Lucy said.

'I know who they are, but I'm not speaking to you about them.' He suddenly seemed bored with the proceedings. 'Doesn't matter anyway, does it? Like I say . . . it's all on me.'

'We want the names of your two mates,' Banks reiterated.

'You can't have them. I'm sorry, but there it is.'

'We also want to know whose orders you were acting under?' Lucy added.

'Eh?' Royton glanced at her, bemused, but as she'd already discovered, he wasn't the best actor. '*No one*'s orders. No one orders *me* around.'

'Oh, I think they do, Leon,' she said. 'In fact, I *know* they do. There are people out there who, if they told you to do the world a favour and jump on a bonfire, you'd do exactly that.'

'I can't help you with any of these daft questions.' For the first time, he sounded vaguely irritated.

'What about the Benton brothers?' she asked.

'What about them?'

'Do you know them?'

'Only as a pair of dickheads who were—'

'Pushing their arses around . . . yeah you told us. But that's not the whole truth, is it. Because a man with your connections, Leon, would also know that the Benton brothers have a bit of a rep themselves.'

'I wouldn't know.'

'Did they owe you something?'

He hammed a frown. 'Why would they owe *me* anything?'

'Because they're professional tea-leaves, Leon. Theft is what they do for a living.'

He grinned. 'Maybe you should give me a medal. Two blaggers less in the world. Everyone's happy, aren't they?'

'I said they were thieves, Leon. I didn't say they were blaggers.'

He greeted this with silence.

'And there was you,' Lucy said, 'pretending like you didn't know them.'

He licked his lips, shrugged.

'Robbed the wrong person, did they?' she asked.

'No further comment,' he replied.

'Very noble of you, Leon, taking the whole rap. Would your mates do that for you?'

'No comment.'

Lucy leaned forward again. 'Good old Bill Pentecost and his cronies, eh? Living five-star lifestyles in penthouse flats, never having to look over their shoulders because there's always some buffoon like you to pay the price for them.'

'No comment.'

She glanced at Banks, who arched a resigned eyebrow.

Lucy stood up. 'Interview terminated, 4.30 p.m.'

Banks switched the tape recorder off and left the room, leaving Lucy with the prisoner.

'Leon . . . we'll almost certainly be charging you with violent disorder and causing grievous bodily harm to PC Cooper and DC Jepson. But it may well be attempted murder in the cases of George and Charlie Benton. You know what that means, don't you? With your record?'

'Never had a bad time in prison yet.'

'We know something's going on, Leon. All this unprecedented violence. Suddenly your gaffers aren't having things all their own way, are they?'

He made an unconvincing show of getting comfy on his chair. 'I don't work for anyone.'

'You certainly won't be where you're going next . . . which might not be ideal from your employers' perspective. Not a good time to be losing their top men, I suspect.'

Chapter 25

While DS Banks headed to the DO to report back to Beardmore, Lucy found herself drawn upstairs to the Robbery Squad office. She went with some minor trepidation. The Squad had been busy as hell over the last few days. By all accounts, the robbery-homicide at the home of Andy Northwood had thrown up more complexities than anyone had expected.

To begin with, the violence had not just been directed at Northwood. A number of his male guests had also been shot and wounded, deliberately so, having first been lined up along a sideboard. And yet, they themselves were proving tricky to trace. It seemed that Northwood had been hosting some kind of drugs and prostitution party at the time, and none of those injured were so routinely involved in criminality that they were comfortable being named as participants; in fact, all of them, by various means, had managed to vacate the premises before the emergency services were even summoned, and doubtless were now receiving treatment from the usual roster of alcoholic, drug-addicted, child-abusing, or just plain incompetent doctors who'd long ago been struck off and these days existed solely for use of the underworld.

It went without saying, of course, that most of the females at the party – the strippers and prostitutes – had also scarpered before the police arrived, in their case with much less difficulty as they hadn't been shot – one had even been reported separately by a passing motorist, who'd been dumbstruck to see a woman clattering along the pavement wearing only a pair of high heels. That said, two local barmaids who'd been hired by Northwood to work as waitresses, and whose status was more legitimate, had remained at the house, and in fact they were the ones who'd phoned the incident in. These two girls now constituted a vital if somewhat unwilling lead for DI Blake, who'd been working with them for several days in her attempts to establish the identities and whereabouts of the other witnesses. But despite this unexpected mass of extra work, Lucy couldn't help feeling that she'd seen less of Danny Tucker for other reasons.

She had *not* given him the brush-off that night of the Robbery Squad party. At least, she hadn't intended to. She'd merely tried to imply to him that this wasn't a straightforward thing for her, and that she didn't want to blunder into an ill-advised relationship. And he hadn't shown any indication at the time that he'd taken it personally. He'd appeared to understand what she was saying. But, whereas beforehand she'd found herself running into him at almost every corner of the nick, now, only a few days later, she rarely saw him at all.

It was entirely possible, she supposed, as she approached the Robbery Squad office door, that she wouldn't see him now either. Most likely he'd be out and about.

But he wasn't.

When she walked in, there were only four Squad personnel present, but Tucker was one of them. He was slumped at his desk, hammering at his keyboard, with his mobile lodged under his ear. On one hand Lucy was glad to see him, but

233

on the other she felt mildly nervous – which annoyed her no end.

'Bloody schoolgirl,' she muttered to herself.

Tucker now caught sight of her and raised a friendly finger.

As she made her way over there, he pointed at the phone and signalled that he wouldn't keep her long. He behaved as genially as ever, but she still couldn't help thinking that there'd been a slight change in his demeanour? Was there something behind his eyes, now? A distance perhaps, which hadn't been there previously?

She tried to put this from her mind while she waited, looking around the office and seeing that the corner formerly dedicated to the Saturday Street Gang had now been commandeered by *Operation Golden Roost*, named after Andy Northwood's premises.

It was adorned wall-to-wall with the usual crime scene photos, mugshots and rap sheets for suspects, maps of the house, grounds and surrounding roads, and pages of hand-written notes, many of which looked to have been scribbled out on the hoof. All of these disparate items were now connected to each other by a complex web of differently hued cotton threads.

It seemed like an old-fashioned way of doing it, but that was the Robbery Squad all over, and at least part of its appeal to Lucy.

But perhaps the most interesting aspect of the miniature incident room was its centrepiece, a whiteboard on which three blown-up e-fits had been grouped together in an inverted triangle. The top two images depicted faces enclosed by red ski masks, with only the eyes visible. There were notations on both: body shapes, estimated height and weight statistics, guestimates about age, and the like.

It seemed vague, but the bottom image was perhaps the vaguest of all; little more than the outline of a head, with no mask, no face, and only a large red question mark in the middle.

Two other Squad detectives were in close proximity. One was Lee Gaskin – *who else*, Lucy thought irritably. He was seated with his feet on a desk, chatting into a phone. He finally noticed her, and if eyeballs alone could convey dislike, his did the trick admirably, but he didn't break off from his conversation. The other was Ruth Smiley, who was collecting print-outs and shuffling them into some kind of order.

'How you doing, Luce?' she said, barely looking round.

'Three, eh?' Lucy replied, still focussed on the whiteboard. 'Thought there were only supposed to be two.'

'Well . . .' Smiley shrugged. 'It's possible there's a getaway man. According to witnesses, the bandits left Northwood's premises, and almost immediately a set of wheels were heard screeching away.'

'Couldn't they just have driven off, themselves?'

'Yeah, course. But the two barmaids were adamant that they didn't hear an engine start up . . . you know, as though there was a car waiting with a driver behind the wheel. But we can't be sure. They were scared to death at the time, both of them. They even gave conflicting accounts of the actual blag. We've not got a lot to go on, to be honest. But we're getting there.'

Smiley didn't seem overly confident, but it still sounded like more fun than dashing around the Hatchwood, locking up sneak-thieves.

'Hey, if it isn't the woman of the moment,' Tucker said. Phone chat over, he stood up, shoving the flaps of his plaid shirt back into his jeans. 'Hear you bagged some heavy muscle today.'

'I bagged a couple of pillocks,' Lucy replied, walking over to him.

Smiley guffawed as she crossed the room towards the door. 'Story of our careers, eh?'

Tucker grinned. 'Still sounds like you're having a good week. Your gaffer's been up here, copying us in.'

'Ahhh . . .' Lucy had wondered if he might, but had still hoped that *she* could be the one to make a possible link between the prisoner downstairs and the Northwood murder. 'So . . . what do you think?'

Tucker frowned. 'About . . .?'

'Well, you're looking for at least two blaggers, aren't you? For Andy Northwood. Northwood was connected to the Crew. Leon Royton's connected to the Crew. His two victims today were the Benton brothers . . . known blaggers.'

'Yeah, Beardmore said the same thing. Could the Benton boys have done the Northwood job, and was today's attack payback?' Tucker gave it some thought. 'What's Royton's story?'

'He's put his hand up to the assaults, and we're going to charge him. But he's not coughing to a connection with anyone or anything else. Said it was a fallout over a snooker table.'

Tucker mused. 'The Bentons are in no state to be interviewed, I understand?'

'One of them's in a coma. The other might be all right to interview tomorrow, or the day after.'

'We'll certainly speak to them,' Tucker said. 'But I'll be honest, Lucy . . . I don't think there's much in this for us. The Benton lads are blaggers . . . no question there. Got lots of form, but they've never used firearms. Certainly not sub-machine guns.'

'First time for everything, surely?'

'I take it you've seen the ballistics report from the Northwood crime scene?' someone interrupted.

Lucy turned and saw that Lee Gaskin had approached, his pitted face written with its usual schoolboy insolence.

'No,' she had to admit.

'Well . . . there's a surprise.'

'How could I have?' she said. 'I'm not involved in the Northwood investigation.'

'In that case,' he said, 'even though it's well outside your remit, allow me to enlighten you. The two weapons we believe were used at Andy Northwood's house are a pair of SIG-Sauer MPX gas-operated sub-machine guns, which can only be classified as high-tech military equipment. Now . . . where do you think a couple of scrotes like the Benton brothers are likely to get kit like that from? The last job they pulled involved a baseball bat and a butcher's knife.'

'The Crew could have provided the guns,' she suggested.

'That's possible,' Tucker said, giving Gaskin a warning glare. 'But the Crew make money from idiots like the Benton boys by ripping them off . . . not supervising them.'

'Anyway,' Gaskin said, 'you seriously saying the Crew would arm the Bentons, and then the first person they rob and kill is one of the Crew's own pals?'

Lucy had no answer for that. For any of it, in fact. Gaskin was being his usual awkward self, but he was right to be dubious, and so was Tucker. The Benton brothers were strictly small-time. And that fact alone should dismiss any possibility they'd attack a Crew associate like Flash Andy.

'Haven't you got something to be getting on with?' Tucker asked Gaskin, who reddened in the cheek before shooting Lucy one final malevolent glance and sloping back to his desk. 'Don't worry, Luce,' Tucker said. 'We'll be interviewing the Bentons when they're fit. Just don't expect a result.'

She nodded. 'Listen Danny . . . there's something else. You're aware this attack on the Bentons is only one of several quite violent incidents recently?'

'Sure. But we're pretty snowed under. I haven't gone through the divisional crime-log in the last few days.'

'There's been a series of assaults,' she said. 'Not all as bad as the one at O'Halloran's, but we're talking a fair number of hoodlum-on-hoodlum incidents.'

'Hoodlum-on-hoodlum?' The turn of phrase brought a half-smile to his face; the first crack she'd seen in his business-like demeanour, though it was only fleeting.

'Look at some of the crime reports taken in the last few days. Dezzy Westerbrook. Don't know if you know him. Crowley lad with form for street robbery . . . three nights ago, someone gave him a kicking outside the Jack of Diamonds pub. The assailant was identified, arrested and charged as Michael Havering. A part-time bouncer, but nothing to do with the Jack of Diamonds. He admitted the assault but wouldn't say what it was about. There's another one. Archie McCrae.'

'Scots Archie?' Tucker sounded surprised. 'Is he still fencing?'

'Maybe not for much longer,' she said. 'There was an aggravated burglary at his flat. Place got wrecked, he got a pasting . . . then they tied him up and poured petrol over him. Only reason he didn't burn, we think, is because the old lady next door called 999 and a divisional van was in the area. Very little was stolen, but he told the uniforms that he didn't know who did it. Later on, neighbours gave descriptions matching Ali Yalfani and Mehdi Amani.'

'We know those two,' Tucker said. 'Right pair of shitheads.'

'Yeah, but it's complicated. Archie insisted it wasn't them.'

Tucker frowned. 'Okay . . . but, I'm not seeing the link.'

Lucy realised that she wasn't explaining this very well, and that maybe, if he was busy – as the Squad undoubtedly were – he was tolerating her presence rather than welcoming it.

'Look,' she said, 'none of these suspected assailants are attached to the Crew the way Leon Royton is, but don't you think this is all a bit suspicious? Known tea-leaves, usually blaggers – or people who work with blaggers – getting a going-over. And then it's always the same thing. They claim they don't know what the cause of the incident was, or they say it was a fallout in a pub or a snooker room, or whatever. This is not your regular kind of crime wave.'

His expression remained blank, which irked her.

'Danny, come on . . . maybe the Crew have put a reward out? I mean for Northwood's killers.'

Gaskin chuckled at his desk. 'Newsflash. Pissed-off gangsters want revenge.'

Lucy tried to ignore him. 'Isn't that relevant?'

'Well, it wouldn't be surprising,' Tucker said.

'Yeah, but this is real crazy stuff. I mean, an awful lot more people are gonna get hurt if it goes on unchecked. Plus, when they *do* find the culprits, they're not going to hand them over to the Robbery Squad, are they?'

'Are we supposed to be bothered?' Gaskin chipped in.

She shot him a vicious stare, to which his only response, again, was to chuckle.

'Look . . . I'm sorry if we don't seem too interested in this, Luce,' Tucker said, sitting back at his desk. 'There's probably something in what you say. But we can only progress the investigation as fast as we can. And ultimately, if the net result is – what did you call it? – a load of hoodlum-on-hoodlum violence, should that really upset us? Plus, if the Crew get these killers first . . . well, like Lee says, it's not the end of everything.'

This was hardly a laudable view for a police officer to take, Lucy thought, but rather to her own surprise, she felt as if she understood it. The bandits who'd hit Andy Northwood's house had been merciless. They'd gone in with heavy firepower and had happily used it. They needed to be taken off the grid one way or the other. It wasn't agreeable to think in those terms, but she supposed she shouldn't be

239

shocked that this was the Robbery Squad's attitude. Some of their previous run-ins with armed gangs were legendary.

Tucker's mobile rang. When he checked it, he started hitting keys on his laptop. 'Sorry, Luce . . . gotta take this. Thanks for the nudge, though . . . seriously.'

She nodded and moved away.

There was no question in Lucy's mind. She *had* damaged her relationship with Danny Tucker. He'd been polite enough, but he'd also been disingenuous. Lucy was no spring chicken when it came to policework, and she knew she'd just come up with a useful lead. The Crew were a fairly typical gang-land organisation; they might be stronger and more influential than most, but they had plenty of weak links. And if they too were hunting for Andy Northwood's killers, those weak links could easily be pressured into giving up vital info.

Lucy had no doubt that this would now become a new line of enquiry. The big difference was that, a week ago Tucker would have thanked her profusely; he'd have called Kathy Blake and given her the good tidings while Lucy was still standing there, maybe even try to bring her on board. Now, he was making as if he couldn't care less.

But it was all to the good that she'd learned this about him, she decided.

As she went back downstairs, it was difficult not to feel disappointed. For all her tough talk when her mother dragged the subject up, Lucy was not an unromantic soul. But she couldn't help wondering if it was a case of her missing an opportunity where Danny Tucker was concerned, or perhaps dodging a bullet.

Chapter 26

Every Monday morning, the twelve underbosses who constituted the Crew's Board of Directors would each despatch a cash delivery to a drop-off point in the back room of a dog-grooming salon in Whiston, Merseyside. Each delivery would constitute that particular section's weekly earnings, all of which, at this stage, existed solely as dirty money.

At the salon, dog-groomer extraordinaire and famously eccentric Crew bookkeeper, Milo Kennedy, would receive and register (in code) each batch of notes, ensuring to make a careful count so that on payday, every head of section, in addition to his monthly salary (from which he would also pay the salaries of his underlings) would receive any bonuses due. The following Thursday, with Milo happy that his records were straight, the cash, which usually totalled in the low hundreds of thousands, would be parcelled in several brown paper packages, and with no cover letter, return address or accompanying paperwork of any sort, be handed to a security detail, who'd deliver it to a private address in a secluded rural area on the outskirts of the Cheshire market town, Knutsford, where they would post it through a specially enlarged letter box in the right-hand gatepost at the front of a cosy, thatch-roofed residence.

The owner of this residence was a certain Margaret Millington, who, as well as being senior accountant at Hooper, Klein and Cromarty, a respected accountancy and business advisory firm in Stockport, also had a sideline as chief money-launderer for the Crew.

Millington never knew the money's source, and never enquired; she didn't even have contact with the delivery boys. She would take charge of the cash, again auditing the delivery and counting it to ensure there were no discrepancies – skimming was one inside job the Crew would never tolerate – keeping her own cryptically coded records, and then, over the next few months, despatched it piecemeal to the various legitimate businesses owned by Ent-Tech Ltd (aka the Crew), such as hotels, nightclubs and restaurants, bars and pubs, bowling alleys, gymnasia, fast-food outlets, tanning salons and the like, where it could be surreptitiously fed into the profits, at which point of course it was all nice and clean.

It perhaps wasn't a fool-proof process but it had served the Crew well for over a decade, with nothing ever going wrong. So, on the afternoon of Thursday November 2, there was no reason at all to take any additional precautions. On this particular day, the transportation duty from Whiston to Knutsford fell to Sam Brodie, a Glaswegian ex-paratrooper who'd worked for the Crew since he'd left the army eight years earlier, and Marty Culvin, a Humberside-born former wrestler and one-time organiser of football violence, who'd now graduated to bigger and better things. As always, to maintain an appearance of normality, having collected the cash from the dog-grooming salon, they would drive first to a Crew-owned garage at Lymm, where they would change into smart uniforms and caps (their pistols concealed in armpit holsters), and continue the journey in a van mocked up to look as if it was part of an official delivery service.

Brodie and Culvin were in relaxed mood as they drove the wooded backroads between Lymm and Knutsford – it took longer that way, but it was deemed better than using the main roads – chatting and bantering as always. And being taken completely by surprise when a rusty old truck, a ramshackle thing that could barely support itself on four rickety wheels, came rumbling out of a layby and jammed its brakes on right in front of them.

The delivery van shrieked to an unceremonious halt.

Brodie, the ex-military man, counselled caution. But Culvin, always quicker to lose his temper, leapt out.

A short burst of warning gunshots split the air.

Culvin spun around. A figure had emerged from the hedgerow on the right, wearing a black leather jacket, dark jeans and a vivid scarlet ski mask with holes cut for the eyes. More worrying, than this, he wielded what looked like a sub-machine gun.

Brodie spotted this in the rear-view mirror, but before he could respond, the truck driver had come upon the delivery van's front-offside. As Brodie tried to shift the van into reverse, his window imploded and a steel muzzle was jammed into his cheek.

Rigid with fear, he rolled his eyes sideways, and was incredulous to see a SIG-Sauer MPX. When he glanced up, an identically clad figure to the first, but slightly taller, leaned in at him.

'Right hand spread on the wheel,' the bandit instructed. 'Where I can see it.'

Brodie's right hand was already on the wheel, so he kept it there and expanded his fingers.

'Left hand,' the bandit said. 'Take the gun out . . . very, very slow. Fingertips only . . . I mean it, mate, you do otherwise, it's the end of you.'

Brodie had survived two combat tours in Iraq and Afghanistan, so though he counted himself a brutal, mean-spirited kind of guy, he also knew from experience when he was facing a cold-blooded killer.

He complied.

'That's it . . . nice and slow,' the bandit said. 'Give it here.'

Again, Brodie complied, handing his Browning 9mm out through the window, where it was snatched away from him and tossed into the nearest bushes.

'Okay . . .' The bandit backed up a half-foot or so. 'First gear . . . into the layby. Very, verrry slowly. You hit the gas, pal . . . I riddle this car end to end.'

As before, Brodie did as instructed, easing the van slowly off the road and into the layby, the bandit walking alongside him, the barrel of the SIG levelled through the open window. Once they were in there, Brodie saw an open space in the hedgerow at the back, beyond which a small parking area nestled between trees.

'Keep going,' he was told. 'Slow as fuck. Don't give me a reason.'

Brodie continued to ease his vehicle forward through the gap, parking on the rugged ground beyond.

'Okay,' the bandit said. 'Get the fuck out. And bring your keys.'

Brodie got out, arms raised.

'Round to the other side of the van. Stand with your pal.'

Brodie edged his way around the vehicle, eyes riveted on the barrel of the SIG. It was the most vicious close-quarter weapon he knew. German-made, he'd occasionally seen it deployed in combat, usually in the hands of terror-ists or guerrillas. He and Culvin were both wearing vests under their uniforms, but that wouldn't make any difference at this range. One blast, and they'd be Swiss cheese.

The second, shorter bandit had frogmarched Culvin into

the parking area behind the van, and now had him up against its flank. Having already extricated his captive's pistol, he was in the process of hurling it into the nearest undergrowth.

A tense silence followed. At mid-afternoon, the road nearby, nothing more than a country lane between farms, remained largely empty. Only birds twittering in the trees disturbed the peace. But even if someone came along, the robbers and their victims would be well-shielded by the partial wall of reddish-gold thickets at the back of the layby.

'You clueless twats!' Culvin snarled, cheeks crimson. 'You got any idea who it is you're stealing from?'

Brodie wanted to tell him to shut it, but was wary of appearing too compliant. Assuming they got through this, he'd have enough explaining to do as it was.

Meanwhile, the taller bandit said nothing as he patted them down for further weapons, pocketing both their mobile phones. The shorter bandit simply watched, SIG levelled.

'Hey . . . shit-for-brains!' Culvin shouted as the taller one stepped back. 'I said you got any idea who you're fucking robbing?'

'On which subject,' the taller one said, 'you!' He gestured at Brodie with his weapon. 'I reckon you've been around long enough to know that sometimes just going home at night is a win, yeah?' He drew a roll of material from his back pocket, and when he shook it out, it was a black canvas sack. He threw it at Brodie's feet. 'So, open the van . . . and fill this.'

'Don't fucking do it, man,' Culvin warned him. 'They want it, let 'em fucking take it.'

But Brodie did exactly as he was told, unlocking the side door and, one by one, sliding the five parcels they'd been carrying into the sack. There was no doubt in his mind that these guys weren't just opportunists. They'd known in advance that he and Culvin would be armed, they'd known in advance the route they would take; on top of that, they were tooled-up in spectacular form. Their intel and proficiency were of the highest order – in which case they wouldn't take any chances they didn't need to; like letting people live if they proved problematic.

It could even be that these guys were so coldly professional they wouldn't take the chance of leaving witnesses anyway.

Sweat greased Brodie's brow. He glanced back towards the road, wondering if he could suddenly dash away. But it was all too open; he'd be cut down before he made it into the layby.

The conviction grew on him steadily that he and Marty were done for.

These bastards were robbing the Crew. You didn't do that, not if you didn't want to be hunted for the rest of your days. In which case, why would they make life easier for themselves by leaving anyone alive who could talk?

And yet, what else could he do but obey?

As tense as he'd ever been on the battlefield, Sam Brodie placed the last package inside the sack, which was now heavy – there was plenty of cash on today's delivery run – and humped it around, lurching forward and dumping it at the bandits' feet.

'Very good,' the taller one said. 'I have to say . . . I was expecting a bit more trouble from you guys. I don't know whether to be relieved or disappointed.'

'Put them shooters down and you'll get more trouble than you can fucking handle,' Culvin snarled.

The taller bandit ignored him, pointing to the nearest line of trees. There was a ditch running along the edge of it. 'Over there. Side by side.'

'Look,' Brodie said, 'you got what you came for. Just go, eh?'

'I said get over there.'

246

Again, the two gangsters knew they had no choice. But even dull-witted Marty Culvin was sensing his pal's unease.

'I'm not going over there,' he said, voice tautening. 'Just so you'll have a clearer field of fire. You going to do me, you'd better do it here.'

The taller bandit glanced at the shorter one. Unspoken agreement passed between them. He looked back and shrugged. 'Okay . . .'

Chapter 27

By origin, Lucy's family were Church of England. Her mother, Cora, during her stripper days having considered herself an outcast from such things, was now cheerfully reconciled with the religion of her youth, and attended services on a steady basis. However, Lucy hadn't been to Church for quite some time, probably not since she'd left school, and she was even less familiar with the Roman Catholic Church of St Clement, which stood on Hudson Avenue on the southern edge of Hatchwood Green – and this was despite it having received considerable police attention during recent years.

It was a sad aspect of the modern age, Lucy told herself as she drove over there.

As recently as her own childhood, churches, even if they were located in poor inner-city districts like this, had tended to enjoy the respect of those living around them. It had been no exaggeration to say that most were once left unlocked twenty-four-seven despite the silver candlesticks on their altars and the poor-boxes in their porches.

Unfortunately, but perhaps inevitably, all that had now changed.

St Clement's had certainly suffered more than its fair share of vandalism and break-ins in the twenty-first century, which, wedded to its allegedly declining congregation and a story that it was now under consideration by the diocese for closure, was an especially melancholy story.

When Lucy got there, it was a surprisingly large building, a tall, narrow, red-brick structure with a steeple, but it looked shabby. The brickwork had eroded and two of the arched stained-glass windows above the main entrance were boarded with plywood. She walked up a short, paved path, passing a noticeboard so scabrous with mildew that the list of Mass times was indecipherable, and, rather to her surprise, found the main door unlocked. Fleetingly she was encouraged by this, thinking it reassuring that the church still tried to provide the haven and sanctuary it had always intended.

Unless it was just that there was nothing left inside St Clement's now worth stealing.

She entered properly via an inner door, the heavy *clunk* of which echoed through the spacious building. Inside, at first glance, the nave was empty, but in contrast to the exterior, very neat and tidy: candles flickered in niches or at the bases of handsomely painted statues of saints; hymn books and orders of service were stacked at the ends of each pew; a noticeboard adorned with children's paintings was attached to the wall behind the baptismal font.

Lucy strolled up the central aisle, approaching the main altar, which was dressed with autumnal bouquets comprising roses and lilies, but also twigs, berries and pinecones.

'Hello, can I help?' she was asked from behind.

She turned, to see that a priest had emerged from a side chapel.

'Father O'Donnell?' she enquired.

'That's me, yes,' he replied, unsmiling.

He was short but stocky, and quite elderly, somewhere in his late seventies, she'd have said, and leaning on a cane. He had chalk-white hair and a white beard and moustache, all of it neatly trimmed. His accent was local, but his voice rather gruff. He showed no consternation at her presence, but he wasn't warm either. As she walked around the block of pews and up the north aisle towards him, his face remained blank, his eyes small and hard, like two blue pellets.

'Good afternoon.' Lucy showed her warrant card. 'I'm DC Clayburn from Crowley CID. Please don't be alarmed, Father. I'm not here to bring bad news or anything like that. It's . . . well, it's a strange one really.'

'I see.' Though, from the priest's unchanging expression, it was difficult to tell whether he actually did or didn't see.

'It's come to my attention that St Clement's has recently been the beneficiary of some . . .' She couldn't help but pose the last part of her statement as a question '. . . some rather generous donations?'

Father O'Donnell didn't so much as blink. 'It happens from time to time.'

'Do you keep a record of these donations?' she asked.

'Yes, we are legally obliged to. But when they're anonymous that's all we can really do.'

'They were anonymous? The recent ones, I mean. Also . . . how much are we actually talking about?'

The priest held her gaze for several seconds without responding, and then, rather unexpectedly, his frosty carapace cracked. He sighed and lowered his head, touching a thumb to his brow as though it was aching.

'I must admit,' he said. 'I've been increasingly worried that something like this might happen.'

'Something like what, Father?'

'Oh . . . I don't know.' He sagged wearily onto one of the pews, and gestured with a loose hand at the one in front, indicating that Lucy should sit too, which she did, rotating sideways to face him. 'I really don't know,' he said again.

'The first time it happened, it seemed like manna from Heaven.' He arched an eyebrow at her. 'You've seen the state of the place?'

'It doesn't look as if things are all they could be.'

'Far from it, I'm afraid. If it isn't too melodramatic a thing to say . . . in former years, the Catholic Church was a beacon of light in hard times, particularly in deprived neighbourhoods.'

'But not so much now?'

He shrugged helplessly. 'Attendances are on the slide. We regularly suffer crime, as you're no doubt aware. The latest missive from the bishop is that if we can't turn things around, we're likely to get closed. It's happening everywhere these days. We have fewer priests, fewer Catholics, parishes are merging. But the last time I thought we faced this danger was in 1959, when the old Manchester Railway that used to run through here was decommissioned and the terraced neighbourhood that stood alongside it got demolished. Of course, they built Hatchwood Green soon after that, so everything looked peachy again.'

'1959,' Lucy said, impressed. 'You've been here that long?'

'I was a young deacon then. No more than twenty or twenty-one. I became the parish priest in 1977. I have to be honest . . . in all that time, I've never known events like *these*.' He shook his head. 'I should have realised they were too good to be true.'

'You're referring to this "manna from Heaven"?'

'Yes.' He sat up straight, bracing himself against the wooden backrest as though to ride out a storm. 'As I say, the first time, it seemed like a Godsend. One morning, we emptied the collection box for the Church Structural Repair Fund – it's over there near the font – and found an envelope inside it that was bulging at the seams. When we opened it, it was crammed with twenty-pound notes.'

'How much would you say in total?' Lucy asked.

'Just over £2,000.'

'And that kind of gift would be unusual?'

'It certainly would here.' He puffed his cheeks out. 'To be honest, in an age when charity very firmly begins at home, I think it would be unusual anywhere.'

'You checked that it was real money . . . not counterfeit?'

'I followed some procedures that we found online. It appeared to be the real deal.'

'And you've no idea who donated it?'

'None at all.' His eyes widened as though he was still surprised by the incident. 'I mean . . . it could have been anyone. Someone could have come into the church during the day; we're open during the week, as you've seen. It could even have happened during Mass. Quite often, it's at Communion when people make donations to our various charities – usually on their way back from the altar rail.'

He relapsed into silence, as he pondered.

'So, you thought this unusual,' Lucy said, 'but not unusual enough to report it?'

'Report it to whom?' He almost laughed. 'The police? The diocese? What could they say? It's not as if it's illegal to make generous donations. But the truth is we were so gobsmacked at our good fortune that we praised the Lord and put it to the best use we could.'

Lucy flipped her pocketbook open, and took out a pen. 'Okay, when would this have been?'

'I've got the details back in the presbytery . . . but it was sometime in mid-to-late October. Around the 19th or 20th. Then, about a week later, it happened again. We opened the poor-box one morning, and it was packed with notes, mostly tens and twenties. This time, it came to about £3,000.'

'And again, you have no idea who the donor was?' Lucy asked.

'No. But that was when I first started to think that maybe there was something odd about it. I was even moved to make a comment in my Sunday sermon.'

'What did you say?'

'It was difficult to know how to phrase it without giving out the wrong message. As I say, as far as I knew no one had done anything wrong. Quite the opposite. I merely said that charitable donations were all well and good, but that I wouldn't want any parishioners to overreach themselves. I said that sometimes charity really does begin at home, and that hard-working people needed to ensure their own were provided for first. I told them that this is serving God too.'

'And you didn't say more than that?' Lucy had been directed towards St Clement's by Reg Murgatroyd, and was intrigued to know how he had found out about these cash gifts. 'You didn't tell your parishioners what had happened?'

'Well, *I* didn't . . .' The priest looked awkward. 'But we have a couple of ladies who come in to clean. They were here when it happened. I suspect they've been rather garrulous on the subject. Word would have got all over the estate, I imagine. Especially after the third delivery . . . as they were the ones who found it.'

'There was a third?'

'Yes, and this was the clincher for me.' He frowned. 'I mean the clincher that something was wrong.' He rubbed at his chin. 'Old Mrs Marmaduke, it was. She arrived at the church on Monday morning, seven o'clock sharp as always. We have a noon Mass each day, you see. So, she was coming in to get the place shipshape. And she found a parcel wrapped with newspaper on the doorstep. There was a message on it in crayon. It said: "For good causes".'

'How much was in it?' Lucy asked.

'We opened it together, Mrs Marmaduke and me. Probably a mistake in retrospect, but it contained . . .' He shook his head with no little regret. 'It contained what I estimated to be around £10,000 in cash.'

Lucy stopped writing. 'You only estimated that?'

He shrugged. 'I haven't counted it yet. I don't even like touching it. It's still sitting in a cupboard in the sacristy. I simply haven't known what to do with it. Do I allocate it as a charitable donation, or do I take it to the police?' He fixed her with a long, querying stare.

'You're looking to me for advice?' she said, caught on the hop.

'You are a police officer, are you not?'

'You say it's still in your sacristy cupboard?'

He nodded.

'I suggest you leave it there for the present.' She stood up. 'Don't let anyone else touch it.'

'Am I to assume this money is stolen?'

'I'm like you, Father,' Lucy said. 'I'm at sixes and sevens. Just because this is an unusual event, it doesn't mean these gifts are the proceeds of crime. But at present we just don't know.'

He sighed again.

'Don't worry,' she said. 'As far as you're concerned, it's now been reported. So, no one at St Clement's is in any kind of trouble.'

He nodded. Clearly, this was some consolation to him, but only a minor one. He wouldn't have been human not to prefer to have been told that he could keep the money.

Lucy walked down the aisle. 'I'll make further enquiries and get back to you.'

'Detective Clayburn!' he called, as she reached the church door.

She glanced back.

He'd stood up and was leaning on his cane. 'We could do a lot of good with that money.'

'I understand, Father. I'll look into it as quickly as I can.'

'Couldn't this be legitimate?' he wondered aloud. 'The world hasn't completely gone to hell in a handbasket yet. Isn't it possible that some wealthy person who wishes to remain nameless has finally decided to give something back to society? That happens, doesn't it?'

'Yes, it happens,' she said. 'But we need to be certain.'

He nodded again, somewhat disconsolately.

'I'm *sure* it happens,' Lucy added to no one in particular, as she strode down the church path. 'Though not in my personal experience.'

Chapter 28

The Astarte was a typical none-too-showy hotel located in central Manchester.

Like many city-centre buildings, it wasn't much to look at from the outside. A huge square block of a thing, standing twelve storeys in height and dominating its own particular corner of skyline. Despite the rather handsome salt-and-pepper granite from which it was constructed, its even rows of tinted windows, and the indigo floodlights that under-lit its soaring outline once evening descended, it lacked any real embellishment or ornamentation, and its owners, Ent-Tech Ltd, preferred it that way.

In their eyes, it was good that the Astarte drew little attention and was mainly regarded as a businessman's stop-over, a place where nothing special ever happened – apart from the board meetings of course, but no one outside the Crew knew about those, and anyway, they only occurred on the top floor. To all intents and purposes, this was the penthouse suite, though in reality no ordinary person had access to it.

It was exceedingly comfortable up there. Not just a business pad comprising an office and boardroom; in addition, there was a bar and hostess lounge, and several ultra-plush bedrooms.

But Frank McCracken, for one, was never overly fond of visiting it.

It wasn't too bad when scheduled general meetings were to be held. Those were usually only for the assessment of annual reports and discussions of routine business. But today's event was a special meeting, called at short notice in response to a growing crisis, and you were never quite sure how these special meetings were going to pan out. Firstly, because Bill Pentecost, Chairman of the Board, would only ever reveal how much he knew when you were face-to-face with him, and depending on what kind of information he'd received, it didn't matter if you were innocent of any wrong-doing, you could still wind up in the frame. Secondly, because a special meeting almost always led to special measures, which, in short, meant that someone was going to cop it. People copped it all the time in this game, quite often on Frank McCracken's instructions, if, for example, they were non-Crew affiliates who'd failed or refused to pay their tax. But there was a certain stratum in the British underworld, which contained men who, while not necessarily untouchable, were deemed to be figures of influence and authority; even the Crew had to be careful how it handled some of these guys, because they too could summon muscle.

It was not that the Crew didn't think they could win any war that might break out; they always had, and always would. But there'd inevitably be disruption. Normal business would be interfered with, cash flow would falter, and the more the conflict spilled into the open, the more likely it was to attract the interest of the police.

Not that the latter hadn't already happened to a certain degree.

In truth, as he'd explained to Cora, McCracken was

already troubled by the way this thing was going. The challenge to their authority was unexpected, admittedly, and the financial losses, while not grievous, were painful. But the response had been cack-handed, in his view. He was beginning to wonder if their august Chairman was finally losing it.

'A church?' McCracken said, as they negotiated the lunchtime traffic around Piccadilly.

'Yeah,' Shallicker replied from behind the wheel. 'Yesterday afternoon.'

'You mean she was going to a service? I mean, I know her mum goes, but Lucy . . .?'

'Don't think it was that. Nobby says she was only in there fifteen minutes.'

'Where was this?'

'St Clement's, Hatchwood Green.'

McCracken sank back into his Bentley's leather-upholstered rear seat. 'Shithole area. Probably been a break-in, yeah? Just doing normal detective stuff?'

'That's what I thought.'

'She hadn't by any chance clocked Nobby and was basically ripping the piss?'

'No way,' Shallicker said. 'He didn't see who she spoke to, but she was only in there quarter of an hour . . .'

'Okay.' McCracken pondered, but ultimately found nothing overly fascinating in what he'd so far learned about his daughter's movements. 'So that's it, then? Nothing else odd?'

'Nah . . .' Shallicker broke off to swing the car across the busy road and veer sharp right, the grilled gate to the Astarte's underground car park rolling upward to admit them. They cruised down a curving concrete ramp. 'In and out the nick, going seeing people round town. Standard cop business. You know Leon Royton got pinched?'

'Yeah, I heard,' McCracken said.

'Seems your Lucy was the arresting officer, but only because she was out and about and she got sent to the incident. She wasn't investigating him for anything.'

'You're fucking joking . . . our Lucy managed to pinch Leon Royton?'

'She's a chip off the old block, Frank.'

McCracken didn't reply.

Ever since he'd discovered that the daughter he'd always known he had but had never seen (except in a photo taken when she was sixteen) had become a police officer, he'd walked an uneasy line. Frank McCracken had never considered himself a family man, primarily because his own family had been the worst kind of low-level, alcohol-addicted, perennially underachieving Salford criminals, whose loser influence he'd divested himself of at the first opportunity. But also because, back during his younger years, his mean looks and strong physique, and his ruthless gangster energy had enabled him to wade through a sea of prostrate beauties – something he'd done ever since, in truth, even now, into his mid-fifties. Though Cora, the only one to get pregnant, might have meant a little more to him than most, her determination to leave him once she knew she was having a child was the kind of defiance he rarely faced, and so had intrigued him even more. But her and her child's departure from his world had only aided and abetted his promiscuous lifestyle all the more. As such, he'd never made an emotional connection with either of them, and in fact had completely lost track of them. So, it shouldn't have mattered last year, when he'd heard that his daughter wasn't just a copper these days, but an undercover detective, and that she was getting in deep with the Twisted Sisters, a pair of brothel queens and Crew associates who would kill you as soon as sniff at you. It really shouldn't have. But for reasons he still couldn't fathom,

Frank McCracken had in due course assisted her rather than allowed for her to be rubbed out.

Why he'd done that, he still didn't know.

Ever since then, McCracken had pestered himself with the question: *Am I a family man after all?*

At present, both he and Lucy existed in a sort of limbo, in a permanently uneasy truce which lasted only because what they knew about each other could be mutually fatal to their careers. No police detective could be trusted by her colleagues if it was known that her father was an underworld bigwig. Likewise, no underworld bigwig could expect to maintain his status if word got out that his daughter was a hotshot copper.

But Lucy didn't make things easy, he thought.

If only she'd remained a plod, going through everyday routines, nabbing shoplifters, telling kids to stop riding bikes on the pavement. That would have been okay, it would have hurt no one. But, instead, Lucy was a bloodhound, a real hunter-killer; she was out to knuckle every name on the list, making it very clear to him the last time they'd spoken – in rather harsh terms, given that he was her father – that he was on that list too, and that the best way for him to avoid trouble lay in him avoiding her.

Not one of these conciliatory coppers, his Lucy.

Yet again, as he increasingly did these days, McCracken wondered just how long this fragile arrangement could last.

'The main thing is,' he said, 'we haven't seen her with any of these Robbery Squad goons?'

They'd now parked up in an empty bay close to the lifts. Shallicker applied the handbrake and switched the engine off. 'None of the ones we know,' he said. 'My gut instinct is she's just doing ordinary CID stuff . . . but even if she wasn't, what would it tell us?'

'I don't know. I'm scrabbling around in the dark here, Mick. We all fucking are.'

They climbed out of the car, all talk of Lucy now suspended because Nick Merryweather was crossing the car park towards them, with two of his own heavies in tow.

Whereas McCracken represented the smoother face of the syndicate, the sharp suit and handsome features, but also the wit and wisdom to be charming and diplomatic, Nick Merryweather, the Crew's whoremaster-in-chief, fulfilled the more traditional stereotype. The brutish outline, shaven head, sunken eyes and leery smile could only belong to an organised crime figure. If that didn't convince anyone, his nickname, Necktie Nicky, ought to, referring, as it did, to his preferred method of despatching opponents: slicing the throat and pulling the tongue out so that it hung down the chest.

'Frank,' he said.

'Nick,' McCracken replied.

They entered the lift together. Shallicker unlocked a steel panel with a special key, and hit the button that would take them express-fashion to the top floor.

'Bill's fucking fuming,' Merryweather said, as they accelerated upward.

'I wonder why,' McCracken replied.

'I wouldn't like to be Benny B.'

'Agreed,' McCracken nodded. 'For lots of reasons. Thick bastard's made things fifty times worse by offering that reward.'

Despite this, on the top floor they were greeted by a cordon of Benny B's security men, who patted them down as was customary at board meetings – not just for weapons, but for recording devices too.

Once this was done, and all minders and bodyguards had been directed into the lounge-bar for a beer and a cold lunch, the underbosses were passed through into the boardroom itself, where a 'no alcohol' rule was in force until business had been concluded.

In total, there were fourteen seats around a long table of polished teak. Excluding those reserved for the Chairman of the Board and for his Secretary and number two, Lennie Trueman, a West Indian guy by origin and one of only two non-whites on the board, but someone who, having delivered almost the entirety of the Liverpool docks on first being recruited, not to mention a considerable portion of the black muscle in both Liverpool and Manchester, had unquestionably earned his lofty position.

Aside from McCracken and Merryweather, the rest of the seats would be occupied by: Larry Harris, who controlled all the firm's loan-sharking businesses; Tom DeSouza, whose remit was cyber-crime and credit card fraud; Adam Gilcrist, who provided firearms to the rest of the underworld; Luke Haynes, who ran all numbers and gambling rackets; Al Reed, whose role was the protection of legit businesses (as opposed to criminal enterprises); Jon Killarny, counterfeiting; Terry Underwood, contraband; Lou Weaver, fencing; and last, but very far from least, East African-born former pirate and smuggler, Toni Zambala, who controlled all the syndicate's narcotic-related interests (if Frank McCracken was seen as an honest achiever among Crew lieutenants, Toni Zambala was the star player; his weekly contributions to company funds often overshadowed all the rest of them put together). One final seat was reserved for Benny B, who, aside from the Chairman and his Secretary, was the only Crew member not expected to produce profits, his role being Head of Security.

As they gathered one by one, they chatted idly, sipping mineral water, but all with at least half an eye on the frosted glass wall partitioning the boardroom from the Chairman's private office, where it looked as if several figures were moving around, their conversation carrying through in low mumbles.

At one o'clock sharp, the office door opened, and Pentecost and Trueman came through alone, closing the door behind them. The Chairman, the eternal grey man, wore his usual grey suit, which of course matched his eyes and his lips and his hair and the steel rims of his square-framed glasses. Trueman, a little on the old side now and heavy-set, his thick, crinkly hair also running to grey, went for similarly sharply tailored suits, though in his case he preferred the flamboyant greens, blues and reds of his youth.

They took their usual places at the head of the table, and a frosty silence reigned. Finally, after sipping some water, Pentecost stood up.

'Afternoon,' he said in his usual emotionless monotone. 'I'm guessing you all know why you're here, but let's cut to the chase anyway. To be frank . . . whoever this fucking Red-Headed League are, their fun in the sun is about to end. At least, it had fucking well better.'

He paused to let that sink in, to let his underlings realise, if they didn't before, that such liberties as these bandits were taking reflected almost as much on those empowered to stop them but failing, as it did on the villains themselves.

'You know my normal position,' Pentecost said. 'I've always had a soft spot for enterprising lads. And I don't mind terribly if certain so-called associates of ours find themselves up against it from time to time. Flash Andy was a case in point. He thought he was a face, but in reality, of course, a total fuckhead. Don't get me wrong, it stank what happened, and we put the word out for info . . . and if we'd got a quick line on who was responsible, I've no doubt we'd have made an example of them by now. However, the money-drop lost yesterday puts this problem into a different league altogether.'

He paused, his narrowly glazed eyes roving across them. 'The bottom line is, gentlemen . . . you steal from our associates, you steal from us. But that's just about tolerable to me if you're punting for a job, or if you're willing to put yourself forward straight away after and offer the usual restitution. But when you steal *from* us, as in right out of *our* pocket . . . well, that's something else altogether.'

Another long pause followed, during which his audience brooded as effectively as they possibly could, faces fixed like gravestones, no one daring to do so much as twitch or fidget.

McCracken pondered what he knew about the previous day's robbery.

It seemed that the cash delivery had been hit on a quiet country lane on the outskirts of Knutsford. It had followed the same pattern as the hit on Andy Northwood's pad: two bandits wearing red masks and wielding sub-machine guns, which Sam Brodie, an ex-army man, had pegged as SIG-Sauer MPXs, the sort of high-tech military hardware that was not commonly found on the streets of the UK. Both the couriers had been shot in the legs even after the cash had been handed over. No one had died this time, because no one had behaved in the same braindead fashion as Flash Andy. But it had still been a pretty sadistic move. The blaggers had done the deed in a wooded area a few yards off the road – they'd certainly plotted the ambush point carefully – and had then simply abandoned their badly wounded victims.

Inadvertently, this ruthless professionalism had helped the Crew, because though taking the target out of sight had clearly been a measure designed to prevent passers-by stopping, and either interfering or maybe, if they'd arrived a little later, assisting the casualties, it had also meant the cops hadn't got there before a Crew clean-up unit had. Both the couriers had had their mobile phones stolen, but there was a radio console inside the van, from which Brodie, hard-ass para to the end, had managed to call for help – after crawling over there with his legs mangled almost to stumps, and heaving himself up into the cab using his arms alone. His heroism wouldn't go unrewarded; he'd be on a company pension for the rest of his life, but it wouldn't console him for the loss of his legs, at least one of which had needed to be amputated.

And nothing was going to console Wild Bill Pentecost.

Okay, the Chairman of the Board hadn't been known as 'Wild Bill' since his youth. He'd strictly forbidden his underlings even to think of him in those terms, quietly advising them that his cowboy days were long behind him. But McCracken couldn't help wondering if they were shortly to see a resumption of all that.

Butchering the Crew's loyal employees was one thing. But butchering employees *and* pinching Crew dollars as well? A mark had just been very drastically overstepped.

Pentecost's cold voice interrupted McCracken's thoughts.

'I see a whole range of blank expressions in front of me,' he said. 'Like a bunch of schoolboys who've been too busy ogling their sexy maths teacher's arse to listen to her lesson. Like you fellas don't have a fucking clue what's going on. Well . . . I'll tell you what's going on. We've got some bad boys on the patch. A regular bunch of renegades. And you lot – my eyes and ears in the world – have no clue who they are, or where they are, or where they've come from, or when the fuck they're going to stop, if they ever do.' He unexpectedly switched his gaze to McCracken. 'Nothing from *you*, Frank? I hear your department particularly lost out during this latest blag.'

'That's true, Bill,' McCracken replied simply.

And it was. Until about a month ago, McCracken had been pulling in some scores. At least ninety grand of the one hundred and fifty lost during the recent drop had come from *his* operation. Pentecost waited for more, but none was forthcoming.

265

'So that's it?' he finally said. 'You shrug your shoulders and get on with life? Not three days ago, you told me that you were going to look into this personally.'

McCracken straightened in his chair. 'I'll be honest, Bill . . . I think we've gone about this the wrong way.'

There was an even longer pause than previously.

'*We*, Frank?' Pentecost wondered. 'Or *me*?'

'We,' McCracken said. 'We're all in this together . . . that's why I'm not taking yesterday's losses personally.'

'Perhaps you can elaborate on "wrong way"?'

'For what it's worth,' McCracken said, 'I think you're dead right to assume this is a bunch of cowboys trying their luck. These are good-sized blags, but I don't see any pattern to it. They're hitting targets of convenience.'

'Targets of convenience?'

'Oh, they clearly know where the money is,' McCracken said. 'They've done their research. But everything's a bit crazy, a bit madcap.'

'I have to agree with that,' Benny B spoke up. 'I don't see any Brink's-Mat type planning behind any of this.'

'Nevertheless . . .' Pentecost swivelled round to peer accusingly at his fat security chief, 'yesterday alone, they walked away with one-fifty K of our cash. *Ours*, Benny. No one else's.'

Benny B reddened and looked at his knees; he was acutely aware that some of the underbosses were now briefing against him. If he'd let his body go to seed, they were asking, how far behind that was his head? Any more foul-ups like this, and his time spent as Bill Pentecost's personal bodyguard when they were juvenile offenders back in Moston would most likely count for nothing.

'And that's my second point, Bill,' McCracken interjected. 'We shouldn't underestimate them. They're clearly good at this. That's why I think we made an error putting out a general reward for intel. If anything, that's proved counter-productive.'

Benny B, whose idea it had been, cut a sideways look at him. 'You'd have done nothing, I suppose?'

'Well, I wouldn't have invited all the criminals of Manchester to eat each other,' McCracken replied.

'Like you've never beaten the shit out of anyone.'

'The point is,' McCracken said, 'it's brought us nothing but misinformation. You put a big reward out for intel, Benny – intel, not *certainty!* – and all it's just been one big opportunity for a whole raft of lowlifes to get rich quick or pay off some old scores, or both.'

McCracken turned to address the rest of the Board.

'We've had vigilante actions everywhere, lots of names named . . . and nothing viable has come from any of it. Accusations are still flying, old firms who've been at peace for God knows how long have become enemies again. It flies in the face of everything we set this outfit up for. But the real problem is that people are getting hurt – as a result of which the heat from the cops is intensifying. A couple of days ago, we lost one of our most useful soldiers. Leon Royton got a false tip that two blaggers from Crowley, George and Charlie Benton, were responsible for these jobs. Leon and his cronies shouldn't have gone in there kicking and punching. A bit of due diligence by Security . . .' he threw another glance at Benny B, '. . . would've shown that the Bentons were way below the league we're dealing with here. But Leon's paid the price, if no one else has. He got pinched for attempted murder. With his record, that means he'll be off the roster for years. We'll miss him, and as long as this disorganised violence continues, more of us will go the same way . . . and we still won't have found out who this Red-Headed League actually are.'

Pentecost remained as inexpressive as ever. 'Whose remit,

Frank,' he said, 'do you reckon this business falls within?'

'As a security matter, it's mainly down to Benny,' McCracken said. 'But *I'm* the one charged with getting us our share from those firms who won't play by the normal rules, Bill. So, it's on me too.'

Pentecost pursed his lips, apparently waiting for something extra.

'I'm gonna tackle this, okay,' McCracken added. 'In fact, *that's* my proposal: that we cancel the reward offer – so that, first of all, we can rein in all these idiot lynch-mobs running around town. And then let me and Benny pool our resources so we can find out what's going on in more level-headed fashion.'

Pentecost gave him another protracted stare, before replying: 'I actually agree with you, Frank . . . offering a reward has backfired. I came to that decision before you did.'

Benny B looked dumbfounded to hear this.

'I wouldn't have expected anything else, Bill,' McCracken said.

'Well . . . good.'

Pentecost began circling the boardroom, another of his favourite tricks: prowling with steady, soundless steps past the rigid backs and stiff shoulders of each of his minions; on at least one such occasion before now, a switchblade had appeared and two disloyal throats had been swiftly slashed (one time, the arterial spray covered half the table and at least three board members seated opposite).

'The reward was withdrawn this morning,' he continued. 'That's why I'm quite happy for you, Frank, to throw your entire team's weight at this problem. I know you'll play it sensible and low-key. So, I've actually taken an executive decision to pull everyone else back. And I mean *right* back . . . thus clearing the decks for a more direct method.' He returned to his chair, and stood behind it, hands on the backrest, and said loudly: 'You can come in now.'

The office door opened, and a trio of people sidled through it.

'In case anyone here doesn't already know these honoured guests, Benny . . .' Pentecost nodded at Benny B, 'perhaps you can enlighten them?'

'Erm, yeah . . . absolutely.' Benny B got to his feet and turned theatrically to the rest of the room.

All three of the newcomers, two males and one female, were dressed smartly in suits, but McCracken – who knew them by reputation, if not personally – was well aware that this was only for show, a temporary disguise by which they could occasionally slide out of the shadows and mingle with the ranks of the ordinary and the sane.

The man on the immediate left was known simply – or so Benny B said – as 'Bojan'. He was about fifty-years-old, and despite his heavy physique, broad chest and shoulders, and his bull-thick neck, he didn't look as if he carried much spare. His scalp was clean-shaven, and his face, which was almost too small for his huge head, was leathery and seamed with old scars. His eyes were tiny and apelike, but there was an odd, greenish glitter about them. It was difficult to tell whether his cruel smirk was a permanent fixture due to some old wound, or a mark of undisguised contempt for the gallery of English gangland lieutenants confronting him. Benny B introduced him as a Serbian-born former spec-ops captain who had served in the Yugoslav war of the late 1990s with 'a specialist urban commando unit called Arkan's Tigers'. If McCracken remembered rightly, Arkan's Tigers had chiefly been notable for the gang rapes they indulged in and their massacres of innocent civilians, but why quibble over details? This trio hadn't been brought here for their sweet and generous natures.

The second one, the woman, was called 'Jocasta', and she was the least familiar to McCracken. She was somewhere in her mid-thirties and clearly of Māori or Polynesian origin. Very handsome, but aggressively so; big-framed, with a statuesque build, dark eyes, strong bone structure, lush black hair done up with carved tribal ornaments, and exotic tattoos adorning her hands, neck, chin and cheeks (and presumably the rest of her). Benny outlined her credentials, which were almost as impressive as her looks. Jocasta was a former 'sergeant-at-arms and a prime shooter' for the legendary Highway 61 motorcycle gang in Wellington, New Zealand. When someone asked why she was over here in the UK, Benny B replied that it might be a while before she could reconcile with her former 'bikie' pals, given that the last time she was Down Under, she'd wiped three of them out in an argument over beer.

The final guest who wore a vaguely loopy grin, was known only as 'Ramirez'. He was perhaps less eye-catching than the other two, being tall, lean and though 'rocking the Jesus look', as McCracken had once heard it described – which meant that he had longish locks, very dark in colour, possibly dyed, and a similarly dark beard and moustache – it was all neat and trimmed, and his hair tied back in a ponytail. Unusually for someone in this particular line of work, he sported no ink, but even so, at this proximity, he gave off an eerie vibe. His smile looked fixed, his eyes hollow and empty – he was like a dead man, a papier-mâché effigy that you might see in Mexico City on *Día de Muertos*. And in many ways, that was quite apt, because Ramirez had previously been a hired gun who had worked for various Mexican cartels, clocking up a phenomenal score card of victims.

Like Jocasta, Ramirez was now in Europe because it had finally got too hot for him back home, in his case because the DEA was on his tail, alongside several dozen vengeful *sicarios*.

As contract killers went, McCracken had seen less conspicuous characters. Even dressed as they were today, as though for formal but routine business, he doubted they could walk down a single street in Manchester, either individually or together, without drawing second glances. But then they were only here for the take-down. The groundwork would mostly be done by his and Benny B's departments, who knew their way around town; the kill-team would come in for the endgame – which would be a kind of relief. These red-headed blaggers weren't playing; it was going to take heavy firepower and a brutal willingness to use it in order to counteract them.

Once Benny B had completed his introductions, Pentecost took charge again.

'I haven't called this assistance in because I don't think we can do this job in-house,' he said tonelessly. 'This is not some indirect criticism of our own people, though I *am* disappointed in the way things have gone up to now. But the plain fact is . . . we all have other jobs to do, without getting distracted, and without risking that we get into the sort of shooting war that could see a whole lot more of us doing time. But this matter needs taking care of, nevertheless. And this threesome will do it. As from this moment, they are fully authorised to use any methods they deem fit to locate these renegades and completely eradicate them. The rest of you, with the exception of you, Frank, and you, Benny – for reasons we've already outlined – can go back to the world and do the job that pays you, and us, so handsomely. And do it better than you normally do, by the way. We've got some lost earnings to make up for.'

And that was it. Without so much as an invite to pop into the lounge-bar for a bit of lunch and/or something to drink, the underbosses were summarily dismissed. They shuffled out quietly, without looking back at the kill-team, who waited alongside the Chairman and the Secretary, and Benny B, of course – who seemed even more diminished than usual in such celebrity company – and watched everyone depart. McCracken was the last to go.

'Problem, Frank?' Pentecost wondered.

McCracken glanced back, pointedly not meeting any of the six glassy-eyed stares directed at him. 'None whatsoever, Bill.'

Chapter 29

As always, the CCTV image was infuriatingly indistinct, but as Lucy watched it again and again on her laptop, she increasingly felt that she was making ground. Perhaps only incrementally, but it was ground nevertheless.

The snippet comprised two and a half minutes of film, black and white, fuzzy, constantly pixelating – all the usual nasties that accompanied modern surveillance footage (unlike the hi-def, full-colour, crystal-clear, super-zoomable versions that you saw on movies and TV shows). But there was no denying that what she was looking at, when she viewed it, was someone in a hooded winter waterproof with the hood drawn up, crossing Langley Street on the night of October 29, and placing a square-looking package on the steps to a formerly grand but now dilapidated entranceway. He then ambled away with hands in pockets, walking across the street, possibly towards the vehicle that had brought him there, which inconveniently was parked out of frame.

On first glance, without having facts to hand, it wouldn't tell you anything. But Lucy, who'd been busy all the previous evening and this morning, had now accrued quite a few facts, and more importantly, thanks to her interview with Father

O'Donnell yesterday afternoon, had started chaining them together.

First of all, she'd made further enquiries with other charitable institutions in Crowley, and it had soon paid dividends. It seemed that in several cases, similarly unsolicited gifts of cash and even jewellery had been delivered to the doors of the needy during the hours of darkness. The recipients included Crowley Family Welfare, the Action on Poverty drop-in centre, Crowley Young Carers, and the Methodist Mission Hall close to the Crowley Emporia, the town's main shopping centre. Will Raglan, one of the helpers down at the Mission, had informed Lucy that he'd heard about similar anonymous donations being made to homeless people – they'd literally been sleeping rough in underpasses or on park benches, and had found the presents waiting alongside them when they woke – and even to private addresses: homes and flats where vulnerable pensioners lived, or where impoverished single mothers were struggling with tribes of rumbustious kids.

This latter suggested to Lucy that it was not just random generosity; it was being targeted, which meant that whoever was behind it had done some serious homework.

In the light of all this, she hadn't felt especially great about continuing to investigate. No crime was evident here. But when she'd heard that Sally Skegg, the bag-lady of Broadgate Green, had walked into a shelter not two nights ago, wearing an emerald and sapphire-studded bracelet, which the staff on duty had estimated must be worth several thousand pounds, it became screamingly obvious that something about this wasn't right. The jewellery itself, which in normal circumstances would have given Lucy her most obvious lead, added nothing; mainly, because in all cases it had gone to private individuals – more homeless, more transients – who had almost certainly sold it on by now, or who, as Sally was currently proving, would be difficult to trace. The institutions themselves had only received cash, the sums varying from a few hundred quid to batches of several thousand. However, the Methodist Mission Hall, the beneficiary of the most generous donation to date – £18,000 crammed into an old shoebox – maintained a single security camera over its front door, and after paying them a visit, Lucy had come away with a copy of the CCTV footage from October 29 on a pen drive. It was this that she was now watching, having further copied it onto her laptop.

It fascinated her to think that the figure depositing the shoebox of cash was almost certainly the same person who'd been donating these expensive gifts across the borough. But that wasn't the only fascinating factor.

Because something else had now cropped up.

Near the end of the snippet, just before the hooded figure vanished from sight, it glanced around, partially in the direction of the camera. Almost certainly, it was unintentional; the guy hadn't realised it was there, and he looked away again just as quickly, so only a glimpse was to be had of his face, but it was sufficient to show . . . fabric.

Lucy watched it perhaps for the fiftieth time. And there was no mistake.

Under this man's hood, he was wearing what looked like a woollen face mask.

A ski mask.

She shook her head as she tried to think this thing through.

It was hardly a smoking gun. It didn't necessarily connect him to Andy Northwood's killers, and with the footage in black and white, she couldn't tell whether that mask was red or not – which was the ultimate frustration. But it was surely worth looking into, especially with other factors slowly coming into play. Without holding any of it in her hand, it was impossible to tell which of the items of jewellery

275

purportedly seen in possession of the town's vagrants might be stolen, but the gem-studded bracelet allegedly spotted on Sally Skegg's wrist had not matched anything recently reported – that was a complete conundrum, unless you considered that it might have been part of the jewellery stolen from the sex workers during the raid on Andy Northwood's house. They'd fled the scene straight afterwards. The house was awash with cocaine at the time, and they likely had form for drug use, or were on parole and such. And this could be the same reason they hadn't reported their missing valuables.

Lucy gave an exasperated sigh.

Okay, when she tried to lay it out like that, it felt tenuous; it was still possible that it was all coincidence. She needed more before she could take this to DI Blake and tell her that she thought she'd caught one of their killers on CCTV.

Which was why she was here now.

She'd been parked on the brick-strewn lot of the boarded-up social club off Hollycroft Lane for the best part of an hour. It was one o'clock in the afternoon. She'd hoped and expected to find her target out and about, in which case she'd simply have driven up alongside him and told him to get into her car. But if he didn't turn up soon, she'd have no option but to knock on his front door, no matter what his objections.

She was looking for Jerry McGlaglen, and this was his home housing estate, though in truth it was little more than a single loop of council properties, with barren slag heaps to the north and west, and Borsdane Wood to the south.

McGlaglen lived at 49, Hollycroft Lane, which was only three or four houses away from where she was parked, so when she suddenly noticed that he'd emerged from the house without her realising, and was already a hundred yards away, she decided that she'd let herself get too distracted by the CCTV.

It was definitely McGlaglen. The distant figure wore a heavy blue overcoat with a Victorian-style cape, and a scarf, but was mainly distinctive for its tall outline and the grey feather-duster mop where its hair should be.

Lucy shoved the laptop and pen-drive into the driver's door pocket, hit the ignition and put her Jimny in gear. She'd only gone thirty yards before the tall figure turned down a ginnel, but knew where this would take him.

McGlaglen wouldn't like her following him, but they were past the stage where he was calling the shots. If she wanted to advance her career, it was time to change the nature of the relationship she had with her most productive informant.

The Robbery Squad seemed like the obvious next step for her. She liked the people in there (with the obvious exception of Gaskin), and she felt she had an aptitude for it. It was merely a matter of proving that, and if she managed to confirm that she was onto something here in relation to Andy Northwood's murder, it could only help. Whether McGlaglen could provide that confirmation, she just didn't know. He was a very useful grass. She and Harry had only been allocated to him half a year ago, when one of the older divisional detectives, his former long-term handler, had retired. But he'd already proved his worth, passing them numerous valuable tips. The problem was that he worked at his own pace, and that was becoming difficult. Lucy couldn't keep on hanging around, waiting for the next time he fancied dropping something her way. And it wasn't just the current case. From here on in general, she'd decided to be more proactive with him.

She pulled off Hollycroft Lane onto the main road and travelled two hundred yards, before veering right onto the parking area alongside The Horseshoe Inn. This was one of those outskirts pubs that were only open these days if they led a charmed life. When rows of terraced pit-cottages had dominated this barren landscape, it had doubtless done a roaring trade, but now the cottages were all gone. The only custom it could draw were locals from the Hollycroft estate, which wasn't the most moneyed in the borough, hence its low-slung roof of moss-eaten slate, its basic red-brick exterior and shabby, overgrown beer garden.

Inside the pub, which was empty save for one or two elderly male drinkers, she found McGlaglen alone in a nook. He hadn't removed either his coat or scarf, and was nursing a pint of mild as he leafed half-interestedly through a crumpled copy of the *Daily Mirror*.

'Hoped I'd find you,' she said.

He glanced up at her, his face falling with remarkable speed. 'I . . . I . . . what on earth are you doing *here*?'

'I've come for a drink,' she said cheerily. 'What'll you have?'

'But I didn't invite you.' His face blanched as he looked nervously around the pub.

'I'm a big girl, Jerry. I don't need invites to visit public houses.' She turned towards the bar, where a brassy-looking woman with white-blonde hair, big earrings and an even bigger cleavage, was mopping the counter. 'Half a Diet Coke please, ta.' The barmaid nodded and moved away. 'Sure you don't want anything, Jerry?'

He nailed her with one of his more theatrical gazes. 'This is a breach of every protocol we ever agreed.'

Lucy looked around, seeing only those few desultory drinkers. 'There's no one else here.'

'Good Lord in Heaven.' He raised his newspaper and sank down behind it. 'Just because we can't see them, that doesn't mean they can't see us.'

Lucy came back with her cola, and drew up a stool.

'You ought to have realised the previous way we did things was too good to last,' she said.

'For heaven's sake,' he hissed. 'What have I done to deserve this?'

278

'Nothing. You always deliver. You're a good snout.'

At which his eyes widened – though not the left one, she noticed, which was discoloured around the socket. 'In heaven's name, woman . . . no one is supposed to know that!'

'Chill out.' She sipped her drink. 'They'll just think I'm some lass who fancies you.'

'Well, yes, obviously . . . because that happens all the time.'

'Tell them I'm your daughter.'

'Miss Clayburn, this is not . . .' He lowered his voice to a hoarse whisper. *'This is not a fucking game!'*

It was the first time she'd ever heard profanity from him, so he clearly *was* upset.

'No, you're right, Jerry.' She too lowered her voice. 'It really isn't. That's why I haven't got time to sit around the nick, waiting on another cryptic email. Not anymore.'

This was too much for the normally affable informant, who stood bolt upright and walked from the pub, struggling to conceal a limp as he did.

Lucy finished her drink. She wasn't being especially kind, doing this to him; that was plain. But it was too easy to let McGlaglen's flowery words and gentlemanly manner create the impression that he was a better kind of person than all the other CIs she'd used. If he was actually different from those other rascals, he wouldn't even be in this line of work. Snouts and grasses were among the least savoury characters the police dealt with. They only ever passed information when they stood to gain. It worked in the police's favour, enabling them to snag or at least become aware of criminals whose activities they might not otherwise have known about, but by its nature – bearing in mind that these were often people the grass knew personally – it indicated just how ruthless such individuals could be. Jerry McGlaglen might pass for a harmless old eccentric, but it would be a mistake to fall for that.

Outside, she found him seated under the shelter of the turning circle that marked the local bus terminus. Uninvited, she sat next to him.

'Christ, woman.' But he sounded tired rather than angry. 'What in hell do you want?'

'Relax, Jerry, okay? No one on this manor knows I'm a copper. Course, if you keep acting like someone's jammed a garden rake up your arse, they'll probably put two and two together.'

He tried to stand up and walk away again. But instead, he gave a gasp of pain and was forced to sit back down. As well as the bruising around his eye and the limp he'd tried to hide, Lucy noticed that a grubby bandage, rather amateurishly applied, swathed his left wrist.

'What happened to you?' she asked.

He sighed. 'Several . . . shall we say, *troubled* individuals happened to be waiting for me outside a hostelry in the centre of town the other night. They gave me . . . I understand the appropriate phrase is "a going-over", calling me a "nonce" and a "poofter" as they did so.'

'Are you saying it was a hate crime? If so, I can take the report now. We'll investigate.'

'It was not a hate crime, Miss Clayburn, because I am well-known around Crowley as being neither of those things.'

'So . . . it was really about your grassing, yeah?'

A car drove past, and he furtively covered his face. 'There are some who know what I do. Perhaps that is inevitable. Until now, it has never had consequences for me. They use me . . . much as you do. But now . . .' he narrowed his eyes, squinting into a distinctly unpromising future, 'something has changed.'

'Did these scumbags say anything else?' Lucy asked. 'Apart from the name-calling.'

'They required information. About several recent incidents.'

'And?'

'I gave them nothing because I knew nothing. I had no clue what they were talking about.'

'What were the incidents?'

'I honestly can't remember. I was, of course, distracted at the time.'

'Well . . . if you don't know anything about any recent or upcoming crimes, do you know anything about donations to charity? Big ones.'

Even McGlaglen, whose poker face was one of the best, glanced curiously round at her.

'Believe it or not, someone's been making charitable donations all around town,' she said. 'And I mean massive. We're talking thousands of quid.'

He gazed at her long and hard. 'Miss Clayburn, I sincerely hope you have not endangered my covert status to ask questions like this? When am I supposed to have become associated with the inner workings of charitable institutions?'

'I strongly suspect the money's stolen.'

'Ahhh . . . well in that case, things are somewhat easier. The felon responsible goes around town in a green hood and carries a bow and arrow. He has a big man with him too. Oh, and a fat monk.'

'I suppose I asked for that, you only being mates with *real-life* thieves and murderers. But I had to try, Jerry, because it's got me bamboozled. Anything you *do* hear, though . . .?' She stood up to leave. 'Can I give you a lift into town? I'm headed that that way.'

'The offer is appreciated, but the answer must be obvious.'

'Okay . . . one thing before I go.'

He rolled his eyes with exaggerated worry.

'These jobs you were asked about . . . by the lads who gave you the kicking. They weren't blags, by any chance?'

'As I've already told you . . .'

'Jerry, you've told me nothing that's of use . . . which I understand is your normal policy if you don't think you're going to earn from it. But that's no good to me . . . so it's time to change the terms of our arrangement. Now, I don't believe I'm putting you in any real danger out here . . . there's no one about. But by my reckoning, the one o'clock from Crowley will be here soon, and there are bound to be a few people get off it, who will almost certainly see you talking to me. So, it's going to suit you to talk fast. The other thing I don't believe is that these guys beat you up and asked you questions so obscure that you can't even remember them.'

He regarded her for a long time, his mouth screwed shut.

This was a different Jerry McGlaglen from the one she'd grown to know. He was frightened, evidently; whoever had beaten him, it had made him realise that, however well he thought he'd protected his real role in this world, there was no such thing as perfect secrecy.

'You're obviously aware,' Lucy said, 'that there've been several violent crimes in Crowley recently? People like you, low-level players, getting kickings for no obvious reason.'

'It is, as they say, a rough old place.'

'The list of victims includes the Benton brothers. And we all know what their speciality is.'

Again, he said nothing.

'None of this could be connected to my case, could it?'

'Oh, I doubt it, Miss Clayburn. Charity and the Crew don't generally go together.'

'You're telling me all this violence is coming from the Crew?'

'Or on their behalf,' he said. 'Or so I've heard. And yes . . . the offences I was questioned about while those hoodlums used my torso for football practice, were armed hold-ups of the Jesse James variety.'

'And the Crew were the victims?'

'I fear I've already said too much.' A car passed by, and McGlaglen averted his face.

'Look, Jerry . . . I can leave you in peace right now, but your problem won't go away. Whoever did you over, they've obviously got you marked as someone who knows stuff. Is it really going to make any difference if you spill the beans? They're bound to come and see you again. And again, and again . . .'

'I – have – no – details – Miss Clayburn!' he shouted. 'Hence the prolonged beating I received.'

She pointedly didn't blink at his tirade, her eyes never leaving his unusually florid face. In time, he was the one who looked away.

'My deduction can only be . . .' he made a hapless gesture, 'that certain associates of the Crew have been robbed in recent days. I have no knowledge who the perpetrators are . . . I had no clue these crimes had even been committed. The rest you know.'

'You were right before when you said this isn't a game, Jerry. One life's already been lost, and several others have come close. We need to deal with it at an official level.'

'It's not just that I *can't* help you, Miss Clayburn. I *won't* help you.'

'Jerry . . . gangs of crims are not going to run around this town doing whatever they want. Now give me something I can take to the bank . . . start by coming to the nick and making a statement about the assault you suffered. If we can pull those tosspots in, we can at least start cracking down on this wave of retaliatory violence.'

'Miss Clayburn, if the Crew learn that I have been talking to you . . . you can count the days I'll have left on one of your dainty little hands.'

'Jerry . . . the way I see it, you need to do anything you can to get these monkeys off your back. So, if you don't want to help me run their bully boys in, perhaps help me to help them. Give me something on these robbers who are targeting their interests.'

Still he said nothing.

'Alternatively, of course, we could start looking at you as an accomplice.'

Even the new browbeaten Jerry McGlaglen looked shocked by this. 'To what, may I ask?'

'How about murder? Flash Andy Northwood? If you know his killers and won't turn them in, how else are we supposed to regard you?'

'You think I wouldn't have given up the murderers' names if I'd known them when those scoundrels were beating the living faeces out of me?'

'Okay . . . how about the murders that haven't yet happened? The ones the Crew will end up committing if they don't get their own way?'

He shook his head wearily. 'I honestly know nothing.'

'At least tell me who the other victims were . . . the other people who've been robbed, I mean. I know you, Jerry . . . you've *always* got your ear to the grapevine.'

'None of this must be official,' he finally said. 'I mean it, Miss Clayburn, no payment, no paperwork . . . none of this has come from me, you understand?'

'I understand.'

'There is an unlicensed money lender in Crowley. A man known simply as "the Shank".'

That sounded vaguely familiar to Lucy, but she couldn't place it.

'I have no knowledge of his real name,' McGlaglen said. 'But it seems that he was handled in the same rough way as Andrew Northwood. Whoever these villains are, they divested him of property, they savaged him . . .'

'Did they kill him?'

284

'I know only what I heard as I lay in that gutter. My assailants wanted information about . . .' and he switched into broad Mancunian, '"them two blags . . . the one at Flash fucking Andy's place, and the one on the Shank".'

'Where can I find this Shank?' Lucy asked.

'Thanks to your regular offices, I have never needed to avail myself of his services. Sadly, all that may now change.'

He huddled into his coat as wind hissed on the grey hummocks of the slag heaps. In the weak November light, he looked pale and wasted.

Clearly this was all he could, or was prepared, to tell her. Lucy decided there was no point dragging things out any further for either of them. At least she had *something* to go on.

'You sure I can't run you into town?' she wondered.

McGlaglen chuckled. 'Forgive me if the appeal of Crowley's various watering holes is now somewhat tarnished in my eyes.'

She turned on her heel.

'Miss Clayburn!'

She glanced back.

He regarded her with sudden curiosity. 'These acts of charity you referred to . . . are they connected to these crimes?'

She shrugged. 'How can I say? You know everything I know.'

'You mention them in the same breath as this wave of attacks against the Crew's interests . . . what else should I conclude?'

'If I'd made the connection, myself, I wouldn't be coming to you, would I?'

He didn't bother to answer that. It wasn't as if such information would be much use with his current problems. He'd previously managed to convince himself that his performance as an eccentric former actor, most often to be found wandering the town's hostelries, would have somehow preserved him from scrutiny. Now he was probably wondering how long it had been since the genial façade had fooled anyone but himself.

Lucy walked back to her car and climbed in.

She sat and pondered the new intel. In itself it wasn't world-shaking. She might have come here to strong-arm Jerry McGlaglen, but he'd still given her the bare minimum: nothing more than another victim's nickname. Okay, that was possibly all he knew and it wasn't insufficient for her to run with, but it was a clear indication of how resilient McGlaglen and his kind could be. He wouldn't be the first CI to have his cover blown, and though some of them inevitably turned up in unmarked graves, the majority seemed to survive. They were as rank and shifty as fog, and just as difficult to pin down. On which subject, perhaps it was time to make a certain phone call.

'Yeah?' came Kyle Armstrong's voice.

'It's me,' Lucy said.

'Who's me?'

'You know perfectly well, Kyle, so stop farting around.'

'Give us a sec.' Briefly, a murmur of other voices faded as he no doubt walked away from the rest of the gang. 'Okay,' he said quietly, 'what do you want?'

'I'll tell you what . . . that favour you owe me.'

'Which favour's that?'

'Don't try and pretend you're clever, Kyle. Some of the people I'm dealing with at present would clear out your bunch of hairy-arsed pillocks with a sneeze. In fact, most of your illegal earnings probably go to them in tax. Now can we get to it, please?'

'Let me guess . . . you want me to return that imaginary, non-existent, totally fucking unimpressive favour that you so-called did for us?'

'Correct.'

'You're ever hopeful, aren't you?'

'I need anything you've got on a loan shark called the Shank.'

'The Shank? Never heard of him.'

'In that case ask around.'

'We don't have too many dealings with loan sharks.'

Lucy found it difficult to believe such a claim. Half the Low Riders were on the dole, half in menial work – and yet the one credential they needed simply to join the chapter was a voracious appetite for drugs, booze and motorbikes, and those were expensive hobbies.

Armstrong spoke again, cutting across her thoughts. 'Any of our lot needs cash, we take care of it in-house.'

Lucy supposed that she *could* believe that. As a group, they earned plenty from the proceeds of crime. If any member needed a bit extra, they probably could provide – for a price.

'Just let me know if anyone's ever heard of this Shank guy, Kyle,' she said. 'It may prick some interest and thereby refresh some memories if you put it around that whoever this guy is, he could go out of business as a result of this. That means all the debts he's owed – none of which are legally binding of course – will get written off.'

She cut the call, started the engine and pulled out of the car park onto the main road. Just to her right, McGlaglen still sat alone, a forlorn figure at the otherwise deserted bus stop. He didn't look round at her, as she drove away in the direction of town.

Five minutes later, her phone buzzed as it received a text. Lucy pulled into a layby to check it.

The text, which was from Armstrong, read:

Shank = Roy Shankhill. 38, Rudyard Row
Careful. Total bastard

She didn't bother texting back to say that, from what Jerry McGlaglen had just told her, Roy 'the Shank' Shankhill was unlikely to be much of a problem to anyone anymore.

Chapter 30

'Lucy . . . what are you doing?' It was Kirsty Banks on the hands-free.

Lucy was sitting at a red light when she took the call. 'Following up those burglaries on the Hatchwood,' she replied.

Banks sounded puzzled. 'Haven't we charged Jordan Burke with those breaks?'

'Yeah . . . but there are anomalies.'

'What kind of anomalies?'

The light changed, and Lucy eased forward into the midday traffic. 'Unresolved ownership issues . . . with regard to the property.'

'Lucy, we've got a backlog of violent crimes from the last two or three days alone. At least three or four of them were left in your and Harry's in-tray. And as Harry's not back off sick leave yet, that means they're all yours.'

Harry.

Lucy could have sworn aloud. Okay, he'd been knocked around and he'd needed an overnighter in hospital, but he'd been discharged yesterday. As it was nothing worse than concussion, a more conscientious officer would not now be resting at home, especially given the recent preponderance of crimes to investigate. They'd have come in and got to it. But not Harry. On no . . . Harry being Harry, he'd take every minute he could.

'Lucy, you still there?' Banks said.

'Look, Kirsty . . . I think there may be something more serious going on here. A kind of connection.'

'Sorry, what are you talking about?'

'A connection between these recent violent offences and the burglaries on the Hatchwood.'

A long silence followed while Banks mulled this over.

'All I can say is that Stan's currently hopping around the office,' she finally said. 'He wants this backlog clearing. So, if I tell him what you've just told me . . . can you give me your solemn guarantee that I'm not going to finish up looking a right plonker?'

'I think this link's genuine,' Lucy replied. 'Trouble is no one's going on the record yet.'

'So, I repeat my first question, what exactly are you doing now?'

'I'm chasing up someone who will. I hope.'

'Okay . . .' Banks paused again. 'But just get your backside in gear, Lucy, okay? I'm not going to trust you indefinitely on this.'

Rudyard Row was one of several narrow byways concealed among former industrial buildings in the centre of Crowley that were barely used in the twenty-first century. It didn't lead *to* anywhere or *from* anywhere, and all the time she'd been a cop, Lucy had had no occasion on which to visit it. Even now that she was actively looking for it, she couldn't go there by car, and so had to leave her Jimny on a backstreet in the vicinity of the Emporia.

From here, it was a ten-minute walk, first across the bus

station and then downhill under one of the borough's many railway bridges. At this point, she was already among shabbier retail units – charity shops, tattoo parlours and the like. With the town centre crowds falling behind her, she took a side street, formerly residential but now comprising two terraced rows of boarded-up shells, and at the end of that cut left along the towpath of the Bridgewater Canal. Fifty yards on, she turned right, walking down a cobbled alley which skirted around Trent & Son, a one-time cotton mill now 'under redevelopment', finally turning right again into the little-known defile that was Rudyard Row.

The first problem, which she only became aware of as she progressed along the Row, was how she was going to locate No. 38. Many of the buildings here were not just derelict, there were no numbers on their doors. It was nearly 2.30 in the afternoon, but the further along she travelled, the further back the hubbub of the town centre receded, and the more abandoned she felt this place was. Some of these aged, eerie structures were still occupied – she spotted an occasional light in an upper window, and fleetingly, from behind a half-open gate in a wall with barbed wire along the top, she heard the distorted cacophony of a too-loud radio, the sort of thing you heard when there were workmen on the premises. But even that diminished as she advanced, until, some fifty yards later, she couldn't hear anything.

The only movement that caught her eye came when she passed a slice of sky between two tall buildings on her right, the lower section of which was bisected by the Archways, a Victorian-age viaduct carrying the Manchester-to-Southport railway. A blue-green, five-carriage caterpillar was currently trundling across it.

A few yards further on, she reached her destination.

The tell-tale numbers were no longer attached to the door, but there was sufficient scaly paintwork remaining to show the outlines where they had once been. The door itself had been damaged: one jamb, presumably where locks had once been fitted, had half-splintered from the wall, and it now hung ajar on a dingy, bare-looking interior.

Lucy pushed the door open.

In front of her, a three-legged stool lay on its side amid crumpled news pages. Beyond that, an uncarpeted stair rose out of sight, to the right of which a side passage led into pitch-blackness.

Ordinarily, Lucy did not like entering any premises unannounced or without authority. But she'd been informed that a crime had occurred here, and she could see from the state of the door that some kind of violence had been done, and so, thanks to the Police and Criminal Evidence Act, which permitted her to enter property to prevent harm or injury, she was covered legally. But, in terms of announcing herself, well – as she was alone, it felt better not to on this occasion. The other option, of course, would be to call for assistance, but that wouldn't leave her looking good if this lead turned out to be nothing.

She ventured forward cautiously, opting to explore the ground floor first, passing the foot of the stairs and staring down the corridor that led into the guts of the building.

For a second, she wondered if she'd just heard something – a slight creak of woodwork maybe. But if she had, it had been infinitesimal, and anyway she couldn't hear anything now.

She proceeded, padding thirty yards along bare floorboards, with only peeling plaster walls to either side, before she came to an internal door, which, when she turned the knob, opened smoothly. On the other side, she found a small, very utilitarian kitchen, little more than a closet space really, with a dirty metal sink at one end, its two taps caked in lumps of hardened paint. The cupboard space underneath the sink, which was visible because there was no door on it, contained nothing but dust and mouse droppings. Close by, on a shelf, a kettle was plugged into a power point; two tins – one containing teabags and one instant coffee, sat alongside that, next to a cup of sugar, an opened bottle of milk which had turned green, and a single mug with what, on closer inspection, looked like fungus growing inside it.

All this was just about visible thanks to the dim light spilling through a single, unshaded window. This gave out into what might once have been a rectangular yard, the narrowest Lucy had ever seen – no more than a gap between buildings – and knee-deep in festering rubbish. There was another door in here, connecting to this yard, but even if it was unlocked, there was clearly no point in trying to exit the place that way.

Then she heard another creak. And this one had not been her imagination.

It was louder than the previous one – a long, low groan of aged timbers; the sort of sound you hear from old floorboards when weight is suddenly redistributed.

Quite clearly, it came from overhead.

She moved back down the corridor to the bottom of the stairs, and waited.

Her eyes had now adjusted to the gloom sufficiently to see a trail of spattered but dried fluid leading up the staircase; or down it, depending on your perspective. It was still too dim to determine a colour, but Lucy had no doubt what she was looking at.

The time for creeping around in here was over.

'Is anyone on these premises?' she called up. 'I'm a police officer and I have reason to believe that a crime was committed here which hasn't yet been reported.'

Predictably, there was no response.

Despite the potential riskiness of the situation, Lucy warily ascended.

'I said I'm a police officer!' she called. 'I'm here to see Roy Shankhill.'

Still nothing.

Lucy was now high enough to see a blank wall at the top of the stairs. When she got up there, she glanced left first, but saw only dripping darkness. When she looked right, it was a similar scene to downstairs: bare boards, peeling walls, but at the far end of the passage, a door stood half-open on a room so filled with stark light that she wondered if a bulb was switched on.

She traipsed towards it, treading as lightly as possible. That made no sense with her having already announced herself, but everything about this place felt wrong. Whatever the creak was she'd heard downstairs, she'd heard nothing similar up here, either on this level or from the one above – but the silence that had replaced it was a brooding silence, a listening silence.

As she approached the door, she was tempted to reach for her mobile phone, but painful experience had taught Lucy that if someone was about to attack you, it was best to have *both* hands free.

She pushed the door open – to the accompaniment of no sound from within, and poked her head around the jamb.

Evidently, this had once been an office of sorts. It contained a desk and a chair, and on the floor against the wall, a free-standing electric fire and a small safe sitting open but empty. There was a large window, which was too grubby to see through properly, though it admitted enough daylight to create the impression, at least compared to the rest of the interior, that an electric light had been switched on.

It served another purpose too; it clearly showed the spent shell casings scattering the floor, as well as multiple reddish-brown stains, which even though dried, still had a clotty texture. Lucy looked further, and saw erratic patterns of damage to the walls, the plaster smashed and hanging on strips of bloodstained paper, the exposed brickwork below peppered with circular holes. Bullet holes, clearly, and by their abundance, not to mention the chaotic spread, bullets fired from automatic weapons.

A key rule of crime detection was never to jump to conclusions, but it was difficult not to immediately think of the red-masked, SIG-toting bandits who had killed Andy Northwood. Whatever debris remained of these slugs, when they managed to prise it out of the walls, that would be all the connection they needed. But Lucy couldn't do that herself.

She went back down the corridor to the top of the stairs, feeling in her pocket for her mobile. But before she could place a call, another long, low groan of timber reverberated downward.

She glanced at the exposed laths above.

Old, half-forgotten buildings like this spoke to themselves all the time, but it was obvious that this wasn't what she'd heard. And now she heard it again. And again, and again – until it became a pattern, the regular tremors of which shuddered through the very walls.

Lucy's scalp prickled as she realised she was listening to what sounded like a rocking chair.

She hadn't passed an upper stair on the way to the office where the blood and bullet holes were, so it stood to reason that any access to the rooms above lay in the other direction, beyond that veil of darkness left of the stairway. Common sense, not to mention procedure, screamed at her that she should get out of here, retreat outdoors and call for support. But she resisted it, that old-school conscience kicking in; she wasn't just some concerned citizen, she was a copper, and she had a crime scene to preserve. Not only that, offenders might still be on the premises, and if she simply exited stage left, what was to stop them slipping out another way?

Face taut with tension, nerves like piano strings, she intruded into that darkness at the other end of the corridor. When she activated her phone light, it revealed a floor, walls and ceiling that were black with rot.

When an open doorway appeared on her left, literally from nowhere, she half jumped.

There was no door in its rectangular frame, just an empty blackness, but Lucy shone her light into it, revealing another uncarpeted stair leading upward.

As soon as she put her foot on the bottom tread, the creaking overhead ceased.

That was almost enough to send her into retreat, but damn it, she wouldn't – not when she'd come this far. Steeling herself with the knowledge that backing off now was no solution whatsoever, she climbed to the top, where a circular skylight was covered by several decades of coagulated autumn leaves – but where the light leaking up from downstairs was just sufficient to show another single door standing ajar by about an inch.

Lucy pushed it open – to be confronted by the ultimate garret room; a narrow attic space, its roof slanted as though it was located right under the eaves, and so much longer than it was broad that it was more like a corridor. A few boxes, thick with cobwebs and crammed with rusty old tools, stood along the left-hand wall. There was nothing else in there, aside from down at its far end, where the rocking chair she had been hearing sat with its back to her, facing another grimy window.

There was a figure in that chair.

Lucy waited for a breathless moment. She didn't know who this possibly could be, but over the top of the chair's backrest she could distinguish a pair of shoulders and a head. No hair was visible, because whoever it was, they were wearing a hoodie jacket and the hood was pulled up.

'Hello,' she said – in a voice so strained that she was ashamed of it. She cleared her throat and tried to sound sterner. 'I'm a police officer. I believe there's been an incident here.'

The figure didn't move.

'If you're able to, I need you to leave this building,' she said. 'It's become a crime scene.'

Still, the figure didn't move.

'Do you know anything about that?'

Again, nothing.

Feeling as if fire ants were scurrying all over her, she ventured forward with footsteps she never even heard despite the hollow floorboards that had amplified the sound of the rockers.

Even as she approached, the figure remained perfectly still.

Lucy couldn't say more; her throat was constricted, her tongue filled her entire mouth. As she came up behind the chair, she saw that it was indeed a human figure. It had arms and legs, and was dressed in jeans and training shoes, both pairs very old and dirty. It also had gloves on, its hands crossed on its lap.

So motionless was the form that in normal circumstances she'd have sworn she was in the presence of a dead man, but the only smell in here was the stagnant air of a derelict building.

'Can't you hear me?' she said, edging her way round to the front. 'I told you, I'm a poli . . .'

The words died on her tongue.

What she was looking at was a department store mannequin, but with its face hacked and slashed to pieces. The implement that had been used for this was still embedded where the right eye had used to be: a pair of rusty old scissors.

As Lucy stood there, bewildered, the chair began to rock

again, stiffly and heavily, back and forth, back and forth. But she only ran when it jerked wildly forward and its occupant threw itself bodily onto her.

As she descended towards the first landing, the echoes of her footfalls drumming behind her like a second pair of feet in fast pursuit, she fought to regain control. She insisted to herself that she wasn't actually running, merely trying to distance herself from a hazardous situation – but she was on autopilot nevertheless, her legs moving in a blur of speed she was barely conscious of generating.

I have not just seen a dummy come alive in a rocking chair.

The thing had been ridiculously light when it struck her; made from polystyrene or balsa wood, and had been utterly lifeless. But whatever had catapulted it out of the chair meant that she was *not* alone, and that whoever else was here, they had no good intentions. This suspicion was further fulfilled as she descended the final stairway to ground-level, almost stumbling in the process – only to see the building's front door now closed. Lucy was sure that she hadn't left it that way. In fact, it could *not* be closed – when she'd found it, hadn't it been broken open?

As she hit the bottom of the stairs, she saw that the upper bolt had been thrown. That explained the mystery. In addition, it was no real problem. She could always draw a bolt back . . . though it might take time, especially if it was stiff.

And then the figure waiting in the dimness just to the right of the door, spoke to her.

'Running's no good,' it whispered. 'Running won't get you anywhere.'

Chapter 31

'Boss?' Spicer said. 'That bloke who wants to see you.'

Bill Pentecost glanced up from the small table in the private dining room at the rear of The Roan Mare, the high-class gastro-pub he owned in Chorlton-cum-Hardy. As always, the table had been set for one; as always, Pentecost, though it was mid-afternoon and he sat alone, was smartly dressed, working his way delicately through a medium-sized portion of roast beef, Yorkshire pudding, boiled carrots and baked potatoes, occasionally sipping from a cut-crystal glass of Merlot. He touched his grey lips with a folded napkin as he considered.

'Sounds like he might have useful intel,' Spicer added.

Pentecost didn't count himself an unapproachable man, especially not among his inner cadre of protectors, but Les Spicer, the senior guard on tonight, knew him well enough not to disturb his dinner unless it was something of significance. Though his meal was only half-finished, Pentecost laid his knife and fork alongside his still folded napkin, and nodded.

Spicer, a typical brutish sort – four-square in shape, with a low brow under his bald head, a flat nose and heavy jaw –

went back through the curtain into the pub kitchen. Pentecost sipped more wine, and brushed an imagined speck from his left cuff. When Spicer returned, he had his sidekick, Alfie Atkins, with him; Atkins was roughly the same shape and aspect, except that he was younger, with greasy mouse-brown hair hanging down past his shoulders. Despite their basic monstrous appearance, both henchmen had been kitted out in specially tailored three-piece suits, which managed to make them look vaguely like members of the human race, but neither were as swish as the chap they escorted between them.

He was somewhere in his sixties, and tall and thin, with two stiff mops of chalk-grey hair, one standing upright from his scalp, the other jutting down from his long, lean chin. But aside from that, he was well-dressed, if a trifle dandified: beneath a caped Victorian-style overcoat, he wore a matching bottle-green blazer and tie, plus pink carnation, over a frill-fronted white shirt. His black trousers were pressed so professionally that the crease down either leg could have sliced paper. His shoes were black slip-ons, and had been polished until they glittered.

For all that, there was something gaunt and tawdry about him. Pentecost ignored the nervous but ingratiating smile, detecting a sour tang of body odour, and then those odd-coloured eyes – which automatically marked this chap as shifty – plus some bruising to his face and a dirty bandage wrapping his left wrist. Whoever this fellow was, he might fancy himself a picture of sartorial elegance, but he was no stranger to the cheap seats.

'I don't know you,' Pentecost said slowly. It wasn't so much a statement as an accusation.

'Erm, no sir,' the dandy replied hastily. 'Please allow me to introduce myself . . . Gerald McGlaglen'

'McGlaglen.' Pentecost steepled his fingers. 'With a name like that, I'd expect some kind of hardcase. Remember that old-time movie star? East London boy, I believe. Looked like he could drop a carthorse with a single punch.'

'I do indeed, sir.' McGlaglen smiled again, another attempt to be ingratiating. 'A slightly different name, as it transpires . . . but a fine exponent of the theatrical art.'

'You look like you should be called Mr Flower,' Atkins put in, sniggering. 'Or Mr Petal.'

Pentecost appraised his guest curiously. 'I know better than most, Mr McGlaglen, that names can be deceptive . . . so we'll judge you not on what you're called, but on what you can tell us. They say you have good information. I sincerely hope I haven't interrupted my lunch for anything less.'

McGlaglen clasped his hands in a humble gesture. 'I always aim to satisfy, sir.'

'You sound like a refined man, Mr McGlaglen. Where do you come from?'

'My current abode, sir, is Crowley Borough, the Hollycroft Brow district. But by origin, I'm an inner-Manchester man. Ancoats, to be exact.'

'Ancoats?' Pentecost arched an eyebrow. 'You take elocution, or something?'

'Not quite, sir . . . in the early days of my adulthood, I sought a career on the stage.'

'Ah, another actor.'

'Only an amateur, sadly. I never had the chance to take it further.'

'Why was that?'

McGlaglen gave a humble shrug. 'Lack of ability, I imagine . . . and there was another reason.' McGlaglen's face reddened. 'A fellow thespian and I collided once, in anger. During a rehearsal . . . over the attentions of our leading lady, no less. I did not just fall from the stage, but down a stairway connecting to the theatre's basement bar. I broke my ankle rather badly.'

'Ouch,' Pentecost said, without feeling.

McGlaglen cleared his throat. 'The incident I refer to was long ago – 1979, in fact. In those distant days, when in pain, one was often treated with morphine. Liberal doses of such.'

'And let me guess, you really liked it?'

McGlaglen gave a sad, foolish smile.

'You've been an addict since '79?' Pentecost pursed his lips. 'I'm impressed you're still alive.'

'It has only been an on-off interest, you understand. I have been able to shake the habit on occasion . . . but, well, when times are hard, it is inevitable that one drifts back.'

'So . . . if times are hard, and you never made it as a professional actor, how've you been able to afford that habit?'

McGlaglen reddened even more. 'I have developed other income streams.'

Pentecost finished his glass of wine and dabbed his lips again. 'And one of those would involve turning in your fellow bottom-feeders to the police.' He nailed the guest with that bone-chilling stare. 'Don't bother denying it, McGlaglen. I already know who you are. I was just interested to see how honest you were prepared to be.'

'Sir . . .' McGlaglen seemed lost for words. 'I assure you, I would never . . .'

'I believe "grass" is the word you're looking for.'

McGlaglen coughed with embarrassment, but also fear, acutely aware of the heavies still standing on either side of him. 'Sir . . . I would never *grass* on anyone like yourself, though I know my profession is anathema to you even so. Please understand, I've had very little option over these difficult years. The morphine quest took me to some terrible places. To acquire it, I several times performed demeaning acts . . .'

'Hah!' Atkins barked. 'Told you he was a ponce.'

'Things I'm not at all proud of.'

302

'But you *are* proud of grassing,' Pentecost said. As before, it wasn't a question.

'Not at all, sir. But as you can tell, I am hardly the sort of man to walk into a bank with a stocking over my head, nor to climb through some elderly lady's window to scrape away what few trinkets she keeps on her mantel.'

'I quite understand,' Pentecost said. 'Couldn't have some old lady catching you in the act. You needed a safer way to make a living.'

'*This* is the reason I am here, sir. I wish to be absolutely frank with you about the role I have played in this drama.'

'And what drama would that be?'

'I understand that you gentlemen are, as the saying goes . . .' McGlaglen lowered his voice for dramatic effect, 'under the cosh?'

'And what do you know about that?' Spicer asked, grabbing him by the collar and twisting it in a handful, constricting his throat.

'Very little, I assure you,' McGlaglen gasped. 'But the little there is I am here of my own free will to share.'

Pentecost nodded at Spicer, who released him.

McGlaglen gasped again, but now with relief.

'And what's it going to cost us?' Pentecost wondered. 'You sharing?'

'Oh . . .' McGlaglen tended to his bruised throat, 'merely my life.'

Pentecost considered. 'Sadly, there are no guarantees in this world, Mr McGlaglen. But I will say this, you police informers might sometimes have your uses. As I told you, we already know who and what you are. So do lots of others. Hence the good hiding you've clearly received. For quite a few years now, your sort have been . . . you like clever words, McGlaglen, so what's a good one here? I know . . . a *conduit*. Your sort have been a conduit between us and the police. If there's someone *at it* who we don't like or approve of, it isn't always convenient to just make them disappear, you understand. So, sometimes we take steps to ensure that people like you do it for us.'

McGlaglen pondered this with a wondering expression, as if he'd never imagined that the info he'd sold to law enforcement over the years might have been fed to him. He'd done well out of it of course, but it was a strange and somehow unedifying thought that, for all his independence of spirit, he might in truth have never been more than another minor cog in the dirty machinery of the underworld.

'Note that I say you *might* have your uses,' Pentecost added. 'Because . . . well, you see, I don't know about you personally. I'd have to check your status with one of my deputies. See where you stand. Whether you've been useful to us, whether you're an asset or a nuisance.'

McGlaglen spread his palms. 'I am here, sir, in an effort to persuade you of the former.'

'So . . .' The Chairman of the Board shrugged. 'Persuade me.'

'There is a female police officer,' McGlaglen said hurriedly. 'A detective constable with Crowley CID. And she is in pursuit of the very gang who have been making your life, and the lives of your associates, so difficult of late . . .' McGlaglen allowed that to hang, hoping to maximise its impact.

'Keep talking,' Pentecost said.

'Well . . . that is essentially it. I could not press her for too much information. That would have made her suspicious, but at present she is following an unusual and rather interesting lead concerning charitable donations in the town. I have no clue how this may be connected to your trouble. But she appears to have made a firm link between that and the murder of Andrew Northwood. Doubtless she knew more, but was not prepared to say.'

Pentecost mulled this over. 'What's this detective's name?'

'Clayburn . . . Lucy Clayburn. As I say, she is part of . . .'

'Yes, Crowley CID.'

The ex-actor could do nothing more now than fidget while they thought this through.

'I reckon you might just have bought yourself some extra time, Mr McGlaglen,' Pentecost said. 'You want extensions on that time, though, you come back to us whenever it's something good . . . you hear?'

'Absolutely, sir.' McGlaglen produced a handkerchief and dabbed at his sparkling brow. 'And may . . . erm, may I thank you profusely . . . for your kind understanding of my circumstances.'

Pentecost sat back and examined his fingernails, while his guest, still mumbling his incoherent gratitude, was steered away through the curtain by Atkins.

Spicer waited and watched his boss, who finally glanced up at him.

'That one,' he said, 'just divulged all his deepest secrets, and through fear alone. He didn't even want paying for it . . . he'd just got spooked. That makes him altogether too talkative, even though he did, in his own way, try to help us.' He paused to think. 'Never been much of a fan of risky situations. No, we need to put Mr McGlaglen on a close-observation list . . . let's see exactly how much he's worth to us. He may not realise it, but from here on he's got to earn the right to survive.'

'What if his intel's sound?' Spicer asked. 'I mean about the cop?'

'That, we also need to discover.' Pentecost sat forward again. 'First job . . . call Benny B. Tell him we may have something.'

Chapter 32

Lucy retreated across the passage until her back struck the wall. The figure, which was bulky and only half-distinguishable in the gloom, lurched awkwardly towards her, and jammed something like a pole or lance across the passageway, smashing it end-on into the plaster on her right, forming a horizontal barrier in front of the door.

The fanlight admitted just enough radiance to show who she was facing. He was a heavyset man in gloves and an overcoat, with a wide-brimmed hat pulled down to his brows. But she could see enough of his face to make out fat cheeks, piggy eyes and strands of sweaty, gingery hair. His complexion was a sickly greyish-white.

He'd frightened her at first because he'd ambushed her, but clearly he was in a bad way.

She now saw that the thing he'd blocked the passage with was a crutch, which he wielded in his left hand, the plastic cuff enclosing his forearm. He had another crutch in his right hand, and was using that one to support himself. When she looked at his legs, which were only visible from mid-shin downward, she saw white casts made of lumpy plaster. Rubber walking-attachments had been fixed to their two soles, but it didn't look like a professional job.

Moisture gleamed on the man's face as he leaned fiercely towards her.

'You really a cop?' he growled.

'I said so, didn't I . . .?'

'You don't look like a cop! You look like a frightened rabbit!' He breathed slowly and heavily; more sweat trickled down his face. 'You on your own?'

Unavoidably, Lucy glanced up the stairway on her left.

'Like what you found up there, did you?' he said scornfully. 'Scared you, did it?'

'I'm not scared.'

'Not much, you fucking aren't!'

She realised that another door, previously hidden, now stood open behind him. An oblong section of wall had simply folded backward, exposing a dim-lit room.

'Something else you didn't expect, eh?' The man gave a strained, pig-like chuckle. 'My panic chamber. My escape route. Call it any of those things, if you like.'

But now it seemed, despite all his bravado, that the effort of trying to frighten her was proving too much. He lowered the left crutch and leaned on it, his angry expression dissolving into one of pain-induced weariness. Filching a pair of glasses hanging down under his coat, he fitted them onto his nose, which she saw was bruised and crooked. He had bruises under both eyes too, ugly green-yellow stains descending onto his cheeks.

'You need these things,' he said, tiredly, '. . . in my business. You never know who's going to come here.' He lumbered backward a foot or so. 'I asked if you were alone . . . but I'm guessing you are. No back-up's come flying in to save you.'

Before she could reply, he manoeuvred himself around

and thudded away on his crutches into the previously unseen room.

'Not, in truth,' he said over his shoulder, 'that you're likely to need saving today.'

Now was her chance to run, she realised . . . if she really wanted to do that. But clearly, he didn't pose as much of a threat as she'd first thought.

She took another second to get herself together, and then followed him through the door, finding herself in another decayed ex-office. This one contained a low table and two chairs. On top of the table, there was an open haversack with several stacks of rubber-banded banknotes lying alongside it. In the wall close by, at floor-level, another concealed door – to all intents and purposes a square section of plaster wall – stood open, revealing a recess in which yet more money was visible. Alongside that, propped upright, there was a pump-action shotgun; momentarily this stopped her short, though if her host intended to use it, he most likely would have ambushed her with it out in the hallway.

'Before you even ask, all this money's mine,' the man wheezed, hobbling to the table. 'I was in the process of collecting it when you showed up.'

Lucy looked around the room. On its far side, a length of dirty rope with a knot tied at the end dangled from a hole in the ceiling; a pull-cord of some sort. Next to that, an ordinary door, made from wood and with a doorknob, stood open on what looked like an exterior brick passage.

'Like I say . . .' the man said, 'this was always intended to be my escape route if anyone ever came here who wasn't supposed to. And this cash . . .' leaning on one crutch, he began loading the money into the bag, 'was my extra supply. Always thought it was a fool-proof plan. Someone knocks, unexpected . . . like you lot. We don't let 'em in . . . always had a good man on the door for that. He gives me the nod,

I come downstairs into here, let you idiots sledgehammer the door down and run all over the building. If you're slow to do that, I help you along. That rope over there's attached to the puppet show on the top floor. If *you* fell for it, why wouldn't someone else? Ought to have bought us enough time to get all this stuff together . . . then out through the back door, down the entry into a private yard and into a vehicle. Leave the area by a different route . . . Bob's your uncle. But it seems like nothing's actually fool-proof. My good man on the door turned out to not be that good after all.'

He grimaced, briefly but intensely; Lucy couldn't tell whether it was an expression of pain or anger, or both.

'For which he too has a paid a severe price,' the man added, 'though not severe enough.'

She walked towards him. 'You're saying someone was shot here? I mean apart from you?'

'No one I'm going to name.' He looked around at her, angry again, almost accusing. 'But thanks to him, I'm now having to do something I never, ever wanted. My son is nineteen years old. He's at Lancaster Uni, studying history and archaeology. Theoretically, he has a normal life ahead of him. Or he *did* have. Now, he's sitting out there in the van, for fuck's sake. Waiting for me. Nervous as hell. And so he should be. Because I've run out of anyone else I trust, I've now had to drag him into something he should never have been part of . . .'

'I take it you're Roy Shankhill?' she said.

He tried to laugh, though it clearly hurt him.

'Regular little Sherlock Holmes, you, aren't you?' He appraised her with near-contempt. 'Are you really the best they can do? Frightened of a fucking dummy, not even sure who it is you're investigating . . .'

'Enough of the lip, yeah!'

309

'I've had *enough* . . . I'll tell you that.'

Even though the money bag was still only half full, Shankhill was visibly exhausted by his efforts. He slumped onto one of the two chairs, his plastered legs protruding out from under his coat like two misshapen sculptures. He patted his sodden brow with a grubby handkerchief.

Lucy studied him, noting what a wreck he was. It irked her that she'd shown fright in the face of the trick he'd played upstairs. She hated it, and was furious with herself, when slimeballs like this got any kind of drop of her.

'You going to tell me what happened?' she asked. 'I presume you want to . . . you didn't have to reveal you were here.'

Shankhill eyed her with uncertainty. 'The fact my lad's out there is the only reason I'm coming clean with you,' he said. 'You were halfway upstairs when you started shouting and bawling that you were a cop. When I heard that, I'll admit I was a bit relieved . . . but for all I knew, you might still have the building surrounded. Last thing I want is Luke getting a criminal record. He's done nothing wrong, you understand? I just asked him to drive me over here so I could pick something up. He didn't even know I rented this place.'

'Assuming he's not blind, he must have half an idea that something bad happened to you.'

'I say again . . . he's not part of this. But he knows enough not to ask questions.'

Lucy walked to the other door, and peered down the outside passage. It turned out of sight about twenty yards along. As Shankhill said, she could imagine it emerging in some disused yard, another hidden space amid this labyrinth of eroded buildings. He might be frustrated that his security was foiled, but the loan shark had chosen his premises well. If the police had ever raided this place, they would have surrounded it first, but there was no guarantee they'd have found that back exit.

When she turned around, he was still breathing heavily and sweating intensely.

'Meds letting you down?' she asked, hardly daring to think what kind of drunken sawbones had tried to put him back together. 'Aspirin maybe? Under a real doctor, you'd probably still be on a surgical ward.'

'Yeah . . . having to listen to bullshit from dumb pigs like you.' Even in his pain, Shankhill was a vile specimen. 'If only your pathetic lot knew how far behind the eight ball you are.'

'So where does that leave *you*?' she wondered. 'I mean, I'm getting paid to be here, and in a couple of hours I'll be back home with my feet up. *You*, on the other hand . . . you've got two shattered legs and a ruined business.'

'And that gives you an edge, does it?' He chuckled again; that grunting, hog-like snort. 'Fine . . . except if you've come to arrest me, tough shit. You'll be lucky to find any evidence of *my* wrongdoings. There's *that*, of course.' He nodded towards the shotgun. 'But you nick me for having an unlicensed firearm and it'll be the least of my problems.'

'I'm less interested in you, Roy, than in what happened to you.'

He took his glasses off, rubbing their lenses with his wool-clad thumbs. 'Like you said, I got shot. During the course of a fucking robbery, would you believe. Here, in my own fucking office. Stamped on my face too . . . like you can't fucking tell.'

'How much did they take?'

'I don't know . . . sixty to seventy grand.'

'When did this happen?'

'Don't bother. I'm not reporting it. Bastards took my jewellery too, even my sodding Rolex!

311

'Your *Rolex*?' Lucy struggled to conceal the impact this made on her. 'Do you have the serial number to hand?'

'I told you I'm not reporting it.'

'That must've cost you a fortune.'

'I'm *not* reporting it!'

'Are you actually serious?'

'Jesus!' he shouted. 'You know what I am, you know what I do. This never happened, all right?'

'What about your injured friend? How badly hurt is he . . . I mean, will he live?'

'I don't have an injured *friend*.' Shankhill stressed the word 'friend', as if whoever it was who'd failed to prevent the blaggers' intrusion had put himself beyond any such favour.

'Where is he?'

'Somewhere he won't want you to find him.'

'You'd better hope he survives.'

Shankhill snorted again, as if this was his very last consideration.

'What would you say if I told you these guys have done this more than once?' she said.

'Wouldn't surprise me. They didn't look like amateurs. But neither will it move me. Not one inch. I'm saying nothing else.'

'Okay . . . all right.' Lucy tried to think this through. 'This never happened . . . at least, officially. But I'd still like to catch them if possible.'

'Good luck.'

'You saying there's nothing you can tell me at all . . . even off the record?'

'Off the record, sure.' He chuckled derisively.

'I can't force you to make a complaint, Roy . . . but I'm sure you'd like the bastards to answer for *something*.'

He finally appeared to mull this over.

'I've just told you they've done other jobs, which *are* being investigated,' she said. 'Give me something to add, and maybe we can bring them in without any of this coming back to you.'

'Okay,' he replied, after some deliberation. 'Okay, but this is all you get: two guys, average size and height, one slightly taller than the other. Heavy clothing . . . dark for the most part. Black leather jackets and gloves certainly. Red woollen ski masks.'

'*Red* wool . . . you're sure?'

'I'll never forget that.' He patted at his forehead again. 'Regular pair of devils, they looked like. Slits for their eyes . . . no mouth-holes.'

'Accents?'

'Local. Northwest.'

'What about the ordinance? I'm guessing they used auto-matic weapons?'

'I'm no expert, but . . . machine-pistols or sub-machine guns, whatever you call them.' He eased himself backward in his chair, which barely seemed to make him any more comfortable.

'Any other witnesses . . . I mean apart from your so-called friend who you're happy to leave in whatever shithole of an unlicensed hospital you've found for him?'

'There *was* one other, actually,' Shankhill admitted.

'Who?'

'Some civvy fuckhead.'

'A civvy?'

'He owed me money. By the looks of it, he was coming to pay me back when they bushwhacked him outside and used him to get through the front door.'

'Name?'

'That's irrelevant.'

'I think I'll decide whether it's relev—'

'*No!*' he shouted, the effort of which set him cringing. 'I'll decide whether it's relevant or not. I'm the one who's near enough lost his legs, okay? I'm the one who now owes the big boys in the field a cut of his business, which he can't pay.'

Which explained to Lucy why he hadn't come out to see her immediately she'd arrived here. He'd thought she might be the Crew. Her own father, no doubt, or one of his henchmen. It also explained why he'd felt relief on learning that she was a cop.

'So, on the basis that I'm having a pretty crap month,' he added, his anger waning in face of his agony, 'I'll decide who I tell stuff to, and how much stuff I tell. You want him so much, go and find him yourself.'

'Roy, have you considered that this civvy might have been in on it?'

'Yeah, sure,' Shankhill scoffed. 'And then pissed himself all over the floor. Go up and look, if you don't believe me. They spared him, and he still pissed himself till he was bone-dry.'

'What do you mean they spared him?'

'Well . . . not only did they not shoot his legs off, they didn't even take his money . . . and he actually offered it to them.'

'He offered it?'

'Yeah. Like I say, he was pissing himself . . . was ready to hand it all over. And it was worth pinching, you know . . . it was a few hundred at least. But they didn't want it. Told him to keep it. After that, when they left, they took our phones and keys, and locked the place up tight to ensure there'd be no quick escape. But that little shit was so scared he almost tore the place down. Searched the entire building trying to find another way out. Snatched his money up first, of course . . . money he owed *me*, even though it was covered in blood. Good luck spending that, you little shit, I thought . . .'

314

Shankhill wiped more sweat from his neck and cheeks. He fiddled two pills out of a foil wrapper, and swallowed them, face creasing at the taste.

'I called to him . . . much as I was able, half-dead as I was. Agonised, wasn't I. Needed any help I could get. Don't know whether he didn't hear me or just ignored me. Either way, didn't matter. He just wanted out. Finally found his way upstairs, got some old tools . . . came back down, broke the front door open, took to his heels. Thankfully, I had a spare mobile down here in the safety room. Almost died getting down the stairs, though. No doubt you've seen the mess I left. Finally managed to make a call.'

He relapsed into haggard silence. Just remembering these events had clearly been an ordeal for him.

'Roy,' Lucy said quietly, 'I really need to speak to this civvy.'

'Forget it. No chance. None whatsoever.'

And on reflection, she supposed that maybe she should have expected that. Whoever, this civvy was, he wouldn't just be a witness to the robbery, but to Shankhill's own dodgy dealings. The loan shark would never give him up. As if in confirmation of that, Shankhill hawked and spat a gobbet of yellow spittle on the floor.

Chapter 33

'Frank?' Shallicker's voice said.

'Yeah.' McCracken was at the wheel of his Bentley when he took the call.

'Remember Gentleman Joe . . . or whatever he called himself?'

McCracken frowned as he tried to navigate the mid-Manchester traffic. 'Gentleman who?'

'Lazenby . . . the Scouse git.'

'Oh yeah, him. What about him?'

'Seems he wants a meet.'

'Ah . . . does he?'

McCracken was pleased, but at the same time mildly frustrated.

It was never his policy to leave his contact details with those individuals whose businesses he was interested in profiting from. His own team made the calls, usually on a kind of schedule: *give the bastards something to think about, leave them a couple of weeks to stew over it, and then see if they're prepared to play ball.* If his memory served, it was now over a fortnight since he'd first introduced himself to Ordinary Joe in that Crowley cocktail bar, so today's outcome was right on cue. But given everything else that was going on, the timing could have been better.

'We can easily tell him to fuck off for a few days because we're busy?' Shallicker suggested.

'No,' McCracken said. 'Could be a hundred-and-fifty grand in this. That'll replace our recent losses. Might placate Bill a little too. Where are you at the mo?'

'Back on the job.'

'How's it looking?'

'Put it this way, I'm intrigued.'

'Something going down?'

'Could be, I'm not sure.'

McCracken pondered. He'd already pulled his big deputy off important duties that morning so that they could both attend the board meeting at the Astarte. It wasn't desirable to be pulling him off them again, especially if the bloke now thought he might be onto something.

'Stick with it, Mick,' McCracken said. 'I'll take care of Gentleman Joe. Did he give a time and place?'

'Yeah . . . you know Crowley Tech?'

'Sure do.'

'There's a staff car park at the back, and there's a lower car park at the back of that. Near the canal.'

'Right near his offices, eh?' McCracken treated himself to a cold smile. 'I love these fucking guys who won't go an extra yard even for *us*.'

'He needs slapping, that's for sure. Now might be the time.'

'When?'

'He says can we do it at 4.30 this afternoon?'

McCracken glanced at the dashboard clock, which read 4.05. 'Suppose so.'

'Frank . . .?' Shallicker asked. 'You carrying?'

'On normal business, why would I be?'

'Do you want me to call a couple of the lads, have 'em hook up with you first?'

'Are you jesting?' McCracken laughed out loud. 'This is Joey the Gent.'

'What if he's got some firm with him?'

'If they're as scary as he is, I'll really be in trouble, won't I?'

'What if he's been talking to the cops?'

McCracken shrugged, as though Shallicker was in the Bentley with him. 'If he has, it's all the better if I'm *not* carrying and *don't* turn up with a team, isn't it? What'll they have? Be his word against mine.'

'Just make sure he's not wired.'

'I *have* done this before, you know.' McCracken hit the brakes, slowing down for a red light. 'Stay in touch about the other stuff.'

'Will do, Frank.'

The line went dead.

McCracken was on the A5145, heading towards Stockport, when he received this call. He'd been en route to see Eddie 'Psycho' Sikes, an old-time robber whose last job had been the infamous £6.6 million Midland Bank Clearing Centre blag in Salford, in '95. Psycho's main usefulness at this moment was not so much his expertise in that field – he'd ended up serving seventeen years for the Salford job, emerging an old man with health issues, which suggested that his expertise wasn't total – but he knew a lot of people, and had a particularly good ear when it came to the up-and-comers, the young buckos, who were more likely than most to throw the rulebook away in an effort to make it big quickly.

'Z-list wankers!' McCracken said, as he spun his Bentley around at Albert Park and headed northwest towards Stretford, and beyond that, Crowley. Psycho could wait till later. He'd need to get his foot down if he didn't want to be late for the RV at Crowley Tech.

McCracken didn't necessarily blame all the woes of the world on the celebrity no-marks who, thanks to social media, now seemed to encircle British youth, endlessly partying: champagne, yachts in the Caribbean, pissing it up in the swankiest hotels on earth, living the high life in an epic, reckless way. But it was no wonder kids today thought they were entitled to the same thing, and just like their cheapjack heroes, seemed to think they would never have to do any actual work to attain it.

Except maybe take down scores from easy targets.

Easy in this case because no one had ever thought that anyone would actually dare.

Unfortunately, for this Red-Headed League, as Wild Bill had christened them, there'd be a big price to pay for such a colossal misreading of the situation. McCracken's job now was to ensure that the right people paid this price. Because, though he never objected to using violence when necessary, it was only ever effective in McCracken's mind when it was targeted. The very last thing they needed now was this whirl-wind of paranoid craziness, with everyone blaming everyone else, opportunist shitheads trying to earn bounties off the innocent, old wounds being freshly torn, various families falling out with each other all over again.

But still, business was business. And Ordinary Joe Lazenby came first.

It was 4.25 p.m. when McCracken drove into central Crowley. A blue autumn dusk was falling, street lights casting their sodium-yellow pall over the late-afternoon traffic. When he turned into the college car park, a succession of vehicles were headed out in the opposite direction.

As such, he had no problem finding a vacant space. He

parked and climbed out, straightening his suit and glancing around. A central tower of lighted windows delineated the stairwell in the college's main building. Closer by, one or two figures sidled between the cars, for the most part academic-types with books and files underarm, carrying keys. None looked as if they were coming over to speak to him. He heard the hum of town centre traffic, but no voice hailed him.

Not that McCracken had expected it. Shallicker had told him the lower car park.

He donned his gabardine overcoat, pulled on a pair of leather gloves and, after locking his car, walked across the open tarmac, finally descending a ramp to a flat, weedy area alongside a waist-high, tubular-steel barrier fencing off a cinder towpath and, beyond that, the dark still waters of the canal. It was now very quiet. The radiance of the road network barely penetrated down to this little-used section.

McCracken strolled into the middle of it and halted.

It was a bold move, but boldness was his way.

And it wasn't as if he hadn't taken precautions.

He'd told Shallicker that he wasn't carrying. That was true. He had no firearm on him at present – Crew under-bosses rarely carried when going about day-to-day business, because if they did and they somehow ended up with the police on their case, that would be one sure way to get the book thrown at them. But with as many enemies as this career could generate, they had to be safety-conscious too; that was why he always wore a Kevlar undershirt.

He scanned left to right, seeing no one skulking around. Lazenby was such an amateur that McCracken had expected to find him waiting conspicuously in a corner, like a schoolboy who'd been sent to stand against the wall. But there was no initial sign of him, which seemed odd – until the vehicle directly in front, one of only two parked down here, growled into action.

Its headlights burst to life, bathing McCracken in dazzling whiteness. But when it lurched towards him, he held his ground, hands in pockets.

Lazenby wouldn't have got where he was if he was completely stupid. He had to know that anything seriously untoward here would not just be the end of him, but of his family too.

And true to form, the vehicle, a beige Ford Galaxy, screeched to a halt just short of McCracken, and the driver's door was kicked open. A figure clambered quickly out. It was Lazenby, though he was more dishevelled than when McCracken had last seen him. He still wore a three-piece suit, but his tie had been stripped off, his shirt was unbuttoned and his jacket was crumpled. There were marks of old bruising on his face, and a smell of alcohol wafted off him. When he raised a Taurus PT 24/7 in his right hand, it shook erratically.

McCracken had to admit to being impressed. The Taurus was a man-stopper, for sure, and not a make you regularly encountered in the UK; Lazenby had clearly cultivated some good connections in South America. Of course, whether he was willing to use it was another matter.

'Very confident of you . . .' Lazenby stuttered, his words slurring as he walked up to his intended target, the barrel barely ten inches from the gangster's heart. 'Coming here alone.'

'You sure I have?' McCracken replied. 'What's that bright red dot on your chest?'

Lazenby glanced down – and never saw the fast right hand, which knocked the Taurus from his grasp, nor the faster left, which dealt him such a slap to the face that his glasses flew off and he went staggering sideways. The next thing Ordinary Joe knew, a knee had rammed into his groin, pile-driving the wind from him, and as he doubled over, an iron claw bunched itself in the material of his collar, and propelled him sideways towards the low barrier, pushing him violently over it.

Lazenby sprawled on the cinder path, crying out in shock and fear. Before he could scramble back to his feet, McCracken had stepped over the barrier after him, dragged him upright and frogmarched him to the canal's concrete edge.

'Fancy an evening dip?'

Lazenby straightened like a flagpole, every muscle taut. 'No, please . . .'

'It's less than you were planning for me.'

'But I can't swim.'

'You can't . . .?'

McCracken paused as two curious passers-by approached along the towpath; two students, by the looks of them, in woolly hats and anoraks, and wearing backpacks. He released Lazenby's collar, laughed and brushed him down.

'Nasty fall, that, sir . . . glad to be able to help, though.'

The youngsters traipsed past, resuming their conversation, vanishing into the evening murk.

'You really can't swim?' McCracken asked, grabbing the Liverpudlian's collar again, and hoisting him up onto his tiptoes. 'Seriously?'

'I . . . I . . . never learned . . .'

'You're as far out of your depth at this level as it's possible to be, aren't you . . . Everyday Joe? I mean, were you actually planning to shoot me? What if the recoil had hurt your hand?'

'I don't . . . I dunno . . .' Lazenby could barely speak, his gaze directed down his nose at the glimmering black surface of the canal.

'Have I really interrupted my schedule for a worthless little pillock like you? Do you know how busy I am, Joe?'

'Was only . . . only gonna shoot if it was you or me.'

'Well, it *is* you or me.' McCracken turned his captive around and marched him across the path, back over the barrier and into the car park. 'So perhaps you should've shot when you had the chance, and not wasted time gabbing.'

Lazenby physically relaxed now that he was away from the water; in fact, he virtually flopped. When McCracken threw him against the Galaxy, he lay over its bonnet like a heap of wet rags.

'And when you'd shot me,' McCracken said, 'what then? Back into your office as if nothing had happened . . . with a body still in the car park, and your fingerprints all over the murder weapon, and gunfire residue on your hands and clothes?'

'Look . . . what do I care?' Lazenby craned his head around, his formerly frightened face written with peevish angst. 'Everything's gone up in smoke. *Literally*. But why am I telling *you*, eh? *You're* the bastard behind it. I mean . . . I was going to play along.' He levered himself upright and turned around, but was so wearied by the confrontation that he still had to lean against the car. 'Your demands were exorbitant, outrageous. But I kind of realised I had no choice. And then you came and did me over anyway. I mean . . . where do you gain from that? Okay . . . dumb fuck that I am, I led you right to my stash and let you pocket a hundred and sixty grand's worth of liquid cash. But all the rest of that gear was worth half a million, at least. And I was going to cut you in. You could have kept on getting paid for months, if not years . . .'

McCracken heard him out in silence, unsurprised but nonetheless disturbed by the unfolding story. 'Someone's robbed you . . . is that what you're trying to say?'

'Don't play the innocent . . .'

'I wouldn't know how to. But tell me what happened anyway.'

323

'Yeah, someone robbed me.' Lazenby hefted himself away from the vehicle, and prodded gingerly at his cheek, which, though it had only been slapped, already looked inflamed. 'Two of your fucking goons followed me to my lock-up.'

'And they lifted a hundred and sixty grand?'

'Everything I had spare.'

'And what happened to the gear?'

Denuded of his glasses, Lazenby struggled to focus on his tormentor. 'You seriously saying you don't know?'

'Indulge me.'

'They torched it, didn't they!'

McCracken felt a creeping sense of disbelief. 'They set fire to half a mill's worth of dope?'

'Yeah, for fuck's sake! And once it had started burning, I had to let it go, didn't I? Else I'd have had some explaining to do when the Fire Brigade arrived. I'm only surprised half the neighbourhood didn't get stoned.'

Noting the glint of Lazenby's glasses lying near his feet, McCracken scooped them up and handed them over. 'Whereabouts was this lock-up?'

Lazenby fixed the specs to his sweat-slick nose. 'Up on the Bellhop. Are you seriously claiming you didn't order the attack?'

'How many blaggers?'

'I only saw two.'

'Ski masks?'

'Yeah.'

'What colour were the masks?'

'Red . . . why?'

McCracken chewed his lip. 'Automatic weapons?'

'You obviously *know* about this.'

'All I know at present is that you, Mr Lazenby, have joined an elite but fast-expanding club.'

Lazenby looked baffled. 'I don't feel too honoured.'

'You should, you're in excellent company.' McCracken strode back towards the ramp.

'Where are you going now?'

'Don't leave town,' the gangster called over his shoulder. 'I couldn't even if I wanted to . . . can't afford it, can I!'

McCracken glanced back. 'You could always walk . . .' He stared at the guy's undamaged legs. 'In fact, I strongly suspect someone's gone to considerable trouble to suggest that's precisely what you should do.'

Chapter 34

'Lucy?' When Danny Tucker answered his phone, he sounded as if he was at the wheel; evening traffic rumbled in the background.

Even though she was outside the front of 38, Rudyard Row, Lucy had no compunction about raising her voice so that he could hear her. 'Danny . . . I've got another crime scene for you!'

'You've got a . . . *what?*'

'An armed robbery carried out by two bandits wearing black leather jackets and red woollen ski masks, and armed with sub-machine guns. Two casualties. Both shot in the legs. Ring any bells?'

'What're you talking about . . . where are you?'

Lucy paced the pavement, stumbling over her words in her efforts to tell him everything.

'Lucy . . . hang about!' Tucker had only heard a few sentences, but he was clearly so surprised that he was struggling to believe her. 'When did this happen?'

'I can't be sure. Sometime in the last month.'

'So . . . what's the story?'

'There's a loan shark called Roy Shankhill. He rents a unit

on Rudyard Row, part of the old industrial site between the canal and the railway. Some time ago, he got robbed, and him and his minder got mown down in the process.'

'How've you . . .' Tucker still sounded stunned. 'Lucy, how've you found this out?'

'Don't worry, I've not been moonlighting on your investigation. Basically, our two cases have converged. Would you believe the common denominator is charity?'

'Charity?'

She told him about Jordan Burke and how at least one of his burglary victims had been the recipient of a generous but anonymous donation.

'You think Burke's involved?' he interrupted.

'Nah . . . he's just an opportunist thief who got lucky. I mean, get this . . .' She went on to describe the Rolex that Burke insisted he stole from Reg Murgatroyd.

'Burke stole a thirty-grand Rolex from a little old man living on a council estate?' Danny repeated, stunned.

'Exactly what I thought. But it seems the Rolex actually belonged to this loan shark, Shankhill.'

'Have you got this character with you now?'

'No . . . he doesn't want to make a complaint. I tried to explain to him that in cases of serious assault, we don't need a complainant to act, but he was adamant. Thing is, Danny . . . he knows he's going to have to answer questions at some point. His crew turned up after the blag and got him away, but they didn't even try to clean up. There're buckets of blood up there, piles of shell casings . . . it's a CSI's dream, I'm telling you. There's even a witness.'

'Who?'

'Some civvy . . . Shankhill wouldn't give me his name, but if we can lift DNA from an old urine sample, though I've no idea if we can or not, we *might* get him that way. And anyway, I think Shankhill will talk eventually. He presumably still rents these premises and there's been gunfire expended all over it. How long can he sit there and keep schtum? I mean, he doesn't like us . . . that's for sure, but he's shit-scared of the Crew, because he owes them his usual tax and now he can't afford to pay it. So, we'll get leverage that way too. But more important than any of this . . . the real shit-kicker is that the blaggers let this civvy off scot-free. They robbed Shankhill of every pound-note he had, but they didn't take anything from the civvy, even though he offered it. I know it's circumstantial, but does that tie in with the charity thing, or what? I mean, Jerry McGlaglen joked with me about Robin Hood . . . but I don't think it's so far from the truth. And listen, there's something else . . . if this team really *have* been donating their takings to good causes, I've got one of them on film.'

'What're you talking about now?'

'I pulled some footage from a town-centre camera. Five days ago, in the early hours of the morning, the Methodist Mission Hall on Langley Street was gifted thousands of pounds in used banknotes by an unknown benefactor. At least, he'd like to believe he's unknown . . . in reality he's on this footage.'

'How much footage is there?'

'Only a couple of minutes, but it's good. I've got it on a pen drive and copied it to my laptop.'

'Do we get a good look at him?'

'Enough to see that he's wearing a ski mask.'

'Red?'

'Can't tell.'

'Shit!' Tucker sounded genuinely exasperated.

'Come on, Danny . . . what're the chances it's someone else? The other thing is . . . his vehicle's out of sight, but there are lots of other cameras in that part of town. We only have to pull all the footage from the night in question, and each car we clock – and at that hour there won't be too many of them – is gonna give us a brand new suspect.'

Tucker was quiet, clearly thinking things through. 'If all this is kosher, Lucy . . . it's the best lead we've had yet. I mean by a country mile.'

'That's what I thought.'

'You're at the scene now, you say?'

'I'm out at the front. Didn't want to contaminate it any more than I already have.'

'Can you secure it?'

'I can stand guard . . . how soon can you get a team over here?'

'I'll get onto Kathy ASAP, and she'll mobilise the Squad . . . but listen, I'm only just round the corner, myself. I'm heading down to the Archways to meet one of my own informants, and the info he's supposedly got sounds as if it's relevant to everything you've just told me. How soon can you get there, because we're due to meet in fifteen minutes?'

'Whereabouts on the Archways?'

'Top of Jubilee Gardens, where it joins Brockle Street. Do you know it?'

'Yeah . . . but I don't know if I can lock this place up.' Lucy re-examined the battered entrance. 'The front door's broken.'

'Just close it, and get yourself down here, pronto. The more I think about it, the more I want you at this meet. Don't worry about Rudyard Row; Kathy'll have someone there in no time.'

'Okay, I'll do my best.'

'Excellent. And Lucy . . .' All the warmth that had been lacking from his voice the last time they'd spoken had returned in cartloads. 'This is great work, babes. Great bloody work. If this doesn't get you into the Squad, nothing will.'

As Lucy tucked her phone away and pondered the doorway, she felt ten feet tall. This time Danny himself had said it: if what she'd done here – and it was all legit, as she'd only been seeking to iron out anomalies from her own enquiries – helped break open the Andy Northwood murder case, that would be another massive score for the Robbery Squad which *she* had put on a plate for them. After that, she didn't see how Kathy Blake could deny her, whether they had a vacancy or not. And if the Robbery Squad folded in a couple of months' time, despite all its recent successes, the worst they could do was bounce her back to Division, so life would go on as normal – ugly notion though that was.

Very ugly, now that she thought about it.

It wasn't just that investigating mundane crime was becoming a drag, Lucy didn't think she could take much more of being stuck with Harry all day. His innate indiscipline constantly invited disaster for the pair of them, while his basic lack of ambition, his determination to get through each shift doing the bare minimum, his endless ruminations on his depressing life while he clock-watched and counted down the days to retirement (even though it was years and years away, for God's sake!) was literally sapping her enthusiasm for the job.

She'd now firmly decided that she needed to be where the action was – like *really* where the action was, and she couldn't help feeling that she'd just taken a very large step in that direction.

But the more immediate problem was how to secure these premises.

There was no way she could fix the door. The main lock was smashed, and though its three internal bolts remained intact, bolts could not be applied from the outside. In the end, all she could really do was pull the door back into its frame by hooking a finger into the damaged section, and hope that its now lopsided shape would jam it there.

Rather to her surprise, this seemed to work.

She stepped back, pleased. Even a relatively light kick would re-open it, but at least it looked closed. And anyway, the Squad would be here in the next few minutes. She half-contemplated waiting for them, just to be sure. But she didn't want to miss Danny's conflab with his grass, especially if they had similar notes to compare.

She hurried along the street. It was now nearly five, and the workmen she'd heard before had seemingly gone home. With no lighting in this district, full darkness had fallen; a couple of times she almost tripped over the age-worn cobblestones, but in due course she passed under the railway bridge, and rejoined the world of lit-up shopfronts, end-to-end cars and hurrying pedestrians. When she got back to her Jimny, she jumped in behind the wheel.

Tucker was indeed close by, but thanks to the early-evening traffic, almost twenty-five minutes had passed by the time she arrived, and she was all but ripping her hair out.

The Archways estate, which comprised ten long, parallel rows of 1930s terraced housing, was long overdue for demolition, not least because of its incongruous location at the foot of six towering, Victorian-age railway arches. Only now, a decade after the houses were left empty, was a plan at last in place to create an inner-city park, and the demolition orders coming through. In fact, the bulldozers were due in the next few days. As such, the whole of the Archways had been fenced off with corrugated metal, though that hadn't stopped the usual skirmishers from breaking in: curious kids, squatters, vagrants and the like. So, there were lots of ways to gain access, though the most obvious one, as Tucker had said, was at the north end of Jubilee Gardens. Here, about three sections of fencing had been flattened.

Lucy pulled up on Felton Lane, just alongside it. Concerned that she was now very late for the meeting, she jumped out and zipped up her anorak as she darted through the gap onto the top of a rugged dirt slope, from which in daytime you could see the whole of the estate, though much of it at present lay in total darkness.

That said, there was at least sufficient light diffusing in from nearby street lamps to show the cobbled surface of Brockle Street running west to east, and the entrances to all the other streets, one by one as you progressed along it, leading north to south. All the place names here sounded more rural or suburban than they actually were: Taberner Drive, Dunwood Road, Brookhill Avenue, Clearwater Way, and of course here, at the point closest to where Lucy now stood, Jubilee Gardens.

In truth, the Archways looked horrible – a sprawl of soulless brick terraces, with tiny yards at their rears and dismal alleys between them – but when in use, it hadn't been hugely different from the neighbourhood she herself had grown up in. She didn't feel out of sorts here as she walked down the slope and crossed Brockle Street. But only when she reached the corner with Jubilee Gardens, already having seen that no one was waiting there, did it strike her as odd that she hadn't seen Tucker's Vauxhall Passat, or indeed any other vehicle, up on Felton Lane. She pivoted around, and squinted down Jubilee Gardens. Her eyes were attuning, and she was able to see a considerable distance, only its farthest depths hidden in the inky caul under the viaduct.

No one was around, and Lucy was puzzled.

According to her phone, it was now 5.30 p.m. By her estimation, fifteen minutes had elapsed since she'd been supposed to rendezvous with Tucker and his contact. That was enough time, if the RV was indeed over by now, for them to have departed, but she'd still have expected Tucker to hang around here to speak with her.

She checked the phone again; there were no missed calls. But it probably wouldn't do any harm to call him, herself. If he was still in conflab at some other venue, the worst that would happen is that he'd ignore her and she'd be diverted to voicemail.

She was about to tap in his number, when what sounded like a clatter of woodwork echoed up the derelict street.

Lucy spun around. At first, she saw nothing different from before, but she walked a few yards along the pavement on the right-hand side, and came in sight of a house on the left where, instead of a front door, there was a visible opening.

This surprised her for two reasons.

Firstly, because most of the houses here were closed up, their front doors and windows either covered with plywood boards or metal, or simply locked and the keys taken away.

Secondly, because she could have sworn that there hadn't been an opening there before.

So, had the door opened just now?

Was it possible that Tucker and his CI had gone into one of the houses to confer? Maybe there was something in there that the CI wanted to bring to Tucker's attention.

Phone in hand, some sixth sense preventing her from pocketing it, Lucy walked down the road, taking a diagonal course as she crossed slowly and warily towards the left-hand side.

Danny didn't say anything about meeting indoors.

She stopped halfway across, almost on level with the house in question. It was indeed an opening; what looked like a plywood hoarding had been levered away, leaving an empty door frame behind it. She supposed it was possible that the wood had simply fallen off through age; the old frame was likely to be rotted through. Perhaps that was the sound she'd heard.

One thing she knew, she wasn't going any closer without making a call first. She raised the mobile to look for Tucker's number; it distracted her for no more than a couple of milliseconds – though that was enough time for a figure to emerge.

The movement drew Lucy's attention up from the phone's facia.

Whoever it was, he was only slightly taller than her own five-eight, and his compact shape was possibly exaggerated by his bulky leather jacket. But there was no doubting the threat he posed. In fact, it was a toss-up which was more terrifying: the blood-red woollen ski mask, or the sub-machine gun with shoulder strap, which he raised to chest-height as he aimed it at her.

It was one of those flesh-freezing moments that police officers occasionally encounter.

Lucy didn't panic, as such – but she was too dumbfounded to make any kind of hair-trigger decision. She finally lurched to the right through pure instinct. The expected hail of bullets did not come, but when she heard a loud metallic *clunk* and a hissed curse, it was the kick-starter for headlong flight. The trouble was that the cobbled road surface was old and trodden and broken, and the toe of her left trainer immediately dug itself into a gap between two stones.

It pitched her down face-first.

Lucy was too adrenalised to feel the pain of the full body impact. She simply rolled with it, turning over and springing back to her feet when she heard her phone skittering away, knowing there was no time to retrieve it. She caught a fleeting glimpse of the gunman, arrested in his tracks as he wrestled with his weapon – at which point, another metallic sound, a healthy *click* this time, signalled that whatever component had jammed had now been released.

Lucy ran blindly down Jubilee Gardens. She put forty

yards between herself and the gunman in what seemed like no time. But she knew that wouldn't be enough.

As the first blazing volley split the night, she knew it wasn't *nearly* enough.

Chapter 35

Lucy zigzagged as she fled, surviving the first fusillade.

He ought to have shot her down; she was moving hell for leather, but no one could outrun a bullet. But by sheer fortune, maybe because of the restricted vision through his mask, his raking salvo missed her by several inches, lead projectiles flashing along the cobblestones to her left.

Panic pulsed through her as she ran. She imagined him turning on his heel, weapon still levelled, needing only to hit the trigger to cross-stitch the entire street with slugs. So thinking, she veered fully right, making straight for the nearest doorway. It looked to be covered with chipboard. There could be anything behind it: a solid wooden door; a steel brace. But to stay out in the open was death. She struck the chipboard full on with her shoulder, a blow that stunned her entire body even though she smashed clean through into the recess on the other side.

Another volley of lead thundered into the doorway behind, tearing the jamb to shreds, rebounding from the brickwork with piercing shrieks.

Lucy barrelled forward through dank blackness, finding her way by extending her hands outward, feeling paper hanging on the walls in rags. As she ran, a desperate thought flickered through her head that the sound of the unsuppressed gunfire might alert someone. But just as quickly, she dismissed it: not in this terrible place, where no one even came in daylight unless they had to, let alone in darkness.

An aperture passed on her left; presumably the doorway to the living room. Another aperture followed; maybe the foot of the staircase. Either way, there was nothing for her there: cul-de-sacs, blind alleys in which he'd easily corner her. She cursed herself for having lost her phone. If nothing else, she'd have used it to light her way. The passage suddenly gave out into a broader space. Lucy sensed greater dampness in here, greater rot, and saw weak yellow light filtered through diagonal planks nailed across a glassless window. Just beneath that, it glinted on the rusting relics of a sink and draining board.

Boots now came clumping into the hall behind her; the heavy rasp of breath through wool.

She whimpered, hurling herself across the derelict kitchen – and colliding with a metal-framed table, which the darkness had obscured. She tangled with it, tumbling down onto a tacky, threadbare carpet.

The booted feet thudded up the hallway.

Lucy leapt back up, grabbed the table by two of its aluminium legs and swung it around three-sixty degrees before releasing it, flinging it at the blacker-than-black oblong of the doorway to the hall – just as the outline of a man appeared there.

Who knew what he saw of the object twirling towards him. But he opened fire all the same, the stroboscopic flash blowing the table every which way, turning it to splinters, to flesh-rending shards. Lucy, meanwhile, had vaulted onto the sink. The unit beneath cracked under her weight, but she ignored it, bullocking her way towards the boarded aperture fists bunched in front of her face in case there was glass she hadn't noticed. The diagonal planks erupted from their moorings as she fell out head-first, taking the stinging blow from the paving stones on the flats of her hands.

Again, adrenaline fogged the pain as she leapt back to her feet, finding herself in a typical terraced house backyard – though there was no easy route to its gate, it was so crammed with rubbish: bricks and masonry, stacks of furniture, mounds of festering household waste.

Hearing movement behind, she threw herself backward, flattening her body against the strip of wall alongside the kitchen window, sucking in two lungfuls of air and trapping it inside her. Sweat streamed down her face as she heard his harsh breathing, sensing him on the other side of the window frame, only inches away as he peered out into the dim yard.

It was anyone's guess how much of it he could see with his restricted vision. His solution was to riddle the entire yard with another strobe-like burst, kicking up multiple divots of filth, hammering ruined furniture into heaps of pulverised scrap.

Lucy, ears ringing to the roar of discharge, could only press herself harder into the bricks, more feverish sweat seeping from her brow. The shooting stopped and she heard him fumbling with something. A metallic *click* indicated that an empty clip had just been disconnected. With a louder *clack*, a fresh one was slotted into place. Then his feet stumped away across the kitchen. With a banging and smashing, the exterior kitchen door juddered in its frame.

She spun, looking for another escape route.

A wooden fence stood beside her. This too had seen better days. It wasn't just rickety; when she threw herself at it, it fell apart like wet paper. The yard beyond was empty. Frantic, she dashed to the open gateway, and through it into a narrow backstreet.

She veered left and ran as hard as she could. But litter was strewn all along the alley: paper; beer cans; bits of carpets; more broken, scattered furniture. She wove between these obstacles with a speed and agility not just born of her years on the hockey fields and squash courts, but also from sheer, blind desperation. When survival was in doubt, it was amazing what physical reserves you could call on.

Unavoidably, she glanced over her shoulder again. He was coming in swift pursuit, so determinedly, in fact, that it looked like he was actually gaining on her. Even in this gloom, the red blob of his head became clearer and clearer. She could distinguish the sub-machine gun clasped horizontally to his chest, the way a paratrooper would carry it on manoeuvres.

He'd be in shooting range in less than a second.

Lucy swerved left into another backyard, with some vague idea that if she could work her way through this house, she'd be on Jubilee Gardens. From there, she could make it to Felton Lane and her car. But this time, where the house's back door and kitchen window stood, there were slabs of perforated steel fixed with brackets.

A moan of horror wheezed from her chest. She again heard the approach of his feet.

She cast around – and spied a coal shed, its door closed but hanging on a single latch. She yanked it open and set it swinging, before turning, bombing back across the yard and vaulting over its five-foot brick wall. She landed in what had once been a flower bed, but was now a tangle of thorns and desiccated weeds. As she did, she heard him enter the next yard and, taking in the swinging door, open up on the shed with everything he had.

Lucy scurried towards the rear of this latest house. There was no metal on the doorway here, only chipboard again. To bludgeon her way through that would alert him, but with no choice, she charged at it. However, before she reached it, she kicked an old metal watering can, which bounced across the yard.

Looking back, she saw the reddish outline of his head pop up over the wall.

He didn't fire – which confused her. Until he withdrew, and she heard a fumbling and clicking as he replaced his latest empty magazine. Then she hit the chipboard headlong, crashing through it with an impact so massive that she literally saw lights in front of her eyes. Dazed and disoriented, she toppled over, landing on all fours, and crawling away from the open doorway at an angle. When she glanced back through the narrow gap this afforded her, she saw him reappear at the wall and level his weapon – and a blinding staccato volley exploded towards her.

Only the fact that she was on hands and knees saved her, the hail of lead peppering the wall above her head, knocking out chunks of plaster and pipework, showering her with brick dust.

Yelping like the animal she felt she was imitating, she waddled across the kitchen floor and into the main hall, where she jumped to her feet and ran. Only to skid to a halt, as the poor light spilling in from the kitchen showed riveted steel instead of a front door.

She heard an impact as he alighted in the yard.

Staring back through the kitchen, she saw him. He'd landed badly, by the looks of it on one knee. He struggled to get up, but still managed to lurch in through the shattered kitchen door.

Lucy went left, barging into what had once been the living room. Though exceedingly dark thanks to the sheet steel covering the window, enough light leaked in to show that finally there was nowhere else to run. She turned helplessly, her eyes only adjusting enough so that she could see how empty the room was; it was featureless save for a faux-marble mantelpiece above the maw of a fireplace. Outside, his footsteps came down the hall.

They were clumsy now, awkward. He grunted with pain and effort. He'd hurt himself and was clearly exhausted. But he still had the gun.

Lucy scampered to the fireplace, the darkest point in the room, squatted down and backed into it, crushing her knees against her chest, wrapping her arms around them to make herself as small and insignificant as she could.

And he came in, puffing, gasping, clouds of breath hanging around him. He limped into the middle of the room, so close that she could smell the rankness of his sweat. But now he seemed puzzled. Perhaps, yet again, that mask, which had to be sopping wet, had prevented him spotting her straight away. He dropped the sub-machine gun to his hip; it swung there from its leather strap. Fabric rustled. Perhaps he was digging into a pocket, looking for a torch or phone. Either way, Lucy realised, it was now or never.

With every vestige of strength left in her gym-toned legs, she catapulted herself up and out from the fireplace, hurtling at him, striking him hard – but taking his shoulder in her chest, which brutally winded her, and sliming her nose and mouth on the sweat-soaked material of his mask.

But Lucy wasn't heavy, and though he grunted with surprise, he tottered rather than fell over. When she wrapped her arms and legs around him, he rammed his elbow into her belly.

The pain was horrible, nauseating. But she clung on, even when he twirled her around like a doll, hacking wild punches into her. Desperate, pushing her face into his, she clamped her teeth as hard as she could on what she assumed would be his nose. She was right, her incisors impressing through the soggy wool, grinding into the cartilage beneath.

His grunts became shrill squeals of pain as, doglike, she worked her head from side to side, yanking and ripping at his tortured flesh. But then, in a massive overhead blow, he brought his fist over. It impacted not on Lucy's skull, which it would surely have crushed, but on her left shoulder

White-out pain sheared through her like a guillotine blade.

She crumpled to the floor, where he kicked her in the ribs, but he too was in pain and the kick lacked power, serving only to flip her over, enabling her to scramble around him on all fours.

He whimpered, turning almost drunkenly as he tried to locate her.

As she wobbled back to her feet, he swung a wild punch. Lucy raised her right arm and trapped his wrist in her armpit, before retaliating with a punch of her own, smacking him full on his damaged nose. Even this impact was less than she'd hoped for. His head hinged backward, but he kept his feet, lugging his arm free, yanking his right glove off in the process and striking back at her. It was another wild haymaker, and this time he connected – though not so much with a balled fist as with an open-handed slap.

He wasn't trying to punch her, she realised, he was trying to grab her by the hair.

The chase was over for this guy. He couldn't risk her getting away a second time. He had to finish her off here and now. It was a stinging impact nevertheless, knocking Lucy sideways, four streaks of agony racing down her cheek as his nails ploughed her.

She teetered away, trying to circle him, but this was an error – as he still had sufficient energy to raise the gun at her. She flew back at him, wrapping her hands around its barrel, desperately trying to push it sideways. He backhanded her across the face. Head muzzy, vision seesawing, Lucy hung onto the weapon, forcing its muzzle away from her, as they turned round and round, as though dancing.

He hissed in rage and exertion.

She headbutted him – again in the middle of his bitten nose.

He choked in pain, his finger reflexively squeezing the trigger, the weapon blasting the room like a miniature howitzer. Plaster erupted from the walls, and with an echoing *spang-spang-spang*, plate-sized holes were punched in the metal shutter, before it blew out of the window altogether. Lucy headbutted him again. He released one hand from the weapon and tried to grab her throat. She slammed a fist into his right eye. He gasped, releasing her but throwing another punch. It caught her in the mouth with sledgehammer force.

Lucy was hurled backward, jarring her spine against the stone mantel. The gunman staggered and half-overbalanced. Tonguing a loosened tooth, blood filling her mouth, Lucy bolted sideways for the window and sprang up and out through its now empty frame, landing heavily on the mangled metal lying on the pavement outside. She forward-rolled over cobblestones, launching herself back to her feet and sprinting away along the street.

With a grunt, the gunman slid out through the window after her.

Lucy zigzagged, but she too was at the end of her strength, her head woozy from the pounding she'd taken. The world spun, and she found herself tottering sideways and tripping over the opposite kerb.

Panting, he trekked across the road towards her, weapon levelled.

'Oh, God . . .' she sobbed.

He was only about five yards away, when he stopped and gazed down the barrel at her.

And then – *BLAM!* – *BLAM!* – *BLAM!*

Three detonations of a different calibre rang along the street.

Lucy watched agog, as the gunman jerked to each impact – before tilting sideways and hitting the cobblestones like a sack of wet cement.

The sub-machine gun clattered down alongside him.

Hardly able to breathe, she levered herself upright, squinting to see through the gloom, not just bewildered – but perplexed, bamboozled, as she tried to figure out what had just happened.

She sensed the gigantic figure advancing down the middle of the road before she saw him.

He too was armed, but in his case with a pistol; he still aimed it two-handed at the prone figure in the scarlet mask. 'You okay?' he asked.

'*You?*' Lucy could scarcely believe it, but there was no mistaking the towering intruder, not when she'd got so up close and personal with him in the past that she'd half-busted his knee with a wrench. '*Shallicker! Mick bloody Shallicker!*'

'Keeping tabs on you's a full-time sodding job, girl!'

Exhausted though she was, Lucy staggered to her feet. 'What's going on? *What the hell is this?*'

Shallicker halted a few yards away, gun still aimed. 'Was hoping you could tell me?'

He looked and sounded genuinely bewildered, something Lucy had never seen in him before.

She turned and regarded the body, her sweat cooling in the November air. The fallen gunman didn't move, the streams of claret that had partially flowed away between the cobbles already congealing. He lay at an awkward midriff-twist, his left hip propped up in line with the front of his ribcage; the sort of contortion which, in Lucy's experience, only the dead could flop into.

She risked edging closer. At least one of the three slugs

Shallicker had fired had penetrated the front of the leather jacket and presumably the sternum underneath. If there was ever a fatal shot, that had to be one. Not that it made this any easier.

'Is this one of them?' Shallicker asked. 'The Red-Headed League?'

She glanced at him distractedly; she ought to have known the Crew would also be gunning for this renegade band. The big minder's pistol was still trained on the prone form; the eyes in his shadowed face shone like moons, so intently was he watching it.

'Be careful,' he warned, as Lucy squatted down and advanced the last couple of yards on her haunches. 'I may need a clear shot.'

'The bloke's dead, Mick.'

'Yeah, I've heard that before.'

Though it was against all the rules, Lucy dug one hand into her anorak pocket, pulled out a latex glove, and after fitting it in place, reached first for the sub-machine gun, which she intended to toss out of harm's way – only to find it still fastened by the strap to its owner's shoulder. Instead, she laid the gun down and reached underneath the guy's chin. Locating the bottom edge of the ski mask, she slowly worked it upward, finally managing to uncover the whole of his face.

When she succeeded, she could only drop back onto her buttocks with a strangled gasp.

Slowly, Shallicker lowered his weapon. 'You cannot be bloody serious . . .'

Chapter 36

Frank McCracken was still in Crowley when he took the phone call. In fact, he was still on the Crowley Technical College car park, sitting behind the wheel of his Bentley. A short time earlier, he'd seen Joe Lazenby's Ford Galaxy come labouring up from the lower parking area, and drive jerkily towards the exit, where it waited what seemed like an age before pulling out into the evening traffic.

In truth, he was letting the bastard off easily. Stripped of his illegal earnings or not, Lazenby owed the Crew money. They'd made a demand of him that day in Hogarth's wine bar; £140,000, if McCracken remembered rightly. And what would their reputation be worth if they simply walked away from that? It was something they'd need to work out, of course. Lazenby wasn't some street-fighting hoodlum whose head they could squeeze in a vice till he came up with a secret stash. But he *did* have other assets: a house, a car, a regular wage through his day job. In due course, by some discreet means or other, they'd get what he owed them. It wasn't as if McCracken had any choice in the matter, especially not the way things were going; he was supposed to be the Shakedown, the tax-collector – he couldn't keep losing out on big paydays.

But in the meantime, he had other problems to contend with.

And then his phone rang.

He saw that the call was from Mick Shallicker. When he answered, he did so grumpily. 'Better make this good, Mick . . . I've had enough bad news for one day.'

'On a Richter scale of bad news, Frank,' Shallicker said, 'this is pretty seismic.'

McCracken didn't reply; he just waited, listening.

'I've just killed a cop.'

McCracken arrived on Felton Lane in what had to be record time for a busy Friday evening. On arrival, he saw that one car was already parked there: Lucy's Jimny. Not wishing to leave his Bentley out in the open, he found an entrance to a backstreet where there was a row of disused garages. He reversed in, halting alongside another vehicle, the Peugeot 307 that Shallicker had been driving. McCracken didn't know what the hell his minder was playing at. Shooting coppers was no-go territory even for the Crew; it only ever happened in extreme circumstances, and with the entire Board of Directors' approval obtained beforehand. But if nothing else, at least Mick had been sufficiently smart to tuck his vehicle up this backstreet, where no one would see it.

McCracken parked alongside the Peugeot, climbed out, locked up and hurried down to Felton Lane. He found Shallicker about a hundred yards along Jubilee Gardens, standing beside a twisted body, the white face of which had been brutalised to some tune, the right eye swollen closed, the nose a mangled, gory mess.

But it wasn't this that stopped McCracken in his tracks.

He leaned down incredulously.

The dead man's dark hair was cut stylishly short, but his

347

soft, rounded features clearly revealed that he was actually not a man at all.

'A bird!' McCracken half-shouted. 'You're telling me it's not just a cop . . . *but a fucking bird!*'

'Before you really blow a gasket,' Shallicker said, 'I doubt she was here on official business. She was wearing this . . .' he held up the red woollen mask, 'and taking potshots at your lass.'

'And where the fuck is *she*?'

'*She's* here!' Lucy snarled, projecting herself away from a nearby house wall, where she'd been leaning, shivering, arms folded tightly around herself. 'And that *bird* had a name. She was DC Smiley from the Robbery Squad.'

McCracken regarded her stonily, as she walked unsteadily across the cobbles towards him.

He was not unaccustomed to seeing his daughter in an emotional state, but this was a whole new level. To start with, she'd been significantly roughed up, sporting several cuts and bruises, including four particularly livid claw-marks down her left cheek. Her hair, which was longer than when he'd last seen it, hung to her shoulders in a straggling, sweat-soaked mop, giving her an untamed appearance. Her shoulders were hunched, partly through pain, he suspected, but also with anger. She was breathing hard, eyes wild and wet – which was hardly a surprise, he supposed, given that one of her own colleagues lay dead at her feet.

For Lucy's part, the last few minutes had seen her barely able to think straight.

She'd just had something very akin to a near-death experience. She'd been chased and shot at, and beaten savagely as she'd fought for her life, literally having to scrap it out like a tigress. The fact that she'd managed to win that nose-to-nose encounter was more explainable given that her opponent had been female, though in truth it explained nothing of real consequence, because now she was enmeshed in a *genuine* nightmare.

She shuddered uncontrollably at the sight of Smiley's corpse.

It was almost beyond her capability to deal with. It defied all logic, every rule of the game. Nothing Lucy had previously believed in before, or at least *thought* she'd believed in, seemed relevant any more. And then of course there was the double act from hell: Shallicker and her father. She might have known they'd be involved in something as demented and perverse as this.

But she didn't quite know enough – not for her liking.

'What's this fucking gorilla been following me around for?' she shouted. 'How are you two bastards involved in this?'

'You snotty bitch!' Shallicker snapped. 'I just saved your arse.'

'We're involved in nothing!' McCracken stuck a warning finger in her face. 'And you'd better watch your tone, my girl. Mick's right – it's thanks to us that you're alive and kicking.'

'Let me guess,' she said. 'You've been trying to find out who's been robbing your mates? Is that why you've been tailing me?'

He shrugged. 'Who was going to make ground on the case, if not you?'

'*Bastard!*' She was so angry she wanted to spit. 'You sodding bastard! You really think you can prey on me like this?'

'I've advised you to mind your tone,' he said firmly. 'I won't say it again.'

'*For Christ's sake . . . there's a police officer dead!*'

'And was she a real police officer?' he wondered. 'Sounds

like she didn't have any qualms about topping one of her own colleagues!'

Lucy stared at the body, still helpless and horror-struck by that reality.

'Who is this anyway?' McCracken asked. 'You said her name was Smiley?'

'Ruth Smiley,' Lucy replied.

'And she was in the Robbery Squad . . . for real?'

'Yes, *for real!*' Lucy's anger flared again. Somewhat pointlessly, she realised. Smiley had hardly behaved like a genuine copper. Not that evening, at least.

'Did she arrange for you to meet her here?' McCracken asked.

'No, she . . .'

At first, Lucy's mouth was too dry to say anything else. In the terrible chaos of flight and fight, and then in the midst this shocking, bloody aftermath, she hadn't had time to ponder how it had all started. Until now.

'That was *Danny Tucker*. Sweet mother of . . .'

Her father eyed her with interest. 'Who's Danny Tucker?'

'DS Danny Tucker . . .' She still struggled to find the words. 'Also with . . . with the Robbery Squad. They were *both* in the Robbery Squad.'

McCracken sniffed. 'And by the sounds of it, this Robbery Squad of yours does exactly what it says on the tin.'

'No . . . *no!*' Lucy blurted, staggering tearfully away. 'This isn't happening.'

McCracken watched her coolly. 'I can see you're under pressure, love. I would be too. But perhaps it's time to set your police loyalties aside and put your thinking cap on, eh?'

She spun back. 'This can't be it! It just can't!'

'Where is he now, this DS Tucker?'

'I don't know, but . . . but . . .' She could barely bring

herself to say it a second time, but she had to face the facts: Danny Tucker had been the one who'd told her to meet him here. No one else.

'Were you getting close to an answer?' McCracken wondered.

'I'd just . . .' Lucy's words trailed off, as she toyed with the idea that maybe Tucker had been shot as well, and now was lying dead somewhere nearby. But she knew that he hadn't. Danny and Ruth had been close. Plus, how weird had it seemed that he'd asked her to come and see him *here* . . . in a Godforsaken place like this?

And there was no denying it: she *had* been close.

Tears dripped down her cheeks as she acknowledged this to herself. Her discovery of the Mission Hall CCTV and her plan to pull the rest of the town centre footage to see which cars were in the vicinity must have been the clincher.

'Something tells me you know stuff we don't,' McCracken said.

'Stuff you'll *never* know!' she retorted.

'Not prepared to share just yet? Okay . . .' he nodded to himself, 'well, let's see if I can prompt you. Another target of this Red-Headed League . . . yeah, they're so well known to us, Luce, they've even got their own nickname, courtesy of Sherlock Holmes, I think . . . was a wannabe drug-supplier called Joe Lazenby. Ordinary Joe. I'd say keep your ears open for that name, but I don't think you'll hear of it much from now on. He's already been put out of business by these characters. But they didn't just rob him of one-sixty K, they also burned his stash of coke . . . half a million's worth. What do you think to that, eh? Is that the sort of public-spirited act you'd expect from the average armed robber?'

Lucy wiped her tears as she listened. Despite everything, her innate copper was fascinated to learn these details. Slowly but surely, it was all making a crazy if horrifying kind of sense?

'Do you know a loan shark called Roy Shankhill?' she asked.

McCracken eyed her warily. "Yeah, we know him.'

'Then you're aware that if he owes you any tax, from now on you'll have to take it in IOUs?'

'We're aware he's been hit,' McCracken confirmed.

'How could we not be?' Shallicker said. 'That was another big earner gone.'

'The point is he had a customer with him at the time,' Lucy said. 'One of his debtors. This lad offered his own money to the robbers while they were there. But they wouldn't take it. Said he could keep it.'

Shallicker sniggered. 'Very John fucking Dillinger.'

McCracken looked less amused.

Lucy walked around the body. The implications were sinking in fast, but they were almost impossible to believe. Police officers robbing the underworld? Who'd heard of such a thing? But the more she agonised over it, the more it all fell into place. The acts of charity. The sparing of the innocent. And the high-end weapons . . . a former army girl like Ruth Smiley would have had better contacts than most in *that* field.

But there were still questions.

Danny Tucker, for one, was disillusioned with police life. Okay, he didn't demonstrate it all the time, but he was livid about the threat the Robbery Squad was living under. Conceivably, that could have destabilised him. But even if it had, how did committing his own armed robberies bring a solution? Sure, the takings were going to good causes, but even so, given that most of the APs were villains, the blags weren't likely to be reported, so it wasn't as if a new crime wave had suddenly hit the headlines that would ensure the Squad's continued existence.

'Whatever,' McCracken said, interrupting her thoughts. 'One thing's certain . . . you can't call *this* in, can you?'

Lucy glanced up at him. 'Are you mad?'

'Are *you*?' By his grave expression, he was perfectly serious. 'One of these bad apples is now dead, but there's at least one other one still running around, and how many more on top of that?'

Again, Lucy tried to resist his unerring logic.

All the evidence pointed to three blaggers and no more, in some cases only two. That didn't mean they didn't have support units out there . . . but surely not? The Robbery Squad were an elite police outfit; handpicked detectives all with superb records. But then, hadn't that been the same of the Flying Squad down in London, on whom the Manchester Robbery Squad had originally been based? She recalled *Operation Countryman* – it had been before her time, back in the 1970s, but it had seen the Flying Squad fall under suspicion, not for carrying out their own robberies, but for taking massive bribes. Only a couple of detectives had been convicted of actual crimes, as she recalled, but comments were still made that semi-autonomous, specialist units of that sort needed much tighter control, that they operated too far outside the police norm and, as such, were always likely to attract edgy characters.

But aside from Lee Gaskin, none of the other Robbery Squad members seemed to fulfil that stereotype.

For what it was worth, Lucy had already decided that Gaskin was the third member of the gang; she'd met some twisted, obnoxious coppers in her time, but he was like a creature from another world. On top of that, if anyone had a *bona fide* reason to engage in a shooting war with the underworld, it was him. But Danny Tucker? Ruth Smiley?

'Look . . .' She struggled to articulate this mass of contra-dictory thoughts. 'Look . . . the Robbery Squad is full of time-served cops who've proved they're solid. There's no way it can be *all* of them.'

'Doesn't need to be all of them to put *you* on Shit Street,' Shallicker said.

'No . . . *this is bollocks!*'

'They've already tried to pop you once, love.'

'They don't need to go that far now,' McCracken added. 'I mean, did anyone else know you were supposed to be coming here?'

Lucy shook her head. 'I don't think so.'

He shrugged. 'In which case, all this Tucker character needs to do now is blame you for this murderous bitch's death.'

'Yeah, but no one'll believe that . . .'

Even before she finished the sentence, Lucy realised that it was nonsense.

Tucker could easily testify that she was supposed to have met him here, and perhaps add some lie that he'd got delayed and sent Smiley instead. Maybe concoct another lie, maybe say that Smiley was concerned that Lucy was going to replace her on the team – which had led to a fight. And good God, they'd ended up having one hell of a fight. Lucy's DNA would be all over the body. Her face had been scratched, so she'd even left skin under Smiley's fingernails.

'No . . . no.' Still she shook her head. 'I *have* to call this in. Even if I'm arrested and investigated, I can sort this out. There must be all kinds of evidence round here that Smiley was shooting at me.'

'Not for much longer,' Shallicker chuckled.

'That's right,' McCracken said. 'This whole estate's going under the demolisher's hammer in a week or so, isn't it? Nothing left but mountains of rubble.'

'Good Lord . . .' Lucy suddenly understood why Danny had wanted her to meet him *here*.

'Besides . . . do you really think it'll get that far?' McCracken shrugged again. 'However many of these bastards there are, you were closing in on them. Oh, they'll make a show of arresting you. But in reality, they still want you dead.'

She shook her head. 'They won't be able to pull that off. Not when I'm in custody.'

'You've just indicated you don't know who they are. Or how many they are. I wouldn't walk voluntarily into their arms, if it was me.'

Lucy tried to think straight. It was too much. It was simply too much.

'Go and get the car,' McCracken told Shallicker, handing over the keys to his Bentley. 'Bring it down to the fence.'

The big minder trudged away up the cobbled street.

'And that's it?' Lucy said. 'You're leaving . . . just walking away?'

'So are you,' McCracken replied, 'if you've any sense. What do you not understand about them trying to kill you? And do you seriously believe that if they've tried it once, they won't try again?'

She couldn't answer, so he turned and walked away.

This jolted Lucy into a hurried pursuit, urging her to shout out an order, to tell him that he needed to stay and give evidence, that he had to help her tell the truth. But she knew it would be futile.

By the time they reached the top of the street, Shallicker had already brought the Bentley down to the gap in the fence. He waited alongside it at the head of the rugged slope.

'*I'm* not leaving,' Lucy said defiantly. 'I *can't*.'

'Isn't like you have a choice,' McCracken said. 'Stay here, they'll pop you. Go to the nick, they'll pop you. Even drive away in your own car, they'll pop you . . . it'll just take a bit longer. So why don't you get in mine?'

Her gaze switched to the Bentley and then back.

'For *real*?' she said. 'You seriously think I'm going to disappear into the shadows with a bunch of hoods like you lot? How guilty would that make me look?'

Her father glanced exasperatedly at his watch. 'I'm going to make two final appeals to you, Lucy. Firstly, to your head . . . you don't know anything about the opposition, either its strength or its disposition. You go back to your nick now, and you'll be walking blind among people who may hate you. In addition, if you think you're just gonna dob Mick Shallicker in for this shooting, you're in for a shock. It will be denied at our end across the board. The gun that fired the fatal shots will disappear, and they'll only have your word for it that he was ever here.'

Lucy couldn't reply. She ought to have realised that the mobsters would look after their own.

'You know *my* form, darling,' McCracken said. 'I'll have unshakeable alibis constructed for both of us by midnight. On top of that, I'll be mightily pissed off if you turn this fella in after he saved your life. You hear what I'm saying? We'll leave you twisting in the wind, completely alone to face whatever nastiness comes your way. It might also occur to you that you'll find it very difficult revealing who pulled the trigger on that cop without revealing mine and your special relationship.'

'We don't have a special—'

'We *do*. Whether you like it or not.' He studied her with his cold, grey eyes. 'Nothing's changed since last time, love. You're my daughter . . . and as soon as word of that gets out, I'm finished as a gangster, and you're finished as one of Manchester's finest. So, you need to engage that cute little head of yours. Secondly . . . I'm going to appeal to your heart . . . or I'm going to try. Because you really ought to consider that Mick here has just gone out on a limb for you.'

Lucy glanced at the towering figure waiting by the car. He regarded her, blank-faced.

'But he took another life in the process . . .'

'In an effort to save you,' McCracken said. 'At which he was successful. And your plan now is to hand him over? In our code – and to a certain extent in yours, I think – you *owe* this fella. Will you be able to rest easily if he goes down for life?'

'I'm a police officer, not a hoodlum. I can't ignore serious offences when they happen right in front of me.'

'Well . . . it's your choice.' McCracken strolled up the slope. 'If the regulations come first, that's fine . . . if you want to be a good little plastic soldier, there's nothing I can do. But *we're* leaving right now, even if you aren't. I have important people of my own to talk to.'

Lucy knew what this meant: he was going to report to the Crew. And that would be it for the Robbery Squad. They'd kill Tucker for sure, but only after torturing him to discover who his confederates were – and then they'd kill them as well.

'Wait!' She scrambled uphill after him.

At the top, McCracken turned again.

'I'm not denying that these blaggers are rogue cops,' Lucy said. 'And I understand why you want them dead . . . but how will that work out for you? A bunch of murdered police officers? Seriously? No one's going to let that drop. You'll be watching your backs for the rest of time. Meanwhile, what's left of the Robbery Squad will be boosted. There'll be sympathy for them, and anger that their colleagues fell in the line of duty.'

'Like we give a shit,' Shallicker said.

'Well that shows how thick you are!' she retorted. 'Look . . .' she focussed on McCracken. 'GMP top brass are seriously thinking about closing the Robbery Squad. One of

357

your worst nightmares will be taken off the table altogether. But you pop a few more of its officers and things could change. They'll say these guys served a purpose after all, that they've got the underworld scared. So, then they won't be shut down – they'll get more men, more resources. They'll interfere with your cash flow like you've never known.'

McCracken remained stony-faced, but at least appeared to be listening.

'But if I can arrest these guys as criminals,' Lucy said, 'and bang them up completely legally, it'll be very different. They'll say the Robbery Squad's corrupt, they'll put what's left of them under the most intense scrutiny they've ever known . . . and those who want them gone because they're an expensive luxury will go at it full steam.' She paused, breathing hard. 'So that's the deal? Kill these Red-Headed blaggers and the Squad lives on? Or let me arrest them and the Squad disappears?'

'You put your case passionately, Lucy,' McCracken finally said. 'I'll give you that. The trouble is . . . we can't leave it to you. You're good, darling, but you're not *that* good.'

'I'm not going to back off . . . I have to do what I think is right.'

He pondered that. 'As long as you know that if you refuse my help now, you're completely on your own . . . though perhaps I can spare a few quid to help your mum with the funeral.'

Lucy stared at him dumbly.

'That's it?' he asked her. 'Mind made up? Okay.'

She gave a single nod in response, and then stood alone by the gap in the fence as, first of all, her father climbed into his Bentley, and the big car wheeled its way through a huge three-point turn and roared off along Felton Lane, and secondly, as Shallicker's vehicle, a Peugeot 307, came barrelling through a gap between two boarded-up units opposite, and followed it.

She ought to have arrested them, she told herself.

Yeah, like that would have been possible.

But they'd spoken the truth. Robbery Squad personnel had been carrying out these violent raids. Robbery Squad personnel had tried to assassinate her because they'd feared she was about to uncover them. Robbery Squad personnel could be on their way here right now, wondering why their girl on the ground hadn't reported back.

With uncannily perfect timing, a police siren commenced yowling in the near distance.

'My God,' Lucy breathed, scarcely able to believe what she was now contemplating.

Before she did anything else, she knew that she should go back down Jubilee Gardens and try to recover her phone, if for no other reason than to prevent it being found in the vicinity of a murdered police officer. Not that it mattered a great deal given that her DNA was clogging said officer's fingernails. But there was no time for that now.

The next question, therefore, was what to do next?

When a second siren joined the first, the pair of them drawing steadily nearer, Lucy dashed to her Jimny, jumped behind the wheel and gunned it away from the kerb.

Chapter 37

The revelation about the blaggers' identities was no consolation to Frank McCracken. In some ways it was good, not least because it meant they could finally bring this business to an end. But in others, it was a choker. It wasn't just that going to war against the Manchester Robbery Squad would cause a ruckus the likes of which the Northwest of England hadn't seen in decades, and that all their income streams would flatline as a consequence, at least temporarily; the main problem was how McCracken was going to explain all this to Wild Bill.

He couldn't outline his discovery of the rogue cops without outlining how it had happened that Mick Shallicker shot one of them, which meant he'd have to clarify why Shallicker had been tailing a low-level divisional detective working from Robber's Row police station.

He was sure he could think up a reason in due course – an anonymous tip-off might be the best option, an unknown and untraceable person leaving them a note about the Robbery Squad. But he wasn't comfortable even with that. Pentecost would want to know much more: why Shallicker had been down on the Archways in the first place, why they hadn't called in a clean-up unit to remove the body and all traces of Crew involvement.

Clearly, a more complex and carefully devised solution was called for.

As he ruminated on this, he received a call. He checked his hands-free, and was barely surprised, though it still sent a chill through him, to see that it came from the Chairman himself.

'Bill?' McCracken said.

'Where are you, Frank?'

'In Crowley . . . chasing up a couple of leads.'

'Anything solid?'

'Well . . .' McCracken hesitated. 'I've heard a whisper – only a whisper, mind – that this could all be down to some London team who are trying to gain a foothold in the north.'

'London, eh?'

Was it McCracken's imagination, or did Pentecost sound even more sceptical than usual?

'I've no more detail, unfortunately, Bill.'

What had seemed like a good idea two seconds ago, didn't any longer. McCracken had been working on the basis that diverting everyone's attention south might just buy him sufficient time to work out an effective cover story. But now, even to his own ears, it didn't sound credible.

'Enjoy making regular four-hundred-mile round-trips, do they?' Pentecost drawled. 'Cost them as much in fuel as they're actually earning.'

'Like I say . . . it was just a whisper.'

'Well, it so happens, Frank, that I've heard a whisper too. And I think this one may have a bit more substance to it. Which is why I'm giving you a call . . . just to put you in the picture, like.'

'Okay . . .?'

'But first a question, Frank . . . what can you tell me about a police detective called Lucy Clayburn?'

361

McCracken couldn't initially respond. The question hit him like a breeze block passing through the windscreen. In fact, he nearly *did* have a collision, sailing blindly past a red light and causing a Fiat Brava to skid onto the pavement, tooting its horn.

'Sorry about that, Bill,' he said. 'Some fucking dipsticks behind the wheel in this town.'

'What about Detective Clayburn?'

'Yeah, erm . . . what about her? Who is she?'

'You don't know?'

It sounded like a loaded question, terrifyingly so – sweat already dabbled McCracken's brow – but it didn't necessarily presage disaster. The older and more paranoid he became, the more Bill Pentecost interacted with his underlings as though routinely mistrustful of their loyalty. Posing questions as if he didn't expect to get the answer he wanted was a tactic designed to undermine confidence, to make people feel constantly as if they were in trouble; and increasingly it was nothing new.

'I don't know every copper in Manchester,' McCracken replied simply.

There was a long pause, which didn't bode well, though it might merely have been more of the same.

'Someone seems to think she was involved in that business with the Twisted Sisters last year,' Pentecost finally said.

'Erm . . . possibly.' McCracken tried to make it sound as though he was struggling to rack his brains. 'What do you mean "involved"?'

'As in she gave evidence against them.'

'She might have. I didn't follow the case.'

'Well . . . this is as much as anyone seems to know about her.'

Sensing a change in tone, as though Pentecost was mildly disappointed – in other words, he didn't know anything about Lucy either – McCracken allowed himself to relax a little. 'Why're you asking me, anyway?'

'I'm asking everyone, Frank . . . I want to know who she is, and whether she's any good or not. And no one's able to tell me.'

'Well . . . if she's a lower rank, just a workhorse . . .'

'Whether she's a workhorse or not, we need to speak to her.'

'I don't get you, Bill.'

'This whisper I've heard is about her. Someone, who I suspect is in a position to know, thinks she's been doing some work on our mask-wearing friends, and not only that, has developed some promising information.'

'Okay . . .' McCracken thought fast: no contact between Lucy Clayburn and Bill Pentecost could ever be a good thing, but there might still be a way he could turn this to their advantage. 'Do you want me to find out where she works . . . perhaps have a discreet word?'

'Oh, I think the time for discretion is past. Besides, someone else is on the case now.'

That wasn't good news, and this time McCracken was barely able to conceal his concern. 'You don't mean those three lunatics Benny B's brought in?'

There was a long, reflective pause. 'Does that bother you, Frank?'

'Don't you think it's a bit heavy-handed, Bill? I mean, this is just a work-a-day copper who may know something.'

'If so, all well and good. By this time tomorrow, *we'll* know it too.'

McCracken sat rigid behind the wheel, oblivious to the darkened streets as they flickered by.

It seemed pointless mentioning to the Chairman that if they adopted a gloves-off approach like this, it would be impossible to backtrack from it afterwards. Pentecost already knew that; as he'd said himself, the time for discretion was past. At the board meeting, he'd advised everyone that Benny B's trio of hired guns were 'fully authorised to use any methods they deemed fit'. In that light, once they'd got what they needed from Lucy, they'd simply dispose of her – assuming she'd survived the actual interrogation – they couldn't possibly risk her going back to the rest of the cops and telling them what had happened. It was nothing less than common sense.

Even so, McCracken felt he had to say *something*.

'Bill . . . don't you think this may be a bit of an extreme measure?'

'Yes, I do, Frank. But we are where we are.'

McCracken struggled to find a further objection. It was a rare occasion indeed when the Crew put any kind of contract on a serving police officer, but it wasn't completely unknown. Not in times of genuine crisis.

'It could really blow up in our faces,' he finally said, somewhat lamely.

'It's already blowing up. There are dickheads wandering the streets saying the Crew are finished.'

McCracken hadn't noticed any of this himself, but he understood the concern even if there was only a hint of it. 'Listen,' he coaxed, 'I know we're in a spot here. But why not let *me* take this lead . . . have a quiet word? You know how persuasive I can be.'

'Doesn't seem to be working on this occasion, Frank.'

'I've hardly had a chance . . .'

'It's too late. Things are already in motion. Besides, a lesson needs to be taught.'

And that was something else McCracken couldn't argue with. Under different circumstances, it was an approach he'd adopt himself. There were way too many wannabes who needed reminding from time to time just who the top dogs in this part of the world actually were. And how better to do it than by demonstrating that even coppers couldn't be allowed to get in the way once the Crew were on the warpath?

'You still there?' Pentecost wondered.

'Where else?'

'Good . . . just thought I'd put you in the picture. Let me know how you get on if you decide to go to London, by the way . . . just in case.'

And the line went dead.

Immediately, McCracken speed-dialled Shallicker.

'Frank?'

'There's a pub on the outskirts of Crowley, on the approach road to the M61, called The Dog and Biscuit. Meet me there.'

'When?'

'Now.'

Before she was anywhere near home, Lucy had already decided that she would go official with what had happened. There was no option but to try and avoid implicating her father or his sidekick, so she was going to claim that an unknown shooter had put Ruth Smiley down at the end of their brutal fight in the house on Jubilee Gardens.

They might find it hard to believe, but they wouldn't be able to prove otherwise. And anyway, everything else was true. She'd got to the Archways through legitimate means, as part of her own investigation, and then they'd tried to murder her. All the evidence would point to Smiley being one of the killers, while Lucy was clean. They could strip-search her if they wanted, but they'd find no gunfire residue on her person. Of course, it was wrong on so many counts, trying to protect a pair of villains like McCracken and Shallicker, even if they had been trying to help her – but if it would also protect her job, what the hell?

The real question was how could she ensure that this

truncated version of the truth arrived with the right people. The obvious person to call would be Kathy Blake, but Lucy thought again about *Operation Countryman*, which had ultimately failed to convict anyone because, or so the rumour-mongers held, the corruption was so extensive within the suspect departments that it was in no one's interest to see it happen. It was almost impossible to imagine that so respected a senior officer as Kathy Blake could be involved in something as crazy as this, but she and Lucy had only become acquainted relatively recently – so there was no certainty there.

In contrast, of course, there was one top cop Lucy *knew* she could trust, and that was Stan Beardmore.

He wouldn't be on duty now; he'd be at home – but she'd called him at home many times, and he didn't mind. There was one small problem, however: all the contact numbers she had for the DI were listed on her phone, which was still on the Archways. She hadn't memorised any of them. In fact, there was only police number she had memorised because she'd needed to call it so often, and that was Harry Jepson's mobile – but she couldn't even call that until she got to a landline, which was why she was now headed home.

She drove across the Brenner estate, her home neighbour-hood, slowly and carefully, constantly checking in her rear-view mirror to ensure that no one had pulled out from a parking space in pursuit. It was 7 p.m., and only twenty minutes had elapsed since she'd left the Archways. On reflec-tion, it seemed doubtful that those sirens had been responding to a lack of communication from Ruth Smiley, as that would mean the bastards were blowing the whole thing wide open before they'd even had a chance to get their story straight. Even when they found her body, they'd have to confer to try and cover their backs, and only then would they feel sufficiently secure to alert the top brass, who, totally bewil-dered, would want a much fuller explanation before they consented to put out an all-points on one of their own officers. Most likely, the office would try to contact her by normal means first, to get her to come in voluntarily, and if that failed, would instruct mobile patrols to try and find her discreetly rather than going at it with the blues and twos. Lucy would have expected all that to take several hours.

But the truth was, she couldn't be absolutely sure.

She cruised to a halt at the end of her road, Cuthbertson Court.

It was vintage suburbia; a quiet cul-de-sac of detached and semi-detached houses, most with front gardens, cars on their drives and curtains drawn against the autumn darkness.

Lucy lived in a bungalow at the far end. But she didn't drive straight down there.

Okay, an official police response to Ruth Smiley's death, with Lucy as the prime suspect, might take hours to get going, but just suppose the Robbery Squad had opted to circumvent all that? Suppose they were simply going to hit her again? She didn't think it possible that anyone who'd turned up at the Archways after she'd left, and had then headed straight here, could have overtaken her – but it wasn't impossible that they'd stationed someone here anyway, just in case.

She edged forward a dozen yards, and halted.

She could now see her bungalow beyond the curve at the far end.

It sat there as normal. There was no sign of anything out of the ordinary. Every car parked between here and there, she felt certain she could account for as belonging to neighbours.

And yet why did she feel so damn uneasy?

Warily, she edged forward. Still nothing moved: in the front gardens she passed, in the darkened spaces alongside the houses, in her rear-view mirror.

367

She finally pulled onto her own drive, and applied the handbrake.

She sat listening, probing gingerly at the four deep rips in her left cheek, but too preoccupied with scanning the front of her property to pay it any attention, in particular the side passage. There was a wrought-iron gate there, but it was closed and only darkness lay beyond.

She climbed out of the car, listening. Rush hour was over, and the estate was quiet, the only sound the rustle of autumn leaves drifting across the blacktop. Lucy walked to the front door and opened it – and it was only then, as she stepped inside, that she sensed a problem.

The burglar alarm did not commence its usual angry chittering.

The box on the wall was dead, its miniature light-show absent, which could only mean that its power cable had been cut. She quickly hit a switch, the hall light coming on – to reveal a rubble of broken pots and ornaments, of scattered papers and torn cushions, not just strewing the hall, but leading into and out of both the lounge-diner and bedroom, and even the kitchen.

Numbed, Lucy waded forward.

Was this a routine break-in, or something else?

At first, she could barely string two thoughts together to provide an answer.

When she came level with the back door, it stood open a couple of inches, having been jemmied: the jamb was shattered, the lock hanging out in tangle of splintered wood. Not atypical of everyday burglars. But there was still something vaguely *professional* about this.

To do the alarm first? How many opportunist thieves had that skill?

Not that it would have made sense for the Robbery Squad to be involved. What the hell could *they* have been looking for? After that last phone call she'd made to Tucker, they knew everything Lucy knew. And they couldn't have expected to find her here, as they were the ones who'd lured her down to the Archways.

However, when she entered the kitchen, she saw something that took this incident entirely out of the realms of the routine.

As before, the entire room had been wrecked, every cupboard kicked in, every drawer pulled out, crockery and cutlery scattered in what looked like a needless frenzy. Even the landline, which occupied a worktop near the door, had been ripped out and thrown wall to wall, until its casing was smashed and its innards hung out. In its place, clearly having finally been discovered in the drawer underneath, lay her telephone and address book. When the intruders had found what they were looking for inside it, it had obviously been abandoned there, wide open, but with a single tell-tale page torn out.

The page on which all entries started with an M.

If Lucy's memory was correct, there was only one of those. *Mum.*

Chapter 38

Lucy and Cora's houses were at opposite ends of the borough, so, though Lucy crossed Crowley at reckless speed, using every short cut she knew, it still took half an hour.

Saltbridge, a residential district, was much quieter than the town centre, and she navigated through most of its network of narrow streets on two wheels, tyres squealing. At the same time, she scanned left and right for anything even vaguely untoward; any persons ducking out of sight, any vehicles speeding away. When she reached her mother's address, a space was available directly in front of it. Thanking God, Lucy slid to a halt, jumped out and, with heart hammering on her ribs, strode quickly to the front door.

It was closed and locked, which might be a good sign, but then again . . .

She peered along the street in both directions, eyes straining hard to ensure that there really was no one loafing around who shouldn't be, no one keeping watch from a side-alley or sitting in a suspiciously parked car. Everything appeared to be normal and the night remained quiet, but sweat still dabbled her brow as she let herself into the house.

Immediately, she heard the television in the lounge.

And then a voice called out: 'Hello?'

It was her mother's.

More relieved than she could say, but still with an over-whelming sense of urgency, Lucy replied that it was only her, closing the front door firmly behind her and, applying the safety chain. She checked in the kitchen first, where the back door was also closed and locked, before going into the lounge.

Cora looked as if she'd just come in from her evening exercise walk, which she usually did with her best friend, Maggie Denton. She was back on her own now, wearing a blue tracksuit and white trainers, and sitting on the sofa with her feet up, a mug of steamy tea on the rectangular coffee table next to her. Her hair was done up in clips, but damp and hanging in strands. Though a news programme was on the TV, Cora's reading glasses perched on the end of her nose as she worked her way through the *Manchester Evening News*.

'Thank God you're in,' Lucy said.

Cora gave a wry smile. 'You thought I'd be off gallivanting somewhere?'

'Well, it *is* Friday night.'

As Lucy said this, she stepped into the lamplight, and Cora saw the claw marks on her face.

'Oh, my God!' The newspaper dropped into her lap. 'What's happened this time?'

'Nothing to worry about.' Lucy moved to the telephone on the sideboard. 'Listen, can you pack an overnight bag?'

Cora stood up. 'What . . . why?'

'Mum, don't argue please . . .' She put the receiver to her ear. 'Just go upstairs, grab yourself some toiletries and a nightie or something, and straight back down here, okay?'

Cora knew better than to resist Lucy merely on principle, but this was a lot to ask. She'd just settled down after a busy week at the MiniMart, and everything she'd just said notwithstanding, she actually *did* have plans for later this evening, because yes, it *was* a Friday.

She removed her glasses. 'So where are we supposed to be going?'

'I don't know, I'm winging things a bit.'

'Lucy . . .'

'Mum . . .' Lucy commenced dialling, 'do you think I'd ask you to do this if it wasn't vital?'

With an irritated sigh, an extra loud one to show that this really wasn't good enough, Cora walked from the room.

Lucy waited impatiently as the phone rang out at the other end.

She had no clue why whoever had raided her house might have an interest in coming here, unless they viewed her mother as the weak point in her armour. Getting to a beloved family member was an obvious way to get to her. If it didn't draw Lucy out, it would still give them massive leverage over her. But somehow, probably because she knew the district better than they did, she'd managed to get ahead of them, and now she intended to keep it that way.

'Come on, come on,' she said into the phone.

'Yeah?' came a sudden, lazy-voiced response.

'Harry!' she blurted, with a gush of relief. 'It's me.'

'Lucy?' He sounded oddly distrustful. She wondered if word had now got around that she was a suspect in the murder of a fellow police officer, or if it was just Harry being cagey because he thought she might be about to enquire when he was planning to return to work.

'Where are you?' she asked.

'Running some errands, why?'

'Have you been back to the office at all? I mean today?'

'Why would I, I'm still off sick?' His tone shifted from cagey to defensive. 'Listen, Lucy . . . just because I'm out and about that doesn't mean—'

'Cut the shit, Harry. Listen to me . . . I need you to get in touch with Stan Beardmore.'

'Eh?'

'I'd do it myself, but I haven't got time to be writing stuff down. I know you've got all his contacts listed on your mobile. So, I want you to call him right now, and tell him this . . .'

In as few words as possible, Lucy relayed the events of the last few hours, from her pulling the CCTV footage at the Mission Hall to her arrival at Rudyard Row, and from Ruth Smiley's attempt to murder her at the Archways to Smiley's own death at the hands of an unknown gunman. All the time, she underlined the importance of her suspicion that certain elements in the Robbery Squad – maybe all of them for all she knew, but at the very least Danny Tucker, Ruth Smiley and maybe Lee Gaskin – had themselves been robbing the underworld.

Harry listened in what could only be described as stupefied silence.

'Lucy . . .' he stuttered when she'd finished, 'you're seriously telling me . . .?'

'Harry, you just heard me, okay! Now please get that info to Stan . . . no one else, and definitely no one in the Robbery Squad, because they're going to be running amok this evening.'

Before she could say more, there was a loud knocking at the front door.

'Shit,' she breathed, as a pair of feet descended the stairway. 'Look . . . wait, Harry.' She lowered the receiver as she shouted at the living room door. 'Mum, don't answer that, please!' But she could already hear her mother fiddling with the chain. *'Mum!'* She slammed the receiver back to her ear. 'Harry . . .'

The phone was dead. There wasn't even a purr of empty air – it was literally *dead*.

Which meant the cable had been cut.

Lucy dropped it and dashed out into the hall. *'Mum!'*

Cora looked round. She wore an anorak over her trackie, but she hadn't yet managed to unchain the front door. Nor had she released the catch, so the door was still closed. Her cheeks paled at the sight of her daughter's evident fear.

'It'll just be the milkman or window-cleaner come for his money,' she said.

'Do not open that door,' Lucy replied. 'Where's your mobile?'

'I don't know. Could be in the lounge, could be upstairs.'

Lucy ducked back into the lounge. She scanned the room. There was no sign of her mother's mobile on the armrest of the armchair, on the coffee table or on the sideboard – and then her eyes fell on the front window.

The curtains had not yet been drawn, and a figure stood on the other side. Two big hands in black gauntlet gloves were spread against the pane like enormous spiders, a face between them glaring through – a face the like of which Lucy had never seen.

What she could see of it under a tangled, tumbling mass of oil-black hair, was female, but also foreign, the features non-Caucasian and deeply tanned – and fringed with savage, terrifying tattoos, possibly Māori in origin. A pair of eyes glared at her with such intensity that they were almost bloodshot. Strong white teeth were bared in a feral snarl.

Lucy was jolted backward, to the point where she almost fell over the coffee table.

Who this person was, she couldn't fathom. But one thing was self-evident; she wasn't solely facing crooked cops here. Not any more.

A terrific *CRASH!* sounded in the hall.

Lucy wheeled back through the connecting door. Cora, who'd been halfway up the stairs, had spun around and stood rigid, one hand clawed on the top of the rail.

'What . . . in God's name?' she stuttered.

Another tremendous *CRASH!* followed.

It was the front door.

Someone was throwing themselves against it, and with such force that its small panel of frosted glass was already riddled with cracks. Another furious blow followed, the entire door frame shuddering.

'Get upstairs!' Lucy shouted, lurching down the hall. 'Find that mobile, and bring my spare staff . . .'

'Staff . . . what're you talking about?'

'Remember, when I moved out, I left some spare kit in the wardrobe in my old room . . . there's an extendable baton in the harness.'

Cora turned and hurried up the stairs.

With the next impact, the door jamb split. With the next, the door itself burst inward several inches, only the chain holding it.

'Who are you?' she shouted. 'What the hell do you want?'

There was no response – no self-identification by a police raiding party, no announcement that a warrant was being executed. That, along with a distinct lack of blue lights outside, and of course, that face in the window, was all that Lucy needed.

She averted her eyes from the mirror hanging in the hall, and rammed it with her right elbow. It shattered, shards jangling to the floor. She swooped down and scooped up the largest as she advanced to the door. It was six or seven inches in length, and curved like a dagger.

As she reached the door, the chain exploded loose, fragments flying in all directions.

Lucy hurled herself against the wood, but was bounced backward by the colossal figure on the other side. Through the expanding gap, she glimpsed a massive bald head on a trunk-like neck, and a barrel-shaped chest. A scarred

375

face, centred around two glittery green eyes, was written with dark, furious glee; it was a madman's face, a mass murderer's face.

So, Lucy slashed it with the shard.

Up, down, sideways.

Animalistic screeches followed as the bear-like form tottered backward, a massive, leather-gloved paw clamped to the wounded visage, blood throbbing between the spread fingers.

Lucy threw herself at the door again, slamming it closed and kicking the lower bolt home, though with the door jamb fractured, it wouldn't hold it for long.

'Lucy . . . what in God's name?' Cora called from upstairs.

Lucy dropped the shard and galloped back down the hall and into the living room, where, without even looking at the window, she flung the tea-mug aside, grabbed the coffee table, and carried it back to the front door. Any second, she expected another attack. Before it came, she ripped the welcome mat up and tossed it behind her, and then upturned the table and jammed it diagonally under the door knob, bracing the lower end in the square concrete impression left by the mat. As she backed away, the next assault commenced, this time accompanied by female shrieks so berserk they were almost equine.

At the same time glass shattered somewhere else in the house.

Lucy dashed through to the kitchen, where half a paving stone had been flung through the main window. A third assailant was in the process of climbing through after it; she saw a gangling body in dark leather, long stringy hair hanging over wizened features, a straggling beard and moustache.

He locked eyes with her, and went for his partly unzipped jacket, beneath which she spotted the handgrip of a firearm. Lucy had no time to think, she simply snatched the heavy,

376

old-fashioned kettle which her mother had recently boiled, flipped its lid, and hurled its still scalding contents into his face. As he roared in agony and grabbed at his eyes, a heavy steel pistol landed in the sink, smashing crockery. Lucy swung at him with the kettle. It bounced across his head, buffeting him sideways against the broken window, the serrated edge of glass biting into his neck.

Eyes screwed shut, one hand clamped to the wound, he rocked perilously on the sill. Lucy levelled the kitchen mop and drove it at him like a spear, catching him end-on in the chest, and levering him backward. He fell out into the yard, landing heavily on the flagstones.

'Lucy!' Cora cried from the hall.

Before Lucy ran back to meet her, she took the gun from the sink. It was a large-frame double-action revolver, a six-shooter, its 50mm barrel inscribed with the make and model, *Colt Anaconda*, no doubt packing the much-feared .44 Magnum cartridges. Lucy had never been firearms-authorised and had never particularly sought to be – the last thing she'd ever wanted to do on joining the police was shoot at someone.

But times change. And so do people.

As she re-entered the hall, her mother was rounding the foot of the staircase, carrying the extendable baton in her left hand and the phone in her right. 'Who do we ring?' she gabbled. 'Who'll—'

Before she could finish, the *boom* of what had to be a sawn-off shotgun reduced the left side of the front door to smithereens, what remained of it swinging inward on warped hinges.

Cora shrieked, falling face-down onto the hall carpet.

Lucy bullocked forward, the Anaconda levelled in both hands. She caught a glimpse of the tattoo-faced woman behind the splintered door, and heard the *clack-clunk* of the shotgun slide.

There was no option; Lucy squeezed the trigger – once, twice, three times.

The recoil was fantastic, the big gun bucking wildly, giving her no real aim, but that was no concern. She was trying to back them off, not kill them – and it seemed to work, because as what remained of the door came apart under the impact, she saw Tattoo diving out of the line of fire. Lucy kept the gun trained on the doorway, as Cora tried to get back to her feet.

'You hit?' She hooked a hand under her mother's elbow, to assist.

'I . . . don't think so . . .'

With another shattering *BOOM!*, a hail of shot ripped through the few fragments of door left, obliterated the banister and peppered the stairway wall with holes. Lucy returned fire as she and Cora backed down the hall, this time one-handed, pumping three more rounds into the smoke-filled blackness outside. The revolver now empty, she tossed it, then turned and shouldered her mother through into the kitchen.

'My God,' Cora moaned, on sight of the destruction there.

'I need that baton,' Lucy said.

Cora pushed it into her hand, and she snapped it open before unlocking the back door and barging out into the night. The third attacker would still be out here somewhere, but they had no choice. At least Lucy had disarmed him.

'Who do we call?' Cora asked again, staggering in pursuit.

'Never mind that . . .' Lucy pivoted, scanning the whole yard. 'If the neighbours haven't called someone by now, God help us! Oh shit . . . *run!*'

She pushed her mother to the back gate. Cora, whose eyes hadn't properly adjusted to the night-gloom, hadn't seen the hellish shape ballooning towards them from the shadows alongside the broken kitchen window.

'I'll go next door,' she suggested.

'*Don't go next door, Mum! Just run!*'

Cora lurched to the back gate, yanking it open, as Lucy moved to meet the tall, rangy figure with the blistered face and slit neck. One hand was still clasped to his wound, but with the other he'd drawn an immense knife, something like a small machete.

Lucy drew her baton to the shoulder, as per the manual.

Even so, it ordinarily would be no contest – but the guy could barely see where he was going. She ducked his first clumsy swipe, and caught him across the left knee with a furious *thwack*. He swore in Spanish as he tottered past her. She straightened up behind him, the manual now going out of the window as she delivered a huge, two-handed stroke to the back of his skull.

He plummeted to the flagstones, landing face-first with an echoing *smack*.

One eye still on the kitchen window, Lucy hobbled across the yard to the shed, and opened it.

Her Ducati M900 glimmered in the shadows. As always, it was fully fuelled and primed, just ready to go. She grabbed her helmet, but as she only had one, she didn't put it on, but hooked it over a handlebar, saddled up and backed the machine out.

The would-be house-invader still lay prone. Lucy spared him one last glance as she turned the bike around, shifted gear and throttled out into the alleyway running parallel at the back. Her mother had progressed about forty yards along it on the left, but only slowly, glancing constantly over her shoulder. When she heard the bike, she stopped and turned as Lucy rode up behind her.

As such, Cora failed to notice a car pull into view at the far end.

Its headlights were turned off, but it was low, sleek, stream-lined. A sports car. What was more, though it filled the alley wall to wall, it accelerated towards them.

379

Cora jumped out of the way as Lucy slid sideways to a halt.

'Here . . .' Lucy handed her the helmet, and then clumsily manoeuvred the Ducati around so that it was pointing the other way. 'Get on, quickly . . .'

'God, Lucy . . . I feel sick.'

'Be sick down my back, just get on!'

The approaching vehicle was two-hundred yards away, encroaching fast.

'*Quickly, mum . . .*'

Cora seemed oblivious to the threat. She struggled to put the helmet on, and half-heartedly looped one leg over the seat. 'You know I don't like—'

'*Do it!* Wrap your arms round me and lean forward . . .'

Less than fifty yards away, the car banged its headlights onto a full, dazzling beam.

'Oh my God, what's that . . .?'

'*MOTHER!*'

Chapter 39

Lucy hit 50mph before she reached the end of the alley, her mother riding pillion but clinging on for dear life with arms cinched around her waist. It was all the more dangerous that Lucy wasn't wearing a helmet, though riding bare-headed could only help if it attracted the attention of a traffic cop.

With the pursuing vehicle only yards behind, they rounded a corner onto Walton Drive, another narrow, terraced street, made narrower still by the cars parked down either side. It was no problem for Lucy as she sped along it, her needle pushing sixty; at 8 p.m. on a Friday evening, she was unlikely to meet oncoming traffic, and the thoroughfare was easily roomy enough for her Ducati. The car behind, a jet-black Jaguar F-Type, had a harder time, though its driver was clearly unconcerned about his fifty-grand's worth of high-performance vehicle, losing a wing mirror and flaying the paint from his nearside flank as he recklessly followed.

At the end of the road, to cut a corner, Lucy screeched the wrong way around the Battle Hill war monument, a brick obelisk encircled by walled-in rose gardens. On the other side lay Crannington Lane, a major artery in this corner of the borough. An approaching van had to take swift evasive action to avoid her, and veered sideways, squealing rubber. As Lucy also swerved to avoid impact, the F-Type roared into view around the other side of the monument, jamming its brakes on, swinging one hundred and eighty degrees. When she skidded to a halt mid-carriageway, she found herself gazing across twenty yards of tarmac at the face of its driver, which was the most hideous thing she'd ever seen: the same bruiser who'd tried to kicked her mother's front door down, but his features now riven every which way, leaving a gory patchwork which looked set to slide apart.

Lucy throttled up, flinging the bike in a U-turn across the middle of the road. As a taxi pulled an emergency stop, she mounted the pavement, circling around the back of it, before bouncing back onto the tarmac, where she swung a right and sped down Battle Hill. A second later, the F-Type reappeared in her wing mirrors, and now it wasn't alone, another vehicle coming full pelt alongside it, a motorbike. Lucy had no clue who this might be, but it would give her more problems; if she'd only been facing the F-Type, there were places she could take her Ducati where the pursuer couldn't go. Not anymore.

At the lower end of Battle Hill, she spun right onto Faraday Road. This was all happening so fast that she had no clear idea yet where she was headed. Robber's Row wouldn't be a bad shout, though that was in the opposite direction, and it wouldn't be easy doubling back with two of them on her tail. At the junction between Faraday Road and Tubbs Lane, a bunch of Friday evening revellers were straggling across in a fancy-dressed procession. She slewed sideways to avoid them, crashing over the kerb and a triangle of uneven pavement, before hitting the blacktop and making the next turn on the edges of her tyres.

Even over the howling engine, she heard her mother's screech of terror.

As they hurtled along Lowrigg Avenue, she risked a backward glance, and now saw only the F-Type – some forty yards behind them.

'Where the hell is . . .?' she said, at the same time glancing left.

The pursuing biker was running neck-and-neck with her, on the pavement.

It was a black Yamaha YZF600, the phenomenally powerful Thundercat. Its rider was the Māori woman. She wore a helmet with goggles rather than a visor, so her facial tattoos were visible, her wild, tar-black hair billowing behind. She levelled her right arm to point at Lucy . . . only no, she wasn't pointing. She was aiming the sawn-off shotgun.

Lucy cut sharp right, veering across the opposing lane and swerving down Claremont Street, which was also narrowed by parked vehicles – only for a car to turn in ahead of her. Cursing, she cut through another gap and mounted the pavement.

A second backward glance showed the Thundercat aping the complex manoeuvre, no more than thirty yards behind her. Lucy didn't hear the shot, but her nearside wing mirror exploded.

Cora squeezed her daughter's waist so hard that she had difficulty breathing.

They sliced left, down a backstreet behind a row of workshops, which was dotted all the way with wheelie bins. Lucy wove her way through like a slalom skier. Behind, the Thundercat rider showed no such finesse, smashing them out of her way one after another. When they hit a short straight, Lucy looked back again. Tattoo was riding no-handed while she slotted new shells into her shotgun. Lucy throttled up, passing the remaining obstacles in a blur, clipping one and sending it cartwheeling, spraying refuse.

Before she reached the end of the alley, which would

disgorge her onto Hansen Road, the F-Type blistered past right to left, clearly aiming for the next junction, thinking to intercept her. As she emerged, Lucy screeched right, heading the other way, at last pointing in the direction of the town centre – but it was miles away yet, and first she had to get around Queen Alexandra Park, which ran alongside an elevated section of the railway.

Behind her, there was a screech and clatter of gears as the F-Type made a rapid three-point turn, and the wild revving of a 599cc engine as the Thundercat swung onto her tail.

She took a right onto Normanton Way. She was sure this led through to Redman's Field, which was a wasteland attached to what had once been Redman's Mill but now had been converted into civic offices. Beyond that lay the park.

The problem was that Normanton Way had now been converted as well.

Fifty yards along it, Lucy skidded to an astonished halt.

The road ended at a row of semi-detached new-builds.

They'd turned it into a cul-de-sac.

With a bestial roar, the Thundercat sped around the corner.

Lucy throttled forward. Cora, barely knowing what was happening, clung to her daughter like a limpet, eyes screwed shut – which was just as well.

The semi-detached house directly in front had an empty drive, with a wooden gate at the end of its side passage. Lucy accelerated up the drive, the gate looking bigger and bigger as she rode headlong towards it. She was doing forty-five when she struck it with her front wheel.

A product of home DIY, it vanished in a cloud of splinters.

The next thing they were tearing down the passage at the side of the house and across a leaf-littered lawn. Lucy ground around a central display of rockery, her rear tyre ploughing a trench in the turf, and then accelerated forward at such speed that she pulled a wheelie as she struck the house's back fence. Its central panel shattered on contact, fragments exploding everywhere as she burst through to the other side.

Semi-dazed, she fishtailed across Redman's field, leaping and swerving over clumpy tussocks of dead grass, but, looking behind, saw the Thundercat emerging through the same gap.

Clearly, Tattoo was in radio contact with the F-Type, because as Lucy closed on Mill Lane, which separated Redman's Field from the open gates to Queen Alexandra Park, the car ballooned out of the darkness on her left, barrelling straight for her. Lucy evaded it with inches to spare, tyres shrieking, and then jammed her brake on, sliding sideways across the road, before righting again, mounting the kerb and shooting through the park gates.

The F-Type growled noisily as it tore around in a U-turn, but Lucy was already flying along the park's main drag. Only now, because there were no lamps inside the park, did she realise that she'd lost her headlight. She had a vague idea of lawns and flower beds spread to either side, but at least the walkways here were broad and smooth, the one she was following spooled out ahead of her like a moonlit ribbon – though she saw it all the more clearly when a powerful cone of light pulsed up at her rear, throwing her shadow far ahead.

In her nearside wing-mirror, Lucy spotted the Thundercat. It was gaining steadily, with the F-Type not far behind. Thoughts racing chaotically, she was flummoxed as to what her next move should be. If she stuck to this route, she would emerge from the park at its southeast end, where there were more housing estates to negotiate before the town centre, but at this rate they'd be within shooting-range before she even got close.

Abruptly, the children's playground loomed up ahead of her, the drag diverting two ways around it via a T-junction. On a whim, Lucy opted to go straight across, leaping a small, grassy bank, landing in the sandpit, which initially gave her no traction, its contents rising in plumes as her back wheel churned, but then she was out of it, carving her way across the rubberised surface, swaying around the swings and round-about, before hitting more grass, ripping through a wall of desiccated autumn vegetation, and heading up the slope of the railway embankment.

'Lean forward!' she shouted back to her mother. '*Right forward!*'

Cora, still adhered to her daughter's back as if she'd been glued, did precisely as instructed, allowing Lucy to take the terrifying incline at full speed, burning uphill, only the night sky in front of them – until they were on the level again, snapping left at the top and running on gravel. With shrapnel machine-gunning behind them, Lucy realised that they were riding alongside the actual railway line.

Close behind, the Thundercat's engine howled in pain and rage as that steel beast also ascended the slope. At least the F-Type was out of the race. Lucy glanced back and down, and saw its lights, marooned on the other side of the chil-dren's playground, receding in her vision. In fact, the whole of the park was disappearing to their rear, which meant they were finally heading into central Crowley – though this in itself was problematic, because once they were past the park, they'd hit the viaduct over the Archways, and after that they'd be in canyons between industrial structures; there'd be no way to divert off the railway, and as this was a frequently used route, that could spell disaster.

Without warning, the open vista on the left gave way to darkened trees; they'd reached the end of the park already. Lucy's last chance was here; she pulled a quick left-hand turn, which, with no headlamp to light the way, was the biggest leap of faith she'd ever taken in her police career.

Cora shrieked as they plummeted through masses of

leafage, rhododendrons and thorns whipping their faces and bodies, the wheels locking as the tyres slid downhill through mulch and rot – too fast to attempt a controlled crash, but then hitting level ground again. To the left stood a railing, beyond which cars rumbled back and forth. Alexandra Way, Lucy realised. They were almost in the centre of town. But even if they reached Robber's Row in the next few minutes, it would not necessarily provide refuge. They could alight in the police station's rear yard, but by the crashing and tearing of fibrous undergrowth as her huge machine descended the slope behind them, the Thundercat rider was still very close. She could easily follow them into the yard, and while they leapt from the Ducati and fled to the personnel door, blast them both with her shotgun.

And then a new inspiration struck Lucy.

It was a shocking thought, in truth – but it was now plain that they were neither going to outfox nor outpace the maniac at their rear.

That left one course of action.

Just ahead, the railing ended where a pair of iron gates hung together on a corroded chain. Lucy ploughed forward through knee-deep layers of autumn leaves, only decelerating late, striking the gates with just enough force for the chain to shatter and the gates to swing outward, but not so that she'd shoot into the middle of Alexandra Way.

Once through, she manoeuvred left, following the pavement, but jumping into the traffic when a gap presented itself. Again, she was heading away from the town centre, but now it was by design rather than default. She swerved left under a railway bridge, and then left again onto Henshaw Hill, at the bottom of which she was among warehouses and scrapyards, all closed for the night. In front, loomed the enormous structure of the XS Stadium, where Crowley Athletic Football Club played, its semi-domed outline silhouetted on the spangled lights of the Whitewood shopping mall and retail park on the other side.

In some ways, this was the worst spot they could lead the killer to: a vast open space in the middle of the conurbation, a gridwork of car parks, slip roads and training pitches, which, at this time of night would be deserted and only poorly lit – a perfect venue for the assassin to perform her dirty work. But in other ways, it was ideal – as Lucy now illustrated; rocketing forward guided by pure geographic knowledge, crossing a stretch of cinders, and curving left onto the approach road to Car Park D, which at last allowed her to open the Ducati up.

With a clatter of steel, the Thundercat leapt onto the blacktop behind her. The shotgun muzzle flashed in Lucy's remaining wing mirror. They were out of range, just.

'Mum, you okay?' Lucy shouted back.

Cora responded by trying to burrow her helmeted head between Lucy's shoulder blades.

Lucy accelerated all the more.

There were no lights on this side of the stadium, so her eyes were failing to adjust with any kind of usefulness, but she knew exactly where she was. Just ahead, the road opened into the car park, though it didn't really 'open' into it, because when the stadium wasn't in use, as now, a low barrier – about two feet in height, made from stainless steel and painted black – was raised from a slot across the tarmac, to prevent shoppers at the mall getting free parking. Lucy was aware of this, but bulleted forward over the final sixty yards, only at the last second diverting left onto the pavement, where there was no barrier of course, and sailing through into the big open space beyond.

The Thundercat rider, in contrast, had no clue the black steel was there.

Even if she saw it in her headlight, at 70mph there was no chance to brake.

She smashed into it full on, the detonation like a bomb blast.

Lucy skidded sideways across the car park in a huge, grit-spurting arc, just in time to see the buckled steel hulk of the Thundercat cavorting end-over-end at colossal speed, a leather-clad body cartwheeling and somersaulting alongside it.

When both objects finally came to rest in hanging shrouds of dust, they were torn and contorted beyond recognition, and had travelled over a hundred yards from the point of collision.

Lucy rode around in an ever-slower semicircle until she too came to a halt, her engine purring, her mother a near-deadweight on her back, whimpering softly.

The scene of disaster lay only twenty yards away.

She stared unblinking at the trail of debris leading from the broken barrier, and the two devastated forms at the end of it. The sweat slowly cooled on her and she was numb all over, but that was down to exhaustion, she was sure.

She felt no guilt, no shame, and certainly no hint of nausea; all these things reported by firearms lads who'd slotted targets in the field apparently eluded her.

All she actually felt now, if she was honest, was a growing concern that the F-Type was still out and about somewhere. As Tattoo had likely been in contact with him until the end, he might be on his way here right now.

'Hang on, mum,' Lucy said. They throttled out of the car park the same way they'd come in. 'This isn't over.'

Chapter 40

The Shed pretty well lived up to its name.

It stood alone, several miles outside Crowley on the north-east side, amid a huge sweep of farmland, which at present was hacked down to an unsightly autumn stubble. It was accessible only by a dirt road running across these undulating fields for about four miles, the other end of which was connected by a farm gate to Hallgate Lane, the main road to Radcliffe. The Low Riders had acquired ownership of both the road and the Shed from a local farmer. Once an old barn with several storage units and stable blocks attached, it had been in a dilapidated state, built mostly from breeze blocks with its roofs made from corrugated tin. However, it was still attached to the National Grid and so had full power, and as the stables had once contained livestock, it also boasted running water. The Low Riders themselves, who had some skilled personnel among their number, had cleaned it up inside, damp-proofing it, lagging and lining the roofs, and installing toilet and kitchen facilities, and a stroboscopic light show to accompany their quadrophonic sound system. Lastly, they had laid a wooden floor and brought in second-hand furniture, along with a pool table and a pinball machine.

Even now, the interior of the Shed wouldn't be to everyone's taste. With no windows and only dimly lit (when the light show wasn't at full dazzle), everything in there, from the couches to the armchairs to the kitchenware, looked ratty and used, and given its location, there were always mice scampering about. The combined smells of patchouli oil, spliff, engine grease and sweaty leather pervaded it. Even when there wasn't a party in progress, rock music, invariably of the heavier variety, thudded in the background.

It was around 9.45 p.m. when Lucy and Cora arrived there, Lucy only finally feeling safe from pursuit when she turned onto the dirt road running through the fields. She'd made her way across the borough ultra-carefully, taking only the back roads to avoid any kind of detection. But when they pulled up on the Shed's muddy forecourt, they were one among fifty-odd other motorbikes. Weird green lighting and thunderous metal emanated from the interior. Only one biker sat outside, an obese slob in his early forties, with a clean-shaved face but a mass of long, stringy hair. He wore jeans and a Low Riders doublet open on an outdated Black Sabbath tour T-shirt, which looked fit to burst, so vast was the ale-gut beneath it. He sat in a deckchair close to the clubhouse's main door, smoking a joint, which he made no effort to extinguish even though he could clearly see that it was Lucy who'd arrived and was now helping a female passenger from the back of her machine.

Cora feebly removed the helmet. Beneath it, she looked white-faced and sickly.

'What's this place?' she asked.

'I don't suppose you remember Kyle Armstrong?' Lucy said.

Cora swallowed hard. She was clearly on the verge of being ill. 'That reprobate . . . thought we were well shot of him.'

'Well, Mum . . .' Lucy led her by the arm towards the door, 'we've all messed up when it comes to getting rid of the dodgy blokes in our lives, eh?'

The biker in the chair took the joint from his lips.

'No helmet, officer?' he said. 'Riding without a headlight? Tut-tut.'

Lucy now recognised him from her teen years. 'Tommy Five-Bellies.'

'Juicy Lucy.'

'Or is if Fifty-Five these days?'

He took another casual toke. 'You here all official-like?'

'Hardly.' Lucy glanced around to check that the road across the fields was still empty. 'Go on, Tommy,' she turned back, 'give us a drag . . . for old time's sake.'

He grinned, showing brown teeth, and handed it over. 'Gotta give me something for it.'

'I will, advice . . . this is illegal.' She dropped the joint and crushed it underfoot. 'Next time I come here, it *might* be official. And then what's going to happen?'

He looked surprised rather than angry, and gazed morosely at the flattened dog-end.

Lucy led her mother inside.

The music in there was deafening, the emerald light disorienting, and the smell of dope and beer and cigarettes so overpowering it was almost a miasma. Her vision took an age to adjust; all she initially saw was a smoky, green-tinged gloom, unidentifiable figures lurching back and forth, others sprawled on couches and armchairs, or sitting at tables.

The pounding music prevented her from announcing their arrival, so all she could really do was stand there and wait to be spotted. But this didn't take long, a figure suddenly disentangling himself from a shapely female form on a nearby sofa, and getting quickly to his feet.

It was Armstrong; he spoke to someone nearby, before

approaching them, tucking his T-shirt into his steel-studded belt, a look of bemusement on his face. Behind him, the girl he'd been necking with also got to her feet. Lucy wasn't surprised to see that it was Hells Kells. She wore denim cut-offs, brown leather cowboy boots, and a T-shirt so short that it displayed her flat tummy and pierced navel. With her flowing blood-red locks, she looked wildly sexy, but also tousled and vexed.

The music was switched off, the sudden silence ringing in all their ears.

The rest of the chapter gradually fell quiet as they too realised they had guests.

Armstrong eyed the twosome sternly. 'I take it you're not here on police business?'

'What would it matter if I was?' Lucy said.

'For one thing, you'd need a warrant to come in here, because you certainly haven't got permission.'

'Well, Kyle . . .' she sighed, 'I haven't brought you a warrant. Instead, as you can see, I've brought you my mum.'

'Your mum?' Armstrong regarded Cora uncomprehendingly. Only now, so many years after he'd last seen her, did he recognise the older woman. 'What the bloody hell is *she* doing here?'

'Hello to you as well, Kyle,' Cora said, disgust at his lack of manners briefly distracting her from her queasy stomach.

'Is this a joke, or what?' he demanded.

'Yeah, sure.' Lucy put an arm round Cora, who she thought might be about to faint. 'The laughs are coming thick and fast. Check Mum out . . . she's rolling in the bloody aisles.'

'Lucy . . . what's going on?' he asked.

'I take it you've got toilets in here?'

'You've come to use the bog?'

'Mum isn't doing so well.'

Armstrong glanced at Cora again, finally taking in her

moist forehead, her grey lips, her waxen pallor. He signalled
to Hells Kells. She arrived at his side like a bullet, but her
expression turned peevish when he asked her to escort Cora
to the Ladies. She scowled at Lucy before strutting off on
her heeled boots, summoning Cora with a hooked finger.

Cora stumbled in pursuit, pausing only to hand Lucy her
mobile phone.

'No one else outside,' Tommy Five-Bellies said, filling the
doorway. 'Came on her own. Apart from the old bird. Well,
I say *old* . . . I wouldn't mind going a round or two with
her.'

'You shut your dirty mouth!' Lucy snapped.

'*Hey!*' Armstrong snapped back. 'Listen, Luce . . .' He
jabbed at her with a finger. 'I've got lots of affection for you,
love, but it has its limits . . .' His words broke off, as he
finally noticed the four gouges on the left side of her face.
'Okay . . . what the *fuck* is going on?'

'I need to lie low for a couple of hours,' she said. 'Maybe
a bit longer.'

'You *and* your mum?'

'I wouldn't have brought her otherwise.'

'Why?'

'It's genuinely better if I don't tell you.'

He regarded her warily. 'So, let me get this right . . . you
want our hospitality for an indefinite period of time, but you
don't feel the need to offer an explanation?'

'The only explanation you need, Kyle, is that I'm calling
in that favour.'

Armstrong frowned. 'You've already done that.'

'I'm calling it in again,' she said. 'And I'll call it in again
after that, if I want to. Don't forget, mate, I'm the police.
The rumour is . . . we can do anything we want.'

'Oh yeah?' Armstrong bared his teeth in an angry grin,
no doubt fuelled by his awareness that leather and denim-

clad figures now clustered around them, the rank-and-file of his chapter.

A lot of it was show where Kyle Armstrong and Lucy were concerned, but she was still surprised when he grabbed her by the upper arm and propelled her roughly down to the far end of the clubhouse, the bikers breaking apart to let him through. When they were several yards from anyone else, he let her go, but forcefully, pushing her back against a wall.

'Try that once more, and you'll get that hand broken,' Lucy hissed, rubbing her bicep.

'Hey, love . . .' His tone was pointedly disdainful, but he spoke quietly. 'I know you, and you know me. We might have had good things once. But we were kids back then, and a lot's changed. You don't come and muscle me in my own place.' He lowered his voice even more. 'Now I don't expect you to bow and grovel, but the very least you can do is show me a bit of respect, yeah? Especially if you want me to cover for you.'

This wasn't a totally unreasonable demand, she supposed.

'We've picked up some heat,' she said.

'What kind of heat?'

'The dangerous kind.'

His brow furrowed. 'And it's on its way as we speak?'

'Most likely not. It doesn't know about this place.'

He eyed her uncertainly. 'You know what we do here? I mean, apart from chug beer, listen to music and ride our bikes. I mean what we *really* do?'

'Course I do.' She'd have been some kind of cop if she hadn't known about the Low Riders' drug-dealing exploits, but at present it was a case of better the devil she knew.

'Yeah, course you do,' he said. 'Like you say, you're the police. Which is all the more reason I'm suspicious.' He knuckled his jaw, a habit she remembered from the old days whenever a conflict was brewing. 'Seriously, Luce . . . you're a copper and you're happy to lay low in a place like this?'

'I'm not happy, but I've no choice. Not at present.'

'This is serious then?'

'Kyle . . . if it wasn't, would I really have brought my mum?'

He assessed her with arms folded. Any fear he might have harboured that this could all be part of some elaborate sting seemed to be fading.

'I could still say "no",' he said. 'I could say the favour's already been repaid, say we don't want this heat, show you the door.'

'You could,' she retorted, 'but you think that'd be the end of it? You only need to sniff the air in here to smell the spliff. You can smell it outside for Christ's sake . . . in which case I wouldn't even need a warrant, would I? Nor would any of the other coppers I'd immediately inform. Then it wouldn't just be Ian Dyke trying to cut deals to save his arse from an epic stretch.'

'So, it's carrot *and* stick, is it?'

'Usually . . . but in your case, no. There's nothing I can pay you with except my good will.'

He looked her up and down, and smiled. 'That might be sufficient.'

'Oh, and what would Kelly think?'

He shrugged. 'Who cares?'

'Who cares? Kyle . . . she stepped into the breach straight after I left. That's fourteen years, you've been with her.'

'She's only a temporary fixture.'

'We may all be if this night doesn't work out for us.'

'This is really that bad?' He sounded sceptical.

Lucy produced her mother's phone. 'If you give me a minute, I'll find out.'

Armstrong waited and watched while she tapped in Harry's

number. It was almost ready to shift to voicemail when an answer came.

'Yeah . . . DC Jepson.' He sounded sleepy.

'Harry . . . it's Lucy.'

'Lucy.' Surprisingly, this only seemed to wake him a little bit. 'What's happening?'

'That's what I was about to ask you. What action is Stan taking?'

A short silence followed. 'How would I know?'

Lucy bridled. 'What do you mean how would you know? Harry, I rang you not two hours ago. Did everything I told you go in one ear and come out the other?'

'Lucy . . . come on.' He gave a dismissive chuckle. 'That sounded like a load of claptrap, to me . . . I've been waiting for you to call me back and tell me it's a gag.'

'Are you telling me you've not spoken to Stan?' At that moment, it was a real struggle not to shriek at him.

'Obviously. You sound like you've lost the plot, love.'

'I don't believe you, Harry!' She tugged at her hair, all but ripping it from her scalp. 'Look . . . me and my mother are in real and serious danger.'

'Come off it, Luce. You're not seriously telling me the Robbery Squad are doing these jobs?' He half-laughed. 'Knocking people off, for Christ's sake . . .'

'Jesus wept, Harry . . . you don't like these guys anyway! You yourself told me not to trust them. Why is this so hard to believe?'

'I didn't say they were blaggers, for God's sake!'

'Neither am I. Just some of them, but I don't know who . . . apart from the ones I've named. That's why I want it to be Division who come and bring us in.'

'Lucy . . . I go around saying stuff like this, I'm going to come over a right dickhead.'

'Well, that'll be a first, won't it!'

'Where's your evidence for any of this?'

'For God's sake . . . Ruth Smiley's dead body lying on the Archways, full of bullet holes, is probably a start.'

'Really?' He sounded more than a little dubious. 'I've been and there's nothing there.'

'You looked on Jubilee Gardens?'

'The whole length of it.'

'Shit!' she said. 'Look . . . they've probably moved it. It's no surprise. There's more than two of them. But they can't have cleaned the site till it's spotless. Get Forensics down there, and you'll find rafts of proof.'

'Lucy . . . I can't call CSIs on the basis of a chat over the phone.'

'Which is why I need you to get me to a place of safety, then I can give you and Stan a full statement.'

'All right . . . okay.' He still sounded reluctant.

'Jesus, Harry . . . I think we need a bit more urgency from you than this. You've just heard me say there's more than one of two them.'

'Yeah, but . . .'

'No buts, mate. There may be a lot more than two of them . . . there are certainly some non-Squad members involved. I ought to know, as they've chased us halfway across town tonight, shooting at us. I mean what the hell's going on. Has no one even reported a motorcycle accident down at the XS?'

'Dunno, do I . . . I'm still officially on the sick.'

'For Christ's sake, Harry . . . just get on the phone to Stan. And do it quickly. These non-Squad people, I have no clue who they are, but they're a whole new level of nasty.'

'I said all right, I'm getting onto it . . .'

'Harry, I've got my mum with me because they attacked her house. If you don't believe me, go and look there. The place has been trashed.'

'I'll check that out too . . .'

'Not till you've told Stan Beardmore what's going on, and got some people out here.'

'Where's "here"?'

'You got a pen handy?' she asked. 'So that you can write this down? Because you sound to me like you've been on the pop.'

'Lucy . . . this is a lot to take in.'

'Try looking at it from *my* perspective! Anyway, you know the Shed?'

'The biker place?'

'Correct. The Low Riders' HQ.'

'You're *there*?' He sounded incredulous. 'And you've got your mum with you?'

'That's right.'

'Lucy, why the fuck . . .?'

'Why do you think? Mine and mum's addresses are registered at the nick, but no one knows my connections to this place.'

'I didn't know you had any connections to it.'

'Just get here!' she all but screamed, cutting the call before he could annoy her further (as if such a thing was actually possible).

Chapter 41

'So?' Armstrong asked.

Lucy slipped the phone back into her pocket, turned, and found not just him, but the entire Low Riders chapter regarding her in fascinated silence.

'Assistance is on its way,' she said. 'I wish I could say it will be here in the next half-hour. It should be. But I don't think that's very likely.'

Armstrong pondered this, and then nodded. 'Want a beer while you're waiting?'

Lucy glanced at a nearby tabletop, where a number of bottles, ice-cold and sweating in the muggy heat of the clubhouse, awaited attention.

'I wouldn't mind,' she said. 'But I'd better not. Might have to drive later.'

Yeah, don't want to risk breaking the law, eh?

She laughed aloud at the sheer nonsense of this. And then, just as quickly, felt like crying.

Seriously . . . what had she got herself into?

Since lunchtime, she'd survived two assassination attempts, but even now – the first time in hours that she'd been able to stand back – she struggled to make sense of how they'd got to this point. There was one light in the darkness: she obviously hadn't been officially blamed for any crime yet, otherwise the police airwaves would be buzzing with it, and even Harry, skiving at home, would have heard something.

'Luce?' Armstrong approached, speaking quietly again. 'If you can give us a bit more info, we might be more use to you.' He nodded at the gathered crowd. 'I know you don't see eye to eye with all these lads. But no one's going to push it if *we're* standing behind you.'

'That would be getting more involved than I think is good even for you guys,' she replied. But she was touched by the earnest look on his face. 'I'm serious, Kyle . . . this is bad. Really bad.'

She noticed that Hells Kells had now returned, minus Cora.

'How's my mum?' Lucy asked.

'Dunno.' The woman glared at her boyfriend. 'Couldn't risk *staying* in there, could I?'

'Don't fret, love.' Lucy looked round and spotted the lavatory entrance. 'You've nothing to worry about from me.'

'I'd better not have. Doesn't make a difference that you're a cop. I'll take a pop at anyone, me.'

Lucy headed over to the Ladies. 'Wouldn't make you stand out tonight.'

Inside, the lavatory was pretty rough-and-ready, with a bare cement floor, white-tiled walls running with condensation and two cubicles constructed from hardboard. Cora sat hunched in a corner, on a pile of straw so rotten it was probably a leftover from when this place was a stable.

'How you feeling?' Lucy asked.

'Awful.' Cora, regarded her daughter with a jaundiced eye; she was still cadaverously pale, but breathing better at least. 'I think I just threw my tea up . . . maybe my breakfast too, and maybe last night's supper. What on earth is going on? Who are those people?'

'Those people or *these* people?'

'They don't look much different from each other to me.'

'They are, trust me.' Cora leaned against a small sink. 'This lot are a Hell's Angel chapter called the Low Riders. They deal drugs for a living.'

'Always knew that Kyle Armstrong was a bad lot. Never liked him when you were both seventeen.'

'Strictly speaking, I was seventeen and he was nineteen. I think that's the real reason you didn't like him.'

'And you're seriously telling me he's going to look after us?'

'Only for the time being. Because the others who are after us are a lot worse. For one thing, they have the power to arrest us.'

Cora was halfway to her feet, but now glanced up, confused. 'They're police officers?'

'Some are. I'm not saying the ones who came to your house were.'

'Oh, my God. Lucy . . . how've you ended up in this mess?'

'It's a long story. So long and convoluted I'm having trouble remembering it all, myself.'

'It's that blessed CID, isn't it?' Cora shook her head. 'I knew it. I said all along . . . the instant you became a detective again, all this would happen.'

'Mum, it's a one-off, all right?'

'Oh, it's always a one-off!' Cora was suddenly red-faced and animated. 'It was a one-off when you got beaten up by that madman in Borsdane Wood!'

'Can we talk about this later? I came in here to check you were okay . . .'

'And do you think I am, Lucy? With you and your bloody

father pulling me one way and then the other!' No longer nauseated, she now felt free to be furious. 'I used to take my clothes off for a living. You know why? Because I was a daft kid who thought she was being a rebel. And I had no shame, and I thought it was an easy way to earn money. But if I'd had any clue that God was going to punish me with you two, I wouldn't just have kept my knickers on . . . I'd have invested in a habit and wimple, and booked myself into a sodding nunnery.'

She stormed out of the tiny room.

'If it's any consolation,' Lucy muttered, 'I doubt I'll be a police officer for much longer.'

Back in the clubhouse, a degree of normality had returned. The music had been switched back on, but at a lower volume. The bikers and their girls talked together as they drank beer and smoked. Armstrong stood to one side with arms folded, face etched with irritation as Hells Kells poured vitriol into his ear. He was only distracted from this, when Cora appeared and pointed at the bottles on the nearby table.

'One of those going spare?' she asked.

'Thought you were feeling ill?' he said.

'Are you a doctor now, Kyle? As well as a layabout and a criminal?'

'Sweet Mary!' he moaned. 'Like today's not bad enough without my ex's mum giving me grief too! Someone give her a bloody beer!'

Lucy was as surprised as anyone to come back in and find her mother with a bottle at her lips.

Before she could say anything, Tommy Five Bellies waddled in as well. 'There's another one here, Kyle.' He nodded at Lucy. 'Says he needs to speak to her ladyship.'

Armstrong looked impressed. 'That was quick.'

But for Lucy it was too quick.

Far *too* quick.

She darted over to her mother, looking to drag her to a hiding place, but it was too late.

Five Bellies went rigid in the doorway, face written with shock to feel the nub of a pistol pressed into the back of his skull. Slowly, clearly acting on whispered instructions, he raised his hands and shuffled forward.

Despite everything in this most shocking day of her life, Lucy was still unprepared for the sight of Danny Tucker, looking swish in a jacket and tie, but his face set like granite as he entered the clubhouse directly behind Five Bellies, one hand clutching the pistol, the other holding aloft his warrant card.

Good God . . . he wanted them to think this was legitimate police business.

'Okay, folks!' he shouted. 'DS Tucker here, Crowley Robbery Squad. Nice and still please.' He glanced towards her, and half-smiled. 'Yeah, that's it, Lucy . . . you too.'

Everyone had frozen. Again, the music fell silent. Armstrong glanced at Lucy, bewildered. 'Okay . . . what the fuck is *this*?'

'You're Kyle Armstrong, I'm guessing?' Tucker said. 'Head honcho of this shithole.'

Armstrong straightened up, chest out. 'President of the chapter actually, pal.'

'Whatever, *pal* . . . you're in trouble.'

'Tell me something new.'

'Nah . . .' Tucker grinned all the more.

Grinning too much, Lucy thought. *You feeling the pressure as well, Danny?*

'I don't mean the playing-at-it trouble you normally get into,' Tucker said. 'I mean big trouble, *real* trouble.'

Armstrong lurched at him. 'You think you know the meaning of the phrase?'

'Save it, fuckhead!' Tucker shoved Five Bellies away and

levelled his gun on Armstrong instead, bringing him to an immediate halt. 'You hairy, unwashed dipsticks are harbouring a murder suspect, which at the very least is perverting the course of justice, and that alone will get you time. Anything else we find while we're tearing the crap out of this place will only add to it.'

But moisture glinted on Tucker's brow. He was being very careful to stay near the door, Lucy noticed. She also saw that he was wielding a Colt Cobra .38 Special, which was *not* police issue. That meant he hadn't officially drawn a firearm before coming here. All the better on one hand – he hadn't yet risked trying to make this thing legal. But on the other, it meant that bodies would not be found riddled with police bullets, which gave him a kind of advantage.

'He's on his own,' Five Bellies said aloud. 'No support units, nothing . . .'

Which was also good news, Lucy told herself.

'One of me's all I need,' Tucker retorted. 'Trust me, I won't need any help making your lives very unpleasant indeed. Back off, all of you!'

The biker crowd, perhaps starting to sense that something was wrong here, had edged a little closer. Now, very grudgingly, they edged backward again.

'Not you, Lucy. You get over here. You're under arrest.'

Armstrong looked at Lucy, baffled. 'Is this above board?'

'No, it isn't,' Cora replied loudly. 'These people tried to kill us in our own house. Now they're pretending they're taking us into custody, but the truth is we won't get to any police station. Not alive.'

The biker president looked even more perplexed. 'Luce?'

'Quit wasting your breath, Armstrong,' Tucker said, eyes darting left and right. The clarity and directness of Cora's accusation had visibly unnerved him.

405

The rest of the chapter stirred uneasily. In some quarters, chains and bats had appeared.

'You're not going to do anything,' Tucker advised them. 'Seriously, you idiots should be thinking about saving your own arses!'

'That's what *you* should be doing, Danny,' Lucy said, her voice deliberately calm.

'Tell your people to back right off, Mr President!' Tucker shouted. 'If they don't interfere any further, there'll be no comeback . . . life for you and your crowd goes on as normal.'

'Even if they're forced to watch you gun me down in cold blood?' Lucy asked him. 'Genuinely, Danny . . . I'm not armed, but neither am I coming with you. So, what are you going to do next?'

He advanced a couple of steps, but many in the chapter were now openly displaying their weapons. Claw-hammers had appeared, lengths of pipe, belts with heavy buckles.

'I'm telling you, Armstrong!' Sweat beaded Tucker's face. 'Keep your people in line.'

'You don't tell me anything in my place,' Armstrong replied.

'A gun's only useful if you're prepared to use it, Danny,' Lucy told him.

'You think I won't?'

'Not in front of all these witnesses.'

Cora turned to the rest of the bikers. 'You think this is normal? He's come here armed, without any kind of back-up. You think this is the way legit coppers do it?'

'I told you!' Tucker shouted. 'I don't need anyone!'

'I think you do, mate,' Armstrong said, one of his colleagues handing him an old-fashioned blackthorn truncheon.

Tucker jammed the pistol straight-armed in Lucy's direction. 'I've got you dead, love! I mean it . . . I *will* shoot.'

'I'm not stopping you,' she said. 'Just make sure you save enough ammo for everyone else.'

'You're a murderer, Lucy.'

'Who you trying to convince, Danny . . . me or yourself?'

'Get over here!' he barked, but his voice had turned hoarse, losing its authority.

She shook her head. 'It's over, Dan. Must've seemed like a good idea at one time, robbing the underworld . . . so you could save the Robbery Squad. Nothing like piling on the violence, eh, so you could make it seem like we really needed an outfit like yours?'

'Are you idiots buying this?' he tried to laugh.

'I think it would have worked better for you if you'd hit ordinary targets,' she said. 'Banks, post offices. Then there'd really have been a need for the Robbery Squad. But you couldn't do that, could you? That would've been a step too far . . . because deep down, you, Ruth and Lee Gaskin, still considered yourself coppers, didn't you? You weren't going to steal from Joe Public. Instead, you were going to steal from those animals who make ordinary folk's lives such a misery. Okay, it wouldn't have got reported straight away, but it would in due course . . . and even though the targets might be undesirables, robbery is robbery, and by then it would be apparent there'd been an awful lot of these crimes, and always with maximum brutality, so it would still be a job for the Squad. But even hitting the undesirables has got out of hand now, hasn't it? Lots of people have got hurt . . . even killed. Including one of your own.'

'You'll pay for that, Lucy,' he said through bared teeth. 'You've no idea how far back me and Ruth Smiley go. For the last time, you are under arrest on suspicion of murder.'

'No, Danny,' she said, *'you're* under arrest.'

Tucker was sweating bullets. He glanced fearfully around

as the crowd openly edged towards him, Lucy at their forefront, her open hand extended for his weapon.

'Give me the gun, Danny,' she said. 'Come on. It's over.'

The eyes bulged in his drenched face. He seemed baffled, as though she was someone he no longer recognised. He stood rigid, gun levelled for several seconds, though it must, to Tucker, have seemed like hours.

Gradually, almost imperceptibly, he began to lower it.

'That's it,' she coaxed him. 'It's better for everyone.'

'Yeah,' he said, the gun at half-mast.

Only for his face to tighten back into a mask of defiant rage. He raised the gun again.

'No!' Cora screamed, barging into Lucy, shoving her aside.

BLAM!

It wasn't a loud shot, but the round struck Cora cleanly and from point-blank range, flinging her to the floor with jackhammer force.

Chapter 42

Kyle Armstrong, who'd managed to manoeuvre himself to one side, was the first to strike.

He lashed down with his truncheon, smashing the revolver from Tucker's grasp. It skittered across the floor as the rest of the Low Riders piled in, flailing with their bats, pipes and chains.

Lucy, who'd quickly righted herself after staggering, was fleetingly frozen by the sight of her mother on the floor, blood pooling out around her, and at the same time by the explosion of violence in front of her: Danny Tucker, a big guy in good shape, dealing out roundhouses to the left and right, felling bikers on all sides, but also taking blow after blow.

When Armstrong caught him in the face with the truncheon, he tottered back, red spume bursting from his nostrils, arms windmilling. The biker president then leapt at him with both feet, ramming them into his groin, putting him down in a curled-up foetal ball, the rest of them laying blows on him with everything they had.

Almost belatedly, Lucy dropped to her knees alongside her mother.

Cora's eyelids fluttered in a face turned alabaster-white.

She was conscious, panting hard, and as yet there was no sign of blood from her nose or mouth, which could only be good. From what Lucy could see, the bullet had gone clean through the left shoulder, the material of Cora's anorak and trackie top rapidly tingeing claret-red.

'Mum, this isn't serious, okay?' she said quickly.

Cora tried to shake her head, but winced with pain. 'Don't . . . don't let . . .'

'You've got to stay conscious! You hear?'

'. . . them kill him . . .'

Tearing off her own anorak, Lucy bunched it up, and as gently as she could, rolling and lifting her mother from the left, she slid it in beneath her shoulder. Cora screwed her face in agony, but it was a necessary action, to staunch the haemorrhage. Lucy then planted a hand on the top wound and pressed firmly downward. Cora whimpered again, but still tried to form words.

'You hear . . . Lucy?'

'Just stay with me, Mum!' Lucy craned her head around. 'Someone get an ambulance please!'

But it was all chaos and rage back there.

'He's . . . your *witness*,' Cora said.

And suddenly, Lucy understood what she was being told.

If Tucker died and they had no proof anyone else was involved, not Lee Gaskin, not anyone; the crimes would go unsolved, and she herself would still be implicated in the death of Ruth Smiley.

'Don't . . . lose him,' Cora whispered, face strained but eyes very much alive.

Lucy turned as she knelt there. Tucker was still curled in a human ball, the bikers kicking, stamping, smashing down with their bats and belts, Armstrong as involved as anyone. Only Hells Kells, of all people, appeared to be trying to restrain them.

'*Kyle!*' Lucy yelled. 'Stop it . . . now!'

Armstrong glanced distractedly round at her.

'Don't you bloody kill him!' she bellowed. *'Don't you bloody dare!'*

But the bikers' blood was up. And why not? These were the Low Riders, an outlaw band, and friends to no one. While this 'phoney cop' – according to real cop, Lucy – had come into their place with a gun, he'd threatened, he'd name-called, he'd shot one of their guests, and even worse, when they'd counter-attacked, he'd laid a couple of them out. One biker still lay unconscious, his crooning woman tending to his head.

'Kyle!' Lucy screeched, but still he didn't respond.

And then, salvation seemed to arrive – in the most unlikely form imaginable.

Beyond the frenzied mob, a familiar figure had emerged through the clubhouse door, and now stood there stunned. It was Harry Jepson, ruffled as ever, wearing a scruffy rain-coat over an unbuttoned corduroy shirt, a white vest showing underneath.

'*Harry!*' Lucy called. 'Harry . . . do something! Stop them!'

Harry finally registered her. He glanced back at the biker pack and the hunched-up figure at their feet, before noticing something else. Quickly, he reached down and scooped it up. The next thing Lucy knew, he was pointing Tucker's .38 at the ceiling.

Two swift shots followed.

They weren't loud – but they were loud enough to attract the attention of the crowd.

'Back off, all of you!' Harry bellowed, swivelling round, pointing the gun at anyone who was close to him.

Almost as one, the biker pack retreated, red-faced, gasping for breath. The bloodstained shape on the ground was still moving, but only slightly.

'Right away!' Harry shouted. 'And drop those punk-arse weapons, right now!'

There was a clattering and thunking, as bats and pipes fell to the floor.

'Okay . . . who the hell is *this*?' Armstrong demanded of Lucy.

'It's okay, Kyle,' she replied. 'Harry, be careful! We don't want you shooting someone too.'

'What the fuck is going on here?' he said.

'We've got to arrest DS Tucker.'

He gazed at her, nonplussed. Then down at the groaning body. He finally recognised the wrenched-around tie, the blood-dabbled shirt and torn jacket. *'Jesus, Mary and Joseph . . .'*

'Harry, he shot my mum!' Lucy said. 'He was going to shoot *me*!'

'Jesus God almighty!'

'Harry . . . just keep your shit together! We have to get Mum to hospital!'

Harry nodded vaguely. 'I've . . .' But he still looked dumb-founded.

'Harry, for Christ's sake!'

'I've . . . got the car outside. But Lucy, what the hell . . .?'

'I'll tell you everything on the way.'

'Okay . . .' He nodded more forcefully. 'Okay.'

'And we've got to take Danny Tucker into custody.'

'Assuming he's fit to walk.'

'You want to leave him *here*?' she asked.

He glanced at the watching bikers, levelling the pistol on them. 'Get back, I said! Drug-addled nutjobs!'

'Listen, Harry . . . they may have saved all our lives.'

There was another groan from Danny Tucker, who now was stirring properly.

'Harry, he's coming round. Get the cuffs on him, please.

412

Kyle, I need some help with my mother. Have you got a first aid kit?'

Rather to Lucy's surprise, while Kyle helped her get Cora to her feet, the person who brought over a green ziplock bag full of medical accoutrements was none other than Hells Kells, though of course she'd also shown a glimpse of humanity during the attack on Tucker.

Lucy wondered if she'd misjudged the woman.

'Don't look too surprised,' Hells Kells said, noting Lucy's expression, but maintaining a typically truculent tone. 'I'm happy to help. Parents can't *always* be blamed for their kids, can they?'

'Kelly was a nurse,' Armstrong explained, after they'd assisted Cora onto an armchair. 'They kicked her out for pilfering prescription drugs . . . on our behalf, I'm sorry to say. But you don't forget your training, do you?'

Lucy herself was a qualified first-aider, all coppers were, but she could only watch in admiration as Hells Kells drew on a pair of disposable gloves and went to work, using surgical scissors to snip away the two sleeves, first Cora's anorak and then her tracksuit top, before swabbing, packing and dressing the wound.

Behind her, Danny Tucker had now been dragged to his feet by Harry, his hands cuffed behind his back. He too could have used some medical attention. Both his eyebrows were swollen, and one had split like an overripe peach. His nose was glutted with blood, and whenever his carmine lips came apart, at least two teeth were visibly missing. Blood also streaked his face from a gash above his hairline. He seemed fully *compos mentis*, but he looked tired and pained.

Lucy walked towards him with a face of bitter disappointment.

'You're under arrest on suspicion of armed robbery,' she said. 'You're also under arrest on suspicion of attempted murder. That'll do for starters, Danny . . . but I'm sure there are plenty more where they came from. And in case you were wondering, you don't have to say anything, but it may harm your defence if you fail to mention when questioned something which you later rely on in court. Anything you do say may be given in evidence.'

'I'm hurt,' he said simply, meeting her eye to eye minus any apparent guilt. 'Surely you can see that?'

'We're dropping my mother off at the hospital first,' she said. 'Then we're taking you straight to the nick. The FMO can check you over. If we need to take you back to A&E, we'll do it team-handed and with an armed escort.'

He half-smiled, before spitting out a wad of congealed blood and what looked like another half-tooth. Cora was now on her feet, her left arm bound and dressed and fixed in a temporary sling. She looked pale, and strangely sleepy.

'I've not given her any painkillers,' Hells Kells said, handing the casualty over so that Lucy could put a supportive arm around her. 'Partly because I don't know what they'll want to give her at the hospital. So, she's hurting . . . don't dawdle.'

'Thanks, Kelly,' Lucy replied. 'I underestimated you.'

The ex-nurse shrugged.

'And you, Kyle,' Lucy said. 'Looks like I'm back in your debt.'

'Get out of here,' he replied. 'Get your ma to the hospital.'

'You know we'll need to preserve this clubhouse as a crime scene?'

'I'll get everyone out. Just go.'

Outside, Harry's BMW, still displaying a damaged windscreen, was parked on the dirt road just beyond the clubhouse's forecourt, parked behind Tucker's Passat. Harry frogmarched the prisoner over there, hitting the fob as he did, the BMW's lights blinking.

'I'll put Mum in the front . . . then I'll go in the back with him,' Lucy said.

Harry nodded, bundling the still-cuffed prisoner into the rear seat, while Lucy eased Cora into the front. The woman was a deadweight on her arm.

'I . . . I think I'm going to faint,' she breathed.

'You've lost a lot of blood,' Lucy said, fastening her in. 'But we're fifteen minutes, tops, from the hospital. Think you can hang on?'

Cora tried to smile, but it barely creased her haggard features. 'Not much choice . . .'

Lucy closed the door, and clambered into the backseat alongside Tucker. Harry jumped in behind the wheel. The engine rumbled to life, the car skidding back and forth as it manoeuvred through a rapid three-point turn. Lucy saw Armstrong and his crowd spilling out of the clubhouse to watch, as they sped away along the rugged trail.

'Thought you were a goner back there,' Harry said.

'I wasn't in any real danger.' Lucy glanced from the window. 'When this is over, ask me nicely and I might tell you what my connection with the Low Riders actually is.'

She looked at the rear-view mirror, and saw his eyes briefly flicker her way, which was strange – almost as if he hadn't been directing that question at her at all.

'What the hell were you thinking?' Harry asked.

'That we had a serious problem,' Tucker replied, sounding groggy, but flexing his left hand, which apparently wasn't cuffed behind his back after all. 'A problem that needing fixing.' Before Lucy could react, he'd produced the .38 Special, and jammed it into her side. 'One way or another . . . and very bloody quickly.'

415

Chapter 43

'You're not seriously telling me you're involved in this too, Harry?' Lucy said. Despite everything, this was still one of the biggest revelations of the day. 'Don't tell me *that*, please.'

Harry chuckled as he drove. 'Liked that little pantomime we put on, did you? About me not knowing these fellas . . . about me not being impressed by their results.'

'You're not that good an actor, pal . . . you genuinely *weren't* impressed.'

'Well . . . it's true. I wasn't. But ultimately, it's not about liking people, it's about picking the side that suits you best.'

The disbelief seeping through Lucy was now replaced by a sense of slow-building rage, mainly at herself; the level of betrayal today was off the scale, literally numbing, and it kept on going up, but perhaps, on reflection, it had been predictable too.

'I've got to give it to you,' she said. 'I never thought *you'd* be able to misdirect *me*.'

'You were a fair opponent, Lucy,' Tucker commented. He'd retrieved Cora's mobile from her and still clutched the .38 against Lucy's ribs, but he'd also drawn a handkerchief and was industriously wiping the blood from his face.

'Don't *you* talk to me, Danny,' she said tightly. 'That's all . . . just don't.'

'No, seriously. You gave us a good run-around. After you killed Ruth this evening, you completely dropped out of sight.'

'I didn't kill Ruth.'

'Well someone did,' Harry chipped in. 'She was just where you said she'd be. Halfway down Jubilee Gardens.'

'It wasn't me.' Lucy's eyes fell on Cora, who, perhaps thankfully, was now slumped unconscious in her seatbelt. 'But I can't say the same for that hit-team you sent to my mum's house. You get my mother involved, lads, and all bets are off.'

Tucker gave a mock-frown. 'We sent no one to your mother's house.'

'Whatever . . . they're history now.'

'Real tough cookie, aren't you?'

'And what are you lot supposed to be?' She couldn't keep the disgust from her voice. 'Coppers . . . who've carried out a series of violent robberies! What special place in hell do they reserve for the likes of you?'

'Thing is . . . some of us need money,' Harry said. 'It's a problem.'

'Your problem, Harry, is you're a total idiot,' she retorted. 'You've made such a bollocks of your life that it costs you a fortune now, just living day-to-day. So, your solution is to steal the money! Jesus, what could go wrong?' She turned back to Tucker. 'Makes *you* a phoney too . . . and it pisses on your so-called charitable donations.'

Tucker half-smiled as he dabbed at his damaged eyebrows. 'Some things are necessary evils. We allowed Harry to skim a little so we could acquire his services.'

'Acquire his services!' she scoffed. 'Is this Harry Jepson we're talking about . . . the guy who wrote the manual on

417

incompetent coppering? What the hell use could *he* be to you?'

Harry's eyes narrowed in the rear-view mirror. 'There you go, underestimating me again. Trouble is . . . this time it's been your undoing, hasn't it?'

'Harry's a handy wheelman,' Tucker explained.

Lucy snorted, but in truth she could have slapped herself. She ought to have seen that all along. The one thing Harry Jepson *could* contribute to a major operation was driving skills. Even so, if they'd been forced to recruit a loose cannon like Harry, it implied that there weren't too many other Robbery Squad officers involved, if any.

'And that's the whole thing, is it, Danny?' she said. 'You and Smiley were the blaggers, Harry was the escape man. I can dismiss everyone else from my enquires . . . like Lee Gaskin, for example?'

Harry laughed aloud.

'Lee Gaskin's an embittered little oik with a personality bypass,' Tucker replied. 'You were right, yourself, when you said he's got mummy issues. It may be that Lee had better reason than anyone to be part of this. But the reality is that losing his brother completely fucked his head up. He came into this job needing a parent figure, and found one in Mandy Doyle, who you then duly erased. As such, he's volatile, awkward and above all, gobby . . . there was no chance on earth we were going to trust a character like that.'

'Obviously not,' Lucy said. 'Only *disciplined* psychopaths for your line of work.'

Tucker showed another of his trademark grins, missing teeth included.

'Three of us were more than enough,' he said. 'Any more cooks than that . . . well, you know.'

'This isn't going to work,' she told him. 'You must realise that? It doesn't matter how effectively you make Mum and

418

me disappear, everything'll come out in the wash in due course.'

'I'm not so sure,' he replied. 'One thing we're really good at in Robbery Squad is improvising on the hoof.'

'You mean winging it?' she countered. 'Making it up as you go along?'

'Isn't that what all good coppers do?' Harry asked.

'Yeah, but *you're* not coppers. Not anymore.'

'I'd love to know where you get off being so uppity, Lucy,' Tucker said, sounding less amused. 'You have no actual clue what's going on here, do you? You still think this was about trying to save the Squad . . . creating a crime wave so we'd be deemed indispensable? Do you really think that's all this was?'

'I don't care, frankly.' And fleetingly, as Lucy regarded the insensible shape of her mother, that was the truth.

It was an ugly thought that suddenly it didn't seem so imperative getting Cora to the hospital – because perhaps no medical treatment would be needed where they were headed now. Of course, it was difficult to equate a thought like that with either Danny Tucker, the all-round good egg, or Harry Jepson, the bone-idle bumbler whose best asset was his sub-standard banter. But in all honesty, now that the shock of revelation was fading, so was Lucy's righteous anger – to be replaced by a dull but rising sense of fear.

'We didn't rob anyone who didn't deserve it, Luce,' Harry said, still in chatty mode. 'Some, we didn't even do a full number on. We let the strippers go unharmed . . . spared a little shit of a Scouse drug-dealer so new to the game he virtually squeaked when he walked.'

'Only saved your full ire for the real players, is that it?' she said. 'Except you didn't, did you? Pimps, bookies, corrupt sports agents . . . second-division idiots you could probably have nicked legally if you'd done some homework on them.'

Harry chuckled. 'Yeah, but that's the whole point.'

'Well, of course. I know any kind of homework's anathema to *you* . . .'

'You think we weren't interested in snaring the big fish?' Tucker said. 'Or better than that . . . hurting them? Really *hurting* them?'

Despite the fear seeping through her, Lucy sensed that they were coming to the crux of it, and forced herself to listen.

'What would you say if I told you there's a certain gangster in this neck of the woods who's basically top of the world?' Tucker said. 'Everything he touches turns to gold, people go out of their way to tug their forelocks to him. I mean, he's Mr Clean at present. Aren't they always? Never gets his own hands dirty these days. But that doesn't mean he hasn't got a finger in a hundred nasty little pies. Doesn't mean he doesn't sell death and destruction on all sides.'

She assumed they were talking about Crew godfather, Bill Pentecost.

'And it doesn't mean he wasn't a real a wild man back in the day,' Harry said.

That settled it, she thought. Hadn't they once used to call him 'Wild Bill Pentecost'?

'When me and Ruth Smiley were young bobbies back in Manchester city centre in the early 2000s,' Tucker said, 'Tony Gaskin was the top man in the job. Only a PC, but everyone liked him, everyone respected him – a real copper's copper. When I got him as my tutor-con, it was the best thing that could have happened. He didn't just show me the ropes, didn't just mentor me . . . he taught me everything he knew, became one of my best mates. A year later, he puppy-walked young Ruth Smiley too, had exactly the same effect on her. And then he got slotted outside that building society – shot through the head, an *unarmed* beat bobby! Talk about one of the biggest losses the service has ever suffered.'

The car fell into silence. Outside, the autumn fields undulated past.

Lucy was again distracted from Tucker's monologue. She wondered where *it* was going to happen. And when. It would have to be soon, because if it wasn't, the next thing they'd be back on Hallgate Lane and the main road network. Surely, they wouldn't risk doing it there? Unless they had somewhere else in mind, and were prepared to chance the main roads for a few minutes. That might give her a brief window of opportunity, she thought . . . Except, what was she going to do: try to jump from a moving car and leave her mother behind?

The lack of viable possibilities only chilled her all the more.

'We were DCs by then, me and Ruth,' Tucker added, oblivious to her inner turmoil. 'But we never caught the trigger-man. We had our suspicions, but . . . we couldn't prove anything.' He snorted with disgust. 'Some people lead a charmed life, don't they? Not just later, when they reach the top level of criminality, but when they're first starting out too . . . when they're wild men looking to make quick scores. But you know, even gangland bosses can get what's coming to them! And that doesn't necessarily mean at the end of a gun. Sometimes it's not possible just to shoot them. Sometimes it's not even desirable. Much better, I think, to do it by slow torture.' He smiled again, very broadly – it really was a much uglier sight now with bloody gaps between his teeth. 'Much better to whittle them down gradually, one cash stream gone here, another gone there. Their finances drying up, an empire cracking, coming apart . . . imagine the end result of that.'

'You seriously think that by hitting these juniors, you'll undermine the senior?' Lucy said, scarcely able to believe this degree of irrationality. 'How long do you think that'll take?'

421

Harry chuckled. 'You're aware Danny's one of the lead investigators on this case? It'll go on as long as necessary, because no one's going to solve it.'

'Seriously, Danny?' she said. 'You think the Crew are so fragile? They've got a thousand ways to earn money. You shut down a couple of conduits, they'll just develop new ones.'

'Oh, I think you'll find they'll be ready to turn on their own long before then,' he replied. 'Even the most powerful players can't withstand failure indefinitely.'

'Danny . . .' She shook her head, though it baffled her that she cared enough to say this; the chances of talking them round when they'd come this far had to be minimal. 'You're getting carried away with your own hatred. I mean, you may think you're doing the right thing . . . hurting the mob, hurting one mob boss in particular, and cleaning out a few mice in the process. But where's the endgame? What's going to happen to *you*?'

'Well, *I'll* be able to pay my debts,' Harry said.

The simple stupidity of that response was a hammer blow to what remained of her hopes, faint as they were. What other kinds of debt were these guys running up during the course of this madness? If Harry couldn't see that . . .

'Nothing for *you* to worry about, Lucy,' Tucker replied. 'Nor your mum. I'm sorry she got involved in this, by the way. I really don't know how that happened.'

'If you've got any sense you'll let her go,' Lucy snapped. 'You'll let me go too . . . as damage limitation. Tonight's been a catastrophe across the board . . .'

'Which has largely gone under the radar,' he said. 'It's Friday night, with all the usual distractions that throws up. Ruth's body's already been moved; it'll soon be moved again, permanently, and then it won't be found . . . I don't like that, but it's necessary. The Archways is about to go under the hammer anyway, so there'll be no crime scene. And all those people back there, those scummy bikers . . . well I can arrange for that place to be raided first thing tomorrow. Lots of drugs on the plot, lots of weapons. Every one of that lot's facing time, and they know it . . . so an anonymous little tip-off beforehand should send them scuttling for cover, should make sure they don't even contemplate trying to contact the police. All we'll find when we get there is an empty barn. Oh . . .' he smiled, 'and your mum's blood of course. All over the floor. That'll be interesting for the CSIs.'

'*Your* blood was on that floor too,' Lucy tried to argue, grabbing at any straw she could.

The panic inside her was becoming palpable; they now had to be a long way from any potential witnesses. At any moment, they'd pull into a siding, where she and her mother would be dragged out into the stubble. But if she couldn't talk them round in moral terms, perhaps she could appeal to their, or at least *Tucker's*, common sense.

'How will you explain that, Danny?' she said. '*Your* DNA at the crime scene! Come on!'

'Well . . . let's see.' He mulled it over. 'Perhaps *I* should lead the raid tomorrow. It only needs to be a small one . . . just me and Harry perhaps. I'll need to get my car back, anyway, so I've *got* to go back there . . . but obviously, I'll say we were looking for you two. Trouble was, a couple of bikers were still hanging around, and they got the better of me. It's not like I haven't got the gashes to prove it. Better still, I can say I got there the previous night – i.e. now – but the whole mob battered me unconscious and kicked me out into the field. That's near enough what did happen, isn't it?'

'We can say you were unconscious all night, and in the morning they'd gone,' Harry put in.

Tucker nodded. 'Along with Lucy and her mum. Neither of them ever to be seen again.'

'See!' Harry looked at Lucy through the rear-view mirror. 'Improvisational thinking.'

Another option had closed, she realised. Her mouth was almost too dry to respond, but she tried anyway. 'You would seriously frame all those people for murder?'

Tucker eyed her incredulously. 'That set of drug-dealing cockroaches? Bloody right I would. You see, Lucy, you and your mum went there this evening to get high and to buy gear . . . and you fell out with them over the price. I'd found out from an informer what you were doing. So, I went over there to try and talk sense to you . . . caught them in the act of giving you a bad time, and got beaten senseless for my trouble. When I woke up, you two had both gone and so had the Low Riders.'

'Love it,' Harry said. 'Perhaps you both legged it, eh, Luce? Maybe that's why they went to your mother's house? Trashed the place, chased you all round town?'

Lucy's blood had turned colder than she'd ever known. To someone who hadn't been party to tonight's real events, this concoction of spur-of-the-moment lies could well have the ring of truth. Most likely, the attack on her mother's house would already have been reported. And it was only a matter of time before someone called in to say they'd seen a biker chasing them, wielding a firearm.

'All coming together, babes,' Tucker said gravely.

'I'm a copper,' she said, trying another tack 'Which means they won't buy it so easily.'

'They might if they find drugs in your house,' Harry said.

Lucy could hardly refute that. And she knew how easy it would be for them to plant a bit of gear.

'They'll go over every wrinkle in the story a dozen times,' she argued anyway. 'If nothing else, they'll find that tell-tale evidence I pulled this morning.'

'Oh, yeah,' Tucker said. 'Your CCTV from the Mission Hall . . . the one you haven't logged in yet.'

'It'll still be found.'

'That *did* occur to me actually,' he admitted. 'Though, I strongly doubt it would mean anything to anyone not in the know.'

Lucy couldn't pretend that this wasn't true. He was correct: not only had she not mentioned to anyone else about the CCTV, but she hadn't told anyone about the link she'd made between the Hatchwood Green burglaries and the Red-Headed League robberies. She'd mentioned to Kirsty Banks that she thought there might be a connection between the burglaries and the recent spate of violence, but crucially, *not* the robberies. In any case, the burglaries were officially closed. She hadn't even formalised this offshoot enquiry by putting her suspicions on paper; in short, it didn't exist.

'However,' Tucker said, 'just in case, and because something else we do very well in Robbery Squad is cover our backs . . .' he rummaged in the pocket behind the front passenger seat, and pulled out her laptop, 'good job Harry found this when he went over to your mum's place after you first called him, eh? We've got the pen-drive too, in case you were wondering.'

'And you thought I was sitting at home, doing nothing.' Harry shook his head. 'Dear me, eh? Lots of police activity on your street when I got there. Good neighbours, you've got. All very concerned. But it was a such a scene that no one noticed me checking your car over.'

Lucy stared at the laptop, helpless.

'As I say,' Tucker said, 'even if someone *did* get hold of this, there's no straightforward connection between your case and ours, is there?'

She shook her head in slow bewilderment.

Unlikely as Harry and Tucker's version of events might sound to her, if she and her mother weren't around to argue otherwise, what choice would the investigators looking into their disappearance have but to listen? Even the Low Riders wouldn't help much. As Tucker said, they'd flee in advance of a possible police raid, and when they learned they were wanted in connection with a double-murder, they'd keep fleeing, maybe heading abroad. Even if some of them were caught . . . well, she hadn't even told Kyle Armstrong why she and her mother had been at the Shed. For all the rest of them knew, she might indeed have been there to buy drugs . . . and Danny Tucker *had* turned up to make arrests, and he *had* been beaten.

'Dearie, dearie me.' Harry still watched her through the rear-view mirror. 'Bet you wish you'd said you'd go out with me now, eh?'

Despite everything, such insolence even managed to break Lucy from her doom-laden reverie.

'Are you for *real*?' she retorted. 'I mean, I always knew you were a bit of a knob, Harry, but deep down I thought you were essentially a decent bloke . . .'

'I used to be a decent bloke,' he replied. 'But decent blokes never get the breaks, do they! I learned that the hard way, Lucy. And you were as much part of it as anyone else. Just think, if me and you *had* got it together, I'm sure I could have persuaded you to leave all this alone . . . before it went tits-up.'

'Enough chit-chat!' Tucker cut in. 'Time to find ourselves a spot . . .'

'Danny!' Lucy blurted. 'I'm making one last appeal to you, as a former friend and colleague . . .'

'I wish I could help you, Lucy.' He was no longer looking at her; she wondered if he suddenly couldn't. 'But you've made it plain from your actions that you're not with us. Therefore, you're against us.'

Instinctively, her left hand stole to the door handle.

'Try and get out the car, if you want, love.' He still didn't look at her. 'But it won't change anything. Except it won't be as clean. Or as quick . . . and that was one thing I was planning in honour of our short time together. To make it quick.'

Lucy's hand dropped to her side. Limp, damp.

Somewhere in her head, a voice was telling her that this wasn't happening, that it was all a massive, elaborate joke, and that they'd suddenly crack up laughing. But a terrible sense of finality was now descending on her. She saw the fields beyond the window in a glaze of moonlight so spectral it almost looked frosty; as if those hunks of scythed wheat were frozen in time – which surely owed more to her warped perception than reality. Not that it mattered either way.

'*Now*, Harry,' Tucker said. 'We don't want to get any closer to the road.'

'There's a spot over this next hill,' Harry grunted.

He cast another look at Lucy through the mirror, but no longer seemed to be enjoying his petty revenge. When she caught his eye, he too glanced away, pretending to focus on the track as they crested this final rise.

A lump rose in Lucy's throat which she couldn't swallow. She would still try to fight; she was adamant about that, but instead of tension building in her limbs, instead of blood pumping, muscles coiling and tensing, she felt weak, tired, hopeless. And what about her mother?

A sob tightened her chest, which, if nothing else, she was determined to contain. With luck, Cora wouldn't even wake before . . .

Beyond the hill, an array of blue swirling lights greeted them.

Harry hit the anchors hard, the BMW pulling a handbrake-skid some thirty yards before coming to a halt.

Tucker blew out a breath so low and raspy that it sounded like his last.

Lucy also, for a second, struggled to breathe. Then, with voice grating, she was able to say: 'What was that about things going tits-up, Harry?'

The flickering blue light played across the barren fields for hundreds of yards, but it emanated from a bank of police vehicles parked side by side in a virtual barricade across the dirt road. A full firearms team, kitted out in ballistics armour and helmets, with visors down, were taking cover behind the vehicles, peering along the barrels of their MP5s.

'Oh fuck . . .' was all Harry could say. In half an instant, the cocky, confident wideboy had turned into a gelatinous wreck. 'Oh fuck . . . oooh fuck . . .'

Instinctively, he released the handbrake, and with a *clank*, shifted the car into reverse.

'Don't think about it,' Tucker barked. 'Where we going, off-road? Just sit fucking tight!'

'What're we gonna do?' Harry stuttered. 'What we gonna say . . . what the fuck . . .?'

'*Shut up!*' Tucker glanced at Lucy. What remained of his teeth bared in a snarl. His injured eyes narrowed. 'This is something to do with those people who attacked your house tonight, isn't it?'

Lucy couldn't answer, because she genuinely had no idea.

'Well, it makes no odds,' he said. 'You killed Ruth Smiley. Her body's only inside one of the houses on Jubilee Gardens. We can still use it. You hearing this, Harry? We can *use* this!'

'I . . . I dunno,' was all Harry could stammer.

Tucker turned another fierce gaze on Lucy. 'Ruth was investigating your links with these biker fucks, and you shot her. Isn't that right, Harry?'

'I . . . I suppose, yeah.'

'I went to arrest you . . . they clobbered me. You hear

that, Lucy . . . you're going down for murdering a fellow police officer. Show me your hands.' When she refused, he pressed the .38's muzzle into her left cheek. 'Show me your fucking hands.'

She complied, and he clapped the handcuffs on her wrists.

'Stay the fuck here, all right?' he instructed Harry, as he dragged Lucy out of the car.

Immediately, they were bathed in the glow of several intense spotlights.

'*Stay where you are!*' came a voice through a loudspeaker.

'Don't shoot!' he shouted. 'I'm armed, but I'm a police officer. Detective Sergeant Danny Tucker, Crowley Robbery. I've got a murder suspect in custody. I'm going to walk her forward so you can see better.'

There was no response as he slowly advanced, right hand clutching Lucy's elbow, left hand holding the .38, loosely and far out from his body. When he was twenty yards away, a lone figure detached from the row of lights and came forward. This too was armoured and helmeted, and it held a Glock in both hands. The figure was semi-silhouetted against the glare of the spotlights, no facial features recognisable behind the Perspex visor, but errant strands of honey-blonde hair dangling over the shoulder pads suggested that it was DI Blake.

'Drop your weapon,' she said, confirming this.

'Ma'am,' Tucker said, 'I regret to report that DC Ruth Smiley was shot and killed earlier this evening, while investigating a new lead connected to the red ski-mask robberies. I know it sounds incredible, but I have strong reason to believe that DC Clayburn was the shooter. As such, I've put her under arrest on suspi—'

'Enough bullshit, Danny,' Blake said. 'I told you to drop your weapon.'

Lucy felt Tucker go rigid alongside her.

She was somewhat surprised, herself. All the bosses she'd known in the past would go with their own team's version of events first, or at least be prepared to hear them out.

Tucker made no verbal response, merely gazed at his chief intently, his nostrils flaring, his lips quivering. But there was no anger there; for a second Lucy thought he was verging on tears.

How could DI Blake not believe him, he was perhaps wondering? They'd worked hand-in-glove for years. They trusted each other implicitly. The only possible answer was that Blake now possessed additional information, and by the looks of this, something pretty conclusive.

Without a word, Tucker pushed Lucy away from him and raised the .38 to his own left temple.

'No!' she shouted, spinning and hitting him in the solar plexus with her elbow, and with both hands clasped together in his throat. 'You don't get out of it that easily!'

The gun dropped as Tucker sagged to the ground, toppling forward in an agonised daze.

Lucy kicked the weapon away, and landed on his back with her knees. What little air she hadn't driven out of him already, expelled with a tortured wheeze.

Panting, she looked up at Blake, who slowly lowered her weapon.

'Detective Sergeant Tucker is under arrest, ma'am . . . on suspicion of robbery, conspiracy to murder, kidnapping, criminal use of firearms . . . you name it.'

'I hear that, DC Clayburn.'

Blake holstered her Glock, lifted her visor, and stepped aside as a bunch of firearms men rushed forward to get him into a pair of plasti-cuffs. As they did, Lucy burrowed a hand into his pocket, to retrieve the keys to her own cuffs and then stepped away, freeing herself. Tucker didn't look at either her or DI Blake when the arrest team hustled him to his feet. Instead, he walked away with head bowed and stumbling feet.

In the background, Harry had emerged from the BMW with his hands behind his head. He sank to his knees as more officers converged on him, shouting commands.

'I also need to report, ma'am,' Lucy said hastily, 'that my mother is in that BMW. She's suffering from a gunshot wound. She was shot by DS Tucker, with *that* weapon . . .' She indicated the .38, which another firearms officer was making safe. 'I don't think it's a serious wound. We've patched it up as best we can, but she's lost a lot of blood and she's none too communicative at present. We could do with getting her to hospital.'

Blake nodded, and relayed the message to the officers now pouring forward from the barricade. One went to the BMW with a first-aid bag; another called an ambulance.

'Had to try something, Lucy,' a voice said.

It was Harry; he too was now in cuffs and being hustled away, but he'd stopped alongside them.

'All my time in this job, and I'm still treated like shit,' he said.

'Don't make excuses, Harry,' she replied. 'It's unbecoming.'

'Easy for you to say that,' he sneered. 'In fact, it's easy for you women full stop, isn't it? What are you two, if not poster kids for the new police service? Young, hot, sharp as razors, educated, ultra-professional. Me, I'm just a fucking dinosaur. White, male, bit rough round the chops, always having to look over my shoulder in case I'm using inappropriate language and the wrong person's listening.'

'I said don't make excuses.'

He ignored her. 'All the dark, wet streets I've worked, all the kickings I've taken. And what have I got to show for it, eh? I'm skint, my ex-wife hates me, my kids don't know me, my bosses don't trust me. Doesn't matter how good I once was, I'm nothing now but an embarrassment. Well . . .' he hawked and spat, 'you may be shot of me now. But don't get too cosy, ladies. Because there are lots more like me, and they're all wondering why the fuck they ever bothered.'

The arrest team, finally irritated, manhandled him away.

Blake took her helmet off, unravelling her sweaty mane. 'I wish I had a cash prize for every bastard I've arrested so up his own arse that he genuinely believed he was only the tip of an iceberg.'

'I doubt Harry believes any such thing, ma'am,' Lucy replied. 'He's just doing what he always does, trying to justify bad behaviour . . . none too impressively.'

'Are you hurt, yourself, DC Clayburn?'

Lucy touched her face. 'No, ma'am. It's nothing.'

'By the sounds of it, you've had a trying day?'

'Well . . . yeah.' Though somewhere in the back of her mind, Lucy couldn't help wondering how the DI was aware of all this.

'Unfortunately, I can't let you go home to get some rest. You need to come back to Robber's Row so we can try to make sense of all this.'

'Yes, ma'am.' Lucy nodded. 'I'd like to go to the hospital first . . . just to see my mother get settled in.'

'That's fine. But come back to the station straight after.'

Blake didn't dally further. She moved away to join a conversation going on alongside the BMW, promptly directing several of the officers to drive over to the Shed, speak to the Low Riders, and take statements from them.

Good luck with that, Lucy thought to herself.

And then something else distracted her.

Beyond the fence separating the farmland from Hallgate Lane, an ambulance had arrived. But it wasn't that; it was the vehicle that had pulled away to make room for it. Lucy couldn't be sure, she'd only caught a fleeting glimpse, but it had looked distinctly like a black Bentley Continental.

Chapter 44

When Lucy came out of the Intensive Care wing, it was close on midnight, and the car park was quieter and emptier than during the daytime. Lights were on in the hospital grounds, and just around the corner at A&E, she could hear a vague commotion as the Friday night furore commenced, but at this section of the building, the only movement came from the last leaves as they fell from the November trees.

A divisional patrol had dropped her off earlier. She hadn't expected it still to be waiting, but a parked vehicle about fifty yards away flashed its lights, and she walked tiredly over there – only to slow down and stop when she saw that it was a black Bentley Continental.

When she turned and headed in the opposite direction, the Bentley cruised after her, pulling up alongside her well before she reached the hospital gate, its window powered down.

'Lucy . . .?' McCracken said from behind the wheel.

She glanced and saw that he was alone, but she kept on walking. 'I haven't got time to talk to you. I've got to get back to the nick.'

'I'll give you a lift.'

'Yeah, right.'

'You got some other wheels round here?'

'I'd rather walk than ride with you.'

He continued to idle along next to her. 'You sure about that? I mean, I'd have thought you'd have a few questions about tonight.'

Lucy stopped and looked at him.

In a few minutes' time, she was going to have to liaise with DI Blake and somehow get this entire mess on paper. It could only help if she knew as much as possible about what had actually been going on. That said, she still only climbed grudgingly into the Bentley's front passenger seat.

'Me first,' McCracken said. 'How's your mother?'

'Do you really care?'

'Listen, love . . .' He didn't glance at her, as he drove them out of the hospital car park. 'I know you like to think it was some kind of sordid one-night-stand that brought you into this world. But it's about time you stopped confusing your own experience of love and sex with everyone else's. Yes, I *care*.'

Lucy rubbed at the back of her neck; she was tired to the bone and aching all over. Continuing to resist him suddenly felt like a pointless, wearisome process.

'It could be worse,' she said. 'The bullet went clean through. No major damage to arteries, nerves and such, though the scapula's broken. She's in intensive care tonight, but she'll be on a visitor ward by tomorrow. If there are no complications, she'll be allowed home in a couple of days. She's obviously going to be incapacitated for a while. Probably best if I move back home for the duration.'

He nodded. 'Okay, that's all you needed to say. Now . . . your turn.'

Oddly, now that she was on the spot, no specific questions hovered at the front of Lucy's mind. Fatigue fogged everything, but, while he was here – in amazingly timely fashion,

434

it seemed – it would have been remiss not to enquire: 'Why do I get the feeling you know a lot more about all this business than anyone else?'

McCracken shrugged. 'I don't know much more, but I've been educating myself as the evening's worn on.'

'Who were those three people tonight?' she asked. Tucker had been adamant that the assailants at her mother's house were not his, and she'd believed him – they clearly hadn't been cops.

'That was a professional hit-team,' he said. 'Called in by a higher power to lean on you, because a little bird told someone that you had a good lead on the Red-Headed League.'

'Professionals, eh? Next time, make sure you pay them in washers.'

'It was nothing to do with me. But I wouldn't have expected them to fuck it up as much as they did. I'm guessing they weren't expecting such spirited resistance . . . which was the right response, by the way. After they'd tortured all the info out of you they could, they'd have killed both you and your mother. And before you say anything else, two of them are still at large . . . which is one reason I'm personally escorting you to the nick. Because the sooner you make it official that these blaggers were bent cops who've now been dealt with, the safer we'll all be.'

'You say two of them are still knocking around,' Lucy said. She thought about the motorcycle pursuit, and its ghastly outcome. She was still numb in terms of personal feelings; weirdly, it now seemed as if it had never happened – as if she'd dreamed it, or someone else had been involved and she'd just watched. 'Does that mean the third one's . . .?'

'Yes. Dead as a frigging doornail. But the good thing is we've been able to turn it to our advantage.'

It was half a second before she could reply to that. 'What advantage?'

'I'll come clean with you, Lucy.' His face remained stony as he steered them through the deserted streets. 'It's not very often my outfit pulls the trigger on a copper. To an extent, we're into new territory with this. We've been scanning the police bandwidths all this evening, just to keep tabs on developments. Wasn't long before we heard that two nutters on bikes were chasing each other in and out of back gardens, and that it had finally ended in a fatal crash down at the stadium. We put two and two together, and got down there ASAP.' He glanced sidelong at her. 'My main concern was that the fatality might be you.'

'Am I supposed to be touched?'

'No, you're supposed to listen . . . for a change. Thankfully, this being a Friday night and all, the local uniforms are busy as hell. It's kicking off in the town centre, so they were only able to spare one patrol to sit on the scene until an investigation unit arrived. That was all we needed. Wasn't difficult to distract this lone unit away just long enough for Mick to check the body . . . and to plant a certain weapon on it.'

'Let me guess,' she said, 'the gun that killed Ruth Smiley?'

'You sound disgusted by that?'

'How *should* I feel?'

'How about grateful?' He glanced at her again. 'I mean, if they ever find out who that biker girl was, they won't be surprised that she was carrying. And as that pistol itself is clean and untraceable, they'll have no reason to link it back to us . . . or to you.'

'Every base covered, as always, eh?'

'Not *every* base,' he said. 'This has been a difficult night for all of us. For example, it will serve all our purposes if you keep schtum about what little you know concerning that terrible trio. Ideally, it'll get written off as someone who had a beef with the Red-Headed League, and made the mistake of thinking you were part of the same outfit.'

Lucy leaned forward, bracing her forehead on her knuckles.

'Are you hearing this, Lucy?' he asked tautly. 'Because I'll be honest . . . I'm a bit concerned that someone may be losing her perspective on how important some of the secrets in our lives actually are.'

'What are you talking about now?' she mumbled.

'This higher power I mentioned before also had a word with *me* earlier on today . . . about whether or not I might know a certain DC Clayburn?'

'Higher power?' she grunted. 'You talking about Bill Pentecost, by any chance?'

'Let's just say it's someone in a position to do the pair of us a real mischief, if he's so inclined.'

Lucy shook her head, unable to believe the negative turns her life had taken in recent times. It was difficult to believe that she'd ever got involved with people like this, but then considering who her father was, maybe, ultimately, it had been unavoidable.

'So?' he persisted. 'On top of what's happened tonight, is there anything else I need to know?'

'You mean have I spilled the beans about our relationship? Of course not.'

'To no one at all?'

'No one.'

'Well . . .' McCracken pondered this as he drove; by the look on his face, he was still bugged by it. 'He's a naturally suspicious character. Especially where his deputies are concerned. Each time he looks one of us in the face, he sees the next Chairman of the Board, or so he assumes.'

Lucy levered herself upright. 'Let's call it what it is, eh? He sees the next Scrote-in-Chief.'

McCracken ignored that. 'Likes to keep us all on edge, nervy . . . even the simplest enquiry's usually framed like a mind-probe. Anyway, to answer your question, I doubt he *knows* anything.'

'I didn't ask that question,' she said.

McCracken ignored that too. 'He's doing his usual thing, imagining treachery and deceit wherever he goes. Always fishing for signs that people haven't been straight with him, always digging.'

'Good to see you're enjoying the world you've made for yourself.'

'It's a world *you're* now part of too . . . whether you like it or not.'

'Tell me about it.'

'Which brings us back to where we were before.'

'Don't worry,' she said, pained by the mere thought that she was complicit in this. 'I'm well aware what's required of me.'

'You sure about that, Lucy?'

'Why wouldn't I be? It's become a habit, telling massive lies under oath.'

'You're telling one little lie,' he corrected her. 'That you don't know who shot Ruth Smiley. After that, everything else will fall into place. Anyway, I don't know why you're looking so stressed by all this. You're still alive, aren't you? Your mother's still alive.'

Lucy sat back. 'I just can't believe it was Ruth and Danny. I mean, they seemed such a straight pair of bats.'

McCracken chuckled without humour. 'None of your lot are straight bats.'

She glared round at him, stung. 'That's not true.'

'Christ's sake, Lucy . . . get real. No one plays a straight bat. Not if they want to get on in life . . . and not if they want to get revenge, that's for damn sure.'

Unwilling to be baited, she gazed from the window. Only to turn and look back at him suddenly. 'Revenge? You just said *revenge*?'

He didn't reply, easing onto the brake as they approached a red light.

'Does that mean . . . does that mean you *know* why Danny and Ruth were doing this?' she asked. 'How is that possible?'

'Lucky guess, I suppose . . .'

'Don't give me that!' Abruptly, even if not entirely sure why, she'd found herself sitting bolt-upright.

'Soon as you mentioned the name "Tucker", it rang a bell,' he said offhandedly. 'I've had dealings with that slime-ball over the years.'

'But how did you figure out that these robberies were about revenge? Even *I* didn't know that. I thought they were about saving the Robbery Squad . . . it was Danny himself who put me right. I mean, it was a stupid, crazy, scattergun type of revenge. It couldn't have had any impact on the Crew. I told him that to his face, but that's all the more reason why I don't see how *you've* managed to work it out, you who've done nothing but listen to police radio chat all night . . . I mean, unless you were a bit more involved than you've admi— *Uhhh!*'

The bitter taste that suddenly flooded Lucy's mouth was all the worse because she knew that she shouldn't be surprised by it, let alone disappointed. And yet, inexplicably, she was.

She pivoted slowly round in her seat to glare at him. 'It wouldn't be a stupid scattergun revenge if it *wasn't* the boss of bosses they were trying to get even with, would it?'

It was astonishing to her now that, not once while she'd been talking to Danny Tucker, had he mentioned the actual name of the gangster they were trying to bring down. She'd thought she knew it anyway; but guesswork could be a pricy pastime in this line of work.

'It was never Wild Bill at all, was it?' she said slowly. 'They could never have hurt him by hitting a few minor leaguers around Manchester . . . but they could have hurt *you*.'

McCracken studied the road ahead.

'You're the Shakedown, after all,' she said. 'You're the Tax-Collector. Mick Shallicker gave it away himself, when we discussed Roy Shankhill . . . "that was another big earner gone". Oh, my God . . .' She shook her head in disbelief; this was yet another aspect of the case that had been sitting under her nose all along. 'Tucker and Smiley were targeting the people *you* would normally target, weren't they? Only they were getting there first. And after that . . . well, it wouldn't matter how many times you and Shallicker nailed them to their granny's grand-piano. They'd already been robbed blind, and in most cases, were half-dead from gunshot wounds, so you still wouldn't get your money. Your contributions to Crew funds would decline, your star status would quickly wane.'

Danny Tucker's words echoed in her mind: *'I think you'll find they'll be ready to turn on their own long before then . . . imagine the end result . . .'*

Still, McCracken said nothing.

'And, of course . . .' Lucy's voice thickened with revulsion, 'what this really means is that back in 2002, Wild Bill Pentecost didn't shoot PC Tony Gaskin . . . *you* did.'

He drove on.

'At least tell me it isn't true!' she pleaded. 'At least try to deny it!'

'What'd be the point,' he replied, 'you've clearly made your mind up.'

'*Dad* . . .' A word which even a few minutes ago would have been completely abhorrent to her slipped out and she barely noticed. 'Dad . . . did you shoot and kill a police officer during an armed robbery in Manchester city centre back in 2002?'

'Shouldn't ask questions like that, Lucy.'

'*Damn it, did you kill that police officer?*'

'What difference would it make?'

'So . . . you did?'

'I didn't say that.' But McCracken was a wily enough operator to avoid looking at her when he said this, the eyes always being windows to the soul.

'I cannot believe I was fathered by an animal like you,' she spat.

'Says the girl who engineered a fatal accident not four hours ago.'

'That was a case of her or me.'

'How do you know it wasn't the same back in 2002?'

'Tony Gaskin was a beat-bobby. He was unarmed.'

He shook his head. 'You know it doesn't work like that. Someone puts his hands on you, won't let you go . . . the next thing, you're doing thirty years. Uh-uh . . . that's your life over as surely as if you'd eaten a bullet.'

'You could have hit just him . . . you could have knocked him out.'

'Who says the robber responsible didn't try to do that? Who says the gun didn't go off by accident? Course . . .' he shrugged, 'I don't know whether it did, or didn't. I wasn't there, so I can't really comment.'

'You must've covered your tracks pretty well,' she said. 'I mean, the Manchester Robbery Squad formed because of that incident. And even *they* weren't able to bring you down.'

'Well, no one's perfect, Lucy. Not even your saintly DI Blake. I mean, just out of interest, how do you think it was that she showed up tonight when she did?'

'I . . .?' Lucy still hadn't been able to give much thought to this not-inconsiderable mystery.

'Maybe someone tipped her off?' McCracken suggested. 'Maybe, earlier this evening, someone advised her that if she wanted to catch the Red-Headed League, she could do worse than put a tail on a certain DS Tucker. Bloody good job they did, isn't it?'

'Like she'd respond to an anonymous tip implicating one of her own men,' Lucy scoffed.

'Who said it was anonymous? Who said the tip didn't come from someone she trusts?'

Lucy was about to scoff at this too, when she remembered the vehicle leaving the scene of the arrests; the one that had looked exactly like the car she was riding in now.

'Seriously, Luce?' He sounded amused. 'You think you're the only police officer I have a relationship with?'

'You and Kathy Blake!' she said slowly. 'Are you kidding me? *You're* her grass?'

'Grass?' He almost choked. 'Good Christ, girl . . . show me some bloody respect.'

'What, then?'

'As rival gaffers, it occasionally makes sense for us to talk. When things are cutting up nasty. You know . . . make the occasional parley. Don't worry . . . this time, it's all approved.'

On a day of life-changing revelations, Lucy had fallen into a state of mind where she could believe just about anything. But there had to be a limit somewhere.

'No chance! Kathy Blake takes your sort down for the sheer fun of it.'

'Correction. She takes cowboys down for the fun of it. I don't run with cowboys anymore.'

'You realise that because of this, the Robbery Squad may now survive?' Lucy tried to sound tickled by the irony of this. 'I only mention that in case their demise was something you were hoping for. The fact they've extricated some of their own rotten elements without relying on an outside investigation puts them in a good light . . . puts the rest of them beyond suspicion. They may still run out of money, but they won't get binned because everyone thinks they're bent.'

McCracken looked puzzled. 'Why should I want the

Robbery Squad to go under? Hey, you're right. I'm the Shakedown. I make money for the firm by taxing these thieving little bastards. But there's an awful lot of them. More every year.' He blew out a weary breath. 'It's hard enough keeping tabs on the old lags, let alone the new kids on the block.'

'And Kathy Blake makes that easier?'

'Sure. Every time she nicks a team, she raises their profile, puts them on our radar . . . and puts them somewhere secure, where they can't duck and dive to avoid us. I mean, thanks to your beloved DI Blake, we've got a big payday coming courtesy of the Saturday Street Gang. That'd be reason enough to stay friends with her, without all the other stuff.'

Lucy closed her eyes as this latest horrific truth struck home.

It was actually *more* than horrific. Gangs like the Saturday Street mob rarely handed over the cash they'd stolen, at least not all of it – and almost never to law enforcement. But the Crew would be a different matter. And they'd be especially difficult to resist once you were in prison, where they and their henchmen could get at you much more easily.

'More to the point,' McCracken said, 'you think it doesn't cut both ways?'

Lucy blinked. 'I'm sorry . . . what?'

'Gets great results, DI Blake, doesn't she? Rolls a lot of teams? Phenomenon, really. I mean, where on earth could she get her intel from?'

Lucy couldn't even begin to reply to this. She didn't *want* to reply. She sought to put the very idea from her mind, but now it was lodged there permanently; not just because it was too disturbing to simply be forgotten, but also because it made a maddening kind of sense.

It was symbiosis, pure and simple.

Blags went off, and DI Blake got the info she needed via the Crew. The blaggers went down, Blake won the plaudits and the Crew got paid because the team who owed them could no longer hide.

'Told you she was no saint,' he said.

'Maybe not . . .' Lucy tried to sound unconcerned even though deep down she knew she'd never view the much-admired DI in the same light as before, if in any kind of light. 'But I wonder if she'll be happy taking those titbits when I tell her you were the trigger-man back in 2002.'

'You think she doesn't already have her own suspicions about that?' McCracken seemed surprised Lucy would even think this. 'I mean, if a DS and a DC thought they were onto something, you telling me a DI wouldn't be . . . particularly a hotshot DI like Kathy Blake?'

Lucy literally could not believe it. Despite everything else she now knew, this was too much.

'So, it's a pay-off too?' she said. 'A few seconds ago, you told me that getting easy access to gangs of robbers would be "reason enough to stay friends with DI Blake, without all the other stuff". Is this "the other stuff" . . . you give her a ready supply of blaggers, and she doesn't investigate the 2002 job?'

McCracken pondered. 'That'd be quite a trade-off . . . if it was real.'

Too dulled to say anything else, Lucy could only gaze bleary-eyed through the windshield until the Bentley cruised to a halt on Tarwood Lane, just across from Robber's Row.

'Why're you looking so troubled?' her father said. 'This way everyone wins. Except for the bad lads who wanted to upset the apple cart, of course . . . and *they'll* not be a problem anymore.'

'Do you know how many ideals of mine have been shattered this evening?'

He snorted. 'Ideals are an expensive luxury. You need to learn that . . .'

'Don't lecture me, gangster!'

'Oh, give it a rest.' He released the central locking. 'That halo of yours is going to end up a millstone round your neck if you carry on like this. Blake can't solve that robbery/homicide from 2002 without proof. I mean, even *you* know suspicion is not enough . . . so don't think too badly of her.'

'One day, there'll be more than suspicion, *Dad*.' Lucy climbed from the car, but leaned back in, deliberately invading his personal space. 'And that's the day you'll get your thirty.'

She slammed the door, and walked around the car to cross the road. As she did, he pulled a U-turn, coming up alongside her on the opposite pavement, his window still down.

'Yo . . . Lucy!'

She looked back one last time.

'A few hours ago, you said something to me like "I'm not going to vanish into the shadows with a gang of hoods".'

'So?'

'So, this whole thing is a game of shadows, love. You need to buy into that soon. Because if you can't, well . . . there're lots of vacancies for coat-check girls.' He winked at her. 'It's not like you haven't got the credentials.'

Epilogue

When Lucy walked round the back of the police station to the personnel door, it was closed, but a single figure in a jumper and jeans stood in front of it, smoking nervously.

It was Lee Gaskin.

As she approached, he dropped his dog-end and smashed it under his foot.

'You seem to specialise in putting our best players out of the game,' he said.

There was accusation in his tone, but for once it lacked both energy and conviction. His pitted cheeks were pale, sallow. That could have been down to the lateness of the hour, but she suspected it was more likely because he was still in a state of shock about Tucker and Smiley.

'Nice mates you've got,' he added, keen to get another jibe in while she was letting him. 'Or so I hear. Bunch of hell-raising, drug-dealing biker scum.'

Lucy tried to formulate an adequate response. The obvious thing would have been to deny it, to say that the Low Riders were *not* her mates. But how true would that be? They *were* drug-dealers, and yet in the space of a month she'd made two deals with them, in both cases to advance her own interests.

'What halo, I wonder?' she asked herself.

Gaskin looked bemused. 'What?'

'I had you pegged as one of them, you know, Lee.' She spoke matter-of-factly, as if conveying ordinary information to him. 'The Red-Headed League, or whatever they end up going down in history as. All along, I had you as a good fit.'

He actually looked scared by that.

'You were pretty thick with Danny, weren't you?' she said.

'That's . . . that's not true.'

'No . . . it is,' she replied. 'You might have pretended otherwise and he might have gone along with that, always bollocking you just to keep up appearances . . . but every time I saw you two together, you were in private conflab. Each time I entered the room, the conversation mysteriously ended.'

He didn't just look scared now, but startled that she could tell such a lie. 'Just . . . watch what you say, Clayburn.'

'No, Lee . . . you watch what *you* say. From now on, let's a keep a civil tongue, eh? Otherwise, who knows what damaging rumours might spread.'

She tapped in the code and entered the station, leaving Gaskin out in the cold.

Loved *Shadows*?
Then don't miss Paul Finch's
other unputdownable reads . . .

A stranger is just a killer you
haven't met yet…

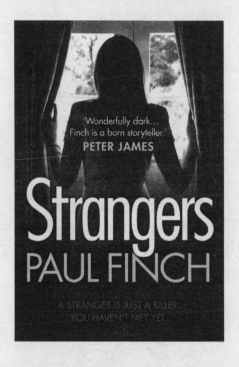

Meet Paul Finch's new heroine in the first
of the Lucy Clayburn series. Read the
Sunday Times bestseller now.

Get back to where it all started with book one of the Heck series, where he takes on the most brutal of killers…

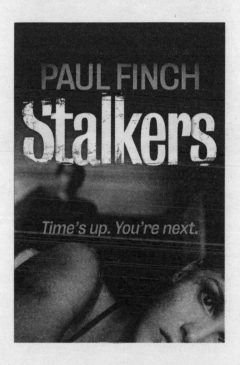

Dark, terrifying and unforgettable. *Stalkers* will keep fans of Stuart MacBride and M. J. Arlidge looking over their shoulder.

A vicious serial killer is holding the country to ransom, publicly – and gruesomely – murdering his victims.

A heart-stopping and unforgettable thriller that you won't be able to put down, from bestseller Paul Finch.

DS Mark 'Heck' Heckenburg is
used to bloodbaths. But nothing
will prepare him for this.

Brace yourself as you turn the pages of
a living nightmare.

Welcome to The Killing Club.

As a brutal winter takes hold of the Lake District, a prolific serial killer stalks the fells. And for Heck, the signs are all too familiar...

Beware the stranger in the night...

DeadMan Walking

PAUL FINCH

A DS Heckenburg thriller

The fourth unputdownable book in the DS Mark Heckenburg series. A killer thriller for fans of Stuart MacBride and *Luther*.

Heck needs to watch his back. Because
someone's watching him...

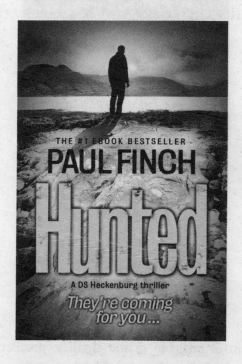

Get hooked on Heck: the maverick cop who
knows no boundaries. A grisly whodunit, perfect
for fans of Stuart MacBride and *Luther*.

Is your home safe?

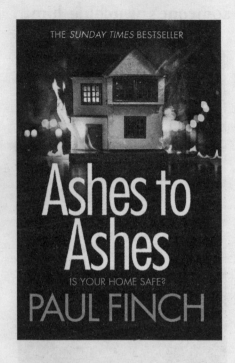